THE
SCAVENGERS

THE
SCAVENGERS
A DEATH & TEXAS WESTERN

WILLIAM W. JOHNSTONE
AND J. A. JOHNSTONE

PINNACLE BOOKS
Kensington Publishing Corp.
www.kensingtonbooks.com

PINNACLE BOOKS are published by

Kensington Publishing Corp.
119 West 40th Street
New York, NY 10018

PUBLISHER'S NOTE: Following the death of William W. Johnstone, the Johnstone family is working with a carefully selected writer to organize and complete Mr. Johnstone's outlines and many unfinished manuscripts to create additional novels in all of his series like The Last Gunfighter, Mountain Man, and Eagles, among others. This novel was inspired by Mr. Johnstone's superb storytelling.

All Kensington titles, imprints, and distributed lines are available at special quantity discounts for bulk purchases for sales promotions, premiums, fund-raising, educational, or institutional use.

Special book excerpts or customized printings can also be created to fit specific needs. For details, write or phone the office of the Kensington Sales Manager: Kensington Publishing Corp., 119 West 40th Street, New York, NY 10018, Attn: Sales Department; Phone 1-800-221-2647.

PINNACLE BOOKS, the Pinnacle logo, and the WWJ steer head logo Reg. U.S. Pat. & TM Off.

First printing: April 2020
ISBN-13: 978-0-7860-5066-6
ISBN-13: 978-0-7860-4375-0 (eBook)

10 9 8 7 6 5 4 3 2

Printed in the United States of America

CHAPTER 1

"Look who's comin' in again," Alma Brown whispered softly to Gracie Billings when the cook walked past her on her way back to the kitchen. Gracie paused and looked toward the front door. It was the second time this week that Jesse Tice had come in the dining room next to the hotel, appropriately named the Two Forks Kitchen. He had become a regular visitor to the dining room ever since his youngest son was killed there some weeks before. Usually, he came in only once a week. "Wonder what's so special about this week?" Alma whispered. They were never happy to see the old man because he made their other customers uncomfortable as he hovered over his coffee, a constant scowl on his unshaven face, while he watched the front door and each customer who walked in. Coffee was the only thing he ever bought. Everyone in town knew his real purpose in haunting the dining room was the chance to see the man who had killed his son. Cullen McCabe was the man he sought. But McCabe was a bigger mystery than Jesse Tice to the people of Two Forks. Everyone knew Jesse as a cattle rustler and horse thief whose three sons were hell-raisers and troublemakers. Cullen McCabe, on the other hand, was a quiet man, seen only occasionally in town, and seeming to have no family or friends.

Alma's boss, Porter Johnson, owner of the Two Forks Kitchen, had talked to Marshal Woods about Tice's search for vengeance against McCabe. Johnson was not concerned about the fate of either Tice or McCabe. His complaint was the fact that Jesse used his dining room as his base for surveillance, hoping McCabe would return. "Doggone it, Calvin," he had complained to the marshal. "I'm runnin' a dinin' room, not a damn saloon. Folks come in here to eat, not to see some dirty-lookin' old man waitin' to shoot somebody."

Marshal Woods had been unable to give Johnson much satisfaction when he responded to his complaint. "I hear what you're sayin', Porter," he had replied. "I reckon you just have to tell Tice you don't wanna serve him. That's up to you to serve who you want to and who you don't. I can't tell folks where they can go and where they can't. As far as that shootin' in here, I told him right from the start that that fellow, McCabe, didn't have no choice. Sonny started the fight and tried to shoot McCabe in the back, but he just wasn't quick enough. I told Jesse I didn't want any more killin' in this town, so I'd have to arrest him if he shot McCabe."

Looking at the old man now as he paused to scan the dining room before taking a seat near the door, Alma commented, "One of us might have to tell the ol' buzzard we don't want him in here. I don't think

Porter wants to get started with him. He's probably afraid he'd start shootin' the place up."

"Maybe we oughta hope McCabe comes back to see us," Gracie said. "Let him take care of Jesse Tice. He took care of Sonny proper enough."

"Meanwhile, I'll go wait on him and take his order for one nickel cup of coffee," Alma said. She walked over to the small table close to the front door. "Are you wantin' breakfast?" she asked, knowing he didn't.

"No, I don't want no breakfast," he snarled. "I done et breakfast. Bring me a cup of coffee." She turned and went to get it. He watched her for a few moments before bringing his attention back to the room now only half-filled with diners. He didn't see anyone who might be the man who killed his son. The major problem Tice had was the fact that he had never actually seen Cullen McCabe up close. When he and his two sons had gone after McCabe, he had circled around them, stolen their horses, and left them on foot. Still, he felt that if he did see him, he would somehow know it was him. When the marshal tried to talk him out of seeking vengeance for the death of his son, Jesse was tempted to tell him that McCabe was a horse thief. He thought that would justify his reason for wanting to shoot him, but he was too proud to admit how his horses happened to get stolen. Every time he thought about the night he and his two sons had to walk twenty-five miles back home, it made him bite his lower lip in angry frustration. When Alma returned with his coffee, he gulped it down, having decided there was no use to linger there. It was already getting late for breakfast, so he thought he might as well go back to join Samson and Joe, who were keeping a watch for McCabe in the River House Saloon.

* * *

It had been several days since he returned to his cabin on the Brazos River after completing his last assignment from the governor's office. The long hard job in the little town of New Hope had turned out to the governor's satisfaction, and Cullen figured it would be a while before he was summoned for the next job. For that reason, he hadn't bothered to check in with the telegraph office at Two Forks to see if he had a wire from Austin. He needed to do a little work on his cabin, so he had waited before checking with Leon Armstrong at the telegraph office. When he was not on assignment for the governor, he usually checked by the telegraph office at least once a week for any messages, and it had not been quite a week since he got back. Halfway hoping there might be a message, he pulled up before the telegraph office and stepped down from the big bay gelding. He casually tossed the reins across the hitching rail, knowing Jake wouldn't wander, anyway.

Leon Armstrong looked up when Cullen walked in and gave him a cheerful greeting. "How ya doin', Mr. McCabe? I got a telegram here for you. Figured you'd be showin' up pretty soon."

"Howdy, Mr. Armstrong," Cullen returned. "Has it been here long?"

"Came in two days ago," Armstrong said as he retrieved the telegram from a drawer under the counter. "Looks like you're fixin' to travel again."

Cullen took only a moment to read the short message from Austin. "Looks that way," he said to Armstrong, and folded the message before putting it in his pocket. "Much obliged," he said, and turned to leave. It seemed kind of awkward that Armstrong always knew Cullen's plans before he did, but since he was the telegraph operator, there wasn't any way to avoid it.

"See you next time," Armstrong said as Cullen went out the door. As curious as he was about the mysterious telegrams the big quiet man received from the governor's office in Austin, he was reluctant to ask him what manner of business he was engaged in. And after the altercation between McCabe and Sonny Tice, he was even more timid about asking. For the most part, McCabe had very little contact with anyone in Two Forks except for him and Ronald Thornton at the general store. McCabe had an occasional meal at the Two Forks Kitchen and made a call on the blacksmith on rare occasions perhaps, but that was about all.

Cullen responded to Leon's farewell with a flip of his hand as he went out the door. All the wire said was that he should come into the capital. That's all they ever said, but it always meant he was about to be sent out on another assignment. So, his next stop would be Thornton's General Merchandise to add to his supplies. As was his usual practice, he had brought his packhorse with him when he rode into town, in the event there was a telegram waiting. Austin was north of Two Forks, while his cabin was south of the town. So, by bringing the packhorse with him, there was no need to return to his cabin. Taking Jake's reins, he led the big bay and the sorrel packhorse up the street to Thornton's.

* * *

Jesse Tice and his two sons came out of the saloon and stood for a while on the short length of boardwalk in front. Looking up and down the street, hoping to catch sight of the man who shot his youngest, Jesse figured it another wasted day. Both Samson and Joe were content to participate in the search for the man called Cullen McCabe as long as their watching post was always the saloon. There was not a great deal of gray matter between the ears of either Joe or Samson and what there was seemed easily diluted by alcohol. Neither son carried the same driven desire their father had to avenge their brother. They generally figured that Sonny was bound to run into somebody he couldn't outdraw in a gunfight and the results would be the same. "How 'bout it, Pa?" Samson asked. "We 'bout ready to go on back to the house?"

"Hold on," Jesse said, something having caught his attention at the far end of the street. At that moment, Graham Price, the blacksmith, walked out of the saloon, heading back to his forge. Jesse stepped in front of Price. "Say," he asked, "who's the big feller leadin' them horses to the general store?" He pointed to Thornton's.

Price paused only long enough to say, "His name's Cullen McCabe." Having no more use for Jesse and his sons than most of the other citizens of Two Forks, he continued on toward his shop. Had he taken the time to look at the wide-eyed look of discovery on Jesse Tice's face, he would have regretted identifying McCabe. As luck would have it, Jesse had asked one of the handful of people in Two Forks who knew McCabe's name. As Price crossed to the other side of the street, he could hear the excited exchange of conversation behind him as the three Tice men realized their search had paid off.

Joe, Jesse's youngest, now that Sonny was dead, ran to his horse to get his rifle, but Jesse stopped him. "Put it away, you damn fool! You're too late, anyway, he's done gone inside the store."

"He'll be comin' back out," Samson insisted, thinking the same as Joe. "And when he does, we can cut him down."

"Ain't I ever learnt you boys anythin'?" Jesse scolded. "And then what, after ever'body in the whole town seen you do it? Take to the hills with a marshal's posse after us?"

"Yeah, but he shot Sonny right there in the dinin' room, and ever'body seen him do it," Joe declared. "Marshal didn't arrest him for that."

"Sonny called him out," Jesse said. "There's a difference. You pick him off when he don't know you're waitin' for him—that's murder, and they'd most likely hang you for it."

Confused now, Samson asked, "Well, ain't we gonna shoot him? Why we been hangin' around here waitin' for him to show up, if we ain't gonna shoot him?"

"We're gonna shoot him," his father explained, impatiently. "But we're gonna wait and follow him outta town where there ain't no witnesses."

"What if he ain't plannin' to leave anytime soon?" Joe complained. "I'd just as soon step up in front of him and tell him to go for his gun—see how fast he is when he don't know it's comin'. Then it would be a face-to-face shootout, and like you said, that ain't murder. Hell, I'm as fast as Sonny ever was," he claimed, his boast in part inspired by the whiskey he had just imbibed. He didn't express it, but he was also thinking about gaining a reputation by gunning down the man who killed Sonny.

Jesse smirked in response to his son's boastful claim. "You don't know how fast McCabe is. You ain't never seen him draw." He had to admit that it would give him great pleasure to have the people of Two Forks see McCabe shot down by one of his boys.

"You ain't seen me draw lately, neither," Joe replied. "I know how fast Sonny was, and I know how fast I am. I'm ready to shoot this sidewinder right now."

"He is fast, Pa," Samson said, curious to see if Joe could do it. "He ain't lyin'."

The prospect of seeing McCabe cut down before an audience of witnesses was too much for Jesse to pass up. Joe was right, he hadn't seen how fast he was lately, and he knew both his boys practiced their fast-draw on a daily basis. There had always been a competition among all three of his sons, ever since they were big enough to wear a gun. Sonny had been the first one to actually call a man out, though, and that hadn't turned out very well. But the fact that Sonny's death didn't discourage Joe was enough to cause Jesse to wonder. "All right," he finally conceded. "We'll go talk to Mr. McCabe. He owes me for three horses he stole. We'll see what he has to say for hisself about that. Then, if you think you can take him, that'll be up to you. If you don't, we'll follow him out of town and shoot him down where nobody can see us do it." They hurried toward Thornton's store, concerned now that McCabe might finish up his business and leave before they got there.

Inside the store, Cullen was in the process of paying

Ronald Thornton for the supplies gathered on the counter when Jesse and his two sons walked in. He had never had a close look at the old man or his two boys, but he knew instinctively who they were, and he had a feeling this was not a chance encounter. He decided to treat it as such until he saw evidence backing up that feeling. He purposefully turned one side toward them while he gathered his purchases up close on the counter, so he could keep an eye on all three. Jesse took only a few steps inside before stopping to stand squarely in front of the door. His sons took a stance, one on each side of him. Thinking the entrance rather odd, Thornton said, "I'll be with you in a minute, soon as I finish up here."

"Ain't no hurry," Jesse said. "Our business is with Mr. McCabe there."

Thornton was suddenly struck by the realization that something bad was about to happen. "Clara," he said to his wife, "you'd best go on back in the storeroom and put that new material away." When she reacted with an expression of confusion, he said, "Just go on back there." Seeing he meant it, she quickly left the room.

Up to that point, McCabe had not reacted beyond pulling a twenty-pound sack of flour and a large slab of bacon over to the edge of the counter, preparing to carry them out to his packhorse. "What is your business with me?"

"Maybe it's about them three horses of mine you stole without payin' me for 'em," Jesse snarled.

"I figured we were square on that count. I paid you the same price you paid for them," Cullen said, guessing Jessie and his boys had most likely stolen them.

"I'm callin' you out, McCabe," Joe blurted, unable to contain himself any longer.

"That right?" McCabe asked calmly. "What for?"

"For killin' my brother," Joe said. "That's what for."

"Who's your brother?" Cullen asked, purposefully trying to keep the young man's mind occupied with something other than the actual act of pulling his weapon. He had faced his share of gunfighters in his time and it was fairly easy to read the wide-eyed nervousness in young Joe Tice's face. The fact that his speech was slurred slightly also suggested that alcohol might be doing most of the talking. Cullen understood the obligation the two brothers felt to avenge Sonny's death, no matter the circumstances that caused him to be shot. There was a chance, however, that he could talk the boy out of a gunfight, so he decided to give it a try.

"You know who he was," Joe responded to Cullen's question. "Sonny Tice. You shot him down in the Two Forks Kitchen."

"So, you're Sonny's brother, huh?" Cullen continued calmly. "Yeah, that was too bad about Sonny. I could see that he wasn't very fast with a handgun. I think he knew it, too, 'cause he waited till I turned around and then he tried to shoot me in the back. He mighta got me, too, but somebody yelled to warn me, so I didn't have any choice. I had to shoot him." He could see that his calm rambling was confusing the young man. He had plainly expected to see a completely different response to his challenge to a face-off. "Yeah, I felt kinda bad about havin' to shoot poor Sonny," Cullen went on. "I've seen it before; young fellow thinks he's fast with a gun and ain't ever seen a man who's a real gunslinger. You must figure you're faster than Sonny was, but I don't know about that. Judgin' by the way you wear that .44 down so low on your leg, I don't see how you could be. How many men have you ever pulled iron on?"

"That don't make no difference," Joe protested. "That's my business." He was plainly flustered by the big man's casual attitude.

"That's what I thought," Cullen said. "This is the first time you've ever called anybody out. Well, we'll try to make it as quick and painless as we can. Let's take it outside this man's store, though." He pulled the sack of flour and the slab of bacon off the counter. "Here," he said, "you can gimme a hand with these supplies. Grab that coffee and that twist of jerky—save me a trip back in here."

Clearly confused by this time, Joe wasn't sure what to do. Accustomed to being ordered around all his young life, he did as McCabe instructed and picked up the sack of coffee and the beef jerky, then started to follow Cullen out the door. Caught in a state of confusion as well, Jesse finally realized that McCabe was talking Joe out of a face-off. "Hold on there! Put them damn sacks down," he blurted, and pulled his six-shooter when Cullen started to walk past him. It was not quick enough to avoid the heavy sack of flour that smacked against the side of his head, creating a great white cloud that covered him from head to toe when the sack burst open. With his other hand, Cullen slammed his ten-pound slab of bacon across Jesse's gun hand, causing him to pull the trigger, putting a bullet hole in the slab of side meat. The hand that had held the flour sack now held a Colt .44, and Cullen rapped one swift time across the bridge of Jesse's nose with it. Stunned, Jesse dropped like a rock.

His two sons stood paralyzed with the shock of seeing their father collapse and Cullen was quick to take advantage of it. "Unbuckle those gun belts, both of you." With his .44 trained on them, they offered no resistance. After laying his slab of bacon on the bar, Cullen took both belts, then picked up Jesse's gun. "Pick your pa up and get him out of here. Take him home and he'll be all right," he ordered, while covering them with his Colt. "There ain't gonna be no killin' here today. And if you're smart, you'll just forget about gettin' even for your brother's mistake. He made a play that didn't work out for him. Don't you make the same mistake." Still numb with shock from the way the confrontation with McCabe turned upside down, Joe and Samson helped their father to his feet. Jesse, unsteady and confused by the blow to the bridge of his nose, staggered out the door with the support of his sons. They managed to get him up in the saddle and he promptly fell forward to lie on his horse's neck. Still covered with flour, he looked like a ghost lying there. Watching the process from the boardwalk in front of the store, Cullen said, "I'm gonna leave your weapons with the marshal and tell him to let you have them back tomorrow." There was no reply from either of the boys and Jesse was still too groggy to respond. Cullen continued to watch them until they rode out the end of the street. It occurred to him then that he hadn't taken their rifles from their saddles. *I hope to hell they don't think about that,* he thought.

"I reckon you're gonna need some more flour," Thornton commented, standing in the doorway of the store. "Maybe some bacon, too."

"Reckon so," Cullen replied. "Flour, anyway. The

bacon looks okay. I'll just cut that bullet hole out of it—might flavor it up a little bit."

"I'll tell you what," Thornton said. "I won't charge you for another sack of flour. That coulda been a bad situation back there, and I wanna thank you for preventing a gunfight in my store."

"'Preciate it," Cullen said. "Now, I expect I'd better get movin'. I'm takin' the road outta here to Austin, and that's the same road they just took to go home. If you don't mind, you can get me another sack of flour and I'll take these guns to the marshal while you're doin' that." He started walking down the street at once and called back over his shoulder, "Sorry 'bout the mess I made in your store."

Still standing in the door, Thornton looked back inside. "Don't worry about that," he said, "Clara's already sweeping it up."

Marshal Calvin Woods was just in the process of locking his office door as he hurried to investigate the shot he had heard several minutes before. Seeing Cullen approaching, he feared it was to report another killing in his town. When Cullen told him what had taken place, the marshal also expressed his appreciation to him for avoiding a shootout with Jesse Tice and his sons. Cullen left the weapons with him, then returned to the store to tie all his purchases on his packhorse. Ronald Thornton stood outside and watched while he readied his horses to ride. When Cullen stepped up into the saddle, Thornton felt prompted to comment, "It looks like Jesse Tice ain't gonna let it rest till he either gets you, or you cut him down."

"It looks that way, doesn't it?" Cullen replied. "I reckon killin' a man's son is a sure way to make him an enemy." He wheeled the big bay away from the hitching rail and set out for Austin.

Thornton's wife was waiting for him when he came back in the store. "Well, you don't know any more about that man than you did before, do ya?" She shook her head impatiently. "You and Leon Armstrong are gonna have to get together to gossip over McCabe's visit to town today, I suppose," she said, referring to the many discussions the two had already had, trying to figure out the man's business. "I'm not sure I like to see him come in the store," she concluded as she pointed to a bullet hole in the floor. "It seems like everywhere he goes, somebody starts shootin'."

"In all fairness, hon," Ronald pointed out, "it's people shootin' at him, and not the other way around."

"I don't care," she said. "It liked to scared me to death. I was sure one of us was gonna get killed and right now I've gotta go to the house and change my drawers."

Thinking it not smart to take another chance on a showdown with Jesse and his boys, Cullen nudged Jake into an easy lope as he set out on the road to Austin. He remembered all too well the day he was forced to shoot Sonny Tice. At the marshal's urging, he had hurried out of town, only to find that the trail to the Tice ranch forked off the road to Austin a couple of miles north of Two Forks. He had managed to pass that trail before they found out he was heading to Austin. It was his intention to do the same today. As he rocked in the saddle to Jake's easy gait, he kept a sharp eye on the road ahead of him. In a short while, he came to the trail leading off to the west and the Tice ranch. He rode past it with no incident, so he hoped that would be the end of it. Time would tell, he told himself, but he was not going to count on it. He had not only killed Jesse's son, but what might be worse for a man like Jesse Tice was the fact that he had made a fool of him twice. There was also the matter of three horses Cullen had taken from the ambush site. *There ain't no doubt*, he told himself, *that old buzzard has plenty of reason to come after me.*

CHAPTER 2

It was time to be thinking about some supper by the time Cullen rode into the capital city of Austin, but he decided it best to take care of his horses first. So, he rode past the capitol building to the stable at the end of the street, operated by a man he knew simply as Burnett. Cullen stepped down from the saddle at the stable door. Having seen him ride up, Burnett walked out to meet him. "Mr. McCabe," he greeted him. "You ain't got no horses to sell this time," he said, glancing past Cullen to see only the one packhorse.

"No, I reckon not," Cullen answered. "Ain't run across any lately. I'd like to leave these two with you overnight. And I'd like to sleep with 'em, if you don't charge too much."

"Sure," Burnett said with a wide smile. "I reckon I charge a little bit less than the hotel does, unless you want clean sheets." He chuckled in appreciation for his humor.

"I 'preciate it," Cullen said. "Maybe you could recommend a good place to get some supper. Last time

I was in town, I ate in the dinin' room of that hotel near the capitol, and it wasn't to my likin'.' "

"You shoulda asked me last time," Burnett said. "I woulda told you to go to Pot Luck. That's a little restaurant run by Rose Bettis between here and the capitol building. That's where I go when I take a notion I don't wanna cook for myself, the Pot Luck Restaurant."

"Restaurant," Cullen repeated. "That sounds kinda fancy." He thought of the place where Michael O'Brien had taken him to breakfast before and all the diners dressed up in suits and ties. Since Burnett said it was back the way he had just come, he commented, "Sounds like I shoulda noticed it on my way down here."

Burnett laughed. "Nah, Pot Luck ain't fancy. It's anything but. It's just a little place next to the hardware store. I ain't surprised you didn't notice it, but if you're lookin' for good food at a fair price, then that's the place to go."

"I'll take your word for it," Cullen said. He followed Burnett into the stables, leading his horses. He unloaded his packhorse and stacked his packs in the corner of a stall. After checking Jake's and the sorrel's hooves, and finding them in good shape, he asked Burnett what time he should be back before the stables were locked up for the night.

"You've got plenty of time," Burnett assured him. "I don't usually leave here till after seven o'clock. I ain't got a wife to go home to, so I ain't in any hurry to go home." Cullen told him he would surely be back before then and started for the door. "Tell Rose I sent you," Burnett called after him.

Cullen found Pot Luck next to the hardware store and he was not surprised that he had not noticed it when he rode past before. A tiny building crammed between the hardware store and a barbershop, the name POT LUCK RESTAURANT was painted on a four-foot length of flat board nailed over the door. A little bell over the top of the door announced his entry when he walked in and paused to look around the small room, half of which was taken up by the kitchen. A long table with a bench on each side, and a chair at each end, occupied the other half of the room. A man and a woman, the only customers, were seated at the far end of the table. They both stopped eating to stare at the man who appeared to fill the doorway completely. A short, rather chubby woman standing at the stove, whom he assumed to be Rose, turned to greet him when she heard the doorbell. She paused a moment when she saw him before she brushed a stray strand of dull red hair from her forehead and said, "Welcome. Come on in." She watched him as he hesitated, still looking the place over. "Since you ain't ever been in before, and you ain't, 'cause I'd remember you, I'll tell you how I operate. I don't have no menus. I just cook one thing. It ain't the same thing every night, but I just cook one supper—just like your mama cooked for you. Tonight, I'm servin' lamb stew with butter beans and biscuits, and you won't find any better stew anywhere else in town. So you decide whether you wanna eat with me or not." She waited then for his reaction.

"I don't recollect if I've ever had lamb before, but I reckon this is a good time to try it," he decided.

"If you don't like it, you don't have to pay for it," Rose said. "Course, that's if you don't eat it."

"Fair enough," he said.

"Set yourself down and I'll bring you some coffee, if that's what you want." He nodded and she suggested, "You'd best set in the chair at the end, big as you are." He took his hat off, offered a polite nod to the couple at the other end of the table, then sat down in the chair.

The lamb stew was as good as she had claimed it would be and the serving was ample for a man his size. The coffee was fresh and hot and she brought extra biscuits. The price was more than fair at fifty cents, considering prices for most everything were higher in a town the size of Austin. When he was finished and paying her, he asked, "Are you open for breakfast?" She was, she said, opening at six o'clock. "Then I reckon I'll see you in the mornin'," he said. "By the way," he thought to say as he opened the door, "Burnett, down at the stable, sent me here to eat."

The night passed peacefully enough as he slept in the stall with Jake, who snorted him awake at about half past five when the big bay heard Burnett open the stable doors. Knowing Michael O'Brien usually came into his office at eight, Cullen decided he would buy himself some breakfast at Pot Luck before he saddled up for the day. He was sure he would prefer eating breakfast with Rose than going to breakfast with O'Brien at the Capitol Diner, where all the customers were dressed up like lawyers. As it turned out, Burnett went to breakfast with him and they took their time drinking coffee afterward. It was a rare occasion for Cullen, but he had to kill a lot of time before O'Brien would be in. Rose's breakfast was as good as her supper had been, so Cullen knew where he would be eating every time he came to Austin in the future. And that would depend upon whether or not he still had a job as special agent for the governor. He still could not know for sure how long the arrangement would last. Granted, he had received nothing but satisfied responses so far, but knowing it to be an unusual position with no formal contract, it could end at any time.

After leaving Pot Luck, he went back to the stable, loaded his packhorse, and rode back to the capitol building. He was still a little early for O'Brien, but Benny Thacker, O'Brien's secretary, was in the office, so he took a seat in the outer office and waited. He refused the offer of a cup of coffee from Benny, since he had drunk what seemed like a gallon of it at Pot Luck. He sat there for about fifteen minutes, conscious of the frequent glances from O'Brien's elf-like secretary. He wondered why the shy little man seemed to be so intimidated by him. Then he recalled the last time he had been in the office. He had walked in just as Benny was coming out and they accidently collided, the result of which nearly knocked Benny to the floor. Further thoughts were interrupted when O'Brien walked in the door. He started to give Benny some instructions but turned to discover Cullen sitting just inside the door when Benny pointed to him. "Cullen McCabe!" O'Brien exclaimed. "Just the man I wanna see. Have you been here long?" Before Cullen could answer, he asked, "Have you had your breakfast?" He hurried over and extended his hand. When Cullen shook it, and said that he had already eaten, O'Brien said, "Benny could have at least gotten you a cup of coffee while you waited."

"He offered one," Cullen said, "but I've had more than I needed this mornin'. Thanks just the same." Impatient now, he was anxious to get down to business. "Have you got a job for me?"

"Yes, sir, I sure do," O'Brien answered. "But first, let me tell you Governor Hubbard is well pleased with the success of this arrangement." He winked and said, "You did a helluva job in New Hope. He's started claiming that the creation of your job was his idea, even though it was mine right from the start. Nobody had even thought about appointing a special agent who reports only to the governor until I suggested it." Without a pause, he went right into the reason for his summons. "This is a special assignment the governor wants you to investigate this time. So let's go on in and I'll let Governor Hubbard explain the job."

Cullen followed O'Brien into the governor's office and the governor got up from his desk and walked around it to shake hands with Cullen. "Cullen McCabe," Hubbard greeted him just as O'Brien had. "I'm glad to see you," he said. "I was afraid my wire hadn't reached you." He smiled warmly. "I'm glad to see you got it." He motioned Cullen to a seat on a sofa, while he sat down in an armchair facing him. "The job I've called you in for is one of special personal interest to me." He paused then to interrupt himself. "You're doing one helluva job, by the way," he said, then continued without waiting for Cullen to respond. "This is a slightly different situation than the problems you've handled up to now. We've got a little situation about a hundred and twenty-five miles northwest of here between a couple of towns on Walnut Creek."

"Where's that?" Cullen interrupted, not having heard of it.

"Walnut Creek is a healthy creek that runs through the Walnut Valley. It's a branch of the Colorado River. I'm sending you to a little town on the west side of that creek, called Ravenwood. It was named for a man who owns many acres of land next to the creek, Judge Harvey Raven. He gave the land for the town to the county officials, along with about one hundred acres for county government business. Of course, the idea was to make Ravenwood the county seat. The problem, though, was that there was already a town of sorts on the east side of the creek where a lot of settlers had farms and homes. They didn't like it much when the county took Raven's offer. Next thing you know, they started having trouble about the water rights. One thing led to another, and pretty soon there were some shots exchanged between the folks that built up Ravenwood and those that wanted the town left on the east side of the creek. So the east-side folks created their own town and called it East City."

The governor rambled at length about the troubles between the two towns, a characteristic Cullen assumed was common to all politicians, but he wondered what it had to do with him. "What, exactly, is it you want me to do?" he asked when Hubbard paused for breath.

"I'm getting to that," Hubbard said. "The problem lies in East City. It's become a town of saloons, brothels, and gambling halls. The mayor contacted my office. East City's crime is spilling over to the other side of the creek, so the folks in Ravenwood petitioned my office for help, also. I sent a delegation up there to meet with the city officials. They concluded that the town was justified in their complaints, but they couldn't recommend any plan of action to improve the situation. We sent a company of Rangers up there to maintain the peace. They set up a camp and stayed for three days. And for three days everything was peaceful. As soon as they left, East City went back to business as usual."

"Ain't there any law in the towns?" Cullen asked.

"Yes, there is," the governor answered, "in both towns. Ravenwood has a marshal and East City has a marshal and a deputy. The problem is, the East City marshal seems to be in control of the whole town and is nothing more than an outlaw, himself. And the town has become a haven for every other outlaw on the run in Texas. As far as we know, the marshal in Ravenwood is an honest man."

"What do you expect me to do," Cullen asked, "if the Rangers couldn't fix the problem?"

The governor glanced at O'Brien and winked. "What you always do," he answered then. "What you did in New Hope and Bonnie Creek—look into the situation and see if there's anything you can do to improve it."

Cullen shook his head and thought about all Hubbard had just told him. "I don't know," he said, not at all optimistic about reforming two towns. It sounded to him that the governor needed a negotiator, and that label didn't fit him. The next best thing was to make one of the towns a permanent Ranger headquarters, and he was about to suggest that when O'Brien interrupted.

"Just ride up there and look the situation over," O'Brien said. "We trust your eyes more than the Rangers'. If nothing else, you can at least report back with a more detailed presentation of the facts."

Cullen shrugged and shook his head again. "Well, I can do that, I reckon. It's your money. I'll see what I can do."

"Good man," Hubbard exclaimed with a grin. "I knew I could count on you. There's a check for your expenses already in the bank. You can pick up your money today. Think you'll be ready to leave in the morning?"

"I expect I'll leave today, just as soon as I pick up my money at the bank," Cullen said.

"Excellent!" Hubbard responded. "Come, I'll show you where you're going." He walked over to the large state map on the wall and pointed to two small dots that looked to be in the very center of the state. Cullen stood for a few minutes studying the route he would take, noting the rivers and streams. When he was satisfied with the way he would start out, he turned and said he was ready to go. "It's early yet," the governor stated. "If you'll need a little time to get ready to go, maybe you'd like to have dinner with me."

"Thanks just the same," Cullen responded, "but I'm ready to go now, soon as I pick up the money at the bank." He didn't think he'd be comfortable eating with the governor. He imagined it would be more awkward than it had been with O'Brien in the Capitol Diner. He shook hands with both of them and took his leave after they wished him a good trip.

O'Brien and the governor stood at the office doorway and watched Cullen until he reached the end of the hall and disappeared down the stairs. "Might be a waste of time sending him up there," O'Brien commented.

"Maybe," Hubbard said, "but I've got a lot of confidence in that man. Besides, it's a helluva lot cheaper than sending a company of Rangers back there for who knows how long."

CHAPTER 3

After a stop at the bank where his expense money was always deposited in his account, Cullen set out on a road he had taken before when he had been sent to Fort Griffin. Had he been able to start out early that morning, he would have thought about possibly riding as far as Lampasas Springs by the end of the next day. But that would have been pushing Jake and the sorrel a little too hard, so he figured to reach the springs around noon the next day. There was a little trading post a few miles west of there on the Colorado River. It was owned by an old man named Blanchard, if he remembered correctly. It wasn't what a person would consider a going business. Cullen guessed it had seen better days, many years ago. He thought it would be worthwhile to stop by and purchase a few things from the old man.

Once he was on the road, he turned it over to Jake. The big bay gelding knew the gait Cullen wanted to maintain and he trusted his master to know when he needed rest. About twenty-five miles out of Austin, Cullen deemed it time to give Jake that rest when they crossed over a narrow creek. He turned him upstream and rode for about fifty yards, stopping at a spot where there was enough grass under the oak trees to feed his horses. Not really hungry, since he had eaten a big breakfast at Rose Bettis's Pot Luck, he settled for a cup of coffee and a strip of beef jerky.

After a peaceful night, he pushed his horses a little harder in order to reach the springs. He estimated the distance to be about thirty miles. He turned Jake to the west at that point, following a healthy creek to the Colorado River. He expected to find the small trading post still there. As he approached the humble building perched on the east bank of the creek, where it emptied into the river, it occurred to him that it was in a bad state of repair. There were weeds and bushes growing up in the yard and the cabin was dark. It appeared to be deserted. When he rode a little closer, Jake whinnied and was answered with a friendly nicker. Thinking it must have come from behind the store, Cullen became immediately alert. So, instead of continuing to ride straight up to the hitching post in front, he angled Jake to pass by the store. Once he rode even with the front corner of the building, he could see the horse grazing on the other side of it. A red roan, it was saddled with the reins left loosely about the saddle horn. He saw no sign of anyone anywhere around the place. Whoever belonged to the horse had to be inside, he decided, and started to ride on by to find someplace else to rest his horses. He went only a couple dozen yards before he pulled up, wheeled Jake around, and rode back up to the front of the cabin and dismounted. His curiosity had gotten the best of him and he decided to find out who belonged to the horse grazing freely beside the cabin.

With his rifle in hand, he stepped up beside the

door, which was standing slightly ajar, and cautiously pushed it halfway open with the barrel of his rifle. He wasn't sure what he might find, but it wasn't at all what he expected. It was a girl, or young woman, he wasn't sure which. She was crouched in the center of what had been the floor of the trading post, hugging her knees up close to her chin. She looked at him with eyes wide and terrified. Not certain what to make of it, he looked around the empty room to make sure he wasn't about to walk into a trap before he stepped inside. When he saw no sign of anyone else, he pushed the door wide and walked in. Even in the dim light afforded by the open doorway, he could see that the young woman was shivering with fear. "Are you all by yourself, miss?" he asked, but she didn't answer. "Are you all right?" Again, she answered with nothing more than a look of terror. "I'm not gonna cause you any harm, miss. I'll help you if I can, but you'll have to tell me what's wrong. What are you doin' sittin' here in this old shack all by yourself?"

When she finally spoke, it was in a voice barely audible and he had to step closer to understand what she asked. "Did Boot send you after me?"

"No, ma'am. Who's Boot?"

"Boot Davis," she answered, her voice gaining strength when she realized that Cullen was not going to hurt her. "I thought you were one of that sorry crowd he runs with, and you were fixin' to take me back to him."

"Maybe you'd best tell me what's goin' on," Cullen said, "and I'll see if I can help you. You can start with tellin' me your name and how come you're runnin' from Boot Davis."

With his offer of help, she responded hopefully.

"My name's Lila Blanchard. Boot and his no-good sidekick, Charley Turner, jumped me outside the Cork and Bottle Saloon."

"Where's the Cork and Bottle Saloon?" Cullen interrupted.

"East City," she answered. "Kidnapped me is what they did. Boot said he was gonna kill me when he was done with me and I knew he meant what he said. But when him and Charley was passed out drunk, I slipped outta the rope he had me tied up to him with. Then I took off. Boot's horse was still saddled, so I jumped on it and ran."

"So, that's his horse beside the cabin?" Cullen asked, and she nodded. "When was that?"

"Two nights ago," Lila answered. "Him and Charley tracked me to a barn I was hidin' in the next day. But I saw 'em when they rode up to the feller's house that owned the farm, so I lit out again. I don't know if they saw me ride out back of the barn. When I heard you come up, I just knew it was them."

"How'd you happen upon this old place?" Cullen asked, puzzled as to why she chose to sit and wait in an abandoned store.

"I didn't happen on it," she said. "I came here on purpose. I didn't know it was gone." She shook her head sadly. "This was home. This was my daddy's store."

"Your daddy?" Cullen reacted. Then it struck him—Blanchard, she said her name was Blanchard. Howard Blanchard was her father. "Your daddy's gone from here, closed up his store, and you didn't know it?"

"I ain't seen my daddy in four years," Lila said. "He told me, if I ran off with Sid Worthy, not to come back home. Sid said he was gonna marry me, but one mornin' I woke up and he was gone." She shook her head as she relived a mental picture of that morning. "I waited there for three days, waitin' for him to come back, till the feller that owns the hotel told me to come up with some rent money, or I was gonna have to get out."

Cullen didn't have to hear what happened next. It was an all-too-familiar story. "So you moved over to the saloon you mentioned."

"Yes, sir," she said. "I didn't have no choice. I went to whorin'. It was the only way I could feed myself."

It was easy for him to understand the situation that he now found her in and why she sat in the middle of the vacant store, hugging her knees, awaiting her fate. Her one desperate hope had been her father, thinking possibly he would take her in and hide her from Boot Davis. When she found him gone, not even certain he was still alive, she had given up and sat waiting for this Boot Davis fellow to find her and punish her. Cullen wasn't sure what he could do to help the desperate woman's permanent plight, but perhaps he could help her immediate situation. "When was the last time you ate?" he asked, and she said she wasn't sure, maybe she had something before Boot snatched her from the saloon. "Well," Cullen continued, "I'm fixin' to rest my horses and cook some breakfast. Reckon you could use a little, yourself."

"Mister, I surely could!" she fairly exclaimed. "Just the mentionin' of it made my belly bark like a dog." She managed a faint smile for him. "You sure as hell came along when I was prayin' for a miracle." She shook her head in frustration. "And I don't even know your name."

"Cullen McCabe," he said. "Pleased to meet you. Let me take care of my horses first, then we'll cook some breakfast. Reckon you could build a fire in that fireplace? Maybe that pile of wood beside it ain't too rotten to make a hot fire." He reached down, offering his hand. She took it and he pulled her up on her feet. His first good look at her told him she might be young in years, but her face reflected the hard times of the profession she had been forced to practice.

On her feet, she began to show a spark of recovery from the state he had found her in. She went at once to the fireplace in the corner of the room and started to arrange some kindling. "I ain't got no matches," she said, so Cullen went outside to get one from his saddlebags. When he returned with it and handed it to her, she asked, "Is that all you've got? I'd better be careful it don't blow out."

"If it does, I'll go get you another one," he joked, glad to see that she was evidently recovering some spunk. It was a disposition he much preferred to that of a helpless victim. "I'll go take care of the horses now. I ain't much of a cook, but I've got some bacon and flour, and I make a helluva pot of coffee."

"Well, bring it on in here and maybe I can put something together that won't kill us," she said, forgetting the fear that had gripped her senses such a brief time before. She felt safe in his presence, this Cullen McCabe. He was a big man, but that was not the reason. There was a calmness about him, a non-judgmental patience that seemed to indicate an inner strength.

Lila showed that she had some skills other than those developed in the bedroom as she took what supplies she could find in Cullen's packs to produce a breakfast of bacon and simple pan biscuits. While they ate, they talked about Lila's situation and what she had planned to do if she was successful in avoiding Boot Davis. "I don't know," she confessed. "I was just runnin' for my life, and when I got here and found Daddy gone, I didn't know what to do. Try to go back to the Cork and Bottle, I guess, 'cause I can't make it on my own. I should have done that when I first escaped, but I guess I panicked."

"The Cork and Bottle?" Cullen asked. "Did you say that was in East City, right across the creek from Ravenwood?" She said that it was, so he asked, "Will you be safe there? It looks like you weren't before."

"As safe as I would be about anywhere, I reckon. I was just in the wrong place at the wrong time. Boot weren't after me, especially, he just had his mind set on snatchin' one of us girls. If it'da been Mabel or Wilma comin' from the outhouse, it'd be one of them in this fix, instead of me." She paused to think about that. "I never was the lucky one and I don't know why he kept trackin' me after I got away."

"You think it might be because you stole his horse?" Cullen casually suggested. The expression on her face told him that it had not occurred to her.

"Damn," she finally uttered. "You think they might hang me for a horse thief?"

"Maybe not," he said. "Especially if we take the horse back and tell the marshal you wanna leave it there for Boot to come get it. Then if he does, you can have him arrested for abductin' you."

The possibility brought a smile to her face. "You think I could really do that?"

"I think there would be a good chance of it," he replied. "Hell, if they were to take it to trial, I don't see any way a judge, or a jury, could blame you for what you did."

"Mr. McCabe, it's plain as day to me that you ain't ever been to East City. They don't have no trials with a judge. There ain't no judge in East City. Micah Moran decides who hangs and who don't." She paused to think about that for a moment. "You said, *we* . . . Do you mean you'd take me to East City?"

"Might as well," he replied. "I'm goin' there, anyway, just as soon as my horses are ready to go."

She fairly beamed, newly excited. "I never believed in angels before, but I'm believin' in 'em now. I don't know how I can ever repay you for what you're doin' for me." Her joy was interrupted then when another thought struck her—one she had forgotten for the moment. "You need to know what you might be getting into. Boot Davis and that animal he runs with, Charley Turner, are a pair of mean customers. I wouldn't feel right about this if I didn't warn you about them."

"I 'preciate the warnin'," Cullen said. "Maybe, if we're lucky, we'll get to East City before they figure out where you are. I expect we'll make East City by late afternoon tomorrow. So if you're ready, we'll get started."

Cullen readied his horses, then took a quick inspection of Boot Davis's red roan. The horse was in good shape, about four or five years old, he figured. "You stole a pretty good horse," he told Lila, as he gave her a lift up. "Pretty fancy saddle, too." He didn't say it, but he had no doubt about the zero possibility that Boot would give up on a search for his horse. It would depend on how good a tracker Boot was, and if Lila had taken any pains at all to hide her trail. In her panic to escape, he would bet that she hadn't. There was a chance, however, since she had left the common road to cut over here to the river. Maybe, if Boot was tracking her, he wouldn't have noticed that she had left the road. "Have you looked in his saddlebags?" Cullen asked.

"No," she answered. "I never even thought about it."

He found that hard to believe. "Let's take a look. He might have some jerky or somethin' in there that you could have eaten." He opened one of the pouches. "Extra cartridges for that rifle," he announced, then opened the bag on the other side. "Well, now," he muttered as he held up a sizable roll of paper money. "Look at that."

"My stars!" she exclaimed, surprised, but not very convincingly, in his opinion.

He dropped the roll of money back in the saddlebag. "Looks like he's got enough money there to buy two or three horses like this geldin' you're settin' on. You reckon?"

"I reckon," she replied, certain that he knew she was already aware of the money. "He oughta owe it to me for what he done."

"You might be right," he said, not really caring if she kept the money or not. His only concern was the added incentive Boot Davis and his friend Charley Turner had to track the woman down.

Cullen returned to the common wagon road that led from Lampasas Springs to Ravenwood and East City. Jake and the sorrel had already worked pretty hard that morning, so he planned to push them on no farther than twenty miles or so. That should put them within a day's ride of East City, if his calculations were right. Then, depending upon what he found when they reached the Cork and Bottle, he might have

Lila off his hands. He could not, in good conscience, abandon her to violent men like Davis and Turner, if it turned out that there was no protection for her at the saloon. He might have to talk the matter over with the marshal of East City before he tried to take on his mission of looking into the situation between the two towns.

He decided he had pushed the horses far enough when he came to a place where two streams met to form the creek they had followed for most of that day. From the ashes of several old fires, they could see that it was a commonly used campground. He took a close look at the clearing where most of the fires had been built and picked a spot near the outer edge where there was a little more cover. Then he pulled the saddles and packs off the horses and let them go to water. While he was taking care of the horses, Lila gathered wood for a fire. Once she had it started, she announced that she was going to go downstream to take care of her personal needs. He filled his coffee-pot with water and set it on the fire to warm. He figured he'd let Lila do the cooking. Convinced that Boot would come after her, he was hoping that the two roughnecks didn't know about her father and wouldn't be looking for her on this road any longer. Regardless, he planned to be ready for a late-night visit, just in case. Along with that thinking, he decided to hobble Boot Davis's horse, as well as his sorrel packhorse. He wouldn't bother to hobble Jake. The big bay would not stray far from him. He had just finished with the hobbling when Lila came back to the camp. She was tiptoeing cautiously along the creek bank, carrying her shoes and what appeared to be her undergarments in her hands.

Seeing his quizzical expression, she explained, "I ain't never been on a horse so long in all my life. And, I declare, this last twenty miles, or however far it was, just about wore my bottom out. I had to wade out in the creek and set it down for a while to put out the fire."

Cullen choked back a laugh and asked, "Did it help?"

"I'll say it did," she giggled, "until I got out again."

"Well, if it ain't too tender to set on, you just go find you something soft and set down, and I'll do the cookin'," he volunteered.

"No, no," she protested. "I'll do the cookin'. It ain't gonna keep me from cookin'. I already owe you more than I can ever pay you." She hesitated, trying to decide whether to say more or not, then went on with it. "I don't know if you're interested, but you know the profession I'm in." He knew what she was about to say, but he let her go on. "What I'm sayin' is, that's all I've got to pay you with, and if you're wantin' . . ." That was as far as he let her go before stopping her.

"That's mighty generous of you, Lila, but that won't be necessary. You don't owe me anything at all." He gave her a little smile. "Besides, you ain't really open for business right now, anyway."

"You can say that again," she cried. "My bottom's sore as a boil."

With an extra blanket Cullen carried and a piece of canvas he used for a shelter in bad weather, they fashioned a bed for Lila. Before she crawled into it for the night, they sat by the fire awhile to finish the little bit of coffee left in the pot. "Was you serious when you said we might leave Boot's horse with the marshal?" Lila asked.

"Yeah," he answered, "we could do that—might make it seem like you wanted to do the right thing." When she cocked her head as if skeptical, he asked, "Why? Something wrong with that?"

"No, I reckon not," she replied, but still with a sense of uncertainty. When he prodded her to say what was bothering her, she finally said what was on her mind. "You ever been to East City?" When he reminded her that he never had, she continued. "Marshal Micah Moran pretty much runs that town and he's been known to go awful light on the wild bunch that likes to hang around there. That is, except for the Cork and Bottle. You see, Marshal Moran is half owner of that saloon, and most of the wild bunch know it. That's why I said I was as safe in the saloon as anywhere else. Moran's got a deputy, Ace Brown, and he's the one that takes care of all the marshal's heavy work. Ace enjoys bustin' up drunk cowhands and farm boys, but it don't seem to keep 'em from comin' back for more."

"What about the ordinary merchants in town?" Cullen asked. "The storekeepers, the hotel, livery stable, barbershop, people like that, are they happy with Moran runnin' the town?"

"It might not be just exactly as they'd like it, but there ain't a lot they can do about it. I reckon they do enough business with the cowhands and the farmers to keep 'em from closin' up and movin' across the creek to Ravenwood. That's where the more respectable folks do their business. At least, that's what I've been told. Ravenwood ain't got but two saloons and it's about twice as big as East City. East City's got two

saloons, too, but Cork and Bottle is the biggest." She
rambled on about the two towns, since he seemed to
be interested in her story. When he asked if there was
a town council, or anything equivalent to one, she
said, "Yep, there's a council. There's even a mayor,
Abe Franks. He owns the hardware store."

As the campfire died down, Cullen realized he had
a pretty complete picture of East City, even if it was
from a prostitute's point of view. He figured her to be
fairly accurate in her description because a prostitute
was more likely to be privy to the dark side of the
town. Just out of curiosity, Cullen asked, "Is there a
church in East City?"

"Goodness, no," Lila exclaimed. "Some folks
wanted to build one about a year ago, but Micah said
no. Said it would be bad for business." She paused to
study his face before saying, "There's one in Ravenwood, if that's what you're lookin' for."

"Just wondered," he said. "Was it just the marshal
that said no to the church, or did the mayor and the
town council decide against it?"

"It was just the marshal that said it," she answered
with a shrug. "But that's all it takes. The council and
the mayor pretty much go with what he says. Tell
you the truth, most everybody who thought about
buildin' a church gave up on it before they got told
they couldn't have one. They already knew what the
marshal would say."

He thought that over for a few moments before
getting up from the fire. "I reckon it's about time to
turn in. I'm gonna take a little look around before I
do, though—won't be gone long." He left her to crawl
into her bed while he whistled Jake up from the edge
of the creek. With only a bridle but no saddle, he

jumped on Jake's back, his rifle in hand. He thought it a good idea to ride a wide circle around the camp just to make sure Boot and his partner hadn't gotten on their trail.

He rode Jake for about half a mile back down the road they had come up. There was no sign of anyone else behind and he figured, if they were being followed, they would most likely be that close. Otherwise, they couldn't watch the camp from much farther away. He left the road then and rode a circle around his camp, maintaining the same half-mile distance. *A nice summer night*, he thought. *I'd appreciate it if we didn't get visitors to spoil it.*

CHAPTER 4

Twenty miles behind Cullen and Lila, her two pursuers sat by the fireplace in Howard Blanchard's abandoned store. Unaware that the woman they chased was only twenty miles ahead, Boot might have decided to press their horses to continue had he known. The fact that the trail they now followed was leading back to East City was enough to satisfy him that Lila was heading back to the Cork and Bottle. He was determined to punish her for the trouble she had caused him, not to mention the fact that she had stolen his horse and his money. "Damn her!" he blurted in anger as he thought about it. "If we hadn't gone back to town to look for her, we'da most likely caught her right away."

"You're the one said she'd run straight back to the saloon," Charley reminded him, "even when I showed you them tracks headin' toward the Austin road. If we'da followed them tracks, we wouldn't be settin' here in this old shack right now."

"Ain't that what I just said?" Boot complained. "I'm gettin' tired of hearin' about you seein' them tracks." He paused to spit in the fire. "I swear, I thought she'd surely circle back and head for town." He wiped his mouth with the back of his hand. "I'm the one that found them tracks that led over here to this shack," he felt the need to remind him.

"Reckon how she knew about this cabin?" Charley wondered aloud.

"I don't know," Boot responded. "I'm more curious to know who them other tracks belong to. There was at least two other horses leavin' tracks around this place and they sure as hell all left here in the same direction."

"Just because we found tracks don't mean them others were here at the same time Lila was," Charley suggested. "And even if they was, there weren't but two of 'em." He shrugged. "Mighta just been one feller and a packhorse."

"I swear, I'll kill that woman if she's run my horse to death," Boot grumbled. He could picture the terrified woman galloping along that road. "There's close to three hundred dollars in my saddlebags and it better be there when I catch up with her."

"Hell, she ain't had no place to spend it," Charley chuckled as he got to his feet. "I'm goin' to bed, if you ain't gonna do nothin' but bellyache all night."

"Yeah, and you can go to hell, too," Boot complained. "It ain't you that lost your horse and three hundred dollars." That triggered another complaint in his mind. "I've half a mind to shoot Art Becker when we get back to East City. That damn horse he lent me ain't worth spit. I don't believe it was ever saddle-broke. I think it'd be better off pullin' a wagon."

"I declare, Boot," Charley japed. "Who else you gonna shoot? Ain't nothin' wrong with that gray. Besides, you picked him out. Art told you to take your pick of all them he had in the corral." He unrolled his blanket roll and spread it in a corner away from the fireplace, the fire in the small store having heated up the room more than enough.

It was late afternoon when Cullen got his first look at East City. The first business they came to, on the south end of the one street, was the stable, owned by Art Becker, according to Lila. She pulled the roan up beside Cullen and they walked the horses slowly up the street. Seeing them pass, Art walked outside to watch them, surprised to see Lila returning to East City riding the red roan he recognized as Boot Davis's. He had wondered why Boot had borrowed a horse from him. Curious as he was about that, he was even more interested in the big fellow on the bay, riding beside Lila. There was going to be hell to pay when Boot found out about her ridin' to town on his horse. *Things might get pretty interesting,* he thought. Something must have happened to Boot, for there was no way he was going to let Lila Blanchard ride his horse. His thoughts came back to focus on the stranger riding the bay, and he wondered if he had something to do with it.

When they had already passed by the stables, Lila asked, "Should I have left Boot's horse at the stable? You didn't pull in, so I didn't say nothin' till we went by."

"No, let's go find the marshal and let him decide what to do with the horse," Cullen directed. "We wanna be on the up-and-up about the horse. Then you might wanna make your charges against Boot

Davis for abductin' you and threatenin' to kill you.
You think?"

Lila hesitated, thinking about the marshal and his
posse, as he called the rough gang of riders who answered to his commands. Boot Davis was a member
of Micah Moran's "posse." "I don't know," she started,
then hesitated again before coming out with it.
"Boot's one of Moran's posse. Maybe it would be
best to just forget about the kidnappin' and rapin',
and just go on back to the way things were before he
snatched me."

"You sure about that?" Cullen asked. It wasn't really
necessary to hear her answer; he already knew she
would not protest her treatment. She was afraid of the
consequences if she attempted to make any charges.
Not waiting for her answer, he said, "Well, we'll go
find the marshal and turn that horse over to him."
He turned to look her in the eye. "You take that
money you found and tuck it in your bodice. As far as
you know, there wasn't any money. You understand?" She responded with a look of fearful uncertainty, so he said, "You're liable to need some extra
money someday, if you decide to leave this town.
And Boot damn sure owes you something." Seeing
the jail ahead on the right, he said, "Let's go in and
talk to the marshal."

"You won't find him in there," Lila said. "This time
of day, he'll be settin' at the back-corner table in the
Cork and Bottle. That's where he always is. Ace
Brown's in the jail, though, if he ain't out walkin'
around town. He's Micah's deputy."

"I think we need to talk to the marshal. Let's go to
the Cork and Bottle. I see it up ahead." He gave her
another look in the eye. "You just remember, you ain't

the one that's done something wrong, so don't be afraid to tell him what Boot did to you." She still looked uncertain. He was afraid she was going to cave in if confronted by Boot.

Cullen tied the horses at the rail and walked Lila to the door. There was a modest crowd at the saloon, for it was still early. But there was an immediate quiet when they walked in. As Lila predicted, the marshal was seated at his regular table, talking to another man. They paused as well when Lila walked in with her formidable-looking escort. Cullen figured the word must have gotten out that she had stolen Boot Davis's horse and left town without telling anyone what she was going to do. The marshal looked Cullen up and down while giving Lila only a quick glance, but he waited for Cullen to speak. His companion did not, however. "Lila, where the hell have you been?" Tom Loughlin, the marshal's business partner, asked.

When Lila hesitated, easily intimidated by the two of them, Cullen answered for her. "I came across Lila a couple dozen miles south of here. To answer the question, where's she been, she's been runnin' for her life. Two of your regular customers kidnapped her when she went to the outhouse a few days ago, and she's been tryin' to get back ever since."

"Is that a fact?" Micah Moran spoke then, staring hard at Cullen. "And just who the hell are you?"

"My name's Cullen McCabe," he answered. "I'm just glad I found her. She didn't have any food and was scared she might run into those two no-goods that abducted her. She was tryin' to get back here to turn the horse over to you."

"That's a mighty interestin' story, ain't it, Tom?" Moran glanced at his partner, then back at Lila, who appeared to be trying to make herself as small as she could. "And who are these two fellows you say carried you off?"

When faced with the two owners of the saloon, one of them being the town marshal, Lila lost any determination she had mustered before. She began thinking about where she would be if they tossed her out to fend for herself. Seeing her hesitation, Cullen answered for her. "Boot Davis and Charley Turner." He saw the immediate alarm in her face.

"Is that what you say, Lila?" Moran demanded.

"It was Boot and Charley," she said. "But I don't think they was out to cause me any real harm. They just had too much to drink and was just foolin' around. They'da probably brought me home before long. I reckon I shouldn't'a got scared and run away from 'em."

Moran nodded, satisfied. "That sounds about the way I figured it to be," he said. "They're both pretty good boys. I think sometimes you women get 'em to thinkin' crazy things, specially when they're too drunk to know what they're doin'. I'll talk to 'em." He turned his attention back to Cullen then. "How 'bout you, Mr. Cullen McCabe? You make it a practice to ride around lookin' for whores to rescue?"

Cullen answered the sarcastic remark with a knowing smile. "Only occasionally, Marshal, when I meet one that's been mistreated by a couple of no-good drunks." He locked eyes with the sneering marshal as both men sought to determine the strength of the other.

"Now that you've brought Lila back where she belongs, I expect you'll be wantin' to get on to wherever you were headin'. Right, McCabe?"

"Oh, I don't know," Cullen replied. "I'm not in any hurry, and I've never been in East City before. I might wanna stick around for a little while, just to see what kinda town you've got here."

"Maybe I can help you with that," Moran said. "It's the kind of town that comes down hard on anybody makin' trouble. Me, or my deputy, will be glad to take care of any troublemakers. Now, don't get me wrong, strangers are always welcome in East City, as long as they obey my rules. But, if I was to give you any advice, I'd suggest you might wanna be gone from here before Boot and Charley get back. I don't hold for back-shootin' and murder, but if a man gets called out for a face-off, that ain't against the law. At least, not in this town."

"I 'preciate the advice, Marshal. It's good to know where you stand. I assure you, I'll keep that in mind, and I guarantee you I ain't gonna call anybody out while I'm in your town." He smiled again. "But I still think I'll stick around a little while, just to see what's here."

He turned to look at Lila, who lowered her gaze, not wanting to look into his eyes. When another woman walked over and took her by the arm, Lila glanced up at him and mouthed a silent thank-you. She quickly lowered her gaze again as the woman led her over to the side of the big room, where a third woman stood watching. After some quick conversation, all three turned and went up the stairs to the second floor. Cullen was sure Lila was finding some comfort from her fellow prostitutes, who no doubt were greatly interested in her plight. His attention was called back when Moran asked him a question.

"If I was to look through my notices when I go back to the office, am I likely to find some paper on you?"

"I'd be surprised," Cullen replied.

Another thought struck the marshal then. "You lookin' for a job?" He had appraised many gunfighters over the years, and it was easy to assume he was looking at another one. This man calling himself McCabe, was a big man, and he wore a Colt sidearm riding in easy reach on his hip. Due to the size of the man, and the effortless way he carried it in one hand, the Winchester 73 went almost unnoticed. Moran thought he might be able to use a man like that, so he said, "If you're lookin' for a job, I might have one for you."

"Doin' what?" Cullen asked.

"Whatever needs takin' care of," Moran answered.

"That could mean just about anything," Cullen said. "I'll think it over while I take a look around town. I'm on a little vacation right now, and I don't know much about this part of Texas. Just thought I'd see what's here."

"The offer might not be open for long," the marshal said, "so you'd best decide quick."

"Fair enough," Cullen said. "I'll do that." He started to leave but paused to ask, "What about that horse Lila rode in on? I'll be glad to take it to the stable for you."

"Yeah, take it to the stable," Moran said, not sure when Boot would be back in town. "Tell Floyd I said to pour you a drink on your way out."

"Thanks, I will," Cullen replied, and stopped at the bar before leaving.

"I heard," Floyd Chandler said before Cullen could relay Moran's offer. "What's it gonna be?"

"One shot of rye whiskey," Cullen answered, and

watched as Floyd filled a shot glass. "Who's the fellow sittin' at the table with the marshal?"

"He's the owner," Floyd answered. "That is, he's the half owner, Tom Loughlin. Marshal Moran owns the other half of the business. Tom's the one who operates the business part of the saloon."

"Yeah? Who's the boss?" Cullen asked before he threw the shot back.

"Marshal Moran," Floyd said with a wry grin.

"That's what I figured. Thanks for the drink." He walked out of the saloon, then took the reins of the three horses and led them back to the stable he had passed on his way in.

Art Becker walked out of the stable to take in the evening air while the sun was still barely visible above the horizon. Looking uptown toward the saloons, he saw Cullen walking toward the stable, leading the horses, one of which he was certain belonged to Boot Davis. His initial thought was that the big man was another outlaw showing up to join Micah Moran's "posse." This especially, since he just came from the Cork and Bottle Saloon. Art stood there waiting, and when Cullen approached, he greeted him. "Good evenin', can I help you?"

"Evenin'," Cullen returned. "I'm gonna be in town overnight, so I'd like to leave my horses with you. These two are mine. The roan belongs to somebody else."

"Boot Davis," Art quickly interjected.

"That's what I was told," Cullen continued. "Anyway, I don't intend to pay for the roan. You don't think there'll be any problem gettin' money for his board, do ya?"

"Nah, there won't be any problem," Art replied, thinking there never was any problem because there never was any pay for boarding Boot's horse. This was a special privilege dictated to him by Marshal Moran. "You just stayin' one night?"

"Don't know for sure," Cullen answered, "but right now that's my thinkin'. I've never been in East City before, so I thought I'd look around, long as I'm here. Any place in town to rent a room and maybe get a decent supper? I noticed that two-story building on the other side of the Cork and Bottle has a sign that says it's a hotel. Is it as bad on the inside as it looks on the outside?"

Cullen's questions caused Art to wonder if maybe he had misjudged him. "Did the marshal recommend the hotel?" Art asked, surprised that he had not, since that was the usual accommodation for his posse.

"No," Cullen answered. "I reckon it never occurred to me to ask him where to get a bed for the night."

Art studied the tall, solemn stranger for a moment before deciding to take a chance on giving him an honest answer. "Mister, if you're really interested in a clean bed and a decent meal that ain't likely to give you belly cramps, stay clear of the hotel. That ain't nothin' but a whorehouse, even though they do serve a little food, if you've got stomach enough to handle it. Moran owns it. He just stuck a sign on it that says 'Hotel.' It ain't got a real name."

"Much obliged," Cullen said, and nodded his head in honest appreciation of the warning.

Confident from Cullen's reaction to his comments, Art ventured to say more. "Like I said, if you're lookin' for a clean bed and a decent meal, there's a lane leadin' off the road to a roomin' house just north of town. It sets back a ways from the main road. There ain't no name on it, just walk on in the parlor and ask for Hortense. She'll fix you up for the night, or for a month. And I know she's got an empty room, 'cause that's where I stay, and the room next to mine ain't got nobody stayin' in it."

"That sounds to my likin'," Cullen said.

"Good. I was just gettin' ready to go to supper. You can go with me and talk to Hortense about a room for the night. We'll take care of your horses right quick, and you can leave those packs in the stall if you want to. It ain't far to walk from here. There's a little path that's a shortcut. We've got time before supper's over." He grinned at Cullen, feeling he had read the somber man correctly, and extended his hand. "Art Becker's my name."

"Cullen McCabe," he said as he shook Art's hand. In spite of what he had been told, he was beginning to think there were honest people in East City. The whole town wasn't evil, and thinking that, he asked, "How long have you been here, Art?" Art boasted that he had been there since before it was called East City. So Cullen figured there had to be more good people who were there before Micah Moran moved in to take over the town.

After the horses were taken care of and they had moved the packs from Cullen's sorrel, Art showed him a footpath behind his stable that followed the creek to Hortense Billings's rooming house. It was a shortcut that saved following the main road around to get there. Hortense was in the kitchen, helping her cook get the food to the table when Art called her.

Wiping her hands on her apron, she walked out into the hallway. "What is it, Mr. Becker?" Cullen stepped into the hall behind Art then, causing her to pause.

"I got a fellow here lookin' for some supper and a room for the night," Art said.

"Oh?" Hortense responded, arching her neck to look around him for a better look at the stranger.

"I realize this ain't exactly a good time to pop in on you," Cullen volunteered. "I mean, right at supper-time without any notice, but I just now got into town. You most likely didn't plan for an extra mouth at the table, so I've got some jerky and coffee in my packs back at the stable I could make do until breakfast." His comment caused both Art and Hortense to laugh.

"I ain't ever seen Annie run short of food, no matter who showed up," Art declared.

"That's right, Mr. . . . ." She paused to get his name. ". . . McCabe," she continued when he supplied it. "I'm sure there's enough, so nobody will go without. I'll show you to your room. You won't need those at the supper table," she added, glancing at the rifle in his hand and the saddlebags on his shoulder. She turned and headed to the stairs, signaling him to follow. He couldn't help marveling at her immediate acceptance, considering the reputation of the town and the population of outlaws there. He figured it had to be that she trusted Art's recommendation.

As Art had told him, the room Hortense led him to was neat and the bedclothes smelled clean. He left his rifle and gun belt on the bed and threw his saddlebags in the corner, then went down to the dining room to find four guests, including Art, seated at the table. They all paused to give him their attention while Hortense introduced him. He received polite nods from all as he sat down in the one empty chair. "I think you'd best move your plate to the end of the table, Mr. McCabe," Hortense said after he had settled in the chair. "I'm afraid you'll have your elbows in Mr. Skelton's plate, if you don't."

Only slightly embarrassed, Cullen said, "I reckon I figured that was your place at the head of the table."

"No, indeed," Hortense responded. "I can squeeze in anywhere. Mr. Billings used to sit in that chair before he passed away."

Not sure how to reply to that remark, he said, "If you say so, ma'am," then got up and moved to the head of the table. Everyone at the table smiled and nodded their agreement with his relocation, especially Mr. Skelton, Cullen assumed. Once the new guest was settled in his chair, everyone got back to the meal before them, and the conversation began once more. Much of it was aimed at Cullen in the form of questions, which he tried to answer in terms as vague as possible. In general, he told them that he was look- ing over a big section of the state to evaluate the prairies most suitable for raising cattle. It was the first thing he could think of.

"I ain't the smartest feller around," Roy Skelton saw fit to comment. "But it seems to me it oughta be pretty simple to figure that out. You need grass and water. Ain't that about it?"

"That's about right," Cullen answered the old gentleman, already wishing he had come up with some other explanation for his presence there. "Course, the company I work for is wantin' me to find water and grass where there's room for some more big ranches. I declare, Mrs. Billings," he said, anxious to change the subject, "Art surely wasn't lyin' when he said this was the best food in the territory."

Sensing his reluctance to talk about himself, Hortense replied, "Well, thank you, sir. I'll tell Annie what you said. Now, I expect we'd better let you eat before it gets cold."

He appreciated her comment, coming as it did when he was beginning to think he had made a mistake in taking a room there. It might have been better to have camped outside of town, where there would be no questions. Since he was looking for answers, himself, he walked back to the stable with Art when supper was over, under the premise that he wanted to check his horses' hooves.

After spending some time with Jake and then his packhorse, Cullen climbed up into the hayloft, where Art was forking down some new hay for Jake's stall. "Hortense doesn't look that old," Cullen said. "How long has it been since her husband passed away?"

"Been 'bout three years, now," Art replied, scratching his head to help him remember.

"What took him?" Cullen asked.

Art paused before answering, thinking how best to put it. "Ignorance, I reckon you'd have to say." When Cullen raised his eyebrows at that, Art explained further. "He told one of them low-down gunslingers of Moran's posse not to use such foul language in front of his wife. Well, that caused the half-drunk louse to make a downright filthy remark to Hortense to see if her husband had the guts to do anything about it. Billings shoulda known he didn't stand a chance against that gunman, drunk or sober. Hortense tried to get him to walk away, but he was too stubborn to turn tail. So you know the rest." Cullen said that he did.

Art had some questions for Cullen as well. "I saw you when you rode into town this evenin', you and one of those whores that work at the Cork and Bottle. That ain't none of my business, and you can tell me to go to hell, but she was ridin' Boot Davis's red roan. I couldn't help wonderin' if Boot is no longer with us, not that that would be any great loss."

Evidently, Art didn't know that Lila had been missing or that Boot went after her. "I don't have any idea if Boot has passed away," he said. "I've never had the pleasure of makin' his acquaintance. But I can tell you how I happened to be in the company of that prostitute. I found her alone about sixty-five miles south of here, just her and that red roan." He didn't tell Art the whole story, explaining why Lila was so far from East City. "I was comin' this way, anyway, so I brought her along with me, and that's the end of that story."

Art considered that, but he was still not satisfied that he had all the details. "But how did Boot's horse get way down there where you said you found it?" Cullen figured it shouldn't have been tough to figure out, but he spelled it out for him. "Oh," Art said, finally getting the simple picture. "Boot grabbed the whore, she got away from him, stole his horse, and ran off with it. You came up on her and brought her back here." Cullen nodded, amazed that it took so much explanation. Understanding finally, Art nodded, too. "You know, McCabe, you ain't done nothin' but help a woman in a fix and return a horse to where it came from." Having allowed that, he felt the need to offer advice. "I don't know how long you intend to stay here in town, but it might not be a good idea for you to be here when Boot gets back. He's liable to think you had somethin' to do with her running off. And I can tell you, Boot ain't a very peaceful man, and if Charley Turner is with him, there's bound to be trouble."

"'Preciate the warnin'," Cullen said. "You strike me as an honest man. Who else can an honest man trust in this town?"

The question caused Art to hesitate before answering. Then he decided there was nothing suspicious about it, so he answered. "What you're wantin' to know is who ain't in cahoots with Marshal Moran and his gang of outlaws. Right?" When Cullen nodded, Art continued. "Well, there's a lot of honest, hard-workin' folks settled around East City. But the folks who've been here in business the longest are me; Joe Johnson, down at the general store; Abe Franks at the hardware store; Cary O'Sullivan at O'Sullivan's; Martin Pearson at the feed store; Stewart Ingram, the postmaster; and Buck Casey, the blacksmith. We make up the town council with Abe Franks as the mayor. So that's who you can trust, if that's what you're drivin' at." He paused and shook his head. "But it's a town council in name only. We don't decide a damn thing. Micah Moran decides what we can and can't do."

"Much obliged," Cullen said, since that was exactly what he wanted to know. East City was as close to a lawless kingdom as he could imagine, with Micah Moran sitting on the throne. The town council was a council in name only, and as such, would never have a prayer of building a respectable town. It occurred to him that the governor had sent him up here when he pretty much knew the situation already.

CHAPTER 5

After a solid breakfast at Hortense Billings's table the next morning, Cullen announced to those seated at the table that he was going to walk around town to see what East City was all about. "Should I save your room for you?" Hortense asked. "Or are you going to be moving on today?"

"To tell you the truth," Cullen answered, "it's been a long time since I've had a nice bed and been able to enjoy some real cookin'. I think I'll stay with you for a few days, if that's all right with you." She was pleased to hear his answer and assured him that he was welcome. "Good," he went on. "I'm gonna take a look around Ravenwood while I'm out in this part of the state, too. But I'm so comfortable in your house, I think I'll still stay here, since Ravenwood is right across the creek." That really seemed to please her.

"Glad to hear it," Art Becker said, just coming in the back door. He was just getting back for his breakfast after leaving earlier to open his stable. "I took a look in his stall," he joked. "Your horse is still there."

"Well, that surely is good news," Cullen came back at him and laughed with him.

"Heard you say you're gonna cross over to Ravenwood," Art said. "Goin' over to rub elbows with the fancy folks, are ya? Over there in the county seat," he went on.

"If it's that fancy, I think I'd best clean up a little bit before I go. And maybe I'll visit the barbershop, too."

"If you want a shave and a haircut, you'll have to get 'em across the creek," Art said. "We ain't got a barber over here where the poor folks live."

"Maybe that's what I'll do, then," Cullen said. "I'll be back for supper this evenin'," he said to Hortense, and took his leave.

"Pork chops tonight," she called after him. When he had gone, she turned to Art and asked, "Who is that man? You know darn well he didn't come here to look for grazing land for cattle."

Art didn't answer until he heard the front door close. "I don't know, Hortense. You might be right about that, but he seems to be on the up-and-up, and he doesn't appear to have any connection to Micah Moran and his bunch. That right there makes him all right in my book."

"He doesn't say much," Hortense commented, "but he's polite enough. I expect he'll move on in a day or two."

"He's liable to move quicker'n that," Art said, "when Boot Davis gets back in town and finds out McCabe brought his horse with him and a whore in the saddle." He saw at once that Hortense had no idea what he was talking about, so he had to tell her the story. It only added to the mystery Hortense already saw in her new tenant and caused her to wonder if Art might be justified in his concern for Cullen.

* * *

Cullen saw immediately that Michael O'Brien and Governor Hubbard had been right on the money when they said the difference in the two towns was like night and day. As he slow-walked Jake down the main street past the courthouse, he saw that Art had been right as well when he said there was a barber in Ravenwood. He spotted it right next to the post office, so he figured he'd go through with what he had threatened in East City and pay for a shave and a haircut. He figured it to be a good investment, because usually the barber knew about everything going on in town most of the time.

"Mornin', stranger," Rodney Blake greeted him when he walked in the door. "What can I do you for?"

"It's been a while since I've bought a shave and a haircut," Cullen said. "I feel like doin' it today."

"Well, you've come to the right place," the barber said. "Don't believe I've seen you in town before. You passin' through, or are you gonna stay with us awhile?" Without waiting for an answer, he stuck out his hand. "My name's Rodney Blake, and I'll be glad to fix you up fit for the church social, or the soiled doves over at the saloon. I can shape that mustache up for you."

"Just shave all the mustache and chin whiskers off and cut my hair off a little shorter, and I'll skip the church and the saloon." He shook the extended hand and said, "Cullen McCabe," then sat down in the barber chair. By the time Rodney had finished, Cullen knew about all the latest news and activities in the town—where to get the best dinner and Rodney's choice of saloons between the two in town. As a final touch, and before Cullen had a chance to stop him, Rodney splashed a high-smelling solution on his face.

Twitching his nose like a bloodhound on a hot trail, Cullen paid the barber, settled his hat on his shorter hair, and went outside to take a look at the town. Before he untied Jake, however, he walked over to the horse trough on the corner of the street and washed his face as vigorously as he could in an effort to rid himself of the aftershave. Satisfied that he wouldn't attract horseflies then, he climbed up into the saddle and slow-walked Jake up the street, looking at the shops and the people coming and going. He decided it was in direct contrast to the streets of East City. Ravenwood appeared to be a normal town, and from the looks of it, probably on the way to becoming a sizable city. *Peaceful* was the word he thought of to describe it. He decided to stop in a large store bearing a sign that identified it as HORMEL GENERAL MERCHANDISE.

James Hormel glanced up toward the front of the store when he heard the screen door open. He paused to take a longer look at the imposing stranger before greeting him. "Good mornin'. Something I can help you with?"

"Yep, I need to buy me a new razor," Cullen replied. "I had to go to the barber this mornin' to get a shave."

"Come on down to this end of the counter and I'll show you what I've got," Hormel said. "Might have something you can use." Cullen followed him to the end of the long counter where Hormel opened a drawer holding several different razors. "Something like this?" he asked. While Cullen picked up the razor and examined it, Hormel continued talking. "Don't believe you've been in before."

"That's a fact," Cullen said. "Never been in Ravenwood before. Looks like a quiet little town. Did I hear about some kinda trouble you folks were havin' a while back?"

"Trouble?" Hormel asked, surprised. "What kind of trouble? The only trouble we ever have is when some of that outlaw riffraff on the other side of the creek crosses over to raise a little hell." When he saw the interested look on Cullen's face, he quickly explained. "Ravenwood's a peaceful little town and we're on our way to becoming a city. I'm on the city council and we're working to make Ravenwood the best place in Texas to settle. We have a little trouble now and then when some of those drunken outlaws come over here. But we've got an honest, hardworking marshal that tries to keep the peace."

"Have you ever tried contacting the governor's office for some help?" Cullen asked, already knowing the answer, but he wanted to hear Hormel's version.

"Oh, we complained to the state, all right," Hormel answered, rapidly warming up to the subject. "They sent two men up here to meet with Mayor Raven and the council, and said they'd go back and report to the governor about the problem. A couple of weeks after that, they sent a whole company of Rangers up here to camp on the other side of the creek. They stayed for three days. I reckon they figured that fixed all the problems, so they left and we're back with the same old problems with that damn Sodom across the creek."

"I'll take the razor," Cullen said, having heard what he needed to confirm what the governor had told him. He dug into his pocket for some money.

"Don't let my ranting give you the wrong impression of Ravenwood," Hormel quickly implored. "Are you thinking about settling in Ravenwood?"

"Just passin' through," Cullen said.

After he left the store, he decided he'd pay a little visit to some of the other businesses, so he would have the opinion of more than one man. Before he was through, he had spent the rest of the morning talking to other merchants, almost everyone but the staffs at the saloons and the hotel. He decided he might as well eat, since it was past noon already, and he had plenty of expense money. Before that, however, he decided to check out the Whistle Stop Saloon, the one the barber had recommended.

There was a small crowd of customers in the Whistle Stop. Cullen walked over to the bar, where half a dozen drinkers were lined up. He stepped in beside a fellow wearing a Stetson Boss of the Plains hat atop long hair that hung to his shoulders. "What's your pleasure, stranger?" Toby Futch, the bartender, asked. His greeting caught the attention of the long-haired man and he turned to take a look at the stranger, but said nothing.

Cullen ordered a single shot of whiskey, a little drink before he went in search of dinner, he told Toby. And when Toby poured it, Cullen was curious enough to ask, "Why do you call this place Whistle Stop? There ain't any railroad around here, is there?"

Toby chuckled, accustomed to the question from strangers. "Ain't got nothin' to do with the railroad. The boss named it that 'cause this is the place to come to wet your whistle." He paused to chuckle again. "There's some talk about the railroad comin' through here, though. Ain't that right, Marshal?"

The man with the hair to his shoulders, turned to Cullen again, this time far enough for Cullen to see the star on his vest. "That's what they say, all right."

Giving Cullen his full attention now, he asked, "What brings you to town, stranger?"

"Just curiosity, I reckon. I've never been in your town before, so I thought I'd stop long enough to see what's goin' on here. My name's Cullen McCabe."

"Tug Taggert," the marshal said. "What line of work are you in? You don't look like a cowhand, or a farmer, either."

"I've got a little place south of Austin, but I've been up north of here visitin' some friends. I'm on my way back home and I decided to take a look at Ravenwood. So far, it looks like a right friendly town."

"We're tryin' to keep it that way," Taggert said.

"Well, I've had my one drink, so I think I'll look for some dinner," Cullen announced. "Any recommendations?"

"It's hard to beat the dinin' room over at the hotel," Taggert said.

"I'll take your word for it," Cullen said. "Much obliged."

Outside, Cullen stepped up into the saddle and took the short ride past the courthouse to the hotel beyond and left Jake at the hitching rail by the outside door of the dining room. He was met by Marcy Manning at the door and asked to leave his firearms on a table nearby. After he left his Colt and his Winchester on the table, Marcy showed him to another small table close to the kitchen door. The beef stew was good, and the coffee was hot, so he took his time to enjoy the meal. He intended to make more stops, although he felt that he had a pretty good picture of the town. He had seen nothing that would lead him to believe Ravenwood was the major cause of the trouble between the two towns. East City was just a town of outlaws, run by outlaws, and he wasn't sure he could do anything to change that. Michael O'Brien told him to just ride up there to look at the situation, and that's what he was doing. He might as well start back to Austin in the morning.

He finished his dinner, collected his firearms, and prepared to head back across the creek to East City when he heard the sound of gunshots. He couldn't be sure, but he thought they might have come from inside the saloon he had been in earlier. With an eye toward caution until he figured out the source, he waited to hear if there were more shots. Less than thirty seconds later, he heard two more. Louder and sharper, he figured they were shot outside the building. Then he saw the source. Two men moved out in the street in front of the saloon, blazing away with six-guns at someone taking cover behind a wagon. When he got a glimpse of the man behind the wagon, he grabbed his rifle and ran toward the Whistle Stop, leaving Jake there at the dining room hitching rail. It was Marshal Tug Taggert and he was not in the best position to defend himself. The two gunmen he faced were obviously hoping he would raise up from behind the wagon to take a shot at them. It wasn't going to be much longer before he would be in the open because the two horses hitched to the wagon were frightened and already rearing frantically. "Come on outta there, Marshal!" one of the shooters taunted. "Stick your head up for me!" He fired three more shots into the side of the wagon.

So intent upon keeping an eye on the marshal, neither man was aware of the big man carrying the rifle running toward them. "Drop your weapons!" Cullen ordered as he approached, which stopped both men from firing momentarily. "Drop 'em right there and stick your hands up in the air! Now!"

"Go to hell," one of them snarled, and spun around to face Cullen. The slug from Cullen's rifle tore into his side before he had turned halfway. In the brief instant while the other man stood stunned to see his partner drop, Cullen cranked another cartridge in and was set to fire. The shooter wisely dropped his pistol and held his hands up.

Stunned as well, Marshal Taggert stepped out from behind the wagon, his handgun aimed at the remaining outlaw. "Get on your knees!" he ordered the gunman, then took a quick look at the man Cullen shot before picking up their weapons. Then he looked at Cullen and confessed, "Damned if you didn't save my bacon! There ain't no doubt about that. It was my fault I let 'em pin me behind that wagon. Mister, I forgot your name, I owe you for sure."

"Cullen McCabe," he reminded him. "I'll help you herd this one to the jailhouse."

Unnoticed by the participants in the gun battle, or Cullen, either, the confrontation was being watched by a man on a horse. Two stores down from the saloon, he sat, holding the reins of two more horses with empty saddles. When it was plain that the shootout with the marshal had failed, he wheeled his horse and loped off toward the end of the street, leading the two extra horses. Thinking the shooting was over, anxious spectators came streaming out of the saloon to see the carnage. Taggert grabbed one of them by the arm. "Go fetch Doc McNair. Tell him there's a wounded man outside the saloon. I gotta get this one locked up." On the way to the jail, Taggert told Cullen what had happened to set up the ambush he blindly walked into. "One of 'em shot a feller they were playin' cards with and shot at me when I started after 'em. I was lucky to jump behind the bar to keep from gettin' hit. Then they ran out the door and I ran after 'em, but I found out too late that they were standin' out there, waiting for me to run out the door." He prodded his prisoner in the back with his six-gun. "Ain't that right? That crooked marshal over the creek sent you two to shoot me."

"That's you that's sayin' that," his prisoner snarled. "We weren't tryin' to kill you. We was just protectin' ourselves."

"We'll see if Judge Raven thinks that," Taggert said. Then it occurred to him to ask, "Where'd you leave your horses?"

"We walked over here," the prisoner spat defiantly.

"So there were three of you assassins," Taggert said. "And your brave partner ran off with the horses when the shootin' started. What's your name?"

"I ain't got one," his prisoner replied. "We was poor where I came from, so my mammy couldn't afford a name."

"Why, you're a regular clown, ain't you?" Taggert responded. "I expect you musta been a bastard and that's why you ain't got no name. But everybody in my jail has to have a name, so I can tell the hooligans apart, so I'll have to give you one. I think I'll call you Cow Pie. You like that name all right?"

Cullen stayed there until the marshal had his prisoner, who still refused to give his name, locked up in a cell on the lower floor of the courthouse. When they walked back outside, Taggert extended his hand. "Man, I appreciate the way you stepped in back there. Everybody else was just stayin' under cover. The city council just voted me the money to hire a deputy, but he ain't startin' till the first of the month. Fine young man—name's Beau Arnett—comes highly qualified. For a while back there behind that wagon, I was wishin' he'd started the first of this month. So I'm damn glad you decided to take a look at Ravenwood." Still gripping his hand, he blurted a question. "Who the hell are you, anyway?"

"I told you, Cullen McCabe."

"I don't mean your name. Hell, I got that. What I mean is, who are you, really? I ain't never seen anybody handle a Winchester rifle like you did when that feller tried to shoot you. He didn't even have to draw, he already had his gun in hand, and he didn't get turned halfway around before you hit him."

"I was just lucky, I reckon, and he wasn't that fast." He shrugged as if to say he had no explanation for it.

Taggert just stared at him for a long moment, a smile on his face indicating he didn't believe him. "All right," he finally said. "Whatever you say, but the least I can do is buy your supper. Whaddaya say?"

"Thanks, Marshal, I appreciate the offer, but after I make a few stops, I've gotta get back to East City. I'm rentin' a room in a boardin'house over there and I told 'em I'd be back for supper."

"East City!" Taggert exclaimed. "I hope you're talkin' about that little boardin'house owned by Hortense Billings." Cullen said that he was and Taggert went on. "Damn, McCabe, you'd best keep your head down over there. If word gets out over there what you done tonight, it won't be safe for you to go to the outhouse. I ain't got a doubt in my mind that Micah Moran sent those two jaspers over here to get me. He's liable to find out that it was you that saved my bacon. The third man, who was holdin' the getaway horses, musta seen you."

"He probably didn't get a real good look at me, but I'll be extra careful," Cullen said, and started back to the dining room to get his horse.

Taggert stood in front of the courthouse, watching Cullen walk away. *I don't know what line of work you're in, but I'll bet my bottom dollar it has something to do with that rifle you're toting,* he thought.

Cullen was thinking about the rugged-looking marshal with the shoulder-length hair hanging like a curtain from under the Stetson hat. He got the impression that he was an honest, hardworking lawman. He liked him. He was the kind of man East City needed, if they could ever successfully rid the town of Micah Moran and his "posse."

CHAPTER 6

Right across Walnut Creek from each other, the two towns were about a mile and a half apart, as the crow flies. There was a road that linked them and there was once a bridge across the creek, but someone had destroyed the bridge. Cullen had discovered it when he crossed there that morning. Now, as he approached the crossing on his way back, he was thinking that someone on the Ravenwood side must have done away with the bridge. And he found that he couldn't blame them. If Tug Taggert knew about Hortense Billings's boardinghouse, he must know other people in East City who are honest hardworking people. There was only one solution for the problems between the two towns and that was to clean Micah Moran and his rotten crowd out of town. It was a simple answer, but he wasn't sure it could be done without a Ranger company permanently stationed there. *That will be my recommendation to Governor Hubbard,* he thought. And with that in mind, he reaffirmed his plan to start back to Austin in the morning.

It was nearing dusk by the time he rode up out of the creek and followed the road into town. As he approached Art Becker's stable, he thought he spotted something odd swaying in the gentle breeze moving the trees beyond the corral. He didn't think he had noticed it before, but he didn't focus on it. When he approached the stable door, he glanced toward the corral again and realized what he had seen. It was a body, hanging from a limb of a large oak! A woman's body! He turned Jake's head toward the tree to get a closer look. It was Lila Blanchard! Hearing a sound behind him, he turned to see Art Becker running toward him. "Hung for a horse thief!" he cried out obviously upset. "It's that whore you brought back here! They hung her for a horse thief, said she stole Boot Davis's horse. Didn't matter she brought it back. Micah Moran said she stole the horse and horse thieves get hung in this town. He won't let nobody cut her down, said to let her hang there, so everybody gets a chance to see her and learns a lesson."

Cullen felt the blood run hot in his veins as he stared at the pitiful corpse when it swayed slowly back and forth with every little change of the breeze. The murder of this innocent young woman was one of the lowest acts of pure evil that he had ever seen. After a long moment, he asked, "Who strung her up?"

"Boot and Charley actually tied the rope around her neck and hauled her up on that limb," Art said. "But it was Marshal Moran that told 'em to do it."

"Did she tell him about gettin' kidnapped and raped and Boot Davis sayin' he was gonna kill her when they were finished with her? And the part where she had to run for her life?"

"Well, I wasn't there when Boot and Charley showed up at the Cork and Bottle this mornin'." He paused to point out, "That ain't my favorite saloon. But it likely wasn't more'n half an hour after you left. Well, like I said, I wasn't there in the saloon, but Wilma Wiggins was. She's one of the women that works there. She said Lila told Moran all about that business with Boot and Charley. Boot said she was a damn liar and she oughta be hung for stealin' his horse. So the marshal told 'em to go do it."

The more Cullen heard of the vicious act on this poor defenseless victim and her killers' callous disregard for human life, the madder he became. This was no longer an investigation for the governor. With this evil act, it was now a personal matter, and he was resolved to see that the perpetrators were made to pay for their deeds. Not planning now to return to Austin in the morning, he pulled his horse up close to Lila's body and put his arm around her. With his other hand, he drew his skinning knife and hacked the rope in two, easily holding the frail corpse in one arm. Seeing what Cullen was doing, Art hurried over to help lower the body gently to the ground. "Whaddaya gonna do?" Art asked, anxiously.

"I'm gonna bury her," Cullen replied. "I think she deserves that."

"Cullen," Art implored, "there's gonna be hell to pay if Moran finds out you cut her down. You'd better bury her somewhere back in the woods before somebody comes along here and sees us. I'll help you dig a grave, but let's get the hell out of the open before we get caught."

"This ain't got nothin' to do with you, Art. You've got no part in it. I'm the one who cut her down and I'm the one who'll bury her. And I want Micah Moran to know it. He can come talk to me about it, if he doesn't like me doin' it."

"Oh, he's gonna be hoppin' mad, all right," Art responded. "Only, I doubt he'll come talk to you. More'n likely, he'll send his deputy, Ace Brown, to come after you—him or Boot and Charley—maybe all three." He wasn't sure Cullen realized he might have signed his death warrant with that skinning knife. And chances were his body, shot full of holes, would be swinging from that limb where Lila's body had been.

"I 'preciate you offerin' to help, Art, but all I want from you is the borrow of a shovel to dig the grave. I'm hopin' nobody notices that Lila's gone from this tree tonight. If you say it happened right after I left here this mornin', I expect everybody's already done all their gawkin' at her. I reckon what I'm tellin' you is there's gonna be a war, and I don't want you or Hortense Billings to get involved in it. So, I won't be stayin' in the boardin'house. I'll go pick up my possibles from there after I take care of Lila. Then, if it's all right with you, I'll sleep with my horses tonight in your stable. Like I said, I think we'll be all right for tonight, and tomorrow I'll be outta there. Is that okay?"

"Yeah, sure it is," Art replied. "But if you're plannin' on being here in the mornin' when they do find out that body's gone, you ain't gonna stand much of a chance alone."

"I'm willin' to risk it," Cullen said. "Now give me a hand with her body. It's already gettin' stiff and I'm gonna lay her behind my saddle, if she ain't too stiff to ride there." They saw right away that wouldn't work, so Cullen ended up holding her across his thighs. Her back pressed against the saddle horn helped secure her. Art went to the barn and returned with a shovel, which Cullen stuck down beside his saddle sling.

Before Cullen pulled away, Art felt the need to

explain something. "Cullen, I might be wrong, but I think you're an honest man. And I wanna let you know I am, too. I reckon I spend more time with Micah Moran's gang of outlaws than anybody else in East City. But that's because I ain't got no choice. I own the stable, and they keep their horses here. I hear a lot of their talk, but I sure as hell ain't one of 'em. So I just want to let you know I ain't gonna say who cut Lila down."

"Hell, I know that," Cullen said. "I already figured that out."

Then Art stood back to watch Jake walk slowly away with the dead woman cradled by the big man and the shovel sticking up like a cavalry flag. He almost called out to tell him he was going the wrong way, since he was heading toward town, but he held his tongue. He shook his head and headed back toward the barn.

Less than fifteen minutes later, one of Moran's posse, Stan Molloy, came riding up, leading two rider-less horses. "Here," he yelled to Art, "take care of these horses!" He jumped down and started to run toward the Cork and Bottle.

"Who do the other two belong to?" Art shouted after him, even though he knew Molloy and two others, Johnny Barr and Sam Polek, rode out that morning, talking about going to Ravenwood.

"Just do what I said and take care of 'em!" Molloy shouted back, in too great a hurry to stop to talk, and luckily, too great a hurry to notice there was no one hanging in the tree.

Art was thankful for that. *Maybe it was on the side of his bad eye*, he thought. Molloy, an especially belligerent individual, wore a patch on his left eye, the result of a knife fight some years before.

* * *

Micah Moran was angry and confused at the same time. Stan Molloy was standing in front of his table, shifting nervously from one foot to the other. "Why do you think it was McCabe?" Moran asked.

"It was him, all right, the same feller I saw walk outta here yesterday when he brought Lila back on Boot's horse."

"But you're tellin' me he was helpin' the marshal, and he shot Johnny and Sam?"

"He shot Johnny, but he didn't shoot Sam," Molloy insisted. "Then him and the marshal arrested both of 'em and hauled 'em off to jail, I reckon. I didn't hang around to see."

"Where the hell were you all that time they were gettin' shot at?" Moran demanded.

"I was two or three stores down from the saloon, holdin' the horses, just like we decided. Johnny and Sam wanted to be the ones that went in the saloon to pick a fight. And I was ready to bring their horses as soon as they shot the marshal, so we could make a quick getaway. It all happened too quick. I didn't have no time to help 'em, far away as I was. Besides, they was supposed to shoot the marshal in the saloon, but I reckon they missed 'cause most of the shootin' was in the street. And that McCabe jasper was waitin' out in the street for 'em. I swear, Micah, it looked more like they was set up, waitin' for us, than the other way around. I got outta there fast, but I didn't know if they saw me or not, so I took off out the north end of town 'cause I didn't wanna lead 'em here. Found me a spot to hide out till I was sure I could come back."

It was a very worrisome report on the planned

assassination of Marshal Tug Taggert. Moran had decided to make that move several days before all this mess with Boot Davis and Lila Blanchard was on everybody's mind. As he thought back, he remembered that Ned Larson was one of the ones who thought it a smart plan. "Might even get one of our boys to run for marshal," he had said. And Cullen McCabe was there. How'd he know to be there? And now, he had lost two good men.

Thinking at first that he should find a quiet secluded spot to bury the unfortunate prostitute, Cullen changed his mind, somehow certain that Lila would approve. Instead of the creek bank, then, he guided Jake to walk slowly behind the backs of the buildings on the one street. It was almost a hard dark by then, so he thought his odds were good that he wouldn't be disturbed in his labor. The sounds of raucous laughter and loud conversation, mixed with the notes of a tinny piano, came to him as he guided Jake to a stop between the Cork and Bottle and the hotel. He let Lila slide down to the ground, then he dismounted, grabbed his shovel, and started testing the ground between the two buildings, hoping to find a spot that wasn't too hard. There didn't seem to be any place better than another, so he went to work on a spot close to the backs of the buildings. It was not easy digging. He wished he had a pick as well, but after breaking through the sunbaked surface, he began to make real progress. It took him an hour to dig a grave that suited him. When it was finished, he laid Lila gently into the grave and uttered a sincere apology for the rough burial. He was still of the opinion that she would approve of this as a chance to come back at Micah Moran and his posse. He could not help feeling that he had a part in her death, for he had brought her back to this hellhole. She had been convinced that she would be safe at the Cork and Bottle, thinking Moran would protect her from Boot Davis. Standing over the mound of dirt, in the darkness of the alley, he promised her that Moran and his kind would not get away with her murder.

As he prepared to leave, he was suddenly overcome with memories of the personal tragedy that resulted in his appointment to serve as the governor's special agent. Fleeting sketches flashed across his mind's eye of his wife, Mary Kate, and their three children: Lucy, nine; Cullen junior, seven; and William, five. Their lives were snuffed out, and their home burned to the ground, by ruthless men such as those surrounding Micah Moran. He had hunted those men down and hung every one of them, but it brought no peace to his mind. It left him with only an empty feeling with no concern if he lived or died. He knew it was this state of mind that the governor saw as an ideal qualification for his job.

His mind came back to reality when he felt a nudge against his back. He turned and gently rubbed Jake's face. The big bay gelding always seemed to know when his partner was visiting that dark place again. "All right, Jake," he said softly, "let's take Art's shovel back. I'm gonna put you in your stall, then I'll go pick up my things from the boardin'house."

Although it was late and well past suppertime, he found there was a plate of food warming for him in the oven. He was met in the hallway by both Hortense and Annie when he came in the front door. "There's supper for you in the oven," Hortense said. "Mr. Becker said that you wouldn't be able to get here till later."

"And we didn't want you to go to bed hungry," Annie said. It occurred to him that it was the first time she had ever spoken directly to him. The serious, almost solemn, attitude they appeared to have made him wonder how much Art might have told them. He would have preferred for them to know nothing about his activities on this evening, so they would be innocent if Moran came to ask questions about him.

"I'm sorry to cause you extra trouble, but I surely do appreciate it," he said. "Did Art tell you that I won't be stayin' here tonight? I just came back to get my things and to pay you what I owe you."

"You shaved your mustache off," Hortense suddenly stated, surprising him. He had forgotten it, himself.

"Yes, ma'am, and cut my hair off, too," he replied.

"You don't have to pay me for the one night. You were just our guest for the night," Hortense said. "Now, come on in the kitchen and sit down before that food dries out." He followed them into the kitchen and sat down at the table. Annie got his plate out of the oven and Hortense sat down across from him. "You know," she said, "as late as it is, you don't have to leave tonight. You might as well stay here."

He was sure now that Art had told them the whole story, and he appreciated their attitude, but he didn't want to take any chance of endangering them, or the other boarders. "Art tell you what I did?" Both women nodded.

"I'm sorry he did," Cullen said. "I don't want you folks gettin' mixed up in any trouble I've caused with the marshal and that gang of his. I'm hopin' he ain't got any idea that I'm stayin' here at your place, so I wanna get out before he finds out."

"I reckon that's the smartest thing you could do," Annie said. "But like you said, Moran probably don't know you're here. So, you oughta be able to stay here tonight and leave town in the morning. I'll fix you some food to take with you and you'll be long gone before anybody knows you've left town." Hortense nodded in agreement with her.

"I'm not leavin' town," Cullen said. "I'm just leavin' your house."

"Are you crazy?" Annie exclaimed. "They're gonna know you cut that woman's body down! You were the one who brought her back to East City!"

"Annie's right," Hortense said. "You might be making a terrible mistake if you hang around this town. They'll blame it on somebody and you're the obvious one. Why are you gonna stay?"

"I've got my reasons," he answered, and got up from the table. "Now, since you ain't afraid to have me sleep here tonight, I'll go upstairs to bed now 'cause I'll be gettin' up early in the mornin'."

"I will, too," Annie said, "so I'll have somethin' for you to eat."

"'Preciate it, but you don't have to get up for that."

"I know it," Annie replied. "But if breakfast in the mornin' is liable to be your last meal, I wanna make sure you get a good one." He left them, still shaking their heads over his stubborn suicidal tendency.

"She's gone!" Charley Turner blurted as he stormed in the Cork and Bottle. "She's gone!" he declared loudly again as he headed straight to the table where Boot Davis was eating breakfast with two other members of the marshal's posse, Shep Parker and Shorty Miller.

"Who's gone?" Boot asked, not really caring.

"Lila Blanchard, that's who," Charley answered him, immediately capturing their attention. "She's gone outta that tree. Somebody's cut her down and hauled her off."

"What about Becker?" Boot asked. "He musta seen who done it."

"You'da thought so," Charley replied. "But he claims he don't know who did it, said they musta done it in the middle of the night. He didn't even know she was gone; till I told him."

"Micah ain't gonna like this," Shep said. "He told ever'body to leave that body swingin' till he said to take it down."

"Hell, I don't like it," Boot snorted. "I've had enough trouble 'cause of that whore. He turned to a table across the room where the two remaining prostitutes were having breakfast. "Mabel!" he roared. You know anything about this?"

Had he taken a closer look at the two women, he might have seen the shocked surprise in both their faces. "No, Boot, it's news to us. We don't know nothin' about it. Do we, Wilma?" Wilma immediately shook her head. When Boot looked away, the two women immediately started speculating on the mystery, themselves.

Hearing the chatter going on between them, Boot barked, "You sure you women ain't planned a funeral somewhere?" When they both shook their heads, he threatened, "If I find out you did, there's gonna be two more funerals." He was distracted then when Leroy Hill came in the back door.

Unaware of the conversation going on in the saloon while he was outside relieving himself of some of the coffee he had consumed that morning, he made a comment. "Hey, I was just out back gettin' rid of some coffee, and I saw somethin' I never noticed before." More interested in the disappearance of Lila Blanchard's body, nobody paid much attention to Leroy's news. He continued, anyway. "I'm standin' there, doin' my business, and I looked over toward the back corner of the saloon, in the middle of the alley. And, I swear, there's a grave back there. At least it looks like a grave. Maybe it's just a pile of dirt. Anybody else ever notice that before?" He was aware then that he suddenly had everyone's attention and he was soon amazed when everyone, including the two women, got up from their chairs and rushed toward the back door. Astonished by the extreme interest they all had to confirm his story, he had no choice but to follow them.

When he saw them standing around the grave and the intensity of the conversation going back and forth across the mound of dirt, he grabbed Shorty by the elbow. "What the hell's goin' on?" Leroy asked.

"Lila," was Shorty's one-word answer before he turned his attention back to what was being said by Boot and Charley.

Still in the dark, Leroy turned to Wilma for explanation. "Looks like Lila's come back to haunt Boot," she whispered. Then she went on to enlighten him on the events of the morning, so far, which properly stunned him, just as they had everybody else. "Of course, that might not be a grave, at all," Wilma continued.

"Might just be a pile of dirt, but I believe it's Lila come home, a-layin' under that dirt."

"Well, I'll be . . ." Leroy started, then moved up beside Boot. "Whatcha gonna do, Boot? What you reckon ol' Micah's gonna do when he finds out somebody cut that whore down and brought her right back to bury her behind his saloon? You gonna dig her up?"

"Yeah, I'm gonna dig her up," Boot answered him. "I wanna make sure that's her in the ground and not somebody just tryin' to jape us. And after that, I'm gonna find that devil that brought her back to East City, ridin' on my horse. I've already got some business to settle with him. Now, I think I've got more." They were interrupted then by a call from the back of the saloon.

"What's goin' on back here?" Micah Moran demanded. "Floyd said somebody cut that woman down." They turned to see the marshal with his deputy right behind him. Boot was quick to explain why they were gathered around the mound of dirt. He told Moran he figured it was the man who brought her back to town, and he intended to settle with him. "I thought he left town," Moran said. "He wasn't here last night, was he? Anybody see him?" No one had. "I think I made it pretty clear to him day before yesterday that it wouldn't be healthy for him to be here when you and Charley got back." He turned to gaze down at the grave again. "Somebody go get a shovel. There's one by the back door." Leroy went at once to fetch it.

Seeing two shovels by the back door, Leroy brought them both and he and Shep went to work on the mound of dirt. Since it was not a very deep grave, it didn't take long before they began to uncover the body. The interested spectators gathered as closely around the grave as they could while staying out of the way of the men with the shovels. "Stop!" Mabel finally yelled when the shovels were beginning to rough up the body. She got down on her knees at the edge of the grave and started clearing the dirt away from the body, until gradually it became fully exposed.

"What's that she's holdin'?" Leroy asked, and they all crowded over the grave to see.

"It's a rope," Shorty said. "It's the noose that was around her neck." He looked back at Moran. "She's holding the rope she was hung with in her hand. Kinda like she's tellin' us to go to hell, ain't it?"

Moran stood rigid, his fists tightly clenched. Somebody in this town was throwing this hanging back in his face. "I wanna get the people who did this," he growled softly. Then raising his voice, he ordered, "Couple of you men pull her outta that hole and fill it up. I'm gonna find out who's responsible for this and we'll have us another hangin'."

"I don't believe there's anybody in this whole town who's got the guts to cut that body down, even in the middle of the night," Boot insisted. "It's gotta be that jasper that brought her all the way back here, and I aim to find out where he hightailed it to when he left here. It was me who got my horse stole. And maybe he brought my horse back, but he didn't bring my money back that was in my saddlebags." At the mention of the money, Mabel and Wilma exchanged a quick glance, having found the roll of money Lila had hidden. "He's holed up somewhere," Boot went on, "and I aim to find him. What was his name again?"

"McCabe," Moran said, "Cullen McCabe. Where the hell could he hide around here without somebody seein' him? I expect he left here and went to Ravenwood."

"Ain't no place he could hide in East City," Charley said. "He wasn't in the stable when I found Lila gone just now. And Becker said he didn't leave his horse there last night. So, hell, he's gone."

"What about that Billings woman?" Ned Larson asked, having just come from the saloon to see what was going on. "She's got a house full of lily-white churchgoers. He mighta took a room there."

"I didn't think about that," Boot said. "That's right, that might be the place he'd get himself a room, since he was too proper to stay in the hotel and it's a little ways outta town. I think I'll take a little ride over there and see if Mr. Cullen McCabe has a room there."

"Why don't you invite him back here to have a drink?" Leroy joked. "He might wanna join up with us."

"You want me to go over there and arrest him, Boss?" Ace Brown asked. "He might put up a fuss and I'll have to shoot him," he said with a wink for the marshal.

"No," Moran said, after a moment's consideration. "Boot's right, he deserves first crack at him. Charley, you better go with him, in case Boot ain't as fast as he thinks he is. I want that lowlife dead." He was still burning inside because of the gall of McCabe to cut that body down after he had ordered it to be left there. "Leroy, you and Shorty take that carcass away from my building and get rid of it somewhere."

"Looks like somebody don't care much for hangin' whores, don't it?" Ned Larson commented to Moran while they watched Lila's body being lifted out of her temporary grave. "I reckon I'll go back in and get some breakfast now."

Moran watched Larson when he turned and walked back toward the back door. He was still steaming over the gall someone had to cut Lila down. *I wouldn't be surprised if you had something to do with it,* he thought. There was no basis for thinking the thought, other than his usual suspicions regarding Ned Larson. Ned had his own gang of rustlers before coming to East City to join up with him. He brought three of his old gang with him, and it seemed to Moran that on too many occasions, he had felt it necessary to remind Larson that he was the boss. Moran felt secure in the knowledge that he had the loyalty of nine hardened gunmen, while Larson had only three. The number of gunmen had been reduced to seven, but as long as the odds stayed in his favor, Larson was obliged to toe the line with the rest of his men. But still a mystery to him was this new arrival, the stranger, Cullen McCabe, and whether he had some connection to Ned Larson.

At the back corner of his corral, unnoticed by the group of men gathered behind the saloon, Art Becker watched the party of outlaws through a cavalry field glass. It afforded him an excellent view of the grave robbery. "That son of a gun," Art muttered in admiration as he focused the lens on his glass. "He buried her right behind ol' Moran's saloon. I'd give a dollar to hear what they said about findin' Lila back home."

Knowing they wouldn't waste time and energy to dispose of Lila's body, Art continued to watch to see who got the job. When two of the men loaded her on the back of a horse and started up the creek, he was sure they would go no farther than they thought necessary to dump the body. Thinking the woman deserved a decent grave, and knowing Cullen wouldn't want her left to the buzzards, he determined to follow their trail and put her in the ground.

CHAPTER 7

"I was wondering how long it would be before that sorry bunch of outlaws would show up here," Hortense Billings said to Annie as she watched the two riders coming up the lane from the road. She opened the front door and walked out on the porch. Annie followed her, and the two women stood there to await their unwelcome guests. "It's the one they call Boot and that no-account that's always with him," Hortense commented.

"Reckon we shoulda brought the shotgun with us?" Annie was inspired to ask, since a more dangerous pair was hard to imagine.

Boot and Charley rode right up to the edge of the porch, plodding through a flower bed in the process. Seeing the stern show of defiance exhibited by the two women, Boot curled his lip into a sarcastic smile. "Well, good mornin', ladies, nice of you to come to welcome us."

"What do you want, Boot Davis?" Hortense demanded, which inspired Boot to chuckle. "State your business here," Hortense demanded again.

"Why, I'm surprised you know my name." It pleased

him to find that she did. It gave him a small sense of fame. "Me and Charley just decided we'd ride over and take a look at your roomin' house, in case we might wanna rent a room with ya."

"Well, I reckon you picked a bad time to come," Hortense responded. "I ain't got any vacant rooms right now. You can try me again next month."

"Just ain't my lucky day, is it?" Boot said with a grin. "But I think me and Charley might as well look the place over, long as we're here, get an idea what you got to offer. You say you're full up. I reckon your new boarder, Cullen McCabe, musta took your last vacant room." He paused to watch her reaction to his statement. "Let's go see his room." Both riders stepped down.

"I've not invited you to step down," Hortense said. "I've not got any vacancies, and I don't expect to have any anytime soon, so you just wasted your time comin' here. I've got no guest by the name of Cullen McCabe. Why don't you try down at the hotel? Maybe he took a room there."

The sarcastic smile returned to his face in response to her cynical remark. "I reckon I'm gonna have to see for myself." He drew his .44 from his holster and came up the steps to the porch. Charley followed his lead and they confronted the two women, now standing side by side, arms folded boldly before them, their backs to the door. Apparently amused by the defiant stance of the two women, Charley grabbed Hortense by her throat and forcefully pulled her out of the way. Annie immediately came to her aid, only to receive a blow on the back of her head from Boot's handgun. Prepared to meet the troublesome McCabe, the two of them stormed into the parlor to find Roy Skelton coming to see what the noise was about. Startled to find himself face-to-face with the two desperadoes, Roy could only stand gawking. "Where's McCabe?" Boot demanded.

"He ain't here," Skelton replied. "Is there somethin' I can help you with?" he asked, for want of anything better to say at that moment. Boot's response was a hand in the middle of Roy's chest, shoving him out of their way. Then they proceeded to stalk into the hallway and up the stairs, kicking every door open as they searched the length of the corridor.

"I reckon he's right," Charley said when they went back downstairs, passing Skelton, who was still standing gawking. "He ain't here." Boot drew his arm back, as if to strike him, causing the frightened man to stumble back against the wall. Laughing at the old man's reaction, they went out the front door to the porch, where Hortense was down on her knees trying to comfort Annie.

"You filthy vermin," Hortense spat at Boot. "You could have killed her."

"Weren't nothin' but a little tap on the head," Boot replied. "Maybe it'll knock a little sense in her head—yours, too. I don't take no sass from women. That'd be a good thing for you to remember." They went down the steps and climbed on their horses. "You're lucky I didn't find McCabe in there," he said as he wheeled his horse away from the porch. "If I hadda, I'da burnt this damn house to the ground."

They turned their horses back through the flower bed to the lane leading to the road. They had ridden no farther than the sharp turn in the lane when they pulled up suddenly, met by a solitary figure seated motionless on a bay horse in the middle of the lane.

Even though they had never seen him before, both men knew at once that it was Cullen McCabe. The shock of the man they hunted suddenly appearing before them caused them both to hesitate. "You lookin' for me?" Cullen calmly asked. There was another moment of indecision on the part of the hunters before they went for their guns. Two quick shots from the Winchester he was holding knocked both men out of their saddles, shot through the chest.

Back on the porch, the two women heard only two shots, for the two assailants were dead before their six-guns cleared their holsters. Hortense helped steady Annie, who was still a little shaky from the blow to her head, as they peered out toward the lane. They were joined a few seconds later by Roy Skelton and they all stared at the two horses with empty saddles, standing in the lane. They could not see the cause of the empty saddles due to the trees that stood between them and the curve of the road. "Cullen McCabe," Hortense whispered softly, without seeing past the horses. A moment later, he appeared around the curve in the path and continued on up to the house.

"Are you folks all right?" Cullen asked after he guided Jake around the flower bed. He noticed some blood on the back of Annie's neck. "Are you hurt, Annie?"

"I got a headache," she replied. "But what happened to those two devils makes it feel a lot better."

"I'm sorry about this," Cullen said. "I didn't want my troubles to involve you folks here. I didn't think they'd look here for me." Seeing Roy on the porch, he had to ask, "Anybody else hurt?"

"No, there ain't nobody else here now, and won't be till suppertime," Hortense said.

"Well, I'm gonna load those two on their horses and take 'em away from here, so Moran won't know where they got shot. Maybe it'll keep him from sendin' somebody else out here lookin' for me."

"Don't worry about us," Hortense said. "It'll be what it's gonna be. Those murderin' hooligans killed my husband and you just made the first payment on what they've got comin' to them."

"I expect you're gonna need some dinner in a couple of hours," Annie said. "I don't cook much in the middle of the day 'cause there ain't usually anybody here but us women and Roy. Sometimes, Art Becker will come over in the middle of the day for dinner, but most of the time he waits for supper. So, if you get hungry, I've got a pot of soup beans on, and I'll bake some biscuits to go with 'em."

"That sounds hard to pass up," Cullen said. "I'll have to see where I am about that time. If I do show up, I'll come in the back door and hope nobody sees me." It was a tempting thought, since there was no place else for him to eat in East City, and his pack-horse and all his supplies were in Art Becker's barn. "I'd best go take care of those two on your front path before somebody spots them."

It took a bit of effort to lift Boot Davis up to lie across his saddle. Charley Turner, being a smaller man, was a little easier. Once he had each would-be assassin lying across his saddle, he used some rope Charley carried on his horse to tie the hands and feet of both men together under their horses' bellies. He wanted to make sure the bodies didn't fall off before he transported them to where he wanted to leave them. Boot and Charley had never seen him before today. He, as well, had never seen them. As he tied

Boot's hands to his feet, that occurred to him, but he had been certain it was Boot because he was very familiar with the red roan he rode. His biggest regret was that the first blood-letting was at the boardinghouse, but on second thought, he realized it was a logical place for Moran's men to look. He had told Art Becker that there was going to be a war. What Art didn't know was that it was not simply an act of revenge for the brutal murder of Lila Blanchard. His plan now was to destroy Micah Moran's evil headquarters for outlaws. It was not going to be easy, with the cards stacked as they were in the outlaws' favor. But he had nothing to lose but his life, and that had been worth less than a nickel from the day his wife and family were taken from him. With that thought in mind, he said, "Let's go to town, boys, your boss is probably worried about you."

"Everything goin' all right, Mr. Johnson?" Deputy Ace Brown asked casually when he walked into Joe Johnson's general store. "I like to keep a sharp eye out, make sure you merchants ain't got no troubles," he said as he casually walked past Johnson to a barrel of apples at the end of the counter. He spent a few moments pawing the apples, trying to find the best ones. When he was finished, he held his selection up and said, "That's a beauty." Then he took another one and said, "Need one for later on." He turned and went back out the door. "Keepin' the peace," he said as he left the store.

"Deputy Brown stopping by to buy some apples?" Doris Johnson asked, flippantly, as she came in the back door.

"Yeah," Joe answered, disgusted. "You know, I would be happy to give an apple to an honest deputy marshal, but I swear that worthless son of a gun just comes in any time he pleases—thinks it's his privilege." She nodded slowly, knowing the anguish burning inside him. They talked often of the unfortunate situation they were forced to endure and talked about closing the store down and moving to Ravenwood, or some other town—anywhere away from East City. But it always boiled down to the fact that they couldn't afford to move and start over again. They weren't the only honest merchants talking about leaving East City, and that only seemed to make their future even more insecure. In the beginning, there was business in their store from the ranches and farms on this side of the creek. But since the takeover of the town by Micah Moran and his gang, most all of those customers crossed over the creek to Ravenwood to do their trading. Over there, you were less likely to get shot by a stray bullet from some drunken cowhand or suffer rude behavior before your wife and children.

"Well," she concluded, "I'm going back in the kitchen. It's almost time to fix a little dinner." A few moments after she uttered the words, the sudden sound of gunshots reached her ears. She turned to face her husband.

"Sounds like they came from the end of the street," Joe said, accustomed to sudden unexplained gunfire. He walked to the front window in time to see two horses galloping down the middle of the street with two bodies lying across the saddles. "Damn!" he exclaimed, causing Doris to run to the window beside him. When the horses had galloped past, they went outside to see Ace Brown running out in the street, waving his arms frantically, trying to stop them. He succeeded in causing the horses to swerve to avoid him, finally stopping them, one on each side of the street in front of the Cork and Bottle.

"It's Boot and Charley!" Ace shouted to the men pouring out of the Cork and Bottle. He grabbed the bridle of Boot's horse and yelled for one of the men to grab the other one. Shep Parker caught the frightened horse.

"Are they dead?" Micah Moran demanded.

"They're dead, all right," his deputy answered. "Shot through the chest, both of 'em. I reckon they musta found McCabe."

"Cullen McCabe," Moran uttered to himself. It was his work, all right. He didn't need any witnesses to tell him that. There was no one else it could have been, and Moran suspected there was motive behind McCabe's arrival in his town. He didn't just wander through to see a common whore back to town. He came here with a purpose, and that purpose was to take over control of the town. Moran was sure of it, and it was the first open challenge he had faced for control of his town, and he was determined to smash the attempt right away. "Ace!" he yelled at his deputy, "come here!"

Ace handed the reins he was holding to Shorty Miller and ran across the street to answer the call. "It's Boot and Charley, Boss," Ace said. "You want me to arrest that McCabe feller?"

"He's the one who done it, don't you think?" Moran replied, sarcastically.

"Yeah, that's what I think," the dull-witted deputy answered. "Sure looks like he got the best of 'em, though, don't it?" When Moran failed to give him any more instructions, Ace said, "I'll saddle up and ride out to that Billings woman's roomin' house. That's where Boot and Charley went lookin' for him, right?"

"That's right," Moran said. "But I doubt he's settin' out there waitin' for you. Those shots sounded like they came from the top of the street. You find him! He can't be far. Track him down, wherever he went. Trackin', that's what you're supposed to be good at. I want to hang that snake."

"I'll get him," Ace said, duly excited about the chance to succeed where Boot and Charley had failed.

"That's what I pay you for," Moran replied. "Kill him, if you have to, but if you can arrest him, I'd like that better. Then we can have another hangin' for the good folks of East City to see what happens when they don't toe the line."

When Ace ran back to the marshal's office to get his horse, Leroy Hill walked over beside Moran. "You reckon me and a couple of the boys oughta go with him to get that feller?"

"No, he oughta be able to arrest one man by himself. I want you boys to search the town in case he didn't run. He might be hidin' in one of the stores, like Johnson's or O'Sullivan's. Matter of fact, I'd search O'Sullivan's first. That's where Johnson, Becker, Franks, and the rest of that town council do their drinkin'. He might be hidin' in one of those rooms back of that saloon. I don't know how Boot and Charley got themselves shot. Looks like they rode right into an ambush. Ace ain't got a lotta brains, but he knows to watch where he's goin'." He glanced at Ned Larson, who said he would go with Steve Tatum and Billy Fish to search the town. The thought returned to him that it was Ned who had suggested that

Boot and Charley should go to Hortense Billings's boardinghouse to look for McCabe. Then there was the shooting in Ravenwood yesterday when McCabe took out two more of his men. That made four men in two days. How did McCabe happen to be there? Did somebody tell him they were going after Tug Taggert?

There was another factor in Moran's thinking, but he wasn't willing to admit it. He preferred to have his men close around him. He was still convinced that McCabe and whomever he was working for were set on taking over his town. And the first thing they would be thinking would be to get rid of him. He didn't know who McCabe was, or where he came from. It wasn't a name he had heard of before, but he had to be a stud horse to take Boot and Charley down. Anybody could hide in ambush and pick a couple of riders off at a distance. But Moran knew that the odds of shooting two riders from a distance and placing two shots squarely in the middle of their chests, were too high to be believed. Boot and Charley had to be facing McCabe, and at a short distance apart. For that reason, Moran wasn't sure he wanted to chance giving McCabe the opportunity to ride in and openly challenge him to a face-off for control of the gang he had assembled. Loyalty was not a common thing among outlaws, and it could be bought for the price of a bullet. Even Leroy felt superior in intelligence when compared to Ace, and Leroy was as simpleminded as could be. But Moran was confident in Ace's fearlessness, strength, and natural ability. "And, Leroy," he called after him, "make sure you check Becker's stable. He stayed there before, he mighta come back there, thinkin' we wouldn't look for him there."

* * *

The stampede of the two horses down the main
street of East City had the effect that Cullen intended,
but he didn't linger to witness it. Knowing there
would be a hasty assembly of an outlaw posse on his
tail, he waited only long enough to see that the two
horses ran straight down the street. The question now
was, in which direction to run? While he thought
about it, he guided Jake off the road and rode toward
the thick growth of trees that hugged the banks of
the creek. The spot he picked to wait in was close to the
footpath Art Becker had made between the back of
his stable and Hortense's boardinghouse. Remembering the invitation she had given him, to come to dinner,
he hoped maybe Art might pick that day to have
dinner, too. With the commotion he had just caused
in town, he figured there was a chance he would. And
if he did, Cullen would see him walking along the
path, and Art could tell him how Moran was reacting
to the trouble he had started. He also had to consider
the possibility of a posse of lawless gunmen searching
the woods between town and the boardinghouse. In
that event, he would cross the creek and hightail it for
Ravenwood. It was unlikely the outlaw posse would be
bold and reckless enough to follow him there. From
his visit in that town the day before, it appeared to be
built by solid merchants and an honest marshal and
was more than double the size of East City. For the
time being, he prepared to wait and see just what his
options would be. As he had told Art, this was a war
he had started. The trouble was, the other side was
the one with the army.

As close as he was to town, he could hear faint noises of heated activity from there and he could imagine that a posse was getting ready to ride. He regretted the fact that one of the first places they were likely to head for was the boardinghouse. He felt a strong obligation to defend it, but that could mean it would be shot to pieces with the likelihood of the women being killed. Their chances were better to escape harm, if Moran's men were allowed to search the house and move on to look elsewhere for him. Thinking about that, he walked down by the creek where Jake was nibbling on some green lily pads at the edge of the water. He gave the bay a few strokes on his neck and said, "I might have started something bigger'n I can handle, boy. Right now, I'm thinkin' about those soup beans and biscuits Annie said she was gonna cook for dinner." He was startled then by a noise up the bank. He pulled his rifle from the saddle sling and made his way carefully up the bank to a position where he could see the footpath. He relaxed as soon as he saw Art hurrying along toward the boardinghouse. His legs plowing through some patches of overgrowth bushes was the source of the noise Cullen had heard.

"Jumpin' Jehoshaphat!" Art bellowed when Cullen suddenly stepped out from behind a thick laurel bush. "You gave me a start." Cullen apologized and Art said, "I'm just glad you're out here in the woods instead of at the house. That's what I was comin' to see and I was gonna tell you to get goin', if you hadda been. Moran's already sent Ace Brown to hunt you down. Leroy Hill was already at the stable lookin' for you. I told him you don't keep a horse there, that I ain't seen you since that first day. I didn't tell him that you've still got a packhorse there." He paused to take a breath before continuing. "It's a good thing we put your packs and stuff in the barn." He paused again in his excitement before asking, "Were you involved in a shootout in Ravenwood yesterday mornin'?" Without waiting for Cullen to answer, he continued. "After you carried Lila's body off last night, Stan Molloy came in. He was leadin' two horses with empty saddles. He didn't waste no time at the stable, just mumbled somethin' about a shootout in Ravenwood and told me to take care of the horses. Then he hotfooted it up to the Cork and Bottle. Did you have any part in that?"

"I happened to be there when it happened," Cullen said. "Two men were tryin' to shoot the marshal outside a saloon, but he came out of it all right and arrested both of 'em." He paused to consider that. "So there were three of 'em, and it looks like they were sent after the marshal, by Moran, no doubt." More interested at the moment about what might be happening on this side of Walnut Creek, he changed the subject. "Ace Brown," Cullen asked, "you say he's already lookin' for me? I reckon he's headed to the boardin'house."

"Yeah, he's gone to Hortense's house 'cause that's where Boot Davis and Charley Turner went lookin' for you." He paused again to comment on that. "You caused quite a stir with that trick and I'm afraid it's gonna cause you more trouble than you can handle. Boot and Charley were a couple of tough customers, especially Boot. I expect there's two or three in that gang of murderers that might wanna make a reputation by killin' the man who gunned down Boot Davis and Charley Turner."

"I expect you're right. The man who shot Cullen

McCabe would make a name for hisself, all right."
Cullen froze when he heard the comment from
behind them. A moment later, Leroy Hill stepped out
onto the path from behind a tree, his six-gun leveled
at Cullen. "I reckon this is my lucky day, ain't it,
Mr. Cullen McCabe?" He glanced at Art then. "You
just step aside, Becker. I knew you was lyin' when you
said you didn't know where he was. I oughta shoot
you down for lyin', and I might, anyway, if you make
the first wrong move." Back to Cullen, he said, "I'll
thank you to drop that Winchester on the ground."
Having no choice but to comply, Cullen dropped his
rifle, wondering why the man hadn't simply shot him.
As if reading his thoughts, Leroy told him why. "If it
was up to me, you'd already be dead. But the marshal
said to arrest you, so we can have a public hangin'. So
you get to live a little bit longer, unless you try somethin'. You do that and you're dead, don't matter what
the marshal said. Now, Becker, ease that gun you're
wearin' outta that holster with nothin' but two fingers
on the handle. Then, before it clears leather, you grab
it by the barrel with your other hand and hand it to
me, handle first." Art did as Leroy directed, and Leroy
quickly took the pistol and stuck it in his belt. "Now
set your ass down on the ground there."

With Art's weapon in his belt and Art on the ground,
Leroy was ready to deal with Cullen. "You ain't said
much, Mr. Cullen McCabe. You ain't as slick as you
thought, are you?"

"I reckon I figured you were all as dumb as Boot
Davis," Cullen said. "I guess I was wrong." Having
been caught like this, he could only hope Leroy would
make a mistake.

"You're damn right you was wrong," Leroy replied.

"You saw how ol' Becker, there, handed over his six-shooter, now let's see if you can do the same thing. You're a pretty big man, but not so big when you're lookin' at the business end of this .44 I'm holdin', ain't that right? So you keep that in mind when you pull that gun up. Nothin' would give me more pleasure than to shoot you down right here."

"All right," Cullen said. "You're callin' the shots. But whaddaya holdin' a gun on him for? Hell, he's on your side."

"The hell he is," Leroy responded. "He led me straight to you."

"He wouldn't be standin' here if I hadn't stopped him. He said he was cuttin' through here on his way to dinner. But ain't no skin off my back if you shoot Moran's stable man. How do you like that, Becker? You thought Moran was your friend." As Leroy had ordered, Cullen started to pull his Colt, but hesitated. "You said pull it out with just two fingers," he said. "I ain't sure I can pull it out with two fingers. Is it all right if I use one finger and a thumb?"

The question confused the simpleminded outlaw. "What are you talkin' about? Pull it out just like he did. Do it with your left hand."

"With my left hand, all right, nice and slow, with one finger and one thumb, just like Art did," Cullen said, and exaggerated the slowness in his movements.

"That's right," Leroy said, "nice and slow. Now grab that barrel with your right hand and hand it to me." He was beginning to wonder if McCabe was as slow in the head as Ace Brown.

Cullen lifted the Colt with deliberate motions, then slowly grasped the barrel with his right hand and eased the weapon toward Leroy. Impatient to the point of frustration with the seemingly thickheaded slowness of the big man, Leroy grabbed the gun and attempted to snatch it out of Cullen's hand. But Cullen held on to the barrel and grabbed Leroy's gun hand, forcing both his hands outward. "Let go!" Leroy blurted. "Damn it, let go, or I'll shoot you down right here!" Realizing at once that he was not able to match Cullen's strength, Leroy held on, knowing now that he was fighting for his life. In a panic, he pulled the trigger on the only pistol that was cocked. It sent a bullet harmlessly into the ground near his feet.

The two combatants were locked in a standoff with Leroy weakening rapidly. In desperation, he aimed a knee at his taller opponent, which Cullen blocked with his thigh. Still, Leroy held on, fighting for his life but realizing he was helpless to free his hands. He managed to continue to struggle until Cullen said, "Becker, pick up my rifle and shoot this piece of crud."

Leroy's eyes spread wide open in fright, held in the powerful grip of his antagonist. Art, having sat stunned throughout the whole contest between the two men, was jolted out of his trance. He got up from the ground, went over, and picked up Cullen's rifle. Knowing then he was about to die, Leroy sank to the ground, releasing his hold on both pistols. On his knees he looked up at the sinister man over him, his eyes pleading like a steer about to be slaughtered. It was especially hard for him to die this way. Never having been thought of as a gunman in the class of Boot Davis, or even Shep or Shorty, he had always talked big. But he was never taken seriously by the other men. This, then, would have been his chance for some respect, had he been able to bring Cullen McCabe in to be hanged. Micah would have had to see him in a different light. Another failure. He felt like crying when he heard the sound of Art cranking a cartridge into the Winchester's chamber.

Cullen held his hand out. "Give it to me," he said. "I knew you couldn't shoot one of your own. I reckon I shoulda shot you when you came walking down this path." Art immediately handed the rifle to him in shocked confusion over Cullen's sudden change. Looking down at Leroy, Cullen asked, "Have you got a horse back there somewhere?"

"Yes, sir," Leroy answered, completely submissive in defeat as his executioner stood towering over him, "back at that sharp turn in the path." Thoughts flashed through his simple brain of his father, who warned him that he was taking the wrong path in life. That path, his pa told him, ended up in hell. *You was right, Pa*, he thought, *it led straight to hell.* When he looked up again to see Cullen staring down at him with the barrel of the rifle only a couple of feet from his head, he spoke softly. "He's a pretty good horse, but you ain't gonna get too much for him. He's gettin' some age on him."

"You think he's young enough to tote you back to your boss to give him a message?" Cullen asked. Leroy didn't answer immediately, he couldn't. Thinking Cullen was playing some sadistic game with him, he continued to stare up at him without responding to his question. He couldn't help thinking about a mental image of Boot Davis and Charley Turner when they came back to town lying across their saddles. That was the kind of message Cullen McCabe sent. "Well, do ya?" Cullen prodded when Leroy failed to respond.

"Oh yes, sir, I surely do," he blurted then, suddenly

realizing that Cullen was talking about letting him go free. "I can take a message for ya!"

"All right, get on your feet," Cullen ordered, and waited until Leroy got up before continuing. "Now, walk back down the path to get your horse." Oblivious to the wet stain that had spread on the front of his britches, Leroy turned and started down the path, with Cullen and Art right behind him. As Leroy had said, his horse was tied in the bushes, just beyond the curve. Cullen untied the reins and held on to them. "Get on him," he ordered, and Leroy eagerly obeyed. Cullen emptied the cartridges out of Leroy's gun and handed it to him. "Can I count on you to give Micah Moran a message?"

"Yes, sir, you surely can!" Leroy answered at once.

"All right, the message is this: The days of East City as the city of outlaws is over. The town is sick of it and so is the state of Texas. If Moran is smart, he'll get out of town now and take the rest of you saddle tramps with him before a company of Rangers sets up camp here permanently. And you might as well tell him not to waste his time comin' back here lookin' for me. I won't be here. You got that?" He turned to address Art. "And the same goes for you, Becker. I won't be here by the time you come back."

"Yes, sir," Leroy answered. "I'll tell him." He hesitated a few moments when Cullen handed him the reins. "I reckon I oughta say I'm obliged to you for lettin' me go."

"Make no mistake," Cullen said. "I let you go because I need to send a message. The next time you come at me with a gun in your hand, I'll kill you. You understand?"

"Yes, sir," Leroy replied. Cullen gave the horse a

slap on his croup and he was off at a lope down the narrow footpath.

Cullen turned to find Art staring at him curiously. "Who the hell are you really?"

"You know who I am," Cullen replied. "The same fellow I was yesterday, Cullen McCabe. I had to put on a little show for that jasper. I'm hopin' he thinks you weren't in cahoots with me at all."

"I don't know about him, but you had me convinced that I was in the same boat with him." He shook his head in relief. "What about all that talk you said about the town and the state of Texas sayin' Moran and his posse had to get out of town? When is all that stuff supposed to happen?"

"I don't know," Cullen replied, "maybe right after you folks in this town decide you've had enough of their kind. I can't see why it's taken you folks so long to decide. I don't even live here, but the hanging of a common whore was enough for me to know I'd had enough of that gang of outlaws. If there's no will to fight, maybe the best thing for the honest people in East City is to cut bait and run. Then maybe the army will bring some cannons in here and level the damn town."

"You can't expect us to fight a gang of murderin' outlaws like Moran's posse," Art felt compelled to say. "Joe Johnson, Abe Franks, Buck Casey, Cary O'Sullivan, Stewart Ingram, and me; we're the major merchants left in this town. What chance would we have against that gang? You had me nervous as hell back there when you told me to shoot Leroy. I'll be honest with you, I don't know if I coulda done it. I mean, with him just sittin' there helpless. I guess I could have if he was shootin' at me." He shook his head, unsure of the consequences that might follow the confrontation with Leroy Hill. "I don't know what Moran might do if he tells him what you said to tell him. It might go hard on all of us honest folks."

Cullen studied the contrite man for a few seconds before replying. "Maybe you're right, Art. I've got no right tellin' anybody what they oughta do. I reckon I'm to blame for any trouble you folks might have. I'll do what I can to make it a one-man fight between me and Moran. At least I'll stick around to see it through. I owe you that. But right now, we'd best get off this path, in case we get some more company right away."

Art had one more thing to say. "I just wanted to tell you that I'll still help you all I can. In spite of what I said, I know it's time to stand up to Moran. I just don't know if we can. But I ain't got no family to worry about, so I oughta be able to step up if I'm needed. Tell you the truth, though, I can't figure out why you're standin' up to Moran. I mean, you bein' a stranger and all, just passin' through, was what you said. Most strangers would just move on, but you're stayin' to risk gettin' shot in the back for your trouble. You're already a marked man for shootin' Boot Davis and Charley Turner. And that was on top of cuttin' Lila Blanchard down from that limb. Did you really ride through this part of the territory lookin' for good grass and water for cattle?"

"Somebody has to do it for the big cattle operations," Cullen said. "It's pretty important to those people not to have a whole town full of cattle rustlers on their doorstep."

"I reckon that's right," Art said after giving it some thought.

"I appreciate your offer of help, Art. I figured

you had some grit." He started to go after his horse but hesitated long enough to say, "I'm sorry 'bout threatenin' to shoot you."

"I'll let it pass this one time," Art joked. "What are you fixin' to do now?"

"Why, Annie said she was gonna cook soup beans and biscuits. And since all my cookin' things are in your barn, Annie's biscuits sound pretty damn good right now."

"Ain't you forgettin' I told you Ace Brown was going to Hortense's?" Art reminded.

"I didn't forget," Cullen said. "But it's bound to be just a matter of time. Might as well go ahead and see what the deputy has in mind."

CHAPTER 8

"I ain't leavin' this place till one of you tells me where Cullen McCabe is," Deputy Ace Brown threatened. "And if one of you don't start talkin' pretty soon, I'm gonna have to get a little rough. Now, where the hell is he?"

"Are you hard of hearing?" Hortense responded. "None of us know where Cullen McCabe is. We told you that. He's not rooming here and he's not eating here. He wouldn't likely be here this time of day, even if he was one of our guests. Why can't you understand that?"

Her retort earned her a hard backhand that knocked her back against the wall. Annie rushed to keep her from falling. "You understand that?" Brown roared. "If I don't get some answers pretty quick, there's gonna be worse than that."

"What kinda law officer do you call yourself?" Roy charged. "Hittin' a defenseless woman. You ain't nothin' but a damn coward!"

Brown turned to scowl at the old man. "You're right. Ain't no need to hit a woman when there's a broke-down old man to hit." Then he gave Roy a rap beside his head with the barrel of his pistol that caused the old man to drop like a sack of potatoes. Both Annie and Hortense went to his side. Ace stood over them, trying to decide what to do to get the information he needed. He was convinced that they knew where McCabe was hiding and there was no limit to what he would do to make them tell. "You folks don't know what it's gonna cost you to keep your mouth shut, do ya? Well, now I'm gonna show you." He holstered his pistol and drew a long hunting knife he wore. Then he reached down, grabbed a handful of Annie's hair, and jerked her head back. With the keen edge of the knife firmly against her neck, he announced, "Now, if nobody don't open their mouth, I'm gonna open her throat." He pressed the knife just enough to draw blood, causing Hortense to try to get to her feet and come to Annie's defense. He waved his knife back and forth, taunting Hortense. "Come on, girlie girl, and I'll chop up both of you." He was determined to accomplish what Boot Davis and Charley Turner could not, and he felt no remorse in the killing of both women and the old man, if that's what it took. Still holding Annie by her hair, an insolent grin spread across his face as he motioned toward Hortense with his knife. "Come on, you old hag." Fighting mad now, Hortense gathered herself, set to spring at him, regardless of the cost. The report of the Colt .44 from the kitchen door behind her, caused her to fall to the floor again.

Not sure what had happened at first, Hortense looked up to see Ace Brown stumble awkwardly, and she flinched again when a second shot ripped into his abdomen. Ace dropped his knife and released Annie to clutch his belly with both hands. Trying his best to stay upright, he staggered out the front door in an attempt to escape. But he made it no farther than the edge of the porch before stopping to support himself on a porch post. Following behind him, Cullen raised one boot and kicked him off the porch to land flat on his face a few feet from his horse. Cullen stood at the edge of the porch for a few moments more, watching him to make sure he was finished before turning back to see if Roy and the women were all right. He saw then that Art had come in behind him and was helping the women to their feet. Cullen walked back inside and extended a hand to Roy, who took the help gratefully, as Cullen pulled him up.

"Is everybody all right?" Cullen asked.

"I ain't never felt better!" Annie declared loudly. "You're a welcome sight, I swear."

Less exuberant, but grateful just the same, Hortense said, "We'd best take a look at that cut on the side of Roy's head. He got hit pretty hard. Are you all right, Roy?"

"I reckon I'll live," Roy answered, and wiped a trickle of blood off his face. "I tell you, though, for a minute there I was seein' stars."

With nothing he could do to help at the moment, Cullen stood watching while they recovered from what might have been a fatal visit from Ace Brown. "I'm sorry I didn't get here sooner," he said.

"You got here soon enough," Annie insisted, wiping the blood from her throat. "That crazy blankethead woulda ended up killin' all of us." She dabbed at her throat again to make sure it had stopped bleeding. "Well," she announced, "I reckon you're all wantin' soup beans and biscuits, now that we've worked up a little appetite. I swear, the marshal's deputy got here right after I pulled them biscuits from the oven, but I'll bet they're still a little bit warm."

They all gaped at her as if she was crazy, but Hortense, better than anyone else, knew she was just Annie. "I guess we do need to eat, but some of us might have lost our appetites."

"Not me," Art confessed, although a little reticent to admit it after Roy and the women had just suffered Ace Brown's traumatic visit.

"I'm gonna take care of the deputy," Cullen said. "Then I'm gonna take a little look-see back toward town to make sure he was alone. Art, I could use your help in loadin' the deputy on his horse." He paused before walking out the door to say, "I'd appreciate some of those beans and biscuits, though. I ain't sure when I'll get a chance to eat again." He didn't express it, but he was concerned by the tendency for Moran and his gang to assume that Hortense's house was his home base. He wanted to change their focus on the boardinghouse, if he could, but he was not yet sure how he could do that.

He walked down the front steps, pushed Ace's horse away from the body, and waited for Art to get there. "He's a pretty hefty load, all right," Art commented. "You wanna throw him across the saddle?"

"No," Cullen answered, having just decided. "I wanna sit him in the saddle, let him ride home the same way he came."

Skeptical, Art said, "He won't hardly stay in the saddle before he gets out of the yard."

"I'm aimin' to tie his feet in the stirrups and tie his

hands to the saddle horn. He might sway from side to side, but I don't think he'll fall off."

"Oh," Art responded, "I reckon that might work." He still seemed skeptical. "We'll see after we get the hard part done—liftin' his big ass up on his horse."

They picked up Ace's body, Art by the shoulders, and Cullen by the feet. Then they lifted the corpse high enough for Cullen to shift the lower body over to rest on the saddle and let the feet drop on either side of the flea-bitten gray gelding. Then Cullen helped Art to lift the upper body up to a sitting position in the saddle. "Can you hold him up like that till I tie him on?" Cullen asked. Art said that he could, so Cullen took the rope from Ace's saddle, pausing to take a look at the project before deciding how best to do what he wanted. Once he made up his mind, he tied one end of the rope around Ace's foot in the stirrup, then pulled it under the horse's belly and took a few turns around Ace's other foot. Then he pulled the rope up across Ace's thighs, took another turn under the horse's belly, coming back to the saddle. After binding the body's hands together, he tied them to the saddle horn. "You can let go of him now," he said. "He might sway like hell, but he won't fall off."

"If you say so," Art replied with a grin for Cullen's handiwork. "Whaddaya gonna do with him?" He figured Cullen had something in mind to have gone to so much trouble when the normal thing would have been to simply take the body off in the woods somewhere.

"I'm gonna help him find his way back home. I know his boss will wanna hold funeral services for such a loyal servant of the people of East City."

Art stayed there and held the gray's reins while Cullen went behind the house to get Jake. He was glad that Cullen didn't take long because he would almost swear that Ace locked eyes with him when he glanced up once. Art honestly believed that the evil in the man lived on after his body was done. It was a feeling he wouldn't share with anyone, and he was damn glad to hand the reins to Cullen when he came back. He stood there a few minutes longer to watch Cullen lead the gray down the path with Ace's body swaying like a rag doll. "I swear," Art said softly, turned around, and went into the house.

With no thoughts of the kind that troubled Art, Cullen was more concerned with the boardinghouse becoming the center of Micah Moran's attempts to get to him. What he feared might happen was the possibility that Moran would send a party of men in big enough numbers to attack the house and burn the occupants out. Even if Hortense survived, she would be without means to support herself, and he knew the blame would lie at his feet. These were the thoughts that troubled him as he led the flea-bitten gray back toward town, even though he knew the way he was returning Ace Brown's corpse was a message to Moran and his posse.

When within a short distance of the south end of town, he had still seen no sign of any other riders watching the trail. It didn't surprise him, for he had a gut feeling that Moran expected Ace to get the job done. As Art Becker had told him, Ace was Moran's bulldog, and no one was better at plugging a skull or breaking a back. Moran used Ace like a weapon and everyone in East City was aware of it. For his purposes on this ride to town, Cullen left the main road and circled the town. There were two reasons for coming into town from the north end. One was his hope to draw Moran's attention away from Hortense's boarding-house, which was south of town. The second reason was the fact that Art Becker's stable was the first business you came to on the south side of town. If he turned Ace's horse loose on that end of town, the horse could well wander straight to the stable and Cullen's planned show for Moran would not be as effective. And he hoped he could send a message that all assassins would be returned in the same state as Boot Davis, Charley Turner, and Ace Brown. Added to the two men captured in Ravenwood, that would be a loss of five of his notorious "posse." He had hopes that it would stop Moran's attempts to kill him, maybe even lessen his men's willingness to go on these attacks.

When he was about a hundred yards from O'Sullivan's Saloon, he looped the gray's reins over the late Ace Brown's hands. Then he gave the horse a swat on his croup that caused it to lope for a few yards, but it slowed to a stop, causing Cullen to repeat the process. Again, the horse loped for a short distance before slowing to a walk. But this time, the horse continued walking, evidently realizing it was back in familiar territory. It had no doubt carried Ace up and down this street countless times. Cullen watched for a while as the horse padded slowly along the street, wandering from one side to the other. As interested as he was in Moran's reaction to his deputy's return, Cullen decided it best not to linger in broad daylight, so he wheeled Jake and started back the way he had come.

* * *

As the meandering horse plodded slowly by O'Sullivan's Saloon, a cowhand from one of the ranches east of town staggered out the door, having spent all he had on whiskey. "Howdy, Ace," he offered. Receiving no return greeting from him, he took a step back to stare at the man on the horse, swaying drunkenly back and forth, side to side, forward and backward. "Damn," he uttered, "he's drunker'n I am." He continued staring, then added, "Unless I'm a helluva lot drunker'n I think I am."

Farther down the street, Shep Parker walked out of the Cork and Bottle, starting to cross the street to Johnson's general store. He stopped suddenly when he caught sight of the horse meandering aimlessly, still some distance up the street. The rider flopped on the horse's neck, then bent backward while leaning toward one side. It took a moment before Shep realized what he was staring at. When he did, he turned and ran back to the Cork and Bottle. "Micah!" he yelled as he ran in the door. "You've gotta come look at this!" When Moran hesitated and started to ask why, Shep blurted, "It's Ace! He's back!" Not waiting for Moran then, he turned and ran back in the street to catch Ace's horse. Catching the urgency then, Moran, as well as Shorty, Leroy, and Stan, who were playing cards with him, jumped up and ran out to see what Shep was yelling about.

In the middle of the street, Shep was in the process of catching the horse by its bridle. Expecting to see Ace Brown triumphantly parading a captured, or a deceased, Cullen McCabe, they were stopped, stunned by the sight of the body flopping back and forth in the saddle. After a moment, Shorty and Molloy hustled out to help Shep while Moran and Leroy remained, still staring at the grotesque spectacle. Leroy couldn't help but picture himself in that saddle, sagging from right to left like a drunk. Had it not been for the fact that McCabe wanted a message delivered to Moran, he was sure he might have returned much like Ace. He had not delivered that message to Moran because he didn't want him to know about his encounter with McCabe on the footpath through the woods. There would be too many questions about why he was spared, when no one else who went up against him was. Moran was already suspicious about Ned Larson and his friends, even to the point of thinking Ned and McCabe were partners in a scheme to take over leadership of the gang. Leroy couldn't afford to let Moran know he had talked to McCabe. As tightly wound as he was, Micah might be inclined to lump him in with Ned's boys. He was still uncertain about Art Becker, not fully convinced that he was not in league with McCabe, in spite of what McCabe had said. But that issue would just have to stew in its own pot. Leroy couldn't say anything to Moran about it without having to tell him how he knew it.

Moran said nothing while his men untied the ropes holding Ace on his horse. Once they got him on the ground, Moran told them to take him away somewhere and put him in the ground. "What about his horse and saddle and all his other stuff?" Molloy asked.

"You can cut cards for all his gear," Moran responded. "Just get him to hell away from here." There was already a small crowd of spectators gathering to gawk at the dead deputy, and the spectacle of his less-than-glorious return could only be a negative reflection on the marshal and his posse.

It didn't help his disposition when Ned walked up to stand beside him to comment. "Looks to me like it's the same result every time somebody goes lookin' for McCabe," he said. "They always come back full of bullet holes. Even when you sent somebody over to Ravenwood to go after that marshal, McCabe was there to welcome them."

"Yeah," Moran said. "Does look that way, don't it? Makes you wonder if there ain't somebody tippin' him off—like maybe they're thinkin' about takin' over this town."

"Oh, I doubt that," Ned responded. "There's too many of us for that."

"There ain't as many as there was a couple of days ago. We've lost five good men in the last two days. At least, I have, and three of 'em were damn good men, Boot Davis, Charley Turner, and now Ace Brown." He paused, then said, "You ain't lost none of those boys you brought with you."

"No, I reckon I ain't," Ned replied. "It's all a matter of luck, I s'pose."

Moran didn't comment further on the subject, but he couldn't discount the fact that, up until Cullen McCabe arrived on the scene, he had an edge over Ned with nine men, compared to Ned's three men. Now that edge was closer with his advantage only four to three. It didn't help matters any that Tatum, Fish, and Ledbetter still had a tendency to keep a bit apart from Moran's men. He hadn't thought much about it until this business with McCabe began. He had to admit that Ned mixed in with him and his men when eating, drinking, and playing cards, but that didn't mean he wasn't trying to deceive them. *You might think you're the man to run this outfit,* he thought, *but you've got another think coming. I'll be keeping my eye on you.*

CHAPTER 9

After delivering Ace Brown's body back to town, Cullen decided he would risk returning to the boarding-house to get some of that food Annie had cooked. His main concern at the present time was the safety of Hortense and her boarders. It was unfortunate that all the attention was drawn to Hortense's plain little two-story house. But it was just bad luck that every killing involved the house, and there seemed to be no way he could divert it. No matter his concern, Hortense, Annie, and the four men who roomed there insisted they were not about to leave their home, come hell, high water, or Micah Moran. "Let them come looking for you," Hortense said. "I won't give 'em any trouble. They can look all they want and maybe it won't take too many more times to show 'em they're wasting their time." All Cullen could do was to try to be ready to intercept anyone else who came looking for him before they got to the house.

When he had finished a healthy serving of Annie's soup beans and biscuits, Cullen went back along the footpath with Art. Art had finished his dinner long before Cullen got back from the north end of town, but he waited for him to return. He hoped to hear about the reaction of Moran and his gang when Ace came riding back to town. Cullen wanted to get some of his supplies and cooking utensils from Art's barn, since he was going to have to set up a camp somewhere not too far from Hortense's place. So he walked with him, leading Jake along behind them. Art had told him before that Moran's men came and went all the time in his stable, and they were never too guarded in their conversation. He often overheard them talk about things they were planning to do. Once, he claimed, he had ridden over to Ravenwood to warn Marshal Taggert about a planned robbery of the bank over there. "If they'da found out I told the marshal, that woulda been the end of this child, and that's a fact," he said.

"What happened?" Cullen asked, surprised that Art had the guts to do that. "Did they try to rob the bank?"

"They rode over there, fixin' to rob it, but when they rode by the bank, Marshal Taggert and about a dozen men with rifles were camped out on both sides of the street. I heard Johnny Barr say it looked like a real hot party they had waitin' for 'em. They just kept on ridin' and came back to East City. From what I could hear, ol' Moran was mad as hell about it."

"I expect he was," Cullen said. "When we get back to the stable, you might find out if Leroy believed me when I said you were on his side. He's dumber'n a stump, but he might notta been fooled. I reckon we'll find out. I'll be hidin' behind the corral, anyway, and if there's any trouble, I'll come as fast as I can. I would like to know if he gave Moran my message. I'm hopin' he'll think there's gonna be more than just one man comin' after him."

"Are you thinkin' about tryin' to clean up the whole town?" Art asked, the thought just having occurred to him.

"I think it needs doin', don't you?" Cullen replied.

"How are you gonna do it, kill all of 'em?" Art asked, but didn't wait for an answer before saying, "You ain't got a chance in a million of doin' that. There's too many of 'em and all of 'em have been to the dance before."

"I reckon you're right," Cullen admitted.

"I know I'm right," Art insisted. "I'm glad you changed your mind."

"I didn't say that. I just said you're probably right."

"I swear, Cullen," Art blurted, exasperated by the man he had taken a liking to and would like to see ride away from East City still alive. "All this started by the hangin' of a whore you didn't really even know."

"You could say that," Cullen remarked. "We're close enough now. I'll stay here with Jake by these bushes. If it's all clear, gimme a signal out the back door of the barn, and I'll come in and get my possibles."

"If there's nobody there, I'll wave like this." He demonstrated. "If you need to wait a little, I'll give you this sign." He held one arm up with his fist balled. With the signals understood between them, Art hurried off to the stable. Cullen stood in the shade of the trees by the creek, watching the back door of the barn. It seemed Art had barely time to get inside when the door opened partway and he saw the all clear signal. He led Jake a little closer to the barn, looped his reins on a bush, and trotted to the barn. Inside, he found Art waiting for him and

the two of them went to the tack room where Cullen's
packs were stored. "You want me to bring your packhorse outta the corral?" Art asked.

"No, I'll leave him here as long as I'm in town,"
Cullen decided. "I'll just take what I need to get by on
in this sack. Jake and I don't wanna be worryin' about
a packhorse." The words had just left his mouth when
he suddenly held a finger to his lips, having heard the
sounds of someone approaching the stable.

"I'll go catch 'em so they don't come in here," Art
whispered. "Most likely somebody ready to leave their
horses for the night." There was a small window in the
tack room wall over a workbench. Taking a cautious
peek, he could see the open door of the stable. "Yeah,"
he whispered again, "it's Shep Parker and Shorty
Miller. They're just leavin' their horses." He hurried
out into the stable and Cullen could hear him greeting them.

"Shep, Shorty," Art sang out. "You fellers fixin' to call
it a day?"

"And not a minute too soon," Shorty answered
him. "I need a good drink of likker. You ain't got any,
have you, Art?"

"Nope, don't carry no whiskey," Art responded,
aware that Shorty was joking. "I know better'n to give
the Cork and Bottle any competition."

"Especially right now," Shep commented, looked at
Shorty, and they both shook their heads.

"Micah's a little testy right now, is he?" Art asked.

"I reckon you could say that, right enough," Shep
replied. "Weren't you here when Ace Brown came
back, tied to his horse?"

"I reckon that musta happened while I was gone

home to get me some dinner," Art allowed. "You mean Ace Brown got shot?"

"He damn sure did," Shorty answered.

"Is that a fact? Do you know who done it?"

Both outlaws snorted in response and Shep answered the question. "The same jasper that's doin' all the killin' around here, that McCabe devil. But Micah's ready to smoke him out in the mornin', and it ain't gonna be just one or two going after him. We're all gonna be on this hunt." He got a sharp nudge with an elbow from Shorty, warning him not to say too much. "Ah, hell, Art's all right. Who's he gonna tell? Right, Art?"

"Right as rain," Art said, "and the horses don't talk much, either." He went suddenly tense when Shorty spoke again.

"I need to get my other bridle out of the tack room," he said. "This 'un's irritatin' my horse's mouth. I meant to swap 'em this mornin' and didn't do it."

Doing his best to stay calm, Art blurted, "I'll go get it for you!"

"Ain't no need to do that. We've gotta take our saddles back there, anyway."

"I just thought I'd save you the trouble, so you could get to that drink of whiskey right away," Art sputtered fearfully, while trying to control his panic. He almost choked then, when he saw Cullen calmly walk out of the tack room and up the alley between the stalls. All they had to do was turn around and they couldn't miss seeing him. Knowing Cullen was counting on him to hold their attention, he kept talking. "I ain't doin' nothin' right now. I'd be more'n tickled to tote them saddles to the tack room."

The offer caused them to hesitate only a moment, and Art was relieved to see Cullen disappear into the stall across from the tack room. "That's mighty neighborly of you, Art," Shorty said, "but I wanna find that bridle." He grinned and added, "Maybe you'd better carry Shep's. He's older'n I am and startin' to look a little feeble." It earned a painful expression and a filthy remark from Shep. They picked up their saddles and bridles and headed for the tack room.

Kneeling up close to the side of the stall, his Colt in hand, Cullen could hear the two outlaws talking in the tack room. "I don't know if it's a good idea to talk much in front of Art," Shorty remarked. "I mean, about what Micah's plannin' to do, and stuff like that."

"I reckon," Shep allowed. "But I ain't worried so much about Art. I don't think he pays attention to half of what we say." He dropped his saddle in a corner of the room. "Did Micah say anything to you about watchin' your back when you're with any of the boys that came in with Ned?"

"Yeah," Shorty answered. "I ain't surprised none, either. I've been lookin' for some kind of trouble ever since Ned and his boys joined up with us. Him being used to callin' the shots, and all. It won't surprise me if him and Micah get to buckin' up against each other. And you know Micah, he ain't gonna tolerate no trouble from anybody. He's already got to thinkin' Ned knows more about this McCabe jasper than he lets on about, like how come McCabe always knows when we're comin' after him."

"It does make a body wonder, don't it?" Shep responded. "But I don't know if Ned's that dumb. If

Micah finds out he knows McCabe, it's gonna be Katy bar the door, and that's a fact."

Finished stowing their tack, the two outlaws left the tack room with not even a glance toward the empty stall across from it. They gave Art a casual wave of the hand on their way out of the stable, unaware of the inspiration they had generated in the mind of the man still kneeling in the stall. The greatest obstacle he had been facing was the fact that he was so badly outnumbered in his fight with the marshal and his posse. There was no way he could face the whole lot of them in a shootout. But after hearing Shorty and Shep discussing their problems, he saw a way to reduce the odds. Why not let the outlaws help his situation by killing one another? The only knowledge he had of Micah Moran and his posse was what he had learned from Art and a few others in town. But it was easy to figure him as a gang leader wary of any challenge to his leadership and quick to put down any threat of defiance. The thing to do now was to think of a way to plant the thought of an actual threat into Moran's head without his knowing where it came from. *I'll have to think about it*, Cullen thought, holstered his Colt, and left the stall.

He met Art on his way out of the stalls. He was coming from the stable door after having gone outside to make sure Shep and Shorty were on their way to the Cork and Bottle. "I swear, a feller could have himself a nervous breakdown if he hung around with you very long," Art declared. "First, Leroy Hill, then this with Shorty and Shep. All they had to do was for one of 'em to turn around."

"I figured I could count on you to hold their attention," Cullen said. "Now, tell me about the fellow they were talking about in the tack room. Ned was his name."

"Ned Larson," Art stated. "Whaddaya wanna know about him?"

"Anything you can tell me," Cullen replied. So Art told him everything he had learned about Ned Larson. And by the time he had finished, Cullen had a pretty good picture of the man. "So he had his own gang of rustlers over in east Texas," Cullen remarked. "Now, he's ridin' as just another hand for Micah Moran."

"That's right," Art said. "And I've heard a little of that talk from some of the other men. They say it was Ned who told Micah to send Ace out to Hortense's house to get you. And they're curious as to how you were in Ravenwood waitin' for Polek and Barr. The bad thing about that is it makes it a big deal about which one of 'em finally gets you. And they figure one of 'em is, sooner or later. You oughta think about that, Cullen."

"You're right, but I'm thinkin' about something else right now." He was trying to come up with a way to make Moran certain that Ned Larson was working with Cullen McCabe to take over his men. "I'd best move along now before somebody else comes in and catches me in town. That wouldn't be good for either one of us. I need to go scout me out a place to set up a camp. I don't wanna get too far from the boardin'-house, in case there's some trouble there." He paused at the back door of the barn when an idea struck him. "Do you go to the Cork and Bottle when you want a drink?"

"Lord, no," Art exclaimed at once. "I don't ever set foot in that place. If I want a drink, I get it at O'Sullivan's, where the rest of the honest men drink."

His answer gave Cullen pause for a few moments, then he asked another question. "Talking about the honest men, and honest businesses, Moran and his men have to go to the other businesses to buy whatever they need. Where would that be? The general store, maybe?"

"I s'pose so," Art replied, wondering what Cullen was getting at. "Even a damn outlaw has to go to the store. He just don't always pay for what he buys," he felt inspired to say, "but the store's the only place to get cigars and tobacco, whatever he needs."

"What's the fellow's name that owns the general store?" Cullen asked. "Is he the kind of man that ain't afraid to take a little chance to try to rid East City of some of its undesirable people?"

"Joe Johnson?" Art responded. "Well, yeah, I reckon he might be. Like the rest of us, he figures it's only a matter of time before all the honest men are gonna be forced to leave."

"I've got something in mind I'd like to try, but I need your help and I need Johnson's help." He laid out the plan he had in mind and Art readily agreed to do his part, since there wasn't a lot of risk involved. He wasn't sure about Johnson, however, but said he'd sound him out on it. "Might not work at all," Cullen said, "but you never know."

As Moran had threatened, he ordered all his posse out of bed and mounted before breakfast the morning after Cullen and Art agreed on a plan. The fact that every one of the marshal's posse would be out of town, with the exception of Stan Molloy, made it more convenient for Art to present Cullen's plan to Joe

Johnson. Moran named Molloy as his new deputy and left him with the responsibility to keep his one eye on the town. Art was just doing his morning chores at the stable when the gang of men arrived to saddle up. As soon as they left, he trotted down the footpath to alert Hortense and the others that Moran was coming to call. Micah Moran was not with the posse when they came to the stable, but Leroy Hill was assigned the extra chore of saddling the marshal's horse. Art was sure he would get to the boarding-house in time to warn them, due to the fact that the footpath was a shortcut, plus the time it would take to pick Moran up.

"All of 'em?" Hortense exclaimed, and she and Annie exchanged concerned glances. "They're coming here looking for Cullen again?" When Art nodded emphatically, she continued. "Why can't they get it in their thick heads that Cullen doesn't have a room here?" She looked at him for an answer, but when he didn't have one, she said, "Well, since the marshal, himself, is coming to call on us, we'll have to be as polite as we can, and let him search the place. Maybe, if he sees for himself that McCabe ain't here, he'll leave us alone after this." She shook her head, exasperated, and pointed toward the table. "You'd better sit down and eat your breakfast while you've got the chance. Everybody else has finished."

They rode into the yard like a cavalry patrol. Moran rode up to the front porch while his men split up and rode around both sides of the house to meet again behind the house. Moran didn't bother to knock and walked right in the front door, where he was met by

Hortense in the parlor. "Well, good morning to ya, Marshal. What's the occasion for the visit on this fine summer morning? If you've brought your posse for breakfast, I'm afraid it'll be a little wait. When you're bringing this many for a meal, I need some notice, so I can prepare enough food." She heard a couple of his men coming in the back door then, led by Ned Larson. One of the men exchanged words with Art, who was still finishing his breakfast.

"I expect you know why I'm here," Moran said. "I'm lookin' for Cullen McCabe, and if I have to, I'll have my men tear this house to the ground to find him."

"There's no Cullen McCabe rooming in this house," Hortense said. "He stayed here one night, three nights ago, but he said he was just passing through, so I imagine he's long gone from East City." She paused when Ned, Shorty, and Duke Ledbetter came in from the kitchen. "But you're welcome to search the whole house, if that's what you want. Mr. Becker has just come back from his stable to eat his breakfast. The only other guest here is Mr. Skelton. He doesn't work anymore. Mr. Pearson and Mr. George have gone to work. You may have met them on your way in from town. So you can go right ahead and search the house."

Moran turned toward the three men standing there. "Anything?" he asked, knowing there was nothing.

"Some of the boys are still tearin' that little barn apart," Ned answered. "Ain't a sign of him anywhere. If he was stayin' there, he didn't leave a trace of it. Leroy and Billy checked the outhouse. He ain't hidin' there. We even looked down at the hog lot, just in case he was visitin' his relatives."

"Go ahead and search upstairs," Moran said, "and

damn it, I mean search, any place a man could hide. Look for clothes or a bedroll."

"They know, of course, that my other men guests have clothes and personal items in their rooms. I hope your men will remember that when they're searching." Moran ignored her remarks and simply signaled his men to go upstairs with a nod in that direction. "Maybe you would like a cup of coffee while your men are searching the house," Hortense offered politely.

"Yeah, I'll take a cup of coffee," Moran replied, and followed her to the kitchen.

They found Annie standing by the stove, holding a poker in her hand. She gave Hortense an inquisitive look when Moran came in behind her. "Marshal Moran would like a cup of coffee," Hortense announced, "while his men are searching the house for Mr. McCabe." When Annie looked dumbfounded, Hortense said, "You remember Mr. McCabe, that big, polite man who stayed with us one night."

"Yeah, I remember him," Annie said, her voice lacking the syrupy sweetness that Hortense affected. She looked at Moran and said, "Set down at the table, yonder, and I'll pour you a cup. There ain't nothin' left to eat, though."

"I'll just take it right here," Moran said, well aware of the show the two women were trying to put on for him. "That way, there's a lot less chance of somethin' droppin' in it by accident." He watched her while she poured it, then took it from her.

Art Becker came into the kitchen then. He had been outside watching Moran's men search. He was not quick enough to disguise the look of surprise he displayed when he saw Moran in the kitchen drinking coffee. "Well, I reckon I'd best be gettin' back to the stable, now that I've had my breakfast. Anything you need from me, Marshal?"

"Maybe you can tell me where your friend Cullen McCabe is. I've got a powerful interest in that mystery man. He rode into my town and folks started dying of lead poisonin'. And it's my job to keep the citizens of East City safe from men like him."

"I swear, Marshal, he ain't no friend of mine," Art declared. "Where'd you ever get an idea like that? He kept his horse in my stable one night, and ain't paid me for it yet. No, sir, I don't know nothin' about his whereabouts. I expect he's long gone from East City. There's too many folks lookin' for him." He turned back toward the door. "I'd best get to work," he said, and was gone.

The search went on for over an hour with no sign that the man they searched for had been there. With no alternative but to admit the hunt was in vain, Moran finally ordered it to stop. "All right, we might as well mount up and get on back to town. We're wasting our time here." The men gladly climbed on their horses, thinking more about getting back to the Cork and Bottle and the breakfast they had given up for this worthless raid. Moran put his empty cup on the corner of the table and looked Hortense in the eye. "If he shows up here again, I'm gonna expect you to let me know. It ain't safe for you if he's in this house. That man's murdered three good men right here in this town. He won't think nothin' about killin' a woman."

"I'll keep that in mind," Hortense said, her eyes meeting his gaze defiantly. He turned and walked out. The two women went to the window and watched until the marshal and his posse of hoodlums rode out of sight.

They turned to see Roy Skelton come in from the outhouse. "Least, they didn't beat none of us up this time," he said.

Hortense looked at Annie, who was still holding the poker in her hand. "Whaddaya still hanging on to that for?"

"'Cause, I was fixin' to lay him among the sweet peas, if he tried to lay a hand on me," she said. Her treatment on previous visits from members of Moran's posse was still fresh in her mind.

"I believe you would have," Hortense said. Then she went over to the corner of the table, picked up the empty coffee cup, and held it up for Annie and Roy to see. Then she threw it against the iron stove as hard as she could, smashing it in pieces. "Nobody in this house will ever have to worry about drinking after that lowlife," she declared.

"Amen," Annie seconded. "I'll sweep it up."

CHAPTER 10

Leroy Hill walked up to the counter in the general store and threw a quarter on it. "Gimme a couple of plugs of that chawin' tobacco," he said.

"Which brand do you want?" Joe Johnson asked. "I got two, and I don't remember which one you usually get." He started to call out the brand names, but Leroy interrupted.

"Gimme the one with the picture of an apple on the package," Leroy said. Since he couldn't read or write, calling out the names wouldn't help. Then, when Joe turned back to the shelves, Leroy stuck a dirty paw in the jar of hard candy on the counter and helped himself to a handful. Moran had ordered the men to pay for their incidental needs in order to show some sense of lawfulness. But to a natural-born thief like Leroy, that order didn't apply to whatever you could steal without being caught at it. He stuck the candy in his pocket, unaware his theft was observed by Doris Johnson, who was standing in the back corner, arranging a display of bandannas. She shook her head in disgust for his sneakiness but said nothing. Just like the apples the late deputy Ace Brown used to help himself to, it was the cost of doing business in East City.

Joe turned around and placed two plugs of chewing tobacco on the counter and picked up the money Leroy had left there. "Will that be all?" he asked, and glanced back at his wife, who was still shaking her head. He nodded, signaling to her, and she started walking casually toward the counter. "I remember how you like that hard candy there," Joe said, pointing toward the jar, which was considerably less than full, and Doris had filled it that morning. "You need some more? Ain't but a penny for three of 'em."

"Nah, I reckon not," Leroy replied. "I reckon the stuff they put in my chawin' tobacco is enough to satisfy my sweet tooth." He started to leave, but Doris stopped him.

"Is this something you dropped out of your pocket?" She made a show of bending down to pick up a piece of brown paper that looked to be torn from a paper bag. "Might be something important." Leroy glanced at it, already certain it was not something he had dropped. Knowing he couldn't read, Doris said, "Let's see what's written on it." Then she read, "'Ned, what are we waiting for?' And it's signed, 'McCabe.'" She looked at Leroy, who was staring back at her with eyes and mouth wide open. "Well, I guess you didn't drop it. Ned Larson must have dropped it when he was in here before. I'll just hang on to it and maybe he'll be back in sometime soon."

"No, no, ma'am!" Leroy blurted, excitedly. "I'll take it to him. Just give it to me." He snatched the paper out of her hand, turned at once, and hurried to the door.

Behind him, Joe and Doris exchanged uncertain

glances. "Well, that went just like we hoped it would," Joe commented. "We'll tell Art that the fish took the bait, but I reckon we'll have to wait and see if it does what he thinks it will do."

"I'm a little afraid Ned Larson might take it out on us, if that simpleton gives him that note," she said, her face now a frown.

"I don't see how," Joe tried to reassure her. "We just found the note. Anybody coulda dropped it in here." He shrugged. "Besides, ol' Leroy, there, is gonna take that message straight to Micah Moran. Leroy's one of Moran's boys. That's why we were lucky he came in the store. We couldn't have picked a better one." He looked at her and grinned. "I especially thought that was a nice touch you made with part of a footprint on that note."

"Well, I had to make it look like it had been dropped on the floor." She could tell by her husband's attitude that he was feeling good about the part they were playing in the scheme to split the marshal's posse into opposing sides. The trick they were hoping to pull might not work as planned. Even if it didn't, it gave him a sense of fighting back. And like the other honest merchants in East City, it was a feeling they needed. She hoped with all her heart that, somehow, the miracle would happen. She shrugged and smiled. "Wouldn't it be something, if this fellow, McCabe, just happened to be the spark this town needed?"

The spark Doris Johnson had referred to was never so bright as the one that lit a raging fire in the veins of Micah Moran. When Leroy had charged into the Cork and Bottle, where Moran was sitting with a couple of the members of the posse, he went straight to the marshal, holding the message out to him. Puzzled, Moran took it from him and glanced at it. In less than a second after, his teeth were clenched in anger, the note crumpled in his closed fist. Looking around him at the lounging men, he seemed to be suspicious of every one of them. Then he got to his feet, knocking his chair over in the process. His heavy eyebrows lowered over his dark eyes like storm clouds building, and he grabbed Leroy by the arm. "Come on," he ordered, and walked him toward the privacy of the storeroom in the back of the saloon.

Closing the door behind them, Moran spun Leroy around and demanded, "Where did you get this?" Leroy wished at that moment that someone else had found the message. Judging by Moran's rage, he thought he was being blamed for its existence. As quickly as he could manage to get the words out, he told him that it had been found on the floor of the general store, that Mrs. Johnson thought he had dropped it, but he certainly didn't. When he got to the part where she read it and said she'd keep it and give it to Ned, Moran said, "You done the right thing. It's good you brought it to me. You tell anybody else about it?"

"No, sir," Leroy responded. "I came straight to you."

"Good," Moran said again, his mind already working. With confirmation for what he had recently come to suspect, he was deciding what steps to take first. Ned must die, and he would take special delight in personally taking care of that. But first, he had to know if any of his men were thinking of siding with Ned. He had to assume that Ned's three men were all in the takeover with Ned. He had to know whom he could depend on in the final shootout. His initial feeling was that it would be a shootout between two gangs, Larson's and his. That reasoning was backed up by the actions of Cullen McCabe. The initial thought he had on the killings of his men pointed that way. For it seemed obvious that McCabe's job was to trim the numbers down to Ned's advantage. Moran had been right all along. Ned Larson was the dangerous one, but McCabe still had to be accounted for. He was Ned's assassin. Moran knew that it was critical that he and his men make the move before Ned did. And it had to be done fast, judging by the note crumpled in his hand. Already, this assassin, McCabe, was asking when they would strike. He opened his fist and straightened the paper out so he could read it again. The time to act was now. With that decision made, he said to Leroy, "I'm goin' up to my room. I want you to go get Shorty, Shep, and Molloy, and bring 'em up to my room. Don't tell anybody why you're doin' it. Understand?" Leroy said that he did. "I don't want any of Ned's boys to know we're onto 'em. All right, get goin'." He followed Leroy out the door of the storeroom and went directly to the stairs, feeling now that a bullet could come his way at any time. He wasn't worried about a direct face-off with Ned or any of the other three, because he knew he was faster with his six-gun. He knew it, and they knew it, and it was one of the reasons he was never challenged as the boss.

As instructed, Leroy walked over to the table where Shep and Molloy were sitting, nursing a bottle of corn whiskey. He told them that Micah wanted them up in his room right away, and not to ask any questions, just go on upstairs. Shorty, however, was sitting at a table with Steve Tatum and Billy Fish. Leroy paused to

consider that, but decided he'd best do as Micah
ordered. So, he walked up behind Shorty and leaned
over his shoulder to whisper in his ear. Feeling him
suddenly hovering over him, Shorty jumped, thinking
it was one of the saloon women. When he saw who it
was, he blurted, "What the hell are you doin', Leroy?
Get offa me."

"I was tryin' to tell you somethin'," Leroy said.

"Well, tell me, then," Shorty replied. "Don't be blowin'
in my ear like that. Hell, I thought it was Wilma wantin'
to take me upstairs."

"Hell, I don't think Wilma ever gets that desperate," Billy joked. It was good for a laugh, but it only
frustrated Leroy.

"Damn it," he said, "Micah wants to see you upstairs
right now." He turned then and headed for the stairs
without waiting to see if Shorty was coming after him.

"Yeah, you better get up there," Steve was quick to
join in the japing.

One who was not, Ned Larson thought it was kind
of odd that Moran wanted a meeting with only "his
boys." So he called after Leroy, "Leroy, does he want
the rest of us up there?"

Leroy paused long enough to answer. "Nope, he
just said them three."

"Well, what's it all about? Did he say?" Ned asked.
Leroy replied that he didn't. It struck Ned as more
than strange. Anytime before this, if there was something to talk over, it was always with the whole gang,
not just the men he had brought to the posse. Feeling
a need for caution now, he told the three remaining,
"Somethin's goin' on with Micah, and I ain't sure it's
gonna be good for the four of us. Might be nothin',
but he's been actin' jumpy as hell ever since that

McCabe jasper showed up. So I'm tellin' you boys to pay attention to what any of 'em might be up to." His warning was received with expressions of total astonishment from the three men who had ridden with him in east Texas. There had always been a feeling of competition between Ned and Micah, but never to the effect that there was any question regarding who was calling the shots for the combined gangs. When Ned saw the obvious puzzlement in their faces, he said, "Just keep your eyes open and be ready for anything. I got a feelin' somethin' ain't right with Micah." A witness to all this, bartender Floyd Chandler was not quite sure what was going to happen. He felt he owed his allegiance to Micah, since he was his employer, but there was nothing he could do to warn him without risking getting shot, himself.

In the private meeting upstairs, there was a similar reaction of confusion as Micah Moran smoothed out the crumpled piece of paper bag with the message written to Ned on it. "Now you know why that damn McCabe knew when anybody was comin' after him. He's in cahoots with Ned and them boys all along, and him and Ned's figurin' on takin' over after he shoots me in the back."

The four men gathered in the room were shocked speechless at first. This possibility of revolt came as a complete surprise, for any sense of competition among them was restricted to Micah and Ned. The rest of the men got along fine, as long as all were enjoying the power they held over an entire town. After a few moments of silence, Shep was the first to comment. "Damn, Micah," he drawled, "we ain't had no idea that them boys weren't nothin' but straight shooters." He turned to look at the others. "Ain't that right, boys?" They all nodded in agreement. Back to Micah then, he asked, "What are we gonna do?"

"I reckon the first thing I wanna know is which one of us are you boys backin', me or Ned Larson?"

"Hell, Micah," Shorty spoke up at once. "You oughta know you don't have to ask us that question. We've been ridin' with you from the first, and we're settin' in pretty good shape right here in East City. And we wouldn't be if it wasn't for you. Ain't that right, boys?" His question was met with enthusiastic grunts of agreement.

"All right," Micah said, "that's what I wanted to know." Still he wanted to be sure. "Ain't none of 'em said anything about this to any of you? Billy or Duke? They always think any idea Ned has is the best one." All four shook their heads in answer. "Good, then it's time we stomp this snake before it has a chance to strike."

"You just tell us how you wanna play this hand," Molloy said. "You're the boss." The other three nodded in agreement.

"Well, I've been studyin' this possibility for a little while, even before we found this message," Moran said. "I'm thinkin' that it's Ned that's wantin' to take over this posse, but maybe Steve and Billy and Duke might just be satisfied to ride with whichever one of us comes out on top." Moran had concerns about the loss of too many of his men, thinking it might weaken his hold on the town. Otherwise, he wouldn't have bothered to take the risk. He would just give his boys the word and they would go downstairs blazing away and take all of them down. He decided to call Ned out to face him in a showdown, thinking that would demonstrate to all the men, his and Ned's, that he was

an honorable man. He didn't consider it a risk on his
part, since he already knew who was the fastest draw.

His decision made, he gave his final instructions.
"We'll go back downstairs now, and I'll return Ned's
message to him. Then I'm gonna challenge him to
face me to decide who's the boss of this posse. An
election by bullets, that's the only fair way to do it. I
want you boys to fan out, so you can keep an eye on
the other three. Make sure none of 'em wants to help
Ned out."

"All right, everybody keep alert till we know what
Micah's up to," Ned cautioned when he heard them
coming back downstairs.

Micah paused briefly when he noticed a difference
in the positioning of Ned's three men. While Ned sat
at a table, facing the stairs, Billy and Steve were leaning casually on the bar, while Duke sat at another
table off to the side of Ned's. Behind the bar, Floyd
was all the way back to the far end. It struck Micah as
an odd arrangement for four men at their ease and
having a drink. All the more evidence in a plot against
him, as far as he was concerned.

Ned Larson watched with considerable interest as
the men descended the stairs and casually fanned out
in the barroom, none of them taking a seat. "What's
goin' on, Micah?" Ned asked. "You boys havin' some
kind of secret meetin' upstairs?"

Moran didn't answer until he came down the stairs.
"Oh, we was just havin' a little discussion about the
way things have been goin' lately. Then we decided to
bring you this little message you musta lost somewhere." He held the piece of paper sack up for him to
see, watching him closely for his reaction. "Reckon
you musta dropped it last time you was in the general

store. And whaddaya know? Leroy found it layin' on the floor."

"What are you talkin' about, Micah?" Ned reacted, obviously puzzled.

"Here," Moran said to Leroy, "hand this to him. Then maybe he'll remember it.

Leroy took the note and gave it to Ned, who quickly glanced at the writing on the piece of brown paper, torn from a bag. Then he read it again more closely. "What the hell?" he uttered in disbelief. "I never saw this message before. I didn't drop it."

"You didn't?" Moran asked, obviously sarcastic. "Maybe the person who was supposed to give it to you dropped it before you got a chance to see it. That was kinda unlucky, weren't it? For you and your friend McCabe. He's wantin' to know what you're waitin' for. I'd kinda like to know that myself."

"Whoa! Wait a minute!" Ned exclaimed. "I don't know what the hell's goin' on here. I don't know McCabe. I ain't ever seen him but once, that day he came in here, and I sure as hell ain't ever talked to him. You're the only one who's ever talked to him." He looked around frantically, looking for some explanation. "Hell, Micah, anybody coulda wrote that message. Leroy's the one who brought it to you. How do you know he didn't write it?"

"'Cause Leroy can't write," Moran answered smugly. "Seems to me you got caught in the trap you was settin', and I expect you're gonna have to answer for it. And right now is as good a time as any."

"Now, hold on, Micah, this is all a mistake. I don't know nothin' about this McCabe message." Then another thought struck him. "Maybe he did try to get it to me, but maybe what he was doin' was callin' me out. Look at it, he says 'what are we waitin' for?' He might be tryin' to say he's wantin' to see if I'll shoot it out with him."

"Well, now, that is another way to look at it, ain't it?" Moran allowed, enjoying Ned's obvious squirming at this point. "Ain't it funny, though, I mean how he knew your name was Ned, and why he didn't pick me to draw against? He knows I'm the boss, and he knows my name 'cause I told him my name. You musta told him you was plannin' to be the boss of this gang."

Desperate now, for he knew he could not beat Moran in a fast-draw competition, Ned looked to his men for support. "Billy, you know there ain't nothin' goin' on between me and McCabe. Right? All of you know that. Right?"

"Nothin' I know about," Billy answered, not sure how far Moran was planning to go with this showdown and whether or not he, Steve, and Duke should be worried as well.

Of the three from the east Texas gang, Duke Ledbetter had known Ned the longest, and he had never thought of him as anything but fair, so he felt a responsibility to speak up for him. "I don't think Ned's mixed up in nothin' with Cullen McCabe. That damn message is a trick you're usin' to turn us against him."

"And I reckon you ain't mixed up in nothin' with McCabe, neither," Moran said. He glared back at Ned then. "Time for talkin's over. Get on your feet, Ned, or take it settin' in that chair."

Everyone in the saloon became tense at that. What had been one gang, one posse, suddenly became two opposing sides. Floyd ducked down behind the bar. Wilma and Mabel scrambled in behind him. The man with the most to lose was Ned Larson. To go up against Micah Moran was akin to suicide, and Ned knew that better than anybody. His options were to turn belly-up like a whipped dog and beg for his life, or to pray for that one moment in time when he bucked the odds. He decided it was better to go out like a man, than to live with the shame of cowardice. He got to his feet. "All right, Micah, but you're dead wrong on this."

"If I am," Moran said, "then you'll be the one standin' when the smoke clears." Ned walked out in the center of the room, poised to duel. Moran stepped over to square up with him. "When you're ready," he said, and stood waiting.

After a few seconds that seemed like minutes, Ned made his move. He succeeded in clearing his .44 from his holster, but Moran's bullet struck him in the gut before he could raise the weapon to fire. Seeing Ned double over, dropping his pistol, Duke drew his six-gun, only to be cut down by Shep Parker, who had anticipated such a reaction. The chain reaction continued when Steve Tatum shot Shep and was promptly cut down by a second shot from Moran.

Billy Fish promptly extended his hands in the air when he saw four guns pointed at him. Stunned by what had just happened, he tried to make sense of it, but was unable to understand how it could have come to this. Ned had warned them that Moran was acting very strange recently, but Billy could not have imagined it would come to this. Of the three of them who had followed Ned here to join Micah Moran's band of outlaws, he alone was standing. And Ned was curled up on the floor, moaning as he lay dying. "I don't know where that message came from," Billy finally managed. "Didn't none of us know anything about

Cullen McCabe. If Ned hadda been talkin' to McCabe, he woulda told us about it."

"What about the note?" Molloy asked him.

"I don't know," Billy replied, and dropped his hands. An instant later, he was struck by four bullets, fired almost like one single shot. He dropped on the floor beside Ned, shot dead.

"Damn," Molloy swore. "When he dropped his hands, I thought he was goin' for his gun." He grinned and reached up to adjust his eye patch.

"I reckon we all did," Shorty said, "since he's got four bullet holes in him. Maybe we shoulda waited to see what he had to say. He always seemed like he was one of us. I didn't ever have no trouble with Billy."

"I swear," Leroy remarked, "I wouldn'ta thought any of them boys was thinkin' about double-crossin' us, especially Billy."

"It's better this way," Moran was quick to reassure them. "We'da never been able to trust him anymore. We couldn't ever be sure that he wasn't in it up to his eyeteeth, just like the rest of 'em. We'll see what happens around here now, see if we hear anythin' more outta McCabe since he ain't got Ned and the other boys to count on."

"If he's got any brains a-tall, he'll just move on and try to find him another strawberry patch to land in," Leroy said. He couldn't help thinking about the message McCabe told him to deliver to Moran, that the days of East City as a place for outlaws were coming to an end. He said a company of Rangers might be permanently based there. Moran would be plenty hot if he heard that. Leroy wished he could tell him what McCabe threatened, but he couldn't without having to explain how he got the message to deliver.

"Might as well get these bodies outta here," Moran ordered. "Strip 'em down and get everythin' that's worth anythin', and we'll divide it up later."

The sudden eruption of gunfire that rang out from the Cork and Bottle caused a wave of concern among the honest citizens of East City. It was not at all unusual to hear a random shot here and there in the town run by outlaws. But this burst of gunfire was enough to worry everyone with a business to operate, with three exceptions. When Art Becker heard the uproar inside the Cork and Bottle, he hurried up the street to Joe and Doris Johnson's general store. "Did you hear that?" Art blurted when he ran in the door. "It sounds like hell broke loose in that saloon."

"We'd have to be deaf not to," Doris replied. "I wonder what happened in there."

"I know what happened," Art declared. "Leroy delivered that note to the marshal, just like Cullen McCabe said he would. I'm just waitin' to see how many got shot."

"I hope Moran doesn't come down here to give us some trouble, if Leroy told him this is where he got that message," Doris said. "He's such a simpleton, there's no telling what he might have said."

"I wouldn't worry about that," her husband reassured her. "With that footprint on it, it looked obvious that somebody dropped it on the floor. And Leroy saw you pick it up off the floor."

"Joe's right," Art said, and walked out to the boardwalk out front to watch the front door of the Cork and Bottle. Joe followed him out. They found they were not the only curious citizens. Looking up the street, they saw Abe Franks in front of the hardware store. Beyond him, there were several people outside O'Sullivan's Saloon, including Cary O'Sullivan. Looking down the street, they saw Buck Casey, the blacksmith. All eyes were staring toward the Cork and Bottle, and all faces carrying the look of deep concern.

Seeing Art and the Johnsons standing in front of their store, Abe Franks walked down to join them. "Now, what do you suppose they're up to?" Abe called out as he walked up. "Anybody know what that shooting was all about? It sounded like a war broke out in there."

Joe and Art exchanged uncertain glances, wondering if they should confess to their involvement. It was Joe who spoke first. "You think we oughta tell the mayor?"

When Art didn't respond right away, Abe asked, "Tell me what?"

Art gave Joe another glance and they both shrugged, so Art said, "I reckon it's safe to tell the mayor what we *think* just happened in the Cork and Bottle." He turned directly to Abe and continued. "We think the shootin' we just heard was the thinnin' out of Marshal Moran's posse goin' on. What we're watchin' for now is to see how many bodies we can count and who's left we gotta put up with." When Abe asked what led him to that conclusion, Art glanced again at Joe and Doris. They both nodded their approval, so Art went on to tell Abe of the hoax the three of them had concocted, with Leroy Hill the scapegoat. "And from the sounds comin' out of that saloon," Art concluded, "it just mighta worked like McCabe said it would."

"McCabe?" Abe questioned. "What's he got to do with it?"

"It was McCabe's idea," Art answered.

The mayor clearly didn't understand. He knew very little about the man called McCabe. Like most of the other folks outside the Cork and Bottle, he had heard the name, but mentioned only as a stranger who brought the whore Lila Blanchard back after she had run away. "McCabe?" Abe repeated. "I thought he was another one of that herd of gunmen who drift through here. Brought that prostitute back for Marshal Moran to hang for a horse thief, is what I understand. And Moran put the word out that McCabe is responsible for the parade of dead men on horses we've had riding through our town. We certainly don't need another gunman to join the outlaw we've got for a marshal."

Johnson looked to Art again to explain, since Art had spent considerably more time with the mysterious Cullen McCabe. Truth be told, Joe and Doris weren't totally sure they were not dealing with another devil, come to destroy their town. "McCabe ain't a gunman. He works for some big cattle company—in Fort Worth, I think," Art said. "He's just passin' through this part of Texas, lookin' over the grass and water possibilities." Even as he said it, he found it hard to believe the story he was telling. "Anyway," he continued, "he didn't bring Lila Blanchard back to be hanged. He found her between here and Austin, down and out, without no food. She had run away from a kidnapper who was fixin' to kill her—took his horse to get away from him. Cullen brought her back here, and the horse, too. Hangin' her for a horse thief was Moran's idea."

"Huh," Abe snorted, still not convinced that Art's judgement of the man was accurate. "What about the dead men roped to their horses to parade down the street? One of 'em was the deputy marshal, for goodness' sakes."

"I don't know, Abe," Art declared. "Ain't nobody come forward and said they saw McCabe shoot anybody." He knew for a fact that he did, but he saw no point in admitting that. "I'll tell you the truth, Cullen McCabe is on our side, and he's willin' to help us drive the outlaws outta East City."

Abe was still unconvinced. He had seen too many outlaws on the run come riding into town and going to the Cork and Bottle. "I hope you're right, Art, but I can't understand the man's motive for helping the people of East City. What does he expect to gain by it?"

The debate was interrupted then when a horse and wagon pulled up to a stop in front of the Cork and Bottle. Art strained to see who was driving the wagon. "Leroy Hill," he announced aloud. "Looks like he helped himself to my wagon and a horse." It was not unusual that he did. Most of the posse used his stable as if it belonged to them. He turned toward Joe Johnson and winked. "Looks like they need a wagon to tote 'em up to the graveyard." They stood there and counted the bodies being carried out and loaded on the wagon, calling off the number as each corpse was piled on. When the count reached the number five, that was the end of it. When they were finished, Shorty Miller climbed up on the wagon seat with Leroy, and they moved away toward the graveyard. "Five of 'em!" Art exclaimed. "And that last one looked like it mighta been Ned Larson—hard to tell from here."

"I didn't see any of them that looked like Micah Moran," Abe said. "There's five less, but we've still got Moran to deal with, so I don't think we're that much better off."

"I reckon it's gonna take a miracle for us to ever get rid of all the outlaws and have a peaceful town," Joe offered. "The biggest mistake we made was moving over here on this side of the creek. We shoulda stayed over there in Ravenwood, but I can't afford to move back now. We need to build another bridge and learn to get along with Ravenwood, and that ain't gonna happen unless we get an honest lawman over here."

"I've got a little more hope than I had before," Art claimed. "I'm thinkin' that shootout in the Cork and Bottle just now looks like a step in the right direction." He grinned at Joe. "That miracle you're wishin' for might be ridin' a bay horse named Jake."

CHAPTER 11

During the time when Micah Moran was eliminating Ned Larson as his chief competition, Cullen was in the process of establishing a camp for himself. The foliage along both sides of Walnut Creek was thick enough to provide reasonable coverage for just one man and one horse. After looking at several possible choices, he decided to make his camp where a tiny stream emptied into the creek. There was not a great deal of grass for Jake, but it was adequate for the short time he planned to stay there.

Since he now had the means to do so, he decided to build a fire and make some coffee to drink with some beef jerky from his packs. It was time to think about his next step, but he wasn't really sure what it should be. It would depend a great deal on whether or not Art took that message to Joe Johnson, and whether or not Johnson had the nerve to pass it along to one of Moran's men. Then it would depend on whether or not it got to Moran. If it did, he could only imagine how he would react. Based upon his initial impression of the marshal, he would bet he would react violently. He knew he should be extra cautious about going back to Hortense's boardinghouse, but it was the best way to check with Art Becker for a report on the bait they sent Moran. *What the hell,* he thought, *nobody lives forever,* and decided to risk a visit to Hortense's supper table. With that in mind, he put his coffeepot and jerky back in his war bag, thinking he'd wait and get a good supper at the boarding-house. There was still a little time before the usual suppertime at the house, so he decided to use it to take a thorough scout around it before riding in. He had to be concerned with the possibility that Moran had men watching the house in the event he did show up again.

He rode Jake slowly along the west creek bank until he was within about one hundred yards of the little shed that served as a barn for Hortense's guests. He stopped there and took a long look around before turning his horse a little farther west to take a wide circle around the house. As he started to cross over to the east side of the creek, he pulled up suddenly when he caught sight of movement through the bushes along the footpath on that side. Deer or horse, he couldn't be certain. He backed Jake up to make sure he wasn't spotted, then focused his gaze on a spot farther along the path where the bushes weren't so thick. In a few seconds, he saw him. Neither deer nor horse, it was Art, on foot, coming home for supper.

He was tempted to call out to him and tell him he came close to being shot for a deer, but he wasn't ready to reveal his presence just yet. First, he wanted to make sure Art wasn't being followed. So he re-mained where he was for a few minutes more, until he felt reasonably sure no one was trailing Art. When he was satisfied that no one was behind Art on the path, he crossed over to that side of the creek and continued his careful circle around the house. He took extra caution when he crossed over the lane leading to the road from town, in front of the house, because of the likelihood that a spy would approach from that direction. When he completed his circle, he left Jake by the edge of the creek and walked to the back door.

"Got enough for one more?" he asked when he eased the kitchen door open far enough to stick his head in, causing Annie to start. He apologized immediately. "Sorry, I didn't mean to startle you like that."

"Cullen McCabe!" Annie exclaimed. "You almost made me dump these potatoes on the floor. What are you doin' sneakin' in the kitchen door like that?" As soon as she said it, she followed it with, "I reckon you ain't likely to come marchin' in the front, though, at that. Well, come on in, I've got plenty of food."

"I apologize again, and I will surely appreciate eatin' some of your cookin'. Of course, I'll pay for it, since I'm not a payin' guest anymore."

"You can take that up with Hortense, but I doubt she'll charge you. You know you're always welcome here. I was just fixin' to put it on the table. You need to go on in there and hear all about the big gunfight in town today."

"Much obliged, Annie," he said, and walked into the dining room to find Art, Martin Pearson, and Franklin George telling Hortense and Roy Skelton all about the incident at the Cork and Bottle that day. They were all startled to see Cullen come in the door.

"Cullen!" Art exclaimed. "You're just the man I wanna see! It went just like you said it would. There's five less of those vultures. We counted the bodies when they carried 'em out." He went on to tell Cullen the whole story on how the message got in the hands of Micah Moran. "Course, Moran came out on top. That is, aside from the fact he lost five of his posse. But they killed Ned Larson and the three men that came with him from his old gang. Moran didn't lose but one of his, Shep Parker."

Martin Pearson spoke up then. "The one called Molloy, that tall, lanky one with the eye patch, he came by the feed store just before I left for supper. He said he was the new deputy, takin' Ace Brown's place and he'd be keepin' an eye on the town from now on." He paused then said, "The one behind his eye patch, if he's anything like Ace Brown was."

It was the news Cullen wanted to hear. His plan had worked better than he had expected. But when Art asked him what he was going to do now, he could only answer, "I don't know yet." It was a problem cut in half, but it was still a helluva problem. Micah Moran alone was a dangerous undertaking. Micah Moran and three gunmen was even worse. He didn't like the idea of turning to the role of assassin to solve the town's problem with a series of sniper shots. That might solve the immediate problem, but there was the chance that it would simply leave East City open for another outlaw to move in and take over where Moran left off. And that was a definite possibility, thanks to East City's reputation as a haven for outlaws. What was needed was a tough, honest marshal to take the responsibility for keeping the law.

When he didn't say more about his plans, Art had to say, "I figured you'd be movin' on to wherever you was goin' when you first got here. For somebody just passin' through, you've done a helluva lot of damage to Moran and his gang. But you've got a bigger target on your back now than you did before. Course, he don't know it was your idea that caused him to kill half his own gang of murderers. But he's convinced it was you that done in Brown, Boot, and Charley. And Molloy told him it was you that done for Johnny Barr and Sam Polek over in Ravenwood."

"I still ain't figured out why you hung around here in the first place," Roy Skelton felt the need to comment.

Because Micah Moran hanged a whore, Art thought, but didn't say it. Instead, he answered for Cullen, "Because he got a taste of Annie's cookin' and he's wantin' more of it."

"And, if you all don't get to the table pretty quick, she's gonna take it back to the kitchen," Hortense said. That was all the incentive needed.

While the discussion at the supper table was in progress, another matter was being discussed in town at the Cork and Bottle. "Why the hell didn't you come to me with this before now?" Micah Moran demanded when Leroy finally decided to tell him Art Becker was in with McCabe. He didn't mention the message he was released to deliver.

"Well, Micah, I swear I meant to, but I didn't think it mattered that much at the time," Leroy whined. "To tell you the truth," he continued, making up the tale as he went along, "I was plannin' to shoot the lame brain. But then I remembered you'd rather have him arrested, so you could hang him. That's why I followed Becker down that path. I figured he was in with that McCabe feller, and sure 'nuff, he led me right to him." He paused then to see if Moran was buying it, but the marshal was still fixed upon him with a steady gaze. So he sought to embellish his tale a little more. "I figured that was how McCabe knew everythin' that was goin' on—Boot and Charley, Ace, and even Sam and Johnny over in Ravenwood."

"Well, why the hell didn't you shoot both of 'em while you had a chance?" Moran demanded.

"I was comin' to that part," Leroy said, wondering how he was going to explain it. Then he was inspired to say, "Like I said, that path back by the creek is so narrow that I couldn't draw a bead on McCabe because Becker was in the way. And I knew it was important to get McCabe. You see, if I'da shot Becker, then McCabe woulda got away, so I needed to shoot him first." Comfortable in his story now, he plowed forward. "Well, I left the path and cut around to get me a spot where I could get a clear shot at both of 'em, you know, like from the side. Only problem is I slipped on some moss or somethin' when I stepped on a rock and I made a helluva noise when I fell. It was enough to spook McCabe and Becker. By the time I got back to the path, they was long gone." He looked at Moran, trying to determine whether or not he believed him. Contrite now, he made his confession. "I didn't come tell you right away 'cause I was ashamed I had a chance to get McCabe and I messed it up."

Moran listened to Leroy's confession with some degree of fascination. All in all, he bought the simple man's story, but it occurred to him to ask one question. "When McCabe was right behind Becker on that narrow path, why couldn't you shoot Becker, then shoot McCabe when Becker dropped?"

Leroy hesitated. That might have been the thing to do. He didn't think of that. Struggling to think of an answer to Moran's question, he decided to just tell the truth. "I swear, that woulda been the way. I just didn't think of that."

Moran shook his head, not at all surprised by Leroy's answer. It was another example of how simpleminded he was. He had gotten one piece of information out of the concocted tale Leroy had spun, however. Art Becker was another source of McCabe's information. He told himself that he should have suspected the owner of the stable all along. The men had become so familiar with him until they were prone to talk rather loosely around him. His first thought was that it was time for another hanging in East City. Concerned about the temper of the community, since being shocked by the sudden civil war in the Cork and Bottle, he decided he would make a show of a trial before the hanging. His intent was to make the citizens of East City believe there was a sense of responsible law and order. Then he would hang Becker on a pole in front of the jail as a lesson to anybody else who might be thinking about helping Cullen McCabe.

"How 'bout it, Micah?" Stan Molloy asked. "You want me to go arrest Art Becker?"

"Ain't no hurry," Micah said. "He ain't goin' nowhere. He's most likely gone to supper right now. He don't close the stable till later, you can pick him up then. Hell, I'll go with you to make sure his friend McCabe ain't with him. Right now, I'm gettin' hungry. Go tell

Lizzie I want my supper." Molloy turned at once to go to the kitchen to deliver Moran's order.

It was already getting dark when Art left the supper table and started walking back to the stable. It would soon be hard dark on that footpath, with the over-hanging limbs of the trees closing over him like a giant tent. *I must have stayed later than I thought,* he told himself. *I might as well just lock up and turn right around and come home.* That thought was immediately dis-missed when he came out of the trees back of his corral and saw a lamp glowing inside the barn. *One of Micah Moran's gunslingers wanting some special favor,* he thought. It had to be someone from town because there were no horses out front. They must be on foot.

He walked around to the front of the barn and walked in to find Micah Moran and Stan Molloy wait-ing inside. "Well, Marshal Moran and Deputy Molloy," Art said as cheerfully as he could affect. "What can I do for you fellers?"

"You can start by puttin' your hands up," Moran an-swered casually. Art, confused, just stood there gaping at the marshal. "Don't make me tell you again!" Moran bellowed, and whipped his .44 out and leveled it at Art.

"Whoa, Marshal!" Art blurted. "What's goin' on? What's this all about?"

"Take his gun," Moran told Molloy.

"He ain't wearin' one," Molloy replied.

"Well, put those irons on him," Moran ordered, and Molloy pulled Art's hands down behind his back and put the handcuffs on him. "Well, Mr. Becker," Moran declared in his most official-sounding manner,

THE SCAVENGERS   157

"you're under arrest. We're gonna give you a fair trial, then we're gonna hang you for your crimes against the town of East City." In total shock, Art's knees buckled and he would have fallen had not Molloy held him up. "You can make it a little easier on yourself if you tell me where I can find your partner in crime, Cullen McCabe."

Fighting to hold on to his emotions, Art managed to respond after a few moments. "Marshal, you're makin' a mistake."

"I don't make mistakes," Moran said. "Tell me where that damn coward is hidin'."

"I swear, I don't have no idea where Cullen McCabe is, and that's the truth. He left his horse here one night, and he stayed at the house where I stay one night. Then he left. I don't know where. He might have a camp somewhere, or he mighta gone to some other town. I just don't know. I swear to God!"

"Is that a fact?" Moran responded. "What would you say if I told you one of my men, Leroy Hill, saw you and McCabe havin' a secret meetin' on that little path behind your corral? What would you say to that?"

"I'd say he was a liar," Art blurted, desperately realizing he was done for. The little weasel, Leroy, must have cooked up some story in order to put the finger on him as McCabe's friend.

"Take him to the jail and lock him up," Moran said to Molloy. Back to Art then, he said, "I'm gonna let you set in that jail for a day or two while you remember where McCabe is hidin' out. Then we'll have a trial for you."

"What about my stable?" Art pleaded. "I've gotta take care of the stock, feedin' and waterin'. Most of 'em belong to you and your men. I'll have to take care of those horses."

"Oh, you won't have to worry about that anymore," Moran said with a smug grin. "I'll be takin' possession of this stable in the name of East City. I'll put somebody in to run it and you won't have the worry of it anymore." Cocking his head toward the door, he motioned for Molloy to take Art outside. "Go and lock him up," Moran ordered. "I'll close the doors and put out the lantern. We don't want nothin' to happen to our horses in our stable."

"Start walkin'," Molloy ordered, and gave Art a shove in the back to get him started. Still in a state of shock, Art almost stumbled, finding it difficult to understand the gruffness in Molloy's tone. Before this, Molloy and all of the other men in Moran's band of outlaws had treated him almost as though he was one of them. It was still hard for him to believe this was happening to him, but after Molloy locked him in the one cell in the tiny jail building, it struck home.

"Stan!" Art cried out when Molloy started to leave. "Stan, you know me. I didn't do nothin'. Hell, Cullen McCabe is as much a stranger to me as he is to you. And I sure ain't done nothin' to get hanged for. Talk to Moran for me. I don't deserve this."

"If you gotta take a dump, do it in that bucket yonder. That's what it's for. I'll get you some water afterwhile. If I don't come back tonight, I'll get you some in the mornin'. I don't know 'bout breakfast, I reckon Lizzie will cook you somethin'." He paused to grin at Art. "You're my first prisoner since Micah made me his deputy. Won't be for long, though— couple of days and we're gonna hang ya."

"Will you talk to Micah for me?" Art pleaded, but

Molloy ignored the question, went out the door, and Art could hear the sound of the padlock snapping shut on the jailhouse door. He had never felt such despair in all his life, locked in a cell, inside a dark little building, and no one knew where he was. It was hard not to blame Cullen for his predicament. He wished now that Cullen had never set foot in East City. He wished the big somber drifter had left Lila Blanchard to shift for herself and never wound up in East City. Gone was the glory he had felt after he and the Johnsons had pulled off the hoax that resulted in the elimination of half of the outlaws who held the town hostage. Life wasn't good before McCabe drifted through town, but it was something he had been used to. And now, his business was lost, and he was lost. He never suspected something as devastating as this could happen to him. With light only from the one window in the front of the jail, and the one small window in the back of his cell, Art sat down on one of the bunk beds. With all hope gone, he dropped his face into his hands and prayed.

While Art languished in the sorrowful ending of his evening, the friend he now regretted he'd ever met was saying good night to Hortense Billings. "That was a mighty fine supper Annie cooked up, but I still think I oughta pay you for it."

"No such a thing," Hortense insisted. "Supper was on me tonight. If you wanna come back tomorrow, you can pay me for that supper."

"I'd like to do that," he replied. "But I don't reckon it's a good idea for me to keep showin' up around

here. I'm afraid Moran and his boys might come
down hard on you, if they found out."

"Who's gonna tell him?" she responded. "Nobody
in this house is gonna tell him. I don't think he'll
make another search. He didn't find any trace that
would make him think you were here. And you said
you scouted around the whole place before you came
in tonight. You can do that again tomorrow before
supper. I'm gonna have Annie cook enough to feed
you and my other guests. So if you get hungry come
on back tomorrow."

"That is mighty temptin'," he admitted. "I might do
that, but only if I pay you for it." Before finding out
how successful their hoax on Moran had been, he
would not even have considered it. But now that the
marshal's posse had been cut in half, he agreed with
Hortense. Moran would not likely come with all his
men for another search. The possibility was stronger
that he would send only one or two men to try to
watch the place. And Cullen was confident that he
could handle two men. But he was not ready to sleep
in the boardinghouse and risk the chance of trigger-
ing a shootout in the middle of the night. He was
concerned that the two women, as well as the other
guests, might be caught in the cross fire.

He said good night and walked back to the creek
where he had left his horse. Depending on when he
got back this way tomorrow, he just might stop in for
supper again. He planned to make another visit to
Ravenwood in the morning. He wanted another talk
with Marshal Tug Taggert. "Besides that," he said to
Jake, "I think you're about ready for a portion of oats,
and I can get 'em over there without worryin' about
somebody takin' a shot at me."

CHAPTER 12

He woke early the next morning and decided to wait to eat breakfast in Ravenwood at the hotel dining room. The meal he had eaten there before was good enough to tempt him to come back again. Feeling no guilt at all for not cooking his own breakfast, he decided that was why the state gave him expense money. He stepped up into the saddle and headed Jake north along the creek, with the idea of approaching Ravenwood from the south. Although breakfast was what he was craving at the moment, he pulled Jake up in front of the marshal's office. There was a lock on the door as well as a handwritten sign that read, GONE TO BREAKFAST. *Well, that suits me just fine*, he thought, remembering that it had been Taggert who recommended the hotel dining room. He figured he might find him there and kill two birds with one stone.

"Yours will come later," he told the bay gelding, remembering that he had promised Jake some oats this morning. He looped the reins over the hitching rail and entered the dining room's outside door. Without waiting to be reminded, he left his weapons on the table provided for that purpose, and while he was doing so, he scanned the busy dining room. He spotted the marshal seated at a table near the back of the room. However, there was another man with him. Since he wanted to talk to the marshal privately, he decided he'd better wait and catch him after breakfast. While he was standing there making up his mind, Marcy Manning saw him and hurried over to welcome him.

"Well, you came back to see us," Marcy greeted him. "I've forgotten your name, but I certainly remember you."

"Cullen McCabe," he reminded her. "If I recollect, yours is Marcy, right?"

"That's right, Mr. McCabe. Let's see where I can seat you." She turned to look over the busy room in time to see the marshal with his hand in the air, signaling her. "Looks like Marshal Taggert has spotted you." She turned back to Cullen and laughed. "Would you like to sit at his table, or do you need to run for it?"

He smiled in appreciation for her humor and said, "I'll risk eatin' with the marshal." Instead of waiting for her to escort him over, he walked on back to the table. "Marshal Taggert," he greeted him.

"Cullen McCabe," Taggert returned. "Have a seat. Are you lookin' for some breakfast?"

"I am," Cullen replied, and pulled a chair back. "I don't wanna interrupt anything," he said, and nodded to the young man sitting with the marshal. Like Taggert, the young man wore a badge.

"Not at all," Taggert assured him. "We're just havin' a little breakfast. Meet Beau Arnett. He's my new deputy, the man I was tellin' you about last time you were in town." Cullen reached over and shook hands with Arnett. Looking toward the young man, Taggert continued. "Beau, this is Cullen McCabe, the man I told you about before. If it hadn't been for McCabe, I wouldn't be settin' here eatin' breakfast with you." He paused to chuckle. "And ol' Cow Pie, back yonder in the cell, wouldn't be there. On the other hand, you mighta been the marshal right now, instead of the deputy, if McCabe, here, hadn't stuck his nose in marshal's business."

"I'm pleased to meet you, Mr. McCabe," Beau said. "Marshal Taggert told me how you stepped in to help him out of a bad spot. I'm glad you did because I've got a lot to learn from him about this job."

"It's Cullen, Beau. I expect it's a job where you never do get to where you know it all, although I expect the marshal is gettin' pretty close."

"Yep," Taggert cracked. "And that's about the time when you start makin' dumb mistakes, like gettin' yourself trapped behind a wagon with two scared horses fixin' to bolt." Conversation halted for a moment then when a young girl came to the table with a cup of coffee and asked Cullen what he wanted to eat. He told her that what they were eating looked pretty good, if the eggs were scrambled. She nodded and turned to go. "And put that on my bill, Polly," Taggert called after her. She turned back and confirmed it with a nod. "Don't even start," Taggert interrupted when Cullen was about to protest. "I told you I wanted to buy your supper when you were here the other day, but you were in a hurry to get back to East City."

Beau Arnett's eyebrows raised slightly at the mention of East City. "Are you stayin' over in East City, Mr. McCabe, I mean, Cullen?"

"Well, I'll have to say I'm stayin' close to East City," Cullen answered. "Campin' on the creek near there, as a matter of fact. I reckon I'm just about as close to Ravenwood as I am to East City."

"What brings you over to this side of the creek today?" Beau asked.

"Breakfast, for the most part," Cullen answered. "That and I brought the marshal some information he might or might not have gotten." Taggert's eyebrows went up at that, and he asked what information that might be. "Well, I don't know if you know the names of the men involved in that shooting." He could tell by Taggert's expression that he did not, so he continued. "The man you have in jail now, the one you named Cow Pie, the name his mama gave him is Sam Polek. The one I shot was Johnny Barr, and the one who got away with their horses is Stan Molloy."

"That is some information I didn't have," Taggert said, seeming to be more than pleased and definitely interested in what else Cullen might have to say. He took a piece of folded paper from his pocket and a stub of a pencil and wrote the names down as Cullen called them out again. "Judge Raven is gonna think I've done some real detective work when I give him these." He wet the pencil lead with his tongue then crossed the *t* in Stan Molloy's name. "Good information, but I think Cow Pie suits that one in the cell better."

The conversation took a brief pause when Polly Peters brought Cullen's breakfast and placed it before him. All three concentrated on the food for a few moments before the talking resumed. "I'm just a little curious," Taggert said. "How did you find out about this? That don't seem like somethin' everybody in town would know."

Cullen hesitated. It was something he had never done before, and he was just naturally more comfortable keeping it to himself. But he decided it probably was best to level with the marshal, since he had decided Taggert was an honest lawman. "I reckon it's time I told you why I'm really in your territory. I don't usually bring it up, if it ain't necessary, and up till now it ain't been." He reached into his inside vest pocket and pulled out a small canvas bag he usually carried in his saddlebags. He pulled a paper out of the bag, unfolded it, and handed it to Taggert.

Taggert glanced at it, and seeing a lot of writing on it, handed it to Beau. "I don't read all that well," he said.

Beau took the document and read over it quickly, then looked up at Cullen before turning toward Taggert. "This says that 'one Cullen McCabe is a special agent of the State of Texas, reporting directly to the governor and only the governor.' And it's signed, 'Richard B. Hubbard, Governor, State of Texas.'" He held it up for the marshal to see. "And it's stamped with the official seal of the state of Texas." Both Taggert and Beau looked from the document to stare at Cullen.

It was the first time he had ever told anyone of his special assignments by the governor's office. And from the reaction he read in the two faces gaping at him, he wasn't comfortable with it now. While he thought of what he should say next, he reached in another pocket and pulled out a piece of velvet material. He unwrapped it to reveal a shiny badge. "They gave me this, too, but I don't ever wear it. I wrapped it in this piece of cloth to keep the shine on it."

"I knew it!" Taggert finally shattered the brief silence. "I knew damn well you weren't no ordinary drifter passin' through town. You came to do somethin' about that rotten den of snakes across the creek, didn't you?" Without giving Cullen time to answer, he went on. "They send a company of Rangers here for three days, and they can't do a damn thing to clean up that mess. So they send one man back to do it?"

"Well, not really," Cullen answered. "I reckon you could say the governor sent me here to take a look at the situation to see how best to maybe clean the lawless crowd outta there for good. My job was to look both of the towns over and make my recommendations, but I turned up some things I reckon I didn't see comin'. So I had to get involved a little more than I'd planned to. There are some good people over there in East City, and I think they're ready to forget about havin' their own town, separate and apart. I think they're ready to build that bridge back across Walnut Creek and be part of Ravenwood."

"There ain't a chance in hell of that happenin' with that damn army of gunmen runnin' the town," Taggert declared. "There's too many of 'em for the Rangers to handle, and so far, the army don't seem interested in our little problems."

Cullen nodded his understanding and said, "Well, there ain't quite as many of 'em anymore."

Interested then, Taggert asked, "That so? What happened to 'em?" He had a feeling he knew the answer to his question, having seen Cullen use a Winchester before.

"There were a couple of different incidents that took place," Cullen said. Then he went on to bring

Taggert up to date on everything that had happened since his first day in East City. Taggert listened with rapt attention as well as a mixture of wonder and disbelief.

When Cullen had finished, Taggert had questions. "So you're tellin' me that Micah Moran ain't got but three men left outta that gang he had?"

"That's the number of men he has since last night, all that's left of the main core of his gang. The trouble is, I expect him to be hiring every lawless drifter that passes through town, the same way he built up his gang before. Another problem I have is I don't know how many customers he's got stayin' in that whorehouse he calls a hotel. They go and come so often till it's been hard to put a number on 'em. Art Becker, the fellow I told you about, he owns the stable, and he says most of the horses there belong to the gang and the customers in the hotel. If I knew there weren't but four of 'em left for sure, I'd ask you if you'd like to help me, and we'd ride in there and arrest 'em or shoot 'em, and that would take care of the problem. But once we got rid of Moran and his men, we'd have to have an honest lawman in there right away to take his place. And we have to make sure the town council is gonna back us. Otherwise, the same old scum will creep right back in. The trouble is, every outlaw in Texas and Oklahoma knows about East City."

"I see what you're sayin'," Taggert said. "It ain't as simple as it sounded at first. I don't know what our city council would say about me gettin' involved in a war across the creek. So I reckon that'll have to be discussed in a meetin'. Might be best if we hold on a little longer till you know a little bit more about how many they've got in that hotel."

Beau Arnett had held his tongue throughout the discussion between Cullen and Taggert, keenly interested in the dilemma that was East City. When it seemed that Cullen and the marshal had talked it out, he made a statement. "It sounds to me that when the time is right to drive those outlaws out of East City, it's gonna be a helluva fight. I just wanna let you know I'd like to be a part of it. And when the time comes to find a lawman to hold the job over there, I don't think you'll find a better man than me."

His statement surprised Cullen, but not Taggert, who could not suppress a smile. He had already seen the drive and the confidence in his newly appointed deputy, and he had to agree with him. He would have thought that Beau might have applied for the job in private with Cullen.

"That's good to know," Cullen said, not quite sure if Taggert would actually encourage such a plan, especially since he would be losing a deputy he just acquired. "I'll pass it along to the governor."

"You know, we hear sounds of gunshots over here from time to time when the wind is right," Taggert said. "I mighta heard that shootout you just told us about. Made me wonder what kinda devilment was happening over there. Never struck my mind to ride over there to see what it was. I'm the marshal of Ravenwood. My job is to keep the peace in this town. I don't have any jurisdiction outside of town."

Cullen thought Taggert felt the need to offer excuses for why he hadn't attempted to do something about Micah Moran. "You were right to take care of your own town. It's best to wait until I contact you for help, after I find out for sure what we're up against. When the time's right, I can officially give you the clearance to participate in a raid on East City." It was not true. Cullen didn't think he had any authority to give the marshal clearance to go to war with the town across the creek. When the time was ripe for it, he wouldn't hesitate to enlist Taggert's and Beau's help in taking Micah Moran down, and to hell with getting legal permission. "I'll keep in touch to let you know what's goin' on over there," he said, as he drained the last swallow from his coffee cup. "Thank you for the breakfast. Good to meet you, Beau." He extended his hand. "I've gotta stop by the stable. I promised Jake I'd buy him some oats this mornin'."

True to his promise, he rode down to the stable where he met the owner, a friendly, mild-mannered man named Jim Farmer. He reminded Cullen of Art Becker, the two could have been brothers. Farmer recognized Cullen as the man who stepped in to back up Tug Taggert when the marshal was under attack. When he found that Cullen was just looking to buy some oats for his horse, Farmer insisted there would be no charge. "Least I can do for the man who kept our marshal from gettin' shot," he said. When Cullen made a mild protest, Jim chuckled and said, "If you wanted a whole sack of oats, that'd be different." Satisfied there was nothing more he needed in Ravenwood, Cullen thanked Jim Farmer for the oats and headed back to his camp on the creek bank south of Hortense Billings's house.

As a precaution, he guided Jake into the trees lining the banks of the creek well north of the spot where he had made his camp. That way, anyone who might be watching wouldn't see him enter the trees right at the camp. He walked Jake slowly along the wide creek, in the shade of the oak trees, until reaching the point where he had left their cover on his way to Ravenwood earlier that morning. About to turn the bay down to the water's edge, he suddenly jerked the horse to a stop. A slight movement he glimpsed through a band of laurel bushes told him someone was at his campsite! Not expecting it, he automatically drew his rifle from the saddle sling and quickly looked all about him, fearing he might have ridden into an ambush. He slid out of the saddle and knelt on one knee, still looking all around him, trying to present as small a target as possible. Still, there was no attack, no shots fired from any direction, so he left Jake where he was and cautiously moved closer to his camp until he could see one man sitting beside the ashes of his campfire, his back turned toward him. Puzzled, for there was no sign of a horse or packs of any kind, he decided he had taken all his precautions because a homeless drifter was snooping around his camp. He promptly stood up and pushed through the bushes and walked down to the water's edge. Hearing him then, the man stood up and turned to face him. Surprised, Cullen blurted, "Roy! What are you doin' out here in the woods?"

"Waitin' for you," Roy Skelton answered. "I was hopin' you'd show up sooner or later."

Immediately alarmed, Cullen asked, "Why, what's wrong?"

"It's Art," Roy replied. "They got him locked up in the jailhouse, and that ain't all. They're fixin' to have a trial for him, then hang him!"

"What?!" Cullen exclaimed. "What for?"

"For helpin' you kill Boot Davis and them others is the word Micah Moran is spreadin' around town. Franklin George came from O'Sullivan's to tell us about it. We didn't know what was wrong when Art never came back from the stable after supper last night. I thought you needed to know," Roy went on. "I didn't have no idea where you were, so I was hopin' you'd come back here. I didn't know where your camp was, so I just walked up and down both sides of the creek. I figured wherever it was, you'd be by the water somewhere. And I found this old campfire, so I sat down and waited. I was hopin' it was yours. Didn't think there'd be anybody else campin' here."

"I'm glad you stayed here," Cullen said, his mind racing. "You did the right thing." He had never expected Moran to take out his vengeance on Art Becker, since Art appeared to have been accepted by Moran and his men as a harmless individual. But once again, Moran had ignited a spark of rage in Cullen's veins, much like the spark he caused with Lila's hanging. This time it hit even closer to home. Art was not only a friend now, but Cullen felt totally responsible for any harm that might befall Art as a result of his actions. All the possible plans of action he had talked over with Tug Taggert that morning were cast aside. If Micah Moran was trying to draw him out of hiding, he was finally successful, for Cullen was damned if he would let Art Becker hang. "They said they would have a trial first?" Cullen asked again to be sure.

"That's what Franklin said. He said Molloy came in O'Sullivan's and told everybody there. He's Moran's deputy now, since you shot Ace Brown. I think Franklin said the trial was this afternoon, and the hangin's gonna be in the mornin'."

There were many dark images swirling through Cullen's brain, memories of devasting tragedies that tore his life to pieces. Painful memories of the half-burned bodies of Mary Kate and the three children among the charred timbers of his cabin came back from the darker regions of his brain, where he tried to keep them. He thought of the men who had destroyed his family, dead now by his hand. But men like that were spawned every day, born to torment and kill, just like the men who reigned over East City. He thought again of the meeting he had with Taggert and his young deputy that morning, and that he had told them to wait to see what would happen after Moran's posse was so severely crippled. None of that talk mattered anymore. This fight had become even more personal. He would deal with it, himself.

He must have been in an angry trance because he suddenly realized Roy was staring at him with mouth and eyes wide open. "Whaddaya gonna do?" Roy asked.

It was enough to bring his mind back to the business of making war. "I'm gonna do what I can to make sure Art doesn't hang," he told him. "Let's go back to the house now. I'll pick up my horse on the way." Roy followed him up the bank and into the larger trees to the place where Jake stood, waiting patiently. Cullen stepped up into the saddle, then he took his foot out of the stirrup and asked, "You wanna step up behind me?"

"No, thanks," Roy replied. "You go ahead. I'll just walk back to the house. It ain't that far."

"Suit yourself," Cullen said, and gave Jake a nudge

with his heel. He wanted to get back first thing to
make sure there was no one harassing Hortense
and Annie, for the same reason they arrested Art.
At this point, he was less inclined to take elaborate
precautions, as he had before. Had it not been for the
threat of harm to the two women, he would have
hoped to find some of Moran's crew lurking about the
boardinghouse. Even as he thought it, he cautioned
himself not to let his anger override his good judg-
ment. When he reached the house, he found there
had been no need for caution, anyway. There were no
unwelcome guests anywhere about.

"Cullen!" Hortense cried out from the kitchen door,
having seen him ride up from the window. "They've
got Art! They're gonna hang him, like they did that
whore!"

"I know," Cullen said as he dismounted. "Roy
told me."

"Where is Roy?" Annie asked, pushing by Hortense
in the doorway, suddenly afraid that something might
have happened to him.

"He's comin' along behind me. He oughta be here
in a minute or two," Cullen said. "Have any of Moran's
men been pokin' around here?"

"We've not seen 'em, if they have," Annie answered.
"Whaddaya gonna do?" she asked, much of the same
opinion as Roy—that it was because of Art's willingness to help Cullen that Art had been arrested.

"I'm gonna go get Art out of that jail," Cullen
declared. Seeing the sinister spark in the solemn man's
eye, none doubted him, and no one asked him how
he was going to do it.

"Will you bring him back here?" Hortense asked,
concerned for Cullen and Art, but also thinking

about the almost certain possibility of Micah Moran and his three henchmen showing up there to look for them.

Cullen had thought of that same probability and he told her that Art would not be staying at the boarding-house. "I'm not sure where we'll end up, maybe the stable, maybe the woods. I'll cross that bridge when I get to it. The main thing I'm interested in right now is keepin' Art's neck outta that noose."

The two women nodded in unison. Always the more practical of the two, Annie asked, "Do you need somethin' to eat?"

"No, ma'am," he said. "I'm not hungry." The two women walked out with him while he stepped up into the saddle. He turned Jake toward the footpath that led to the stable and left the yard at an easy lope.

Roy walked up from the creek in time to see him ride away. "Where's he goin'?" he asked when he reached the two women.

"He said he's gone to get Art outta that jailhouse," Annie answered him.

"Lord of goodness," Roy sighed. "I hope he knows what he's about. He ain't got much chance ridin' into that devil's town and ridin' back out alive."

"I don't know," Annie declared. "I'm thinkin' we oughta be feelin' sorry for the marshal and his men."

As for the man they worried for, he had every in-tention of riding out alive, and with Art alive, as well. He made his plans as he rode along the narrow foot-path that served as Art's shortcut between his stable and his "family" at the boardinghouse. Knowing for sure he was a walking target anywhere he showed up in the town of East City, whatever he did had to be done after dark. The one thing he counted on was the accuracy of Roy's and Hortense's accounting of the story. If there was a chance they decided to hang Art today, instead of tomorrow, then he was too late to do anything to stop it. It might already be over. The notion of having a fake trial was just for Moran and his trash to enjoy themselves, as well as an attempt to persuade the honest folk of East City that he wanted to give every man a fair trial. Cullen had a pretty good idea about who the judge would be, His Honor, Micah Moran, and the bar would remain open throughout the trial. The more he thought about it, the madder he got, so much so that he had to calm himself down again to decide what his plan of action should be.

His hands shackled behind his back, Deputy Molloy on one arm and Shorty Miller on the other one, Art was led across the street from the jail to the Cork and Bottle. Already being harassed by his two guards, he did his best to walk straight and keep his eyes on the ground in front of his feet. "You gonna plead guilty or innocent, Becker?" Shorty japed. "If you get down on your knees and beg like a little dog, you never know, ol' Micah might let you take a shot in the head, instead of swingin' on that rope." He cocked his head and grinned. "Make it a little quicker," he added. Art made no reply. As far as he was concerned, he was already dead.

"Tell the marshal where Cullen McCabe is and he might let you go back to runnin' your stable," Molloy said, knowing that was what Moran would really like to know.

Art remained mute. He knew that was no option.

He was dead regardless of what information he coughed up. Moran owned half of the saloon and the hotel next to it. With Art's death, Moran would own the stable, too. With one more little detour for their amusement, the two guards walked Art toward a set of deep wagon tracks that still held rainwater from two days before. With his guards walking on either side of the widest rut, Art was forced to walk up the middle of the rut. Try as he might to tiptoe from one of the muddy sides of the rut to the other, he was unable to keep from sloshing through the muddy water. His dilemma was enough to delight his guards, leaving them still laughing as they delivered him to the makeshift courtroom.

To complete his farce, Micah Moran was seated at a table alone, facing two rows of barroom chairs set up for the "jury" and any spectators brave enough to come to witness the trial. There was an empty chair beside his table that was supposed to be the witness stand. Of the spectators, Art saw only two friendly faces, Abe Franks and Joe Johnson. He could guess that they were there under duress—the purpose, to make a show of involving the town council. The other spectators were a couple of drifters who stayed for an overnighter in the hotel next door to the saloon. "Everybody come to order," Moran announced. "This court is in session. We're tryin' Art Becker for his part in the murder of Boot Davis, Charley Turner, Ace Brown, and Shep Parker. How do you plead, prisoner?"

"You know how I plead, Moran," Art responded with as much defiance as he could muster. "This is all a bunch of horseshit. I never killed nobody and I never helped Cullen McCabe kill nobody. And ain't nobody seen McCabe kill those fellers, either."

"Is that all you've got to say for yourself, just a

bunch of lies?" Moran barked. "We'll see what the witness says. Call the witness." At that command, Leroy Hill came up and sat down in the chair next to the table. He was still holding a glass of whiskey. Moran continued, obviously enjoying himself with the charade. "Did you, or did you not, witness the prisoner havin' a secret meetin' with Cullen McCabe on that little path behind the stable?"

"Yes, sir, I did," Leroy answered, and took a drink from his glass of whiskey.

"Well, tell the court what you saw," Moran commanded.

"Him and McCabe havin' a meetin' on the path," Leroy replied.

"Damn it," Moran railed, "tell us about it!"

Not really happy to talk about that meeting on the footpath when he had tried to capture Cullen McCabe, Leroy took another belt from the glass of whiskey. "Well, sir, I was suspicious about Becker, so I tailed him when he went home to eat. And sure as shootin', he met that feller McCabe before he got halfway to that boardin'house where he lives. I was tryin' to get a clear shot at McCabe, but Becker kept gettin' in my line of sight, so I had to hold fire and McCabe got away."

"The main thing is you saw the two of 'em plannin' a murder, right?" Moran asked.

"That's right, Micah, I mean Your Honor," Leroy said, and immediately got out of the chair. He walked back toward the bar to the cheers of the two spectators from the hotel.

It was too much for Art to remain quiet. He jumped to his feet and yelled out at Leroy. "You lyin' little weasel, why don't you tell the honorable judge there the truth? About how you came sneakin' out of the bushes when I ran into McCabe on that path, and about how he took your gun away from you. And had you cryin' like a baby before he let you go with a message to take back to Micah Moran." Talking as fast as he could, that was as much as he could get out before he was jerked off his feet and given a hard backhand by Molloy.

"All right, Becker," Moran said. "You're so damn anxious to talk. Why don't you tell the court where Cullen McCabe is hidin' out? You do that and tell me who else is in cahoots with McCabe, and I'll lighten up on your sentence."

Art didn't respond right away. He could not help thinking about talking himself out of a hanging. But he didn't actually know where Cullen was camped. He might buy some mercy by revealing Joe and Doris Johnson's part in the hoax that led to Ned Larson's killing. He glanced over at Joe Johnson, seated next to Abe Franks, and met Joe's nervous gaze back at him. It was easy for Art to imagine that Joe was having the same thoughts as he was. He looked back at Micah Moran, sneering at him, and knew that no matter what he confessed to, Moran was going to hang him. "I ain't got no idea where Cullen McCabe is hidin', and I don't know anybody that's helpin' him," he stated. He dropped his gaze to his shackled hands, still cuffed but now resting in his lap. If he had looked again at Joe Johnson, he would have seen the rigid emotion drain from his face.

"You ain't leavin' me no choice," Moran said, disappointed. He had predicted to his men that Art would squeal like a stuck hog to save his neck. "The court finds the defendant guilty as hell, and the sentence is hangin' by the neck till dead." Then he added, almost cheerfully, "Hangin's tomorrow mornin' after breakfast." He took a drink of whiskey to make the verdict official, then ordered, "Drag him outta here!"

Johnson attempted to make eye contact with Art when Molloy and Shorty stood him up and hustled him out the door. He was hoping to silently convey his appreciation for protecting him and his wife, but Art never lifted his head. The two town council members got up to leave, but Moran stopped them before they reached the door. "You see that, Mr. Mayor? I tried to give him the chance to clear himself and help the town. You merchants have to see that it ain't always easy to keep murderers like Cullen McCabe out of our town. Sometimes a hangin' or two is what it takes. If you know anything about this McCabe gunman, it's your duty to let me know before he kills any more innocent citizens."

"Marshal," Abe answered him, "we don't know a thing more about Cullen McCabe than you do. He just showed up one day with that woman you hung before. We figured he was just another drifter passing through town. And I sure as hell don't have any idea if McCabe killed any of your men or not." He started to turn to leave, but paused to say, "And I don't think for a minute that Art Becker had anything to do with it. In my opinion, you're hanging an innocent man." Abe had no real occasion for direct contact with Cullen. But he knew about the farce Joe and Doris had pulled off with the note Art brought them. That was because they had confessed it to him. He also knew they held McCabe in high regard. As far as Joe Johnson was concerned, he had nothing to say.

Moran was not pleased by their lack of cooperation

in the capture or killing of Cullen McCabe, but there was nothing more he could do to persuade them. After hearing Abe's comments on the trial, he was tempted to hang him alongside of Becker. "Well, maybe Becker will have time to think about it tonight before we hang him in the mornin'," he said, straining to hold his temper.

Outside, as they walked back toward O'Sullivan's for the drink they both decided they needed, Johnson said to the mayor, "Abe, how long are we gonna take this before we do something about it?"

"I don't know," Abe answered honestly. "Not much longer, I guess, but I don't know what else we can do about it. We've asked the Rangers for help and contacted the governor's office directly and you can see how much help they've all been." They walked a little farther, both thinking about their situation, then Abe spoke again. "I guess we can hope they'll have another argument between themselves and finally kill each other off." The mayor paused at the door to O'Sullivan's. "Do you think that McCabe fellow is still around, or do you think he's figured he's done enough and moved on?"

"I don't know, Abe," Joe said. "I suppose Art coulda told us more about that, if they hadn't arrested him." He shook his head and thought aloud, "It was kind of nice having our own gunman for a change." They went inside, knowing Cary O'Sullivan would be interested to hear how the trial went.

CHAPTER 13

As Cullen had anticipated, there was not much activity in the stable. Every one of Moran's men were no doubt at the Cork and Bottle. He was sure that's where Art's trial was being held. But he took the precaution to leave Jake in the trees by the creek while he slipped up behind the barn and entered the same way he had on a previous visit. Most of the stalls were already filled and the horses fed, another sign that Moran's men had taken care of their horses early, so they wouldn't have to come back after the trial. This worked in Cullen's favor, for he figured he could be a little bold in his plan. He left the stalls and went to check the front door to the barn. Finding it locked, he was double sure he wouldn't be disturbed, so he went back out the back to get his horse. Leading Jake inside the back door, he put him in one of the few empty stalls and pulled his saddle off as a precaution. If for some reason, someone had to return to the stable that afternoon they would not likely notice an extra horse in the stalls, unless maybe the horse was saddled. After he made sure Jake had water, he took a bucket he saw hanging on a nail and fetched some grain for the bay to eat. Thinking about the oats Jake had in Ravenwood that morning, he said, "Don't you go gettin' used to eatin' grain twice a day."

After Jake was taken care of, he looked in the other stalls to pick a horse for Art to ride. The horse he selected was a blue roan, almost totally black. The owner had left the saddle on the rail between the stalls. All set then, as far as their riding horses were concerned, he looked in the rest of the stalls, looking for his sorrel packhorse, but with no luck. So he went out to the corral where he found four horses, his sorrel among them. "Reckon you weren't good enough to rate a stall. I hope they fed you." He decided to take the sorrel inside and put it in the stall with Jake, thinking they knew each other well enough. Once that was done, and the sorrel was fed, too, he went to get his packs and packsaddle from the barn where Art had put them.

Thinking he had done all he could in preparation for the jailbreak he was planning, there was nothing left to do but wait. With that in mind, he went to the tack room and searched the workstand under the window, where Art kept some hand tools. In one of the drawers, he found what he was looking for, Art's cavalry field glass. Then he climbed up into the hayloft and went to the open door. With no way to determine how long the trial would last, or even if it had already started, he sat down beside the door and watched what he could see of the street.

He had not been at the door long when he spotted the two men walking Art out of the saloon, heading across the street to the jail. With the use of Art's field glass, he could see the two guards talking every step of the way. Art, on the other hand, looked lost and despairing. It was enough to fire Cullen's rage once more and he felt his hand tighten on the glass he held. In the middle of the street, they stopped and the two guards pointed toward something while their mouths continued jabbering away, broken by fits of laughing. Using the glass, Cullen followed the line pointed out until he spotted what they were pointing to. It was a rope, with a noose formed on one end, dangling from a large pole in front of the jail, a pole Cullen had never seen there before. The sight of it infuriated him and he had a strong urge to limber up his rifle. The shots would be easy at that distance. It was hard to sit there and watch, but he reminded himself that his objective was to get Art out of town in one piece. So he waited, and watched the two men walk Art to the jail and take him inside. Less than two minutes passed before the two guards came back outside. One of them closed the padlock on the door, then they returned to the saloon. *Hopefully for the rest of the night,* Cullen thought, but that was not to be the case. About an hour later, he saw one of the original two men come out of the saloon, carrying what looked to be a cup of coffee and something wrapped in a cloth. It surprised him to see they were feeding Art his supper.

Inside the jail cell, Art Becker sat, dejected and fearful, afraid to meet his rendezvous with the noose Molloy and Shorty had taken such great delight in pointing out to him. Edgy as he was, he jumped, startled when he suddenly heard Molloy unlock the big padlock outside. Expecting more harassment, he was surprised to see the coffee and ham biscuits Molloy brought with him. He made no move to get up from the bed he was sitting on until Molloy motioned for him to come to the front of the cell. "I brung you some supper," Molloy said. "Come here and get it."

Expecting a trick of some kind, Art came to the front of the cell when Molloy pushed the coffee and a couple of ham biscuits through the bars. Still expecting a trick, Art reached out very carefully and took them. Then he stepped back quickly, still wary of Molloy's intent. "Ain't no trick to it," Molloy assured him. "We weren't gonna let you go hungry on your last night alive. Micah ain't as hard as he lets on. He was really hopin' you'd help us find McCabe, so he wouldn't be murderin' nobody else. That would be better for the whole town. I'm pretty sure I could get him to let you go free, go back to runnin' your stable, just like it was, if you'd tell me where we can find Cullen McCabe. Whaddaya say?"

"I told you I can't tell you where he is, because he's gone," Art said, not believing the seemingly compassionate outlaw for even a moment. "He didn't say where he was goin', most likely it's way to hell away from this damn town."

All trace of compassion evaporated from Molloy's face and he spat, "You're makin' one helluva dumb mistake, Becker. What the hell's he holdin' over you?"

"Molloy, you know damn well, just like I know, Micah Moran ain't gonna let me go, even if I did know where McCabe is. He figures he owns my stable now. He's gonna hang me in the mornin', no matter what I say."

"You got that right!" Molloy responded, irritated that Art hadn't been fooled by his charade. "And me and the boys are already bettin' on how many times you kick your feet before you croak."

"I'll tell you somethin' that you can tell that lowdown

skunk you work for," Art said, fully angry now. "I wrote that message that Leroy found and took to Moran." When Molloy looked as if he wasn't sure what he was talking about, Art clarified it. "You know, that one from McCabe to Ned Larson, that asked Ned what they were waitin' for."

"How do you know about that note?" Molloy demanded.

"I just told you, you damn fool. I wrote it and dropped it on the floor in the general store. And you toads believed it and started shootin' each other, just like the fools I knew you were—gunned down half of your own gang. You and your friends think about that while I'm swingin' on that rope." In spite of his certain fate, Art experienced a feeling of triumph over his executioners. It felt good, a welcome uplift in his spirits and he favored the gaping Molloy with a wide satisfied smile. "Thanks for the coffee and biscuits," he said. "I didn't expect 'em." So mad he couldn't say anything at that moment, Molloy turned on his heel and charged out the door. Several minutes later, Art heard the sound of the padlock closing. He smiled to himself when he realized the brainless brute had been so mad that he forgot to lock the door and had to come back to do it.

"What do you mean, he wrote the message?" Micah Moran demanded. "How did he even know about that message? Somebody musta told him about it!" He looked accusingly around the table at the three remaining men in his gang. "One of you shot your mouth off. Who was it? You might as well own up to it.

Who was it? I'll go over to the jail and he'll tell me who it was."

"Maybe he was just guessin' about that message, Boss," Leroy said.

"No, hell, he weren't," Molloy insisted. "He told me everything that was on it, the part about 'what are we waitin' for' and all. I believe he wrote it."

Moran was burning inside. He had worked to build up a gang big enough that no law agency wanted to challenge him. And he had thought Larson was the man he needed with the three men he brought with him, killers all. He forced himself to think rationally. Becker might have written that message, but Moran was certain that McCabe was behind it. McCabe was still the man he wanted. Calming himself to regain his self-control, he looked around the table at the concerned faces of the remnants of his once-powerful posse. He would rebuild, he told himself. "Never mind what Becker said," he finally told them. "It doesn't make a lot of difference, anyway. It was just a matter of time before Ned made his move to take over. I told you, I'd been seein' signs of it for a while. Better to have it settled and out of the way sooner than later. We'll watch Art Becker swing in the mornin' for his part in this trouble, then I'll rebuild my posse back to where it was. But in the meantime, we're gonna flush out Cullen McCabe if we have to burn the town down to find him."

Surprised that he had any appetite, Art ate the last of the second ham biscuit and swallowed the last gulp of coffee. He didn't know if he had been wise in spilling his guts about the message he had caused to be delivered. But it made him feel good to think he had taken down Ned Larson and his men, not to mention Shep Parker. He had kept Joe and Doris out of it and taken the entire blame. The only thing that could have made it better would have been the chance to tell it to Micah Moran in person. He hoped his part in that shootout might inspire Abe Franks and the rest of the council to stand up to Moran and his gunmen.

There was nothing for him now but to wait for morning and face whatever was waiting for him on the other side. He had thought about trying to break out of his cell. He had plenty of time to try because Molloy didn't sleep in the marshal's office. He stayed in the hotel, close to the drinking, gambling, and prostitution. But after testing every foot of the cell walls, he couldn't find any weak places where he might force the bars apart far enough to squeeze through. If he had his steel pry bar that he kept in his stable, he might have been able to spring the cell door loose. But with no tools, he was pretty much a possum in a cage.

He wasn't sure he wanted to go to sleep, even if he thought he could, not wanting those last hours to slip by unnoticed. So he sat up on the bunk and waited. He could hear the raucous sounds of drunken laughter and loud swearing coming from the saloon across the street. After a while, the moon must have lifted up over the horizon because he could see splinters of light showing through the cracks of the shuttered window in the marshal's office. It was not enough to light his dark prison. After a little longer in his solitude, the feeling of triumph he had enjoyed began to fade away and he started to sink into his prior mood of despair. He realized that he was not ready to die and there was nothing he could do to prevent it. He put his head down into his hands and prepared to pray, only to be jolted by the sudden sound of splintering wood, followed by another one of equal clamor. Then the heavy front door, metal hinges and all, was wrenched from the doorframe. Backlighted by the bright moonlight, the doorway was filled by a powerful image that could only be Cullen McCabe! Too stunned to speak, Art stared in shocked amazement. "Are you ready to get out of here?" Cullen asked, his voice calm in contrast to his actions. He lifted his boot again and gave the sagging door a kick that sent it slamming against the wall and out of his way.

"Cullen!" Art blurted. It was all he could say for a long moment. "Cullen, I shoulda known you wouldn't let me die in here!" he finally managed. Then he brought his mind back to the barricade still to be overcome. "The cell door," he exclaimed. "You gotta find somethin' to pry it open." All of a sudden so close to freedom, he became fearfully worried that his escape might be blocked by the locked cell door. "You need a pry bar!"

"Let's try this," Cullen said, still calm in contrast to Art's excitement. He walked over to a large key hanging on a nail on the wall, then came back and unlocked the cell door. Art rushed out of the cell and stood shaking with the excitement of his escape. He only nodded rapidly in answer when Cullen asked if he was all right. "Good," Cullen said, and went to the front door to take a quick look out across the dark street toward the lights of the Cork and Bottle. Satisfied the patrons of that saloon were making too much noise to have noticed the uproar he had created with his rather unsubtle entrance into the jail, he turned back to the business at hand. "Let's find you a weapon," he said, and began searching through the desk drawers, since the gun cabinet on the wall was empty of everything except a box of cartridges. In one of the bottom drawers, he found what he was looking for, a handgun and holster. "Here, put this on. If we're lucky, we won't need it." He took the box of .44 cartridges from the gun cabinet and started toward the door. "You ready?"

"Damn right!" Art blurted. "I couldn't get no more ready!" He followed Cullen out the door, surprised to see the two saddled horses plus Cullen's packhorse waiting at the hitching rail. Still finding it hard to believe his escape to be so easy, at least for his part, he couldn't help taking nervous glances toward the saloon, expecting shots to fly at any moment.

Noticing Art's worried looks toward the Cork and Bottle, Cullen sought to calm him. "They're makin' such a noise in the saloon I coulda blasted that door with dynamite and they wouldn't have heard it. As long as they're havin' such a good time over there, I think it'll be all right if we go back to the stable before we leave town, and you can get any clothes and things you're gonna be needin'. I've already got everything we'll need to camp with for a while."

"Where are we goin'?" Art asked as he stepped up on the black horse. Before Cullen could answer, Art said, "This is Ned Larson's horse. I always figured Larson had to have him a black horse to match that Morgan Moran rides."

"Is that a fact?" Cullen replied. "I doubt he'll miss it, but Marshal Moran might still try to hang you for a horse thief." Then, answering Art's question, he said, "I don't know for sure where we're headin'. I'm just

thinkin' about gettin' you away from here right now."
He climbed on Jake and wheeled him away from the
rail, heading for the stable.

With no one in the street and the town buttoned
up for the night, with the exception of the two saloons
at the opposite ends of the street, they rode quietly
away from the jail. When they got to the stable Cullen
told Art they'd best tie their horses out behind the
barn. Then, while Art picked up the personal articles
he kept at the stable, reluctant to leave them behind,
Cullen went through the stable and opened all the
stalls, chasing the horses out the front of the stable. It
was hard for Art to watch. Cullen had to remind him
that the horses weren't his to lose, even as he opened
the corral gate. "I reckon," Art replied. "I just spent so
many years tryin' to make sure this didn't happen."

"It might buy us a little more time," Cullen said.
"I'd like to make sure they scattered, but I reckon if
we try to stampede 'em, they *would* hear that in the
saloon. If we had the time, we'd cut all the cinch straps
on these saddles, but I reckon it would be best for us
to get goin' while everything's still quiet."

Art tied his raincoat and the few personal items he
wanted to take with him onto Cullen's packhorse.
Then they rode away from the stable on the narrow
footpath that led to Hortense Billings's house. Both
of them agreed that they should take the time to let
Hortense and the others know what had happened,
and Art could pick up some extra clothes. Cullen was
sure they would want to know that Art was still alive.
In the deep darkness under the trees, Cullen let Art
lead them, since he knew the twists and turns in the
path so well.

With no idea what the hour was, only that it was

late, they arrived at the boardinghouse to find it totally dark, everyone having gone to bed. It didn't stay that way for long. Hortense's two hound dogs came out from under the back porch to alert the house. Art tried to quiet the baying hounds, but he was not in time to prevent a couple of lamps from flaring into light in two separate windows. As Cullen and Art dismounted, the lamps left the windows and showed up together in the kitchen. The door opened slightly, and Annie demanded, "Who's out there?"

"It's me and Cullen," Art answered her. "We figured we didn't have nothin' else to do, so we thought we'd pay you ladies a visit." Cullen, as well as Annie and Hortense, was surprised by his show of carefree bravado.

"Did they knock you in the head?" Annie demanded. "That bunch of scum will sure as hell be out here lookin' for you. This is the first place they'll look."

"We know that," Cullen assured her. "We planned to stop just long enough to let you folks know that Art's gonna miss his appointment with that necktie party in the mornin'. Then we'll be on our way." He knew that what Annie had just said was very likely what would happen. Moran and his crew would be here to look for them. It had troubled him as he thought about that possibility on the ride from the stable.

Having been awakened by the sound of the dogs barking under his window, Roy Skelton came down to stand in the kitchen door behind Hortense and Annie. "I swear," he exclaimed upon seeing who the women were talking to. "Danged if he didn't do it, just what he said he would do!"

It was a little longer before Pearson and George joined them, their rooms being on the front of the house. Like Roy, they wanted to hear how Art had escaped. He was about to give them a blow-by-blow accounting of it, but Cullen cut him short, and pushed to get started. "I don't know how long it's gonna be before they discover you're gone, and how long it's gonna take them to round up their horses. So, to play it safe, we need to get away from here right now." He turned to Hortense then. "When they show up here, don't give 'em any trouble. If they wanna search the house, let 'em. Don't give 'em any reason to get rough. I'm sorry to have to leave you like this, but it's better than havin' a shootout here."

"I understand," Hortense said, "and I think I like our chances better that way. Have you got anything to eat?" Cullen said he had some jerky, flour, and coffee in his packs, and maybe, if they were lucky, they might find some rabbits, squirrels, or a deer to hunt. "I've got bacon in the smokehouse. You'd best take some with you." He tried to refuse it, but she insisted. "Won't take me a minute," she said, and ran immediately to the smokehouse.

Art, basking in the glory of his escape, appeared to be disappointed when Cullen said it was time to ride, but a grin reappeared on his face and he said, "They locked me up in the jailhouse and went to the saloon. Afterwhile, Cullen come up and kicked the front door off its hinges and unlocked the cell door. We went to the stable and let all the horses out. End of story."

Cullen tied the side of bacon onto the packhorse, and they rode out of the backyard, heading for the creek and the prairie beyond.

"Oh shit!" Stan Molloy blurted when he approached the jail and saw the gaping black hole where the heavy oak door was supposed to be. "Oh shit!" he repeated, and ran the rest of the way, drawing his .44 as he ran. Just before reaching the step up to the door, he stopped running and took a more cautious approach. The full moon was now higher in the sky and more directly over the center of the roof. Consequently, there was just enough light falling on the doorway to permit him to see only a few feet inside the office. Fearing an ambush waiting for him inside the jail, he pressed his body against the wall to the side of the doorway and tried to peek inside. He was still unable to see anything inside the room. "Becker!" he called for no reason other than he didn't know what else to do. When there was no answer, he knew he was going to have to go inside. He couldn't go back to the Cork and Bottle and tell Micah Moran he didn't check inside because he was afraid he'd get shot. At this point, he wasn't sure that Becker was gone. He might still be in the cell. He had to be sure, so he knew he had to go inside. There was a chance that he might get shot. But if he didn't go in to check, he was sure to get shot when he reported that to Moran. With no concern for the time he might be wasting, he called again. "Becker! You in there?" He waited for a minute or so, then reached in his pocket for a match. He struck it on his belt buckle and carefully held the burning match at arm's length before him. When nothing happened, he followed it inside the building to discover it was empty, no Becker inside the cell, and the cell door standing open with the key in the lock. When the flame started to flicker down, he pulled out another match and lit it off the first one. Then he used that match to light the lamp on the desk. Fearing the wrath of Micah Moran to come down on them all, he took the lamp in hand and walked inside the open cell. Standing in the middle of the cell, he turned around in a circle, as if hoping to see Becker hiding somewhere, in a room where there was no place to hide.

Fearing the worst, he left the lamp on the desk, still lit, and walked back across the street to the saloon, pausing a moment when a horse trotted in front of him. It didn't strike him as odd, his mind occupied with how Moran was going to react to the news he was bringing. He continued on to the saloon, his mind so locked on the escape that he paid no attention to the two horses walking between the saloon and the hotel.

Inside the saloon, Micah Moran was sitting at a table talking to Jeb Dickens and Riley Pitts, two bank robbers on the run from Arizona Territory. The hour was late, and Moran had been drinking since supper, but he had no desire to retire for the night. He would sleep late in the morning. And when Molloy had asked what time he wanted Becker out for his hanging, Moran had told him whenever he got up and had his breakfast. "There ain't no hurry," he had told Molloy. "Let him stew a little longer over gettin' his neck stretched. Besides, I wanna make sure the town council gets a chance to see it. I wanna make sure everybody's come to work in time."

Sitting at the table now with the two young men from Arizona, Moran was already in the process of re-building his posse of outlaws. Jeb and Riley had just come from Tucson, where they were chased by a posse of angry vigilantes. Having heard of East City, Texas, as a haven for outlaws on the run, they headed there straightaway. It had turned out to be a lucky decision, they thought, for they found that Micah Moran was hiring new members for his outlaw posse. A fair monthly payment, plus occasional opportunities to pull a job and receive a portion of the profit. Added to this was the benefit of various goods and services at the expense of the merchants in town, a room in the hotel with hot-and-cold-running prostitutes. And your boss is the town marshal.

"So, whaddaya say, boys?" Moran asked. "You wanna ride with my posse?"

They didn't have to think about it, or even look at each other before replying. "Yes, sir," they said almost in unison. Then Riley, who was Jeb's elder by two years, spoke for them. "Yes, sir," he repeated. "And I don't mind tellin' ya, you got yourself two good men. Me and Jeb has been makin' a livin' offa cattle ranchers, sheepherders, banks, and anyplace that had a payroll. Ain't that right, Jeb?" Jeb nodded, grinning proudly.

Unimpressed, but in desperate need of gunmen, Moran asked, "You ever kill a man? Either one of you?"

There was no hesitation on Riley's part. He answered right away. "Yes, sir, we've been shot at plenty, and there's been times when we had to kill a man before he killed us." He looked at Jeb again for confirmation, and as before, Jeb nodded profusely.

"How many times have you had to kill?" Moran asked, already of the opinion neither of them had ever killed.

"I don't know," Riley fumbled. "Once or twice, I reckon. You remember, Jeb?"

"Once or twice," Jeb repeated.

Although certain now that he was talking to two

greenhorn would-be outlaws that may have robbed a candy store in addition to that one bank they were now on the run from, Moran was not in a position to be choosy. He needed men. He could cull them out after he was fully strong again. "All right, boys, welcome to my posse. The first thing you've gotta know is, I pay the bills, so my word is law. Any of my men will tell you that. Understand?"

"Yes, sir." Almost in unison again.

Moran picked up the whiskey bottle in the center of the table and filled three glasses. "Let's have a drink on it." They tossed the whiskey back and slammed the glasses back hard on the table. "Tomorrow mornin' you'll get a chance to see what happens to those who cause me trouble."

Sitting at another table closer to the door, Shorty and Leroy sat, working on another bottle of whiskey. Both of them were interested spectators of the hiring of the two new men. "Damn if those two ain't the greenest gourds I've ever seen," Shorty commented. "I hate to think we've got so desperate that I'd have to depend on one of them to back me up."

"Yeah," Leroy said. "Look at ol' Micah givin' 'em the evil eye. Two months ago, he'da run 'em outta here to go back to the farm." Further discussion was halted when Stan Molloy suddenly burst into the front door, looking as if he had seen a ghost. "What's the matter with him?" Leroy uttered as Molloy stopped and looked around until he spotted Moran, then went straight to him.

"He's broke out!" Molloy blurted. "Becker's gone!"

"What the . . ." Moran uttered as he came to his feet. "What are you talkin' about?"

"He's gone!" Molloy repeated. "He ain't there no more!"

"What do you mean?" Moran pressed. "You mean he's dead?" His first thought was that Art had somehow killed himself, because there was little chance that he had found a way to break out of a locked cell inside a building locked from the outside.

"I mean he's gone!" Molloy insisted, frustrated that Moran didn't seem to understand simple English. "I went to check on him and the door was open and the cell empty!"

Moran's face flushed red, but he said nothing. Instead, he ran immediately to the door, thinking his deputy must be drunk or crazy or both. He had to see for himself, and right away, that Molloy was wrong, too drunk to know what he had seen. Moran had suffered too many defeats in the few days since Cullen McCabe had entered his world. His patience was at an end when it came to the somber stranger who continued to thwart his every move. With his gun drawn, he ran out the door. Alarmed as well by Molloy's frantic announcement, Shorty and Leroy jumped to their feet and followed Moran out the door, weapons ready to fire. Confused by the sudden charge out the door, the two newly recruited members of the posse looked at each other in astonishment, then jumped up and followed the others.

The first thing Micah Moran noticed, when he ran out on the dark street, was the sight of a couple of horses, standing unattended, casually watching the men pouring out of the saloon. His mind occupied with Molloy's announcement, he didn't bother to wonder about their presence in the street. Before he was halfway across the street, he could see the lamp sitting on the desk through the open doorway. Just as Molloy had, he went inside to see for himself and was back standing in the damaged doorway when Shorty and Leroy arrived. "He's right," Moran confirmed. "The dirty rat is gone." He stepped outside and looked up and down the street. It occurred to him then. "Where the hell did all these stray horses come from?"

The five men gathered at the door of the jailhouse all looked around, too, aware of the unusual number of horses as well. "I know where one of 'em came from," Leroy suddenly announced. "That's my buckskin yonder. Somebody's turned the horses outta the stable!" He started toward the horse, but the buckskin decided it was enjoying its freedom and turned to trot off toward the other end of the street. Leroy ran after it. Shorty and the other men started looking for their horses, but Moran yelled at them to go to the stable first to see if they were all out, or just the ones they saw in the street. Leroy was already too far up the street to hear the order, but the other men headed for the stables. Jeb and Riley led the pack, eager to please their new boss. When they reached the stables, they found the corral gate open and the barn door open as well. There were a couple of horses milling around the front of the stable. They were quickly herded back in and the men prepared to go back to catch the rest of them.

"Grab some rope," Shorty yelled. "I didn't see no bridles on them other ones." Already in a panic to save their horses, the other men ran in the barn to fetch rope from their saddles.

Equally as frantic to retrieve his horse, a four-year-old Morgan gelding named Satan, that stood fifteen hands high, Moran caught Riley Pitts by the arm when he ran by him. "Are you any good with that rope?" When Riley said that he was born and raised on a cattle ranch, Moran said, "Good, you stick close to me." The marshal was no good with a rope, and he was desperate to find that Morgan. Even though Cullen had not thought it worth the risk to make enough noise to stampede the horses out of town, his emptying of the stable proved to be more effective than he had anticipated. It gained several hours for him and Art, since the horses scattered about town before finally ending up along the creek bank. By the time they were all rounded up, it was only a half hour or so before sunrise.

Some of the early risers in town, like the black-smith, Buck Casey, were treated to see the curious horse roundup by Moran's men on foot, as they herded the horses toward the stables. At the precise time they drove the horses by him, Buck was standing on the one step before the jailhouse, staring with wonder at the smashed-in door. He had already gone inside when he saw the jail was open and found that the prisoner was gone, and he was anxious to spread the word about his discovery. Knowing Art Becker could not have done this by himself, it was not diffi-cult to guess whose work it was. *Cullen McCabe* was the name that came to him. *Art had escaped!* He was eager to tell Abe and Joe, especially. He started to return to his shop when he saw Micah Moran walking behind the herd of horses. Thinking he might risk getting shot, Buck still could not resist asking the question. It was in his nature. "Mornin', Marshal." He nodded back toward the jailhouse door. "Does this mean the hangin's canceled?"

Moran jerked his head around sharply to stare menacingly at Buck. "No, damn it," he answered. "It means it's delayed." He continued walking toward the Cork and Bottle, but stopped before taking more than a dozen paces to turn back and say, "And you'd best get started to repair that door. So anybody that wants to can kick it in," he added sarcastically.

"Yes, sir, Marshal, I'll get right on it," Buck responded. *I hung that door on those hinges, myself,* he thought, *so anybody couldn't have kicked it in. It took a hell of a man, who was mad as hell, to kick that door in.* He headed back to his shop, wondering how long it would be before Joe Johnson opened the store. He couldn't wait to tell him the news. The dark sky was already starting to lighten up with the promise of the sun's appearance. Buck looked toward the distant hills on the eastern horizon and thought, *Looks like it's going to be a good day.*

It was certainly an interesting day, at least for two young outlaws on the run from Arizona Territory. The reason they had made East City their destination when they had fled was stories they had heard of Micah Moran and his outlaw posse. The picture they had formed of the outlaw empire was vastly different than the scene they witnessed today. To begin with, the marshal's posse had been reduced considerably, down to the marshal, and in their young eyes, three washed-up-looking saddle tramps, one of whom had only one eye. Never having met Boot Davis, Charley Turner, Ace Brown, or any of the other hardened gunmen who rode with Moran until recently, their picture of the posse was not intimidating.

"You know what, Riley?" Jeb saw fit to remark. "Micah Moran needs me and you a lot more than he realizes. And from the looks of those three he's got left, that ain't much of a posse. I think we mighta landed right where we wanted to."

Riley grinned back at him. "I can't say as I disagree, partner, and the sooner he finds out, the better."

CHAPTER 14

It was a good day, indeed, that greeted Art Becker as he awakened after a couple of hours' sleep. He rolled over and sat up to discover Cullen kindling a fire. "Mornin'," he said.

Cullen looked over at him. "Mornin'," he returned. "I'll get some coffee workin' here in a minute, then I'll fry up some of that bacon Hortense gave us. How 'bout it? Think you could use a little coffee?"

"I surely could," Art answered. "And I don't care if you make a good cup of coffee or a sorry one, it'll be the best cup of coffee I've ever had in my whole life. When you kicked that door in, it sounded like the whole jailhouse blew up. But it turned into music like the angels sing. I ain't never been so glad to see anybody as I was when you came through that door."

"Damn," Cullen replied, "I reckon I better pay attention to what I'm doin'." He could well appreciate Art's good spirits, considering what he had expected to happen to him on this morning. He had no real notion of how far ahead of Micah Moran and his posse he and Art had gotten during the remainder of the night just passed. But he had decided to stop by this little stream that made its way down a narrow ravine in a line of low hills. It offered good water and there was plenty of grass for the horses. He had decided that, as well as the horses, he and Art needed to rest. And if they were not as far ahead of their pursuers as he hoped, and had to defend themselves, the top of the ravine would be a good place to do it.

"What can I do to help you?" Art asked.

"Well, I ain't exactly cookin' up a big breakfast here," Cullen replied. "I'll let you cook your own bacon. How 'bout that? And I've got some hardtack in one of those packs we can fry in the bacon grease. It won't be like you'd be gettin' back at Annie's table, but maybe it'll keep the sides of your stomach from rubbin' together."

"That suits me just fine," Art said as he caught the cup Cullen tossed to him. He watched his mysterious rescuer, compelled to wonder why this complete stranger had risked his life to save his. "You know," he felt the need to say, "I don't know if I thanked you for gettin' me outta that jail. But if I didn't, I wanna thank you now."

"Well, you're welcome, but if it wasn't for me, you wouldn't have been in that jail. So I sure couldn't let you hang just because that little rat I shoulda shot surprised us on the path back to the house. The question right now is what to do next." He was thinking about where to leave Art while he returned to finish what he had started.

"Whatever you say, partner," Art said. "I would like to get my stable back, but I reckon we'll be on the run for a spell, till Moran gives up on findin' us." He filled his cup with coffee when the pot finished boiling. "I hate to give up my room at Hortense Billings's board-in'house, though. I don't know when I'll ever get back there, maybe never." He took a sip of the hot coffee. "I reckon it won't do no harm to talk about it now, since I might not ever go back, but I've got a soft spot in my heart when it comes to Hortense. I was even thinkin' I might wanna see if she'd consider hookin' up with me." He looked up at Cullen and added, "You know, marriage."

Cullen was surprised to hear that affirmation come from the mild-mannered stable owner. He hadn't noticed any obvious signs of Art's affection for the spunky landlady in the short time he had spent at her house. He was not sure how to respond to his confession. Finally, he spoke his mind. "You know, Art, you're talkin' like you ain't ever goin' back to East City, like you and me are gonna have to leave the territory for good. I'm plannin' to go back. I've got unfinished business to take care of in your town. And what I'm hopin' is that, since you showed 'em the guts you had to take Moran's boys down, maybe it'll encourage Abe Franks, Joe Johnson, Buck Casey, and some of the others to fight to get rid of Moran for good. I'm thinkin' you and the others aren't quite ready to give up on East City." He paused, then added, "I think that would be a pretty good pairin', too, you and Hortense."

"You think so? She might take a broom to my backside, if I was to ask her." He paused to picture it, then returned to the subject of taking back their town. "I don't know, Cullen. I ain't sure we're strong enough to go up against Moran, even if he ain't got all the men he used to have. They're still cold-blooded gunmen and I ain't even there to help 'em. I don't see any chance of it."

"I'm not talkin' about Franks and the others doin' it all by themselves," Cullen tried to explain. "I'm plannin' to draw Moran out to settle it. I don't expect the townspeople to take that gang on themselves. And I don't expect to drag you into any shootouts with those gunslingers, either. Right now, we have to decide where you can go to be safe for the next few days. Do you know anybody in Ravenwood?" He could see that his statement had Art confused.

"Well, yeah, I know Jim Farmer," Art said. "He owns a stable over there. I used to be partners with him before I got the bright idea to build my own stable in East City." He grunted an amused chuckle and said, "You can see how that turned out."

"You still get along with Farmer?" Cullen asked, thinking the split might not have been a friendly one.

"I reckon," Art answered.

"Think maybe he'd let you stay in his stable for a little while, till things in East City get under a little better control?"

"I expect so," Art said, scratching his head while he considered it. "If he don't, my sister will let me stay at the house. She's his wife. But I'd just as soon stay in the stable."

Cullen didn't say anything for a few moments while he paused to wonder if he really had heard what Art had just said. "Jim Farmer is your brother-in-law?"

"He married my sister, Rena," Art stated simply. "I reckon that makes him my brother-in-law." Cullen couldn't help shaking his head when he thought about his meeting Jim Farmer. At the time, his first thought was that Farmer reminded him of Art, even to the extent they could have been brothers.

"Good," Cullen said. "We're goin' to Ravenwood right after we eat this fine breakfast." Art looked disappointed, and it occurred to Cullen that the mild little man wanted to stay with him when he went back to East City. Cullen didn't want to risk Art's life again with any meeting he might have with Moran or any of Moran's men. He worked better alone when it came to what he planned to do, anyway. Foremost in his mind was to check to see if Hortense and her little family were not being threatened by Moran. He was bound to go there to search for him. Thoughts of his family came back to haunt him. He feared a fate for Hortense and Annie like the fate of his Mary Kate and the children. There was a good possibility that things would get pretty nasty before he was through with East City, and he didn't want to have to worry about Art's safety, too. Of concern also, however, was Art's newfound courage. Cullen did not want to discourage him, or make him feel he was not thought of as dependable. So he said, "I'll look around to see how things are settlin' down over there. It's easier for one man to scout out the place. Then I might need you to help me if it comes to goin' up against the posse. Whaddaya think?"

"You can count on me," Art said at once. "If it comes to the town squarin' off against Moran and his gang, I wanna be in on it."

"I knew I could count on you," Cullen said. "When I need help, you're the first one I would think of."

That seemed to satisfy Art, and he settled back to eat his bacon and the hardtack Cullen had fried. After a while, he began to think about everything that had happened in the last few days, especially to him, and he was prompted to ask a question. "Cullen, somethin' I ain't figured out, why are you takin' on East City's fight with Micah Moran? You didn't know anybody here before you rode in with Lila Blanchard. And you said from the first, you ain't plannin' to stay. How come you're riskin' your life to help us?"

"I don't know, Art, sometimes I do crazy things, I reckon. I ain't got anything better to do right now."

"I reckon you're the first crazy man I ever had any use for," Art declared. "I'd hate to see you get yourself shot while you're in one of your crazy spells."

When breakfast was finished, they saddled up and set out for Ravenwood. They would have to ride back a few miles in a more northeastern direction, since they had ridden west of the town the night just passed. Cullen was not overly worried about the chance they might meet Moran and his posse coming after them. But he decided not to double back on their own trail, just in case Moran was a better tracker than he figured. He doubted Moran could track them during the night, at any rate.

"I declare, Art Becker," Jim Farmer acknowledged when he walked out of the stable to meet the two riders approaching. He grinned when he saw his brother-in-law. "Reckon had I better notify Marshal Taggert that one of them outlaws from East City is in town?" He chuckled and winked at Cullen. "I was thinkin' it was about time you gave up on that devil's playground across the creek and came back to work with me."

"Howdy, Jim," Art returned. "I'm glad to see you're still in business since I left."

"Hell, business has picked up since you left," Jim joked. He nodded to Cullen, then said to Art. "I see you met up with the feller who saved Tug Taggert's bacon." Art gave Cullen a look of surprise. He knew only that Cullen had shot one of Moran's men in Ravenwood, but he didn't know anything about saving the marshal's bacon. Before he could comment on it, Farmer continued talking. "You gonna be able to visit Rena while you're here?"

"I expect so," Art answered, "since I'm plannin' on sleepin' with my horse for a couple of days or more in your stable. That is, if you don't charge too much."

Jim looked genuinely surprised when he heard that, but he continued to jape with his brother-in-law. "Is that a fact? I reckon I'd best clean up the bridal stall and throw down some fresh hay." Cullen was glad to see there appeared to be no friction between the two ex-partners. Jim turned his attention to Cullen then. "Glad to see you back in town, even with the company you're keepin'." He winked at Art. "What brings you two back to Ravenwood?"

"I reckon I'll leave Art to tell you that," Cullen answered.

When Jim looked at Art then, Art chuckled and said, "I just broke outta jail and Cullen thinks I oughta lay low for a while."

"What were you in jail for?" Jim asked. "Anything serious?"

"Well, I reckon you could say so," Art answered with a wide grin on his face. "They was plannin' on hangin' me this mornin'." Confused, Jim automatically looked at the black horse Art had ridden in on. Reading his thoughts, Art said, "No, it ain't for stealin' the horse. They don't even know about that yet, I don't reckon."

Cullen couldn't help noticing that Art was enjoying his new notoriety and before he started to fill Jim in on all the events that led to their appearance at his stable, he interrupted. "Well, I'll leave you two to catch up with everything. If it's all right with you, I'll leave my packhorse here with you, Art. I'll get my war bag with the few things I'll need and I'll head out."

"What's your hurry?" Jim asked, totally unaware of the urgency of their appearance in Ravenwood. "You'd be welcome to take dinner with us at the house. My wife would be tickled to have you join us." He paused to issue a chuckle. "I don't know about her brother, though."

"'Preciate it," Cullen said, "but I expect I'd best not linger—as good as it sounds. Art, I'll be in touch as soon as I see how things are gonna go." He untied his war bag from the packhorse and tied it onto Jake, then he promptly climbed on the bay. "Much obliged," he said, wheeled the horse, and started off down the street at a comfortable lope.

In spite of his intent to mount an early search party for the escaped prisoner and his conspirator, Micah Moran found himself still delayed in East City. It had taken well into the morning to round up all the stray horses and drive them back to the stable. Even then, they were not at all certain that they had recovered all of them. His posse were all stumbling around, nursing hangovers from a night of celebrating the hanging to come, as well as a night with no sleep at all. Moran, himself, was not exempt from the suffering his men were experiencing, having imbibed too heavily, too. But he was driven by the burning desire to kill Cullen McCabe. The recapture and hanging of Art Becker would be satisfying, but secondary to the death of McCabe, preferably by his hand. He had overheard grumbling between Shorty and Molloy, that it was useless to saddle up and go after Becker and McCabe. They thought they were too late to catch them now and tracking would be unlikely. But Moran was convinced that Becker and McCabe would go straight to Hortense Billings's house from here to pick up anything they needed for their escape. "I reckon we're ready to ride, Boss," Stan Molloy said, interrupting Moran's thoughts.

"Get the men in the saddle, then," Moran replied. "We'll head to that woman's boardin'house on that little path behind the stable."

"You reckon we oughta load up a couple of packhorses?" Molloy asked. "How long you reckon we'll be gone?"

"No," Moran answered, not willing to wait another minute longer. "We need to get to that boardin'house as soon as possible while the trail's fresh. If we don't find 'em hidin' out around there somewhere, we'll try to pick up their trail from there. We'll send back here for supplies then."

"Right," Molloy responded, although with very little enthusiasm. He then risked Moran's ire by making another comment. "When you come to think of it, with Becker and McCabe on the run, they're just gettin' rid of our problem for us. With McCabe gone, things will just get back to normal. Whaddaya think, Boss? Ain't that about right?"

"Get ready to ride," Moran answered. "We've already lost too much time. You and Shorty ain't got sense enough to know that the folks in this town need to see Art Becker swingin' from that pole. That's what it takes to keep 'em in line." Molloy turned and started toward the four men gathered at the front door of Art Becker's barn, their horses saddled and waiting. Having second thoughts, Moran stopped him. "You tell them to get ready. You're gonna stay here and keep the peace in town till we get back," he ordered. It had struck him that, as a matter of insurance, one of his men should always be there to be seen by the merchants. And Molloy, being the deputy, was the logical choice to stay. "And you be damn sure everybody sees that you're watchin' the town."

"Right, Boss," Molloy responded, this time with considerably more enthusiasm. "I'll get 'em ready to ride." Nothing could have made him happier at this particular moment with his head pounding like someone was inside it, trying to get out, and a load of liquid contents in his stomach that threatened to erupt at the same time. Already planning his day, he told himself that as soon as the posse pulled out, he was going to get a dose of the hair of the dog that bit him. Then he would get Lizzie to cook something for him to see if he could hold it down. Then he was going to get some sleep. With all those thoughts in his head, he walked up to the four men waiting at the barn. "Micah said, get on your horses."

"I swear," Leroy complained, "oughta let 'em go and be done with 'em."

"You can tell Micah that," Molloy said. "He might let you stay here and keep an eye on the town with me."

"Whaddaya mean, with you?" Shorty asked. "You ain't stayin' here."

"I hate to let you boys down," Molloy japed, "but we can't leave the town without any protection. Micah says I gotta stay and protect the town. Makes sense 'cause I'm the deputy marshal. Folks respect me. They wouldn't pay you no mind." He stood back and laughed at the two of them as they reluctantly climbed up into the saddle.

Standin' a little apart, saying nothing, but listening to the conversation going back and forth between the three older members of the posse, Riley Pitts and Jeb Dickens climbed on their horses, as well. "These jaspers act like a couple of old men," Riley said aside to Jeb. "We can damn sure outdrink 'em, and I expect we can outshoot 'em, if it comes to that. All we need to do is get a chance to show Micah what we can do." Jeb nodded his agreement. When Micah climbed up on the big Morgan named Satan, he signaled for Shorty to lead out to the path. That was in case McCabe might be waiting somewhere on the narrow little footpath in ambush. Shorty had always assumed he led because Micah thought he was the best tracker. Jeb and Riley moved their horses in line as close to Moran's as they could.

Molloy stood watching them ride away until he could no longer see them. Then he turned and headed as fast as his aching head would permit to the Cork and Bottle. When he went inside, he found Tom Loughlin, Micah's partner in the saloon, seated at a table with a couple of cowhands from one of the ranches east of town. Molloy figured they were most likely out of money and were trying to talk Loughlin into granting them some credit. There were no other customers in the saloon, which suited Molloy just fine. He went to the bar and told Floyd to pour him a stiff drink. "I thought you boys had drunk all the whiskey you could hold for a week," Floyd cracked as he poured the whiskey. "What you doin' back here? I thought you were goin' after Becker."

"Micah and the rest of 'em went after Becker and McCabe. I'm stayin' here to look after the town, and I ain't in no mood to put up with any trouble."

"Well, I don't know if drinkin' more of that corn whiskey is gonna do you any good. Maybe you oughta get Lizzie to make you some coffee instead, maybe a little somethin' to eat along with it, if you can hold it down."

"I was thinkin' about doin' that, but I need a little hair of the dog first," Molloy insisted. "Pour me another one."

"All right, but if you ask me . . ." That was as far as he got before Molloy cut him off.

"Damn it, I didn't ask you," he blurted. "Just pour the damn drink!" Floyd said no more, shrugged, and poured the glass full. Having seen Molloy's short temper before, he didn't say anything further. The belligerent deputy took his glass of whiskey and sat down at a table a few feet from Loughlin and the two cowhands. He didn't bother to acknowledge Tom. None of the posse had much to do with Micah's partner, even though he had a half ownership in the saloon. He had been the one who originally bankrolled the building of the Cork and Bottle. It was a feeling among the posse that it would only be a matter of time before Micah decided to retire him with a bullet in his head. After taking another stiff drink of the corn whiskey, Molloy decided he'd better get some coffee and food inside him. "Floyd!" he roared out. "Go tell Lizzie I need somethin' to eat, and I need some coffee to go with it." His words were followed out of his mouth by the contents of his stomach which splattered across the entire surface of the table. Molloy wiped his mouth with his sleeve and swore. "Damn," he blurted, "and tell her to bring a mop and a bucket to clean this mess up."

Tom Loughlin, as a rule, made very little noise in the saloon he owned half of. Like everyone else in town, he was in fear of Micah Moran. And he especially avoided contact with the outlaws that frequented his saloon. But this disgusting exhibition was too much to ignore, so he commented, "Lizzie's busy getting ready for dinner, Molloy. I think it would be a good idea if you went up to your room and slept it off." He glanced at the two cowhands sitting with him before adding, "You'll be driving off our customers."

Molloy was in no mood to be corrected. "Our customers? You mean Micah's customers, don't you? You snivelin' old bastard, I'll let you know if I wanna hear anything outta you. Lizzie!" He shouted as loud as he could. "Get your lazy behind out here and clean this up." His howling brought Wilma and Mabel from the back room to see what the fuss was about. Seeing them, Molloy shouted, "You two come clean this up."

"Clean it up, yourself," Wilma responded. "You did it."

"Why, you low-down slut, I'll make you lick it up," Molloy threatened, and got up from his chair.

"I think that's about enough outta you," one of the cowhands sitting with Tom spoke up then and got to his feet. "You'd best do like everybody's been tellin' you and go on to your bed, wherever that is."

"Well, now," Molloy said. "You reckon you're man enough to make me?"

"I reckon I am," the young man said. "But it wouldn't be a fair fight. You're too drunk to stand up on your own. You'd best get on outta here. You'll feel better after you sober up."

"Is that so? You're pretty good about tellin' people what they oughta do, ain'tcha? I see you're wearin' a gun. You any good with it?"

"It don't matter if I am or not. This ain't gonna come to any gunplay," the cowhand quickly replied. "I don't use my gun for nothin' but killin' snakes."

"That's too bad," Molloy said, "'cause I use mine for yellow-belly cowboys." He drew his six-gun and shot him in the stomach. Stunned, the young man bent double and collapsed and Molloy turned to aim his .44 at the unfortunate cowhand's friend, who immediately put his hands in the air.

Tom Loughlin stood up at once and stood in front of the frightened cowhand. "He ain't lookin' for no trouble. Put it away!"

They stood for a long moment, glaring at each other, Molloy's .44 still leveled at Loughlin. At the bar, Floyd stood rigidly fixed, not certain what to do. There was a double-barreled shotgun within his easy reach, only a few feet away, but he was hesitant about going for it. Molloy was obviously deciding whether or not to shoot the half owner of the Cork and Bottle. No matter if the posse held low regard for Micah's partner, he couldn't let a drunken outlaw shoot him down. He was saved from reaching for the shotgun when Molloy lowered his gun. "Get him outta here before I cut you down, too," he ordered the wounded man's friend. He looked at Loughlin and said, "You're lucky I ain't in a bad mood." Then he pushed him aside and stalked into the kitchen to confront a frightened cook.

Loughlin exhaled a sigh of relief as the tension that had gripped the almost-empty saloon eased with Molloy's departure. He turned to the wounded man's friend, who was stunned speechless. "You'd best take your friend to get some help," Loughlin said. "Mabel, get him a bar towel to help stop that bleeding." Back to the dumbfounded cowhand, he said, "There ain't no doctor here, but if he can stay on a horse, there's one across the creek in Ravenwood. Here's a couple of dollars to pay the doctor." With Floyd, Mabel, and Wilma's help, they managed to get the wounded man into the saddle, leaning forward on his horse's neck, and they started for the road leading to Ravenwood.

"I don't know, Tom, you think he'll make it?" Floyd asked.

"I doubt it," Loughlin answered. It was not the Cork and Bottle's policy to pay the doctor's bill for patrons shot in their establishment. But he was especially sickened by Molloy's blatant murder of a customer. He and Micah had discussed the savage disregard his men had for human life before, but Micah had maintained that the nature of his posse was what maintained the peace in East City. Loughlin planned to talk to Moran about this incident when he returned. He turned to Floyd and repeated, "I doubt it." They could still hear Molloy grumbling in the kitchen while Lizzie tried to sober him up.

CHAPTER 15

Lying on his belly, on a sandy rise on the west bank of the creek, Cullen McCabe watched the column of outlaws emerge from the trees along the narrow footpath and ride out into the yard behind the house. From his position, not quite fifty yards away, he could see each rider clearly. And with his rifle ready, he could easily pick one or two of them off before they took cover. He hesitated to do that, however, thinking he was reluctant to ignite a gunfight that might cause Moran to take cover inside the house. And that might result in injuries to Hortense and Annie, if only for the purpose of retaliating for the loss of his men. It was perfectly clear to him that the solution to East City's problems was the complete extermination of Micah Moran and his rats. And at this point, he would not hesitate to start the process, but the safety of Hortense, Annie, and Roy was too important for him to make his fight here. So he decided he would hold his fire as long as there was no threat to any of those three.

As Micah Moran rode around Shorty, pulled his horse up before the kitchen door, and dismounted,

Cullen watched the rest of the men file into the yard behind him. He counted four men riding with Moran. Art had told him that Moran had only three men left, so that meant he had picked up another man already. Then he remembered that Art had described Moran's new deputy as a one-eyed man who wore an eye patch over his left eye. From his sandy rise by the creek, he could easily see there was no man wearing an eye patch. That had to mean that Moran had picked up two new men, and he had left the one-eyed deputy in town. He had to consider the possibility that Moran might have picked up more than the two he could now account for. It wasn't likely, however. He would have probably brought everybody except the one man left to cover the town.

He watched while Moran and his men searched around the house. Finding no trace of him or Art, Moran sent two of the men to search inside the house. Cullen guessed Moran didn't go in, himself, because of the risk of someone hiding behind a bed, waiting to ambush him. The temptation to thin out one or two of the notorious posse was strong, but Cullen couldn't risk it. Moran was bound to hold Hortense and Annie as hostages and shoot Roy. So all he could do was sit and watch, waiting to fire only if he was forced to. After what seemed a long time, the posse mounted up again and left, following the tracks he and Art had left when they rode away during the night before. When he was sure the posse was going to continue their tracking, he whistled Jake up from the trees behind him and rode across the creek to the house.

"Good Lord in heaven!" Annie cried out when she

saw Cullen ride up from the creek. Out the kitchen door she ran, in a panic, thinking he wasn't aware that Moran was just there. "Cullen," she exclaimed, "they was just here lookin' for you!"

"I know, Annie, I saw 'em. They're gone now, tryin' to follow our trail away from here." Considering the possibility they might decide not to follow their tracks very far, he said, "I just wanted to make sure you folks were all right and then I'm gone."

"We're all right," Annie said. "But you'd better not stay here long. They might be back."

"I know. I'm leavin' right away. Thought you and Hortense would like to know that Art is all right. He's stayin' in Ravenwood with his brother-in-law."

"His brother-in-law?" Annie responded. "Art ain't never said anything about a brother-in-law." She thought another couple of seconds and said, "He ain't ever said anything about havin' a sister."

"Well, he's safe where he is," Cullen said. "I'll be on my way. Just wanted to know you were all right." He turned Jake back toward the footpath and disappeared into the trees.

Behind Annie, Hortense came to the kitchen door and asked, "They come back?"

"No," Annie said.

"Well, who were you talking to?"

"Cullen."

"Cullen?" Hortense responded. "What were you talking about?"

"Art," Annie answered. "He said Art's all right. He's stayin' with his sister."

"Sister?"

* * *

Some doubts returned to his mind as he rode the narrow footpath back to town. He had made his decision to mount a one-man war on Moran and his posse primarily for a personal reason. The trial and planned hanging of Art Becker, after the brutal hanging of an innocent woman, had turned this assignment into a personal war. He wasn't sure how O'Brien and the governor would react to his method of eliminating the problem he was sent to investigate. But he saw it as the only way to put a halt to it right away. Moran was already hiring new men to ride with him. And now, as he approached the rear of Art's stable, he was thinking of the opportunity to eliminate Moran's deputy.

When he rode around to the front of the stable, he reined Jake to a halt when he saw a man on a horse, leading another horse with a second man on it. The man being led was evidently hurt, for he was lying on the neck of his horse. They were heading for the road to Ravenwood. His first thought was the man had been shot, and it didn't surprise him. Evidently, it was business as usual in East City. He wondered if Moran's new deputy apprehended the shooter. If he did, he had no jail to put him in. Then he corrected himself, for the deputy could lock him in the cell.

After the two riders passed, he nudged Jake again and headed for the Cork and Bottle, thinking that to be the place he would most likely find the deputy. He figured the most dangerous part of this trip for him was the ride up the street to the saloon because he would be shot on sight by anybody who worked for Moran. However, he went unnoticed by the few people in town with the exception of Buck Casey, who walked out to the front of his shop to watch him ride by. "Cullen McCabe," Buck muttered to himself, astonished to think he would show up in town after he was positive it was McCabe who busted the jailhouse door. He was further amazed when he saw Cullen pull up before the Cork and Bottle and dismount. "Lordy, Lordy," he muttered. "I think I need a drink." He pulled his blacksmith's apron off and hustled over to the Cork and Bottle.

Cullen, his rifle in hand, paused for a brief second at the door to survey the room before entering. The only people he saw were the bartender, talking to Tom Loughlin standing at the end of the bar, and two women seated at a table in the center of the room. When he stepped inside, all four faces turned to stare at him and all conversation stopped. From the kitchen, he could hear the drunken rambling of a male voice. He took a few more steps to stand closer to the center of the saloon, then stopped again to listen. There was still not a word spoken by any of the four he saw, only the continuous rambling of the man in the kitchen. "Who's in the kitchen?" Cullen asked.

Answering immediately, Wilma said, "Stan Molloy." Then she emphasized, "*Deputy* Stan Molloy."

Cullen nodded, then called out, "Molloy! Get out here!" There was no response right away, so he called out again.

This time the one-eyed deputy walked out of the kitchen and demanded, "Who the hell is hollerin' my name?" Then he stopped short when he saw the imposing figure standing in the middle of the room.

"Cullen McCabe," Cullen answered. "You lookin' for me?"

Dumbfounded, Molloy did the only thing he knew to do and reached for his gun. The .44 slug from Cullen's rifle struck him in the middle of his chest, causing him to take a couple of steps backward. His gun, only halfway out of his holster, dropped back in it as his knees buckled and he sank to the floor. Cullen's rifle immediately swung around to cover Floyd and Loughlin. "Lizzie, don't!" He heard the cry from Wilma behind him and turned to discover the skinny little cook standing at the kitchen door, holding a shotgun. "He's the man who brought Lila home," Wilma said, and Lizzie immediately put the shotgun down on the floor.

Cullen nodded to Wilma, then, with his rifle still leveled at Floyd and Loughlin, he asked, "Who else is here?"

"No one else," Loughlin answered.

"He's all right, McCabe, he ain't like Moran and his crowd." Cullen whipped his rifle around to discover Buck Casey standing at the front door. He raised his arms to show Cullen he wasn't armed.

Cullen recognized him as the man he had seen in front of the blacksmith shop. Responding to Buck's statement, he turned back toward Loughlin and said, "You need to find you a better partner, if you're plannin' on stayin' in this town."

"I run this place the best I can," Loughlin felt compelled to answer. "I can't help it if we attract so many of the least desirable customers."

Buck came on in the saloon and walked up to Cullen. "I'm Buck Casey. I got a little blacksmith shop you just passed on the street back there. I'm on the city council. Tom Loughlin's all right. I don't know how he got himself in a business deal with Micah Moran. He don't like to talk about it. Does he, girls?" He paused to grin at Wilma and Mabel. Back to Cullen then, he chuckled and said, "I'm the feller

Moran told to fix that door you kicked in last night. You must have a kick like a mule."

"Glad to meet you, Buck," Cullen said, then asked, "What makes you think it was me?"

Buck answered with a wide grin, "Ever'body in town knows who kicked that door open. Couldn'ta been nobody else."

Cullen knew who Buck was, but he had never talked to him. According to Art, Buck was one of the honest men in town, and Cullen was glad that he was because he felt he was a little careless in smoking out Stan Molloy. *Coulda got shot in the back twice*, he thought, *once by a skinny little woman with a shotgun, then again by a blacksmith standing at the door.* He was going to have to be more careful from now on and the first thing he wanted to know was how many he was up against. He figured Buck could tell him. "I saw Moran and his men out at Hortense Billings's house a little while ago. He had four men with him. Do you know if he's picked up any more that I oughta be watchin' over my shoulder for while I'm in town?"

"Nope," Buck answered. "Four's all he's got, now that you put the 'Out of Order' sign on ol' Molloy. He wouldn'ta had four, but there were two young fellers in town that were wantin' to join up, I reckon. 'Cause they rode out with Moran and Shorty and Leroy. But tell me where Art Becker is. Is he all right? I was tickled pink when I got to my shop this mornin' and got a look at that jailhouse."

"Art's all right," Cullen said. "He's in a place where nobody will likely bother him." He decided not to tell everybody exactly where Art was. He remembered that Moran had once sent three men to Ravenwood in an attempt to kill the marshal. "He's gettin' kinda

itchy about takin' your town back to the honest folks,"
Cullen said. He hoped that might encourage Buck
and other council members to scrape up some grit.
He needed the whole town in on this deal to throw
the outlaws out of East City for good. "Art's waitin' for
me to give him the word when you folks are ready to
fight. He wants to be in the middle of it." He could tell
that Buck was thinking hard about what he was saying.
What he needed was to get most of the other people
committed to saving the town as well. "I wanna go talk
to the mayor while I'm in town right now. I need to
see where he stands before I take on the rest of Micah
Moran's gang. I don't know how long they're gonna
try to track Art and me before they come back to
town. From what I saw out at Hortense's , they weren't
packed up to stay out long, and I don't think Moran
will stay away from town very long anyway."

"Ain't you gonna hang around town awhile longer?"
Buck asked. "I'd be proud to buy you a meal at O'Sullivan's."

"Well, I appreciate that, Buck, but I don't aim to
hang around here very long. I've got a target on my
back for any one of Moran's men that sights me. And
I ain't bulletproof, so I have to be able to pick my
fights."

"I understand," Buck said, but Cullen doubted that
he did. He suspected that Buck thought he was going
to challenge all five of them to face him in the street
for a shootout. "I'll drag ol' Molloy outta here for you,
Tom," Buck said to Loughlin, who was still studying
the strange man that was Cullen McCabe.

"I'll give you a hand," Cullen said to Buck, and they
each grabbed a wrist and dragged Molloy's body out
the front door. They left it on the boardwalk in front

of the Cork and Bottle, so Moran could see it first thing when the posse returned. Then Buck, already invested in the overthrow of Marshal Micah Moran's regime, walked with Cullen when he led Jake up the street to the hardware store.

Abe Franks looked up when he heard them come in the door of his store. He knew without being told that the big man with Buck was Cullen McCabe. He was not sure if he wanted to talk to the mysterious killer of some of the key members of Micah Moran's posse. In spite of Art Becker's and Joe Johnson's high regard for the dangerous drifter, Abe was not sure that McCabe was not just another lawless gunman. And that his interest in East City was the same as the devil running it now. From the looks of it, it would appear that Buck Casey had also jumped on the Cullen McCabe bandwagon.

"Hey, Abe," Buck sang out. "Cullen, here, is wantin' to talk to you about somethin'."

Abe put down the new saw he was removing from a wooden crate and walked up to the front counter to meet them. "I heard a rifle shot a little while ago," he said. "Did that have anything to do with you?"

"As a matter of fact," Cullen answered, sensing the mayor's caution in talking to him. Before he could say more, Buck interrupted.

"Yes, sir," Buck started, "that shot you heard created a vacancy in the deputy marshal's job. Stan Molloy has officially retired." He chuckled at his humor. It served to convince Abe he had been right in his opinion of Cullen.

"That's puttin' it kinda bluntly," Cullen was quick to say. "I reckon anybody given the choices I was given would most likely make the choice I made."

"That's right," Buck said. "Molloy went for his gun and Cullen cut him down."

Abe cast a frown at Buck, much as he would a precocious child, before addressing Cullen. "Is that what you specialize in, Mr. McCabe? Are you a fast-draw expert?"

From the mayor's curt manner, it was obvious to Cullen that Franks saw him as merely one more lawless individual seeking to take advantage of a town already a haven for outlaws. "I don't fancy myself as anything more than a man who's seen enough trouble in your town to know that there ain't but one direction it can go in. And if the people in East City don't do something about it pretty quick, it's gonna be too late to save your town." He let that sink in before adding one more comment. "And I don't figure I'm a lot quicker to draw my handgun than the next fellow, so I've got a lot more sense than to try to find out. Molloy got shot because he didn't have enough sense to know he couldn't beat a rifle already out and cocked."

His statement gave Franks pause to reconsider the manner of man he faced, but not completely. "As a stranger just passing through East City, it strikes me as odd that you seem so interested in our town's troubles. Are you thinking about settling here, if we are successful in ridding the town of Micah Moran and his kind?"

"No, sir, I'm not. I've got some property south of Austin that requires my attention. I'll be headin' back there pretty quick now." He didn't go into any detail, since his property was a small cabin in various states of repair, that he worked on between assignments from Austin. "It just appears to me that now's the time to do something. The big posse that Moran had has been cut down to him and four men."

Abe interrupted then. "You mean that *you* have cut down to four men."

"I'm afraid I have to give most of the credit for that to Moran, himself. He's the one who took Ned Larson and his boys out of the picture."

Still eager to be part of the discussion, Buck was quick to inject, "Don't forget Boot Davis, Charley Turner, Ace Brown, and Stan Molloy," he said. "That's four of a kind that's hard to beat in any poker game. Don't try to tell me you didn't take care of them."

Wishing he had left Buck back at the Cork and Bottle, Cullen replied, "Most of that business was a matter of luck." Back to Franks, he said, "The main thing is that it's time to strike Moran when he's at his weakest, and that's right now before he has time to build up his gang."

Skeptical at first, Franks could not help softening his attitude toward the solemn man, thinking he might have no selfish motive after all. So he allowed himself to talk earnestly about the town's problems for a few minutes. "Even if Moran and his men were gone, what would keep the next outlaw gang from moving in to pick up the pieces where Moran left off? Then it would start all over again."

"You need a strong, honest man to fill the job of maintaining the peace, just like they have across the creek in Ravenwood," Cullen said. "I don't reckon I have to tell you that."

"And that would be you, right?" Abe was swift to jump on that, his skepticism returning in a heartbeat.

Cullen shook his head and favored him with a tired smile. "No, Mr. Mayor," he said patiently. "Like I told you,

I don't plan on staying here. I've got other business to tend to somewhere else. But I know where you might find the kind of man you need to protect your town."

That tweaked Abe's interest. "Oh? Where's that?"

"Marshal Tug Taggert just got a new deputy, a fine young fellow. He's strong and won't stay a deputy very long. His name's Beau Arnett. He'd be a good one for you folks."

"How in the world do you know that?" Abe responded.

"I was over there a couple of times. I met him, young fellow, seems to have the right attitude for what you're lookin' for. And Marshal Taggert thinks he's highly qualified." That was all the explanation Cullen offered.

In spite of his natural caution, Abe allowed his mind to think about that idea for a moment. The thought of East City operating in a peaceful existence, like Ravenwood, was something he had given up in despair long ago. "You think this Beau Arnett would be interested in taking the job of marshal here in East City?"

"Don't know for sure," Cullen answered, "but he said he was interested." He realized he was making a recommendation on nothing more than a gut feeling about the young man, but he believed it would be a good match. "Seems to me you folks over here oughta get together with the folks in Ravenwood again, patch up any differences you've had, make the two towns one big city. It would be good for both of you, and it would sure as hell pick East City up."

Abe considered all that had been said in the short time Cullen had been in the store, especially the idea of combining with Ravenwood to become one city.

The two parts of town could be joined by one big bridge and commerce could travel back and forth. In another moment, however, reality returned and he said, "Sounds good, I reckon, but the fact is, we ain't rid of Micah Moran yet." He looked at Cullen directly and confessed, "It might seem a simple solution to a man like you, but the men who would have to confront Moran and his gunmen are men like Joe Johnson and me—hardly gunmen."

Buck interrupted again. "Don't forget about me. I ain't afraid to go up against 'em. And Art Becker, he's already showed a lotta grit. Hell, I say we tell Micah Moran his day in East City is over and it's time for him to pack up his posse and get outta town."

"Use your sense, man!" Abe responded. "That would be the quickest way to get shot down. Do you think Moran will even debate the issue? Him and his four gunmen would put that protest down before you got it out of your mouth. We need the backing of the army, or the Rangers to set up here to enforce our demands."

"We tried that already," Buck reminded him, "and look how that went."

"That was because when the Rangers camped here, all they were doing was policing the town against any lawbreaking," Abe said. "We weren't actively trying to force the marshal out of East City for good. When the Rangers felt like Moran and his deputy were keeping things peaceful, they left. And they're not likely to come back anytime soon to help us run the marshal out of town. If we try to go up against Moran without help from the state, it'll just be a shootout between Moran and his four gunmen against any of our merchants who feel brave enough to do it."

"What do you say to that, McCabe?" Buck pressed.

"I expect he's probably right," Cullen said. "I'm afraid you might lose some of your honest people in that kind of gunfight." The expression on Buck's face told him how disappointed he was to hear him seeming to back off. But Cullen realized that the businessmen of East City would risk suicide in demanding a show-down with Moran and his kind. He knew then that he was going to have to carry the fight alone to keep Abe and his fellow storekeepers from being killed. He wasn't even sure now that it had been a good idea to talk to Franks, after all. In spite of making a great effort to hide it, Abe had clearly let his mind wander to a vision of a town without Micah Moran. Cullen was afraid the reality of his situation might serve to discourage the mayor more when it came to taking steps to uproot the marshal.

Evidently of the same mind as Cullen, the mayor said, "I think it would be best to call a meeting of the town council tonight to discuss our problem and find out how many are ready to take action." This he addressed to Buck.

Thinking he might have done more harm than good, Cullen said good day to the mayor and left his store. Buck followed him outside. "Whaddaya aimin' to do now?" he asked.

"I'm aimin' to get outta town right now," Cullen said.

"Ain'tcha gonna wait for Moran to come back?" Buck asked, obviously disappointed to hear Cullen was leaving. "Or at least come to the council meetin' tonight."

Obviously, Buck was still thinking that he was going to stand in the middle of the street and challenge

Moran and his four men to face him in a gunfight. "There's some things I need to check on out of town. In the meantime, don't you go gettin' yourself in a fix you can't get out of when Moran and his men come back here. He ain't gonna be too happy when he finds Molloy by the front door. He's liable to shoot the first person he sees. So go to that meetin' and find out if the others are ready to fight."

"We're ready to take our town back," Buck stated confidently. "We'll give Moran the word that his time here is finished. At the meetin' tonight, we'll decide how best to make him understand we mean it."

"Buck, make sure you tell everybody to come to that meetin' with a weapon." He stepped up into the saddle and left Buck standing there, watching him ride away.

Still a little disappointed that Abe didn't put his complete trust in McCabe, Buck's lips parted in a mischievous grin, thinking about Moran's reaction when he saw what McCabe had done to the jailhouse door. *Maybe, if I hurry before it gets too late, I can fix up another surprise for him,* he thought.

As Cullen had speculated, Micah Moran and his four men were not prepared to pursue Art and him for very long. With Shorty acting as scout, they had no trouble finding tracks leading away from the boarding-house. The trouble for Shorty was too many tracks, coming and going on a trail back along the creek. He was able to follow some of those tracks only to have them end in the small clearing where Cullen had made a camp. "He was here, all right," Shorty said, in an effort to justify his skill as a tracker.

"Yeah, but he ain't here now," Moran said, visibly irritated. "So, where'd he go from here?"

"I don't claim to be no tracker," Riley was prone to say, as he studied the tracks leading in and out of the campsite. "But it looks to me like these tracks was left by one horse. There oughta be more tracks if there was two horses."

"Well, that's right," Shorty said. "That's what I was fixin' to say."

"Looks to me like maybe Riley oughta be our tracker," Moran cracked. "We'll just have to turn around and go back to where this trail split off that other one before the creek."

They went back and picked up the original trail and followed it until it left the creek and headed west, staying with it until they lost it where it crossed a wide stream. "We shoulda thought about bringin' somethin' to eat," Leroy commented, when after a considerable amount of searching, they had still not found the place where Cullen and Art had left the stream. "We're liable to be out here a helluva long time before we catch them two."

With his patience already in short supply, and hungry as well, Moran reined his horse to a halt in the middle of the stream and sat gazing out toward the west. Then he looked up the stream and considered another possibility. What if McCabe just continued riding up that stream for a long distance before leaving it and then cut back to return to the camp they had discovered close to the boardinghouse? They had never caught McCabe at Hortense Billings's house, but he was convinced that it was McCabe's base. That thought caused him to speculate further. What if McCabe, having sent him and his men off on a fruitless chase, was taking that opportunity to double back to East City and make his move against the one man left to maintain his hold on the town? What kind of condition was Molloy in, if that happened? He was still half-drunk when they left that morning. It was clear to Moran that McCabe's sole purpose in showing up in East City was to kill him and take over his operation. He decided at that moment. "We're goin' back!" He announced it loud and clear. No one asked why—they were all hungry and still hungover. Still thinking it a possibility that McCabe might have gone back to Hortense's house, he said, "We'll head straight back to that boardin'house. We'll get something to eat there."

CHAPTER 16

"They're back," Annie sang out when she saw Micah Moran's dark Morgan gelding come up from the creek. The two new members of his reduced posse appeared right behind him. "Don't look like they had a successful hunt," she reported as she threw the dishwater out, having just cleaned up after the midday meal.

"I sure hope they didn't catch up with Art and Cullen," Hortense said when she walked to the kitchen door to look over Annie's shoulder. "They might have killed them."

"No, ma'am," Annie insisted. "They didn't catch 'em. If they had, they'd be leadin' their horses back with 'em."

"I guess you're right," Hortense decided. "I wonder why they came back here, instead of going back to town?"

"They're comin' back to pay us another visit," Annie said. "They've gotta make sure Cullen and Art didn't double back on 'em. Better tell Roy. He's asleep on the front porch. He ate so many biscuits with that ham gravy on 'em that they weighed his eyelids down."

"I'll tell him," Hortense volunteered, and went back down the hall toward the front door. Hearing Roy talking to someone, she paused to listen.

"I ain't lyin'," she heard Roy say, so she continued on to the front porch to find Shorty Miller and Leroy Hill seated on their horses, facing the porch. They had evidently been sent to cover the front, in case Art and Cullen were inside the house.

"Don't you lie to me, you old buzzard," Shorty threatened him. "We know they doubled back here."

"I told you, I ain't lyin'," Roy insisted. "They ain't here."

"You heard what he said," Hortense stated. "They ain't here. If you had the brains God gave a jackrabbit, you could see there ain't any horses back of the barn. Or did you think they walked back?"

Leroy favored her with a slow grin. "You're a sassy little spitfire, ain't you? For all I know, you mighta cut their horses up and cooked 'em for supper. Now I expect the marshal is gonna want us to search your house again to see if those jaspers are hidin' under a bed somewhere. Most likely under your bed, sweetie pie. Wouldn't you say, Shorty?"

"Wouldn't surprise me a-tall," Shorty replied. "She's built like she could give a feller a good ride."

"You watch your mouths," Roy reacted. "You saloon trash ain't fit to talk to a lady. Cullen McCabe, or Art Becker, ain't neither one of 'em here. I done told you that, so get your sorry carcasses off the property and leave honest folks alone."

"Did you hear what that old buzzard said to me?" Shorty responded.

"I sure did," Leroy said. "He talks like he thinks he's better'n us, don't he?"

"Sounded like it to me," Shorty said. "I know I feel like he's insulted me. I think he's called me out to a face-off. You got a gun, old man? Go get it and we'll settle this little argument right quick." Looking confused, not sure if Shorty was serious or just amusing himself at his expense, Roy could not respond. After a few seconds, when he still didn't, the smile faded from Shorty's face and he threatened, "You get your gun, or I'm gonna shoot you down where you stand."

Roy froze for a few minutes, unable to move, as Hortense watched in horror. When the two outlaws continued to stare at the unfortunate old man, he slowly started to turn toward the door. "Don't you dare go get that gun!" Hortense scolded. "You go in the house and stay there!" Then back at Shorty and Leroy, she railed, "You filthy animals, treat an old man like that, go away and leave us alone. Cullen and Art aren't here."

"I told you, old man," Shorty said, ignoring her. He drew his .44 and put a shot in the back of Roy's leg as he was going in the door." Roy went to his knees and fell in the doorway, accompanied by the laughter of both outlaws. Hortense went to his aid at once, pulling him inside the house and slamming the door shut behind her.

Hearing the shot, Moran kicked his horse hard and charged around the house but pulled up sharply when he found Shorty and Leroy, still sitting on their horses and seeming to be in a laughing fit. "What the hell was that shot?" Moran demanded.

"Ain't nothin', Boss," Leroy replied. "Shorty was just helpin' that old man into the house."

Moran was not amused. "You damn fool. If McCabe is hidin' around here somewhere, he sure knows we're back now."

"Sorry, Boss," Shorty apologized, "I didn't think about that."

"Maybe if he is hidin' somewhere, and he heard that shot, maybe it'll make him come out to see what happened," Leroy suggested.

"More likely make him run again," Moran said. "You two go on in the house and search it again, just in case they did come back here." They got off their horses and went into the house and he rode back around to the kitchen door, where Jeb and Riley were waiting. Annie was no longer standing at the kitchen door. He dismounted after telling his two new men to stay there and keep their eyes and ears open.

He found Annie in the kitchen, helping Hortense in an effort to stop the bleeding in Roy's thigh. He could hear the sounds of Shorty and Leroy upstairs making their search of the bedrooms. From the thuds of crashing furniture their less-than-gentle touch was evident. Concerned with Roy's suffering, Hortense ignored the obvious destruction overhead. Moran paused only a moment to consider the wounded man before going over to the stove and the coffeepot sitting on the edge of it. He picked it up and shook it back and forth before opening the lid to make sure it was empty. When he saw that it was, he banged it back down on the edge of the stove. "My men and I haven't had anything to eat. You're supposed to be in the business of sellin' bed and board, so we're gonna need something to eat."

Both women looked up at him, amazed he could be so insensitive to the suffering his men had caused.

Annie was the first to respond to his request. "You're too late. We done served the midday meal."

"That's all right, you can start cookin' supper. My men and I are hungry."

Hortense looked up at him, her face tense and strained with anger. "It's not time to fix supper yet. Can't you see we're busy here trying to treat this poor man those animals of yours shot just to amuse themselves?"

Moran's dull expression never changed as he bluntly responded, "It doesn't take but one of you to wrap a rag around his leg. The other one can get up from there and find us somethin' to eat. Start with makin' a pot of coffee."

"I'm sorry," Hortense replied. "We're not open for business right now. You'll have to go into town to find something to eat."

There was no hint of emotion in the baleful face that looked down at her as she knelt beside Roy. Consequently, she had no chance to protect herself when he suddenly struck her with a brutal backhand that knocked her flat on the floor. Shocked, Annie cried out in anger, "Stop! You dirty coward! I'll get you some food. Just wait a minute!" She reached for Hortense. "Are you all right, honey?" Hortense, too stunned to answer, could only stare at her while she tried to recover.

"Make the coffee first," Moran said, still with no evidence of emotion.

"You're lucky you caught me without my poker," Annie informed him, "or you'da been thinkin' about somethin' besides coffee."

He drew his hand back, prepared to strike her, but hesitated when Hortense came to her senses enough to cry out, "Don't hit her! We'll get your damn food for you. Give us a minute to take care of his wound."

"He can wait till later," Moran said. "What you're gonna do now is fix me and my men somethin' to eat. Tie that rag around his leg. He'll die of old age before that bullet in his leg kills him, and I'm hungry now."

"You go ahead and make some coffee," Hortense said to Annie. "I'll help Roy into the parlor, then I'll help you cook up some bacon and eggs, with some pan biscuits. That'll be the quickest." To Roy, she said, "I'm gonna help you into the parlor and you can rest on the sofa, then I'll see what we can do for that wound after they leave."

"I'm sorry, Hortense," the suffering old man murmured. "I'm sorry, I ain't no help to you."

"You just try to rest," she said as she walked him into the parlor, letting him use her as a crutch. "I'll check on you to make sure that bleeding has stopped." When she came back, she saw that Moran was still standing in the kitchen, watching the progress of his breakfast. "I'll roll out some dough," Hortense said to Annie, "and you scramble up some eggs."

"It's mighty lucky we've got some eggs," Annie said, "with this many poppin' in on us all of a sudden. Wonder how come they didn't just ride on back to get some of that good food at the Cork and Bottle? I hear Lizzie is just a wonderful cook," she added sarcastically.

"If you'd keep your jaw from flappin' so much, you'd get the cookin' done a lot quicker," Moran said, watching their every move to make sure there were no shenanigans with his food.

"If you would go wait outside, I'd get the cookin' done a helluva lot quicker," Annie informed him.

He gave her a long hard look before saying, "You know, I don't like you a helluva lot to begin with. You and that smart mouth of yours are liable to get you more trouble than you wanna handle. Hey!" he barked at Hortense when she suddenly left the room. "Where are you goin'?" She said she was just going to check on Roy to make sure his bleeding was under control. "Well, get back here quick," he ordered.

"How's he doin'?" Annie asked when Hortense returned.

She replied that he was doing about as well as could be expected for an old man with a bullet wound, "I'll keep checking on him, maybe take him a cup of coffee when that pot finishes boiling." They continued with their food preparation under the watchful eye of Micah Moran, while upstairs the noisy searching of every inch of the house went on. Thinking she heard a whimper from the front room, she said, "I'd best take another quick look at Roy," and left the kitchen again. When Moran again asked where she was going, she told him she'd be right back. He said nothing in response. She returned in a minute and reported to Annie. "He's just in a lot of pain, but there's nothing we can do with this going on."

Moran walked out of the kitchen. Hortense and Annie looked at each other, both hoping he would stay out of the kitchen until they were finished cooking. They were startled a few moments later by the sound of a gunshot inside the house. Both women started toward the door only to be met by Moran returning from the parlor. "He ain't in pain no more," Moran announced matter-of-factly. "Now you don't have to run back and forth and you can get the cookin' done."

Shocked by his casual demonstration of callous concern for the life of the gentle old man, both women went weak-kneed, holding on to each other for support to keep from collapsing. Even Annie's tough shell was cracked by the cold-hearted act of casual execution, leaving her unable to speak. It seemed to the two women that it was an eternity between the sound of the shot and that of Shorty and Leroy hustling down the stairs. It was actually only seconds before they rushed into the kitchen. "What was that?" Shorty blurted.

"Nothin' but that old man in the parlor," Moran answered. "You and Leroy drag him out on the porch. We're fixin' to have somethin' to eat in a little bit, if these women will shake their behinds 'stead of standin' around like a couple of tombstones in a graveyard." He cocked an eye at Annie and said, "Which is where they might end up, if they don't."

Cullen was still some distance from the boardinghouse when he heard a shot ring out. There was no doubt where it had come from, so he nudged Jake for a little speed. He had taken the main road from town, instead of the shortcut along the footpath. It was a little longer that way, but he figured if Moran and his men were coming back, he would be at a disadvantage on the footpath. He might shoot the man in the lead, but then he would still have four others shooting at him.

When he came to the lane from the main road that led to Hortense's house, he turned onto it in time to hear a second shot, and he decided this one came from inside the house. When he came to the curve where the lane wrapped around a grove of oaks, he guided Jake into the trees and dismounted, He thought it a good idea to scout the house first, instead of riding straight in. As soon as he moved halfway through the trees, he saw the two horses standing at the front porch. "Damn," he muttered, "they did come back here." With two in the front, that meant the other three were at the back of the house, or maybe all inside. His concern now was the cause of the shooting he had heard. His concern was immediately answered when the front door swung open and Shorty and Leroy came out, dragging a body. He couldn't get a good look at the victim, but it was not one of the women, so it had to be Roy. He felt a sharp pang of anger when he watched the two outlaws drag Roy out on the porch and leave him there. Wishing he could release his anger, he pulled his rifle up and dropped the front sight on Leroy's chest. *I should have killed him when I caught him back on that footpath,* he thought. He lowered his rifle, unable to risk any endangerment of the women's lives. The fight would have to be fought somewhere other than here. Since there was pretty good cover where he now stood, he decided to wait them out right where he was, until they moved on.

There was much to think about. They had killed Roy. Possibly they had killed Annie and Hortense as well. The thought of it caused his veins to throb with anger. He had no way of knowing. And what if Moran was still there when Martin Pearson and Franklin George came home for supper? He needed to get Moran and his men out of that house, but didn't know how to do it without putting the women's lives in danger. The afternoon was wearing on; soon it would be suppertime. He would have to start watching the lane behind him to keep Pearson and George from walking into a hostage situation. Fortunately, the front door opened before either of the two boarders came home, and Shorty and Leroy came out of the house and got on their horses. They rode around the house and soon Cullen saw all five of them ride out of the backyard and onto the footpath to Art's stable.

He waited until they were completely out of sight before he left the cover of the oak trees and rode up to the front porch. With a worrisome feeling of dread, he quickly dismounted and hurried up the steps. There on the porch, he saw the body. The poor unfortunate man had been shot in the forehead. In a hurry to find Annie and Hortense, he didn't look at Roy's body close enough to notice the wound in the back of his thigh. The first thing he saw when he walked into the parlor was the bloody stain left on the sofa. Anxious more than ever now, he rushed down the hall to the kitchen to be met by Hortense with a double-barreled shotgun aimed at him. "Hortense!" he yelled. "It's me, Cullen!"

Rigidly determined before he yelled, she started to collapse when she saw it was him. He caught her by the arm to support her with one hand while he took the shotgun from her with the other. "Cullen," she gasped, "I thought it was that monster coming back. I swear I was gonna kill him if he did."

"If that shotgun didn't kill him," Annie said as she stepped out from behind the door, gripping her trusty poker, "I was gonna finish the job." He helped Hortense over to sit at the table. Annie, the stronger of the two women, went back to the stove. "I was just fixin' to make us some coffee when we heard you come in the front door. There was still some in the pot, but I'm makin' us some fresh. Me and Hortense both need a strong drink and since we ain't got any whiskey, we're settling for coffee. Didn't want what was left in the pot. I made it too weak," she said, paused, and added, "And there was spit in it."

"I'm just happy to see both of you still kickin'," he said. "I'm awful sorry about Roy." He was even more sickened about it when they told him how he came to be murdered. Cullen took a closer look at both of them then, noticing the welt and broken skin on Hortense's face and thinking it could have been a lot worse. When he looked hard at Annie, something looked different about her. He wasn't sure what it was until he looked closer. "Broke?"

"Reckon so," she said. "Feels broke." She reached up and gently touched her nose with a fingertip. "The marshal rapped me with the barrel of his pistol when I told him I'd fed men like him before."

Already regaining strength as a result of Cullen's presence, Hortense perked up enough to elaborate. "That's not exactly the way she said it. Moran said something about proving we could whip up something in a hurry to feed his men. And Annie said, it wasn't the first time she'd had to slop hogs." They both giggled when she told it. "It was a bloody mess on her face till she cleaned it up. I thought he had killed her."

"Takes more'n that to kill this ol' she-bear," Annie boasted. "That jackal better hope he don't ever come around here again. Me and Hortense are gonna get us a gun belt, and we'll be ready the next time he shows his face around here."

"I'm hoping you won't get the opportunity," Cullen said. "I was hoping they wouldn't come back here after they broke off their search for Art and me."

"I think they came here 'cause they were hungry," Annie said, "and they didn't wanna eat that slop Lizzie cooks up at the Cork and Bottle."

"Maybe so," he allowed. Her mention of the name brought to mind the image of the skinny little cook standing behind him with a shotgun that looked bigger than she. Thinking of her, and looking at Annie, caused him to wonder if all women cooks were naturally ornery. "I expect I'll go on into town to see what the marshal and his posse are up to tonight. But first, I'll take care of poor ol' Roy." He shook his head. "I swear, there just ain't no excuse for men like Moran to live on this earth. I'll find Roy a nice spot under the trees."

"We're gettin' ready to fix supper," Annie said. "You can eat somethin' after you bury Roy." When he hesitated, thinking he didn't want to waste too much time before going into town, she prodded him to stay. "You need some good food, and I've got some beans soakin' on the side porch since breakfast. They'll be ready to cook with some ham right about now. I'm fixin' to roll out some biscuits and blackstrap molasses." She paused then and gave Hortense a wink. "You know, when the marshal and his hogs wanted somethin' to eat, I reckon I plum forgot about those beans and ham."

"I expect it would be downright impolite to say no to that invitation," Cullen said, surprised that they all three could find humor after what the women had just suffered through. *Just the joy of survival I suppose,* he thought as he went out the back door to get a shovel and pick from the barn.

Martin Pearson showed up when Cullen had a hole dug about half the size he wanted. After the women had told Pearson what had occurred there that afternoon, he came out to find Cullen and pitched in to help. Hortense told him that she and Annie decided to have a little ceremony over the grave the next day. They finished up the grave and laid Roy in it, then covered him up. Martin said he would carve a tombstone for him out of some pine boards in the back of the barn.

"That was a powerful waste of time, weren't it?" Jeb Dickens said, his voice low so as not to be overheard by the other posse members. He pulled his horse over closer to his friend Riley Pitts.

"You got that right," Riley responded. Expecting to ride on a real posse to catch up with the two men Micah Moran was obsessed with killing, all this posse did was ride around in circles. The net result of the chase was a poor meal at that boardinghouse and a lot of bellyaching about how hungover everybody was. And now, back in East City, they rode down the middle of the street, past the jail with its broken door. Someone was sitting in one of the two rocking chairs on the front porch of the Cork and Bottle. In the shade of the porch roof, it was hard to tell who it was until they were pulling up to the hitching rail. It turned out to be Stan Molloy, Moran's one-eyed deputy. He looked like he was sitting in the chair, but he didn't appear to be actually relaxing comfortably.

Asleep or passed out, he showed no sign of awareness that the posse had ridden right up to the hitching rail.

"Molloy!" Moran yelled at the corpse as he dismounted, but there was no response from Molloy.

"He's drunker'n a skunk," Leroy said to Shorty, "stiff as a board."

"He's gonna sober up pretty damn quick when he finds out Micah's back," Shorty replied. They both stood by the rail to watch what was going to be an entertaining event. Moran was already steaming mad as a result of their wild-goose chase.

"Molloy!" Moran yelled again as he went up the two steps to the porch but stopped suddenly when he was close enough to see Molloy's bloodstained shirt. Furious now when he stared at the empty eye socket staring back at him, he kicked the chair over and stormed into the saloon.

"I swear," Leroy muttered. "He ain't drunk. He's dead."

"McCabe," was all Shorty could say.

They went up on the porch to look at the body. "He don't look right," Leroy said.

"He looks dead," Shorty replied. "That's what he looks like, and I reckon we'd best haul his ass off the porch. Micah's already about to blow the roof off."

Still thinking Molloy looked different, Leroy studied the corpse carefully. "He's wearin' that patch on the other eye. Maybe that's why he didn't see McCabe comin' after him." He looked around at the other three. "I reckon we oughta dig a hole for him." No one seemed eager to volunteer.

"Hell, me and Jeb'll do it," Riley spoke up. "We gotta take the horses to the stable, anyway, so we'll throw him on a horse and plant him down by the stable somewhere.

"Before you do," Shorty said, "I wanna take a look at that eye. Molloy was mighty particular about anybody seein' what was behind that patch—always said it was his evil eye and if he ever looked at you with that eye, you'd be a dead man."

"Did you believe that?" Leroy asked.

"Hell, no," Shorty replied. "Are you japin' me?"

"I did," Leroy admitted. "Leastways, I didn't see no sense in puttin' it to the test."

Shorty struck a match and held it close to Molloy's face. "I swear," he uttered, "ain't nothin' but a hole—ain't no eyelids or nothin'."

At the jailhouse, diagonally across the street from the saloon, Buck Casey stood at the back corner of the building, chuckling to himself. He saw the five returning possemen when they rode by his shop, so he immediately hurried over behind the jail, eager to see their reaction to the deputy's welcome. After his meeting with McCabe and Abe Franks, Buck had hurried back to the Cork and Bottle, thinking to arrange a little surprise for the marshal. Unfortunately, Molloy's body was already getting stiff, so he couldn't work with it as well as he had planned. After some strain on his part, he had managed to get the corpse in a position that appeared to be sitting. When he had done the best he could with it, he stepped back to admire his work. *Well, you ol' devil spawn,* he thought, *you're just as ugly dead as you were alive.* He paused to take another quick look in the window to make sure no one was aware of his preparations. Looking back at the corpse, he muttered, "Needs somethin'." Then he decided and moved Molloy's eye patch over to his good eye.

Observing the reaction to his handiwork now, he felt it had been well worth his effort, as well as the risk of having been seen while in the process. The reactions of the members of the posse were what he had hoped for, especially Micah Moran's. He imagined he could almost feel the marshal's rage at this distance. He watched until the two new members of the posse carried the body off the porch and hefted it up on one of the horses, then led the horses to the stable. He chuckled the whole time, giving no thought as to whether or not his prank might cause additional harassment by the marshal.

CHAPTER 17

"What the hell did you volunteer us to bury this one-eyed drunk for?" Jeb asked as they led all of the horses down to the stable.

"Hell, I figured I'd rather take care of the horses and ol' Molloy than stand around that saloon listenin' to Moran rantin' and ravin' about the way the folks in this town don't respect him. Always ends up blamin' Cullen McCabe for everythin' that don't go the way he wants it to."

"Well, he's right, ain't he? He had a damn good thing goin' here before McCabe showed up. That's what Shorty says," Jeb said.

"I ain't sayin' that ain't so," Riley protested. "I'm just sayin' I'd just as soon let Moran get some of that anger out when I don't have to listen to it."

"Well, I don't feel like diggin' no hole to put this dead dog in," Jeb complained.

"Hell, I don't either and I ain't plannin' to. They ain't gonna know where we buried him, or even *if* we buried him. We'll ride up the creek a ways and dump him in the woods far enough to where you can't smell him when he ripens up."

They found an old stump hole a good way up the creek that was almost deep enough to take half of Molloy's body. So they dumped him in headfirst. "At least, we left him with his better-lookin' side showin'," Riley commented.

When they started back to the Cork and Bottle, Jeb said, "I'm gonna go to the store before he closes up. I need some smokin' tobacco."

"I'll see you back at the saloon," Riley said. "I need a drink of likker after all that work we done diggin' that grave." They parted when they reached the street.

When Jeb got back to the saloon, Moran was still fuming over the loss of another one of his men, his anger intensified by the condition in which he had found his deputy. The display that someone had arranged for him was more infuriating than the actual loss of his man. It was an insult to his authority to be made fun of in a town he owned. Jeb walked inside just in time to witness the dressing-down of Floyd, Wilma, Mabel, and Lizzie for having no notion that someone was having their fun with Molloy's corpse right under their noses. As was customary, Tom Loughlin had retired to his room upstairs beforehand. "The whole town has got to thinkin' they don't have to toe the line," Moran fumed. "We might have to do a little reeducating in this town. They've forgotten who runs it."

When there was a brief pause in Moran's promises of threats to come against those who would befriend Cullen McCabe, Jeb spoke up. "They're havin' a town meetin' tonight at O'Sullivan's. Was you plannin' to be there?"

Moran didn't answer right away, pausing as if he

had been dealt another clue of a merchant uprising. "How do you know that?"

Jeb told him that he had gone into Joe Johnson's store for some smoking tobacco. When he was looking around the shelves for anything else he might want, he overheard a man Johnson had been talking with tell Johnson there was a meeting of the town council that night.

"And he said O'Sullivan's?" Moran asked, interested at once.

"O'Sullivan's," Jeb repeated. "That's what he said."

"I wasn't notified of any meeting," Moran fumed. "I'm the town marshal, and I wasn't notified about a town meetin'." He looked around him defiantly. "Well, I'm damn sure goin' to that meeting!" He looked back at Jeb. "What time?"

"The feller didn't say," Jeb answered. "After everybody closes their stores, I reckon."

"Who was the man who told Johnson about the meetin'?"

"I don't know," Jeb replied. "I ain't been here long enough to know anybody's name, but he favored the feller that runs the blacksmith shop."

Buck Casey, Moran thought, *the joker.* That's probably who it was, all right. He remembered Buck's rather flippant attitude when he saw him in the street after the jailbreak, when they were rounding up the runaway horses.

After supper, Abe Franks left his house and went to O'Sullivan's Saloon for the hastily called meeting of the town council. When he got there, he saw that Cary

O'Sullivan had pulled several tables together to form one big one for the members to sit around. Buck Casey and Joe Johnson were already there and Martin Pearson arrived shortly after Abe. Cary offered beer to anyone who wanted it and everyone did, so Cary's bartender, Freddy Lee, brought a tray to the table. As he was coming back to the bar, Stewart Ingram, the postmaster, walked in and snagged a beer from Freddy as he went past the bar. "Just like the mail," Buck Casey couldn't resist saying. "Always late."

After Ingram was settled, Abe looked around the table and commented, "Well, that's everybody but Art Becker and I reckon everybody knows why he isn't here." There were ordinarily seven members at these meetings. The odd number made it easier to have a majority if there was a vote on something, but without Art, they were six in number.

"Does anybody know where Art went when he broke outta jail?" Joe Johnson asked.

"No, nobody, but maybe Cullen McCabe," Buck Casey said, "since he's the one who broke him out."

"I'd like to know that, myself." The statement came from the front door. They all turned to see Marshal Micah Moran walk in the door, accompanied by Leroy and Shorty. The tension at the table immediately increased. Moran marched back to the council table, his forceful stride like that of a man in charge. "Evenin', gents. I apologize for bein' late, but I wasn't notified about a town council meetin' tonight. And I know it wouldn't be an official meetin' if the town marshal wasn't here. Right?" He glanced back at Shorty and Leroy. "You boys go on over to the bar and have a drink while me and the council are talkin' about things." He pulled a chair back from the table and sat down. "Well, now, Mr. Mayor, I reckon you can call the meetin' to order, now that everybody's here." He graced the surprised merchants, who were momentarily struck dumb, with a smug smile.

Not at all prepared to deal with the marshal when he called the meeting, Abe Franks tried to maintain some decorum, nevertheless. "There were a couple of reasons you were not notified of this meeting, Marshal. In the first place, you were out of town until this afternoon, late. And we didn't think you would be interested in attending, anyway, since there was no plan to discuss any matters of law enforcement. We, as merchants, wanted to discuss matters related to merchandising and ways to do more business with the people living around us in the county. I imagine that would be something you hold no interest in."

"Is that so?" Moran responded. "Well, that's where you're wrong, Mayor. I'm interested in everythin' that goes on in this town. And if I'm gonna do my job of keepin' the peace, I damn sure better know about everythin' you shopkeepers got on your minds." He paused to sweep the nervous faces with a threatening stare. "And I mean everything," he emphasized. "'Cause I'm the only thing keepin' you men safe in your stores and your families safe in your homes." He paused again to see if the mayor, or anyone else at the table, had anything to say about that. When no one offered any comment, he continued. "All right, good, we'll get on to another matter we need to discuss. We just had us a serious jailbreak and a convicted criminal was broke outta jail, and he's still on the run. You need to know that helpin' Art Becker in any way is a hangin' offense, and if I find out anybody is helpin' him, I'll stretch his neck for aidin' and abettin'." He waited a few moments to make sure everyone understood that. "Now we need to talk about that gunslinger, Cullen McCabe. Is there anyone at this table who doesn't think McCabe killed my deputies and possemen?" Again no one spoke. "I didn't think so."

Abe interrupted then. "I think, to be fair, we have to admit that no one here actually saw McCabe kill anybody."

"Is that so?" Moran scoffed. "Maybe you think they all committed suicide."

Buck Casey couldn't resist. "That might be what happened," he commented. "'Cause anybody goin' after McCabe is the same as committin' suicide." His remark was followed by a few quiet chuckles.

Obviously heating up a little, Moran said, "You're a funny man, ain't you? Like to make a lotta jokes, right? Maybe like that little joke you pulled with the body of Deputy Stan Molloy?"

"I'm afraid you've got me there, Marshal. I don't know what you're talkin' about," Buck maintained. "Did somethin' happen to Deputy Molloy? I mean, after he got shot in the Cork and Bottle? I'll admit, I did see that. That was another one of them suicides we were talkin' about. Damn fool Molloy drew on Cullen McCabe—death by suicide." That crack brought a few more chuckles.

Moran's brow knotted in an angry frown as his eyes fixed on Buck. Over at the bar, two interested spectators watched, scarcely believing what they were witnessing. "That fool's talkin' hisself into a pine box,"

Shorty said, "and I mean right now in a minute. What the hell's wrong with him?"

"Blacksmith," Moran stated as he stared threateningly at Buck. "I don't like jokes and I don't like jokers. They're the same as cockroaches to me, and when I see one, I stomp the life out of it."

"It ain't gonna be long now," Leroy said, a grin already forming on his face.

The mayor interrupted again at that point, afraid Buck was going to provoke Moran into a killing. "I think we're getting too far off our agenda. Let's get back to the business we came here to discuss tonight." He read the storm warnings in Moran's eyes, and wanted to strangle Buck, but he decided he'd better address the issue at hand, since Moran had unwittingly introduced it. "All right, next on the agenda, since the marshal wants to discuss law enforcement, we'll take that up now. Did you all bring weapons as requested?" He waited then while every member of the council, including himself, placed a pistol on the table in front of them. A look of pure astonishment appeared on Moran's face when he realized there were six guns to compete with his one. He instantly thought of Shorty and Leroy at the bar, now his only way to reduce the odds.

The two possemen were as stunned as their boss when the council produced their weapons. A moment later, they were even more at a loss when they heard the solid contact of a double-barreled shotgun on the bar behind them. "Just relax and enjoy your beer, boys," Freddy Lee advised.

"What the hell is this?" Moran demanded. Accustomed to a cowering look in the face of each merchant he directly confronted, he now looked around the table, confused by the determination he saw in every face.

"Just a way to make sure the votes are counted correctly on any issues we vote on tonight," Abe informed him. "Marshal Moran introduced it, so shall we go ahead and discuss the issue of law enforcement? How many say aye?" All five of his fellow councilmen replied with *aye*. "I say aye as well," Abe continued. "None opposed, so let's get on with it." Not sure what was going on, Moran held his tongue for a few minutes.

"Mr. Mayor," Cary O'Sullivan spoke up. "I make a motion, or whatever you call it, to decide the term of the present town marshal."

"I second the motion," Buck Casey said. "And I think it's time we voted on whether or not we wanna keep Micah Moran as the town marshal. Based on his performance in keepin' outlaws out of our town, I'd like to call for a vote on whether or not to keep him in his present position."

Unable to believe what he was witnessing, Moran sat dumbstruck as the men he had totally intimidated for two years casually voiced their opposition to him. His natural inclination was to draw his .44 and end this travesty of a hearing. But the presence of six weapons at point-blank range against his one was enough to still his hand. When he glanced back at the bar, he readily saw that Shorty and Leroy were of no use as backup to him, due to the shotgun leveled at them in the hands of the smiling bartender. He realized his helplessness without his small army of possemen. Still, he was certain that if he got out of this meeting he had so unwittingly attended, he would once again retain his advantage. Even with just four men left, he knew he could strike whom and when he wanted. And after a couple of the suddenly high-and-mighty town council members were found dead and burned out, the rest of this cowardly group of store-keepers would be begging him to save them.

"I propose we should terminate Micah Moran as marshal of East City, and anybody he's named deputy after the sudden demise of Stan Molloy. I propose his termination be effective as of right now with a sever-ance pay of one dollar." Buck smiled smugly at Moran during the whole time of his proposal.

"Are there any seconds to that?" Abe asked.

"I second it," Joe Johnson spoke up. "And I want to propose an addendum to the motion, that Moran and his gang have until midnight tonight to get out of East City and never come back." The motion was called to a vote by a show of hands. Again, it was unanimous.

"While we're at it," Martin Pearson said, raising his hand, "I propose we officially revoke the sentence of death for Art Becker that was the result of a kangaroo court run by outlaws." Again, there was unanimous passage of the motion.

"Well, Marshal, or should I say, mister?" Abe ad-dressed the baffled outlaw. "You've heard the ruling by the town council, so come midnight tonight, you shall be gone from this town." He paused, then said, "Sooner would be better."

Still stunned by a revolt by the men of the town, men who had cowered before him until the curse of Cullen McCabe had been cast upon him, Moran could not find words adequate to speak his rage. He sat, stone-faced for a long moment before respond-ing. Then he finally rose to his feet, preparing to

speak before he left. "You damn fools. Don't you
know who you're messin' with? I don't know who put
this horseshit into your dumb skulls. Nobody tells me
to get out of a town that I, by God, own! All you've
done here tonight is make it hard on yourselves from
now on. Nobody elected me marshal when I came
here. I made me the marshal and that's how it's gonna
be from now on. Only, it ain't gonna be as easy on you
as it was."

"I figured you wouldn't have sense enough to get
the hell out of this town when they gave you a chance
to." Moran turned when he heard this and found
himself facing Cullen McCabe. Cullen was not alone.
Art Becker was with him, as well as a tall stranger, all
three with weapons drawn—Cullen's rifle leveled at
Moran. When they walked on into the saloon, the
young stranger moved to disarm Shorty and Leroy
while Cullen continued on to the table in the back.

"Have a seat right over there at that table," Beau
Arnett told the two at the bar. He pointed to a table
against the wall. "Take your beer with you and sit
there quiet till I tell you you can go."

"Who the hell are you?" Shorty demanded defiantly.

"I'm the man who's gonna raise a knot on the side
of your head if you don't do what I tell you," Beau
answered.

"What the hell is he doin' here?" Moran demanded
of Abe when Cullen walked back to the table.

"Maybe you'd better ask him," Abe answered, not
sure, himself, and wondering now if the meeting had
gotten out of his control.

"You shoulda got out of town when the council
told you to," Cullen said. "Now, you ain't got no choice.

You and your friends are goin' to jail to await trial for the murder of Lila Blanchard and Roy Skelton, and the attempted murder of Art Becker—plus holding an entire town hostage. Add robbery to that. I reckon that's enough right there to get you a ride on a noose. So take your left hand and ease that .44 outta your holster real slow. And if you're thinkin' about takin' a chance with it, please do. It would save us a lot of trouble."

Moran was trapped. He knew he was a dead man if he tried to make a move with Cullen's rifle already aimed at him, as well as six handguns, all pointed in his direction. He eased his pistol out and Cullen took it from him. Still not ready to go willingly, Moran said, "You ain't no lawman. You can't arrest me."

"I'm not arrestin' you, he is." He nodded toward Beau Arnett. "This is Deputy Marshal Beau Arnett," Cullen said for the benefit of those men seated at the table. "I'm just helpin' him."

"You can't hold me for trial," Moran insisted. "There ain't no judge in East City." Abe didn't comment, but he was thinking the same thing.

"That didn't stop you when you held that trial for Art Becker, did it?" Cullen charged. "But that ain't the case here. You're gonna be held in the Ravenwood jail and tried by Judge Harvey Raven."

Equally as worried as Moran, Shorty called out, "They ain't got no authority on this side of the creek, Micah. That's another county. This deputy can't arrest nobody in East City."

"That's right!" Moran exclaimed. "He's got no jurisdiction over here. Me and my boys can walk right outta here."

"That's where you're wrong, Moran," Cullen said.

"The deputy and Judge Raven both have been granted special jurisdiction by the governor, himself, to rid this town of you and your lawless crowd." He paused to give him a little smile. "Besides, even if they didn't have the authority to arrest you, I'd shoot you down like the mad dog you are before you reached the door." Thinking of Lila and Roy and Art, he meant what he said. As far as the part about special jurisdiction from the governor, that wasn't entirely true. He had exaggerated his authority to Tug Taggert in order to get the loan of Beau for the arrest. Thinking of possibly killing two birds with one stone, he was hoping to place Beau in the position of marshal of East City. He was convinced he was the right man for the job.

"What about the other two?" Joe Johnson asked, thinking of Jeb Dickens and Riley Pitts. "They just joined up with Moran. I don't know if they've done anything to arrest 'em for, unless we can arrest 'em for just ridin' with him."

"I reckon that might be up to the town council," Cullen replied. "If nobody knows of anything they've done against the law, I'd be inclined to let 'em go with a warning, as long as they agreed to leave town and never come back. What do you say, Deputy?"

Beau responded in the manner Cullen hoped he would. "I was thinkin' along those lines, myself. From what you've told me about those men, I'd be satisfied to let 'em go, if they understand they'll be arrested on the spot, if they show up in town again. You say they're young men. Maybe this might serve to show them the folly of riding on the wrong side of the law."

Cullen watched Abe for his reaction to Beau's response. He was satisfied to see Abe nod his head in agreement with Beau. "All right, Deputy," Cullen suggested then. "Late as it is, I reckon we could hold these three in the jail here overnight, if that's all right with you." Beau said that sounded like a good idea, but he was surprised that Cullen kept asking his opinion on each step taken with the prisoners. He was prepared to do whatever Cullen said.

"Buck, over there, is the blacksmith," Cullen went on. "He ain't got around to fixin' the front door, but the cell room will hold 'em till mornin'. I'll volunteer to guard 'em, then you can take 'em across the creek in the mornin'. Of course, I'll be glad to help you with that chore, too, if you want me to."

"Hell," Buck spoke up. "I'll volunteer to guard 'em, too."

"Me, too," Art Becker volunteered. "I'd enjoy settin' all night with those sidewinders."

Cullen could well understand why both men would enjoy the satisfaction of watching Moran and his two killers sweat it out in the tiny jail cell room. It would help him out as well. "If you both will stay and make sure they don't get out of that cell, Beau and I could pay a visit to the Cork and Bottle to see if we can have a word with those two young boys Moran just hired. While we're there, we'll see if Lizzie will fix 'em a farewell breakfast in the mornin' before we start."

"Too bad I didn't bring but one set of handcuffs," Beau commented. "But I reckon we could use some rope to tie those two fellows with. I've got some rope on my saddle."

"I'll get it for you, Deputy," Buck quickly volunteered, thoroughly enjoying the arrest of Marshal Micah Moran. "Which horse?" Beau told him he was riding the gray.

Once the prisoners were secured, they were marched out of the saloon and down the street to the jail, accompanied by all seven of the town council, plus a few curious townsfolk. On the way, there were a couple more volunteers for guard duty. It was a joyous night for East City, and most of the town's residents weren't even aware of it.

Hearing the sound of people in the street, Jeb Dickens walked to the door of the Cork and Bottle to see the cause of the noise. He wasn't sure he was seeing correctly at first, since he had been drinking ever since supper. "Riley," he called out after a few seconds, "come look at this."

"What is it?" Riley called back, not eager to get up from his chair.

"Come here!" This time it was a command. "It looks like a lynchin' party and it looks like Micah and Shorty and Leroy are the guests of honor!"

That was enough to bring Riley out of his chair right away. He rushed to the door, thinking Jeb might be too drunk to see straight. "Damn it all . . ." he uttered. "It is Micah! They're takin' him to jail!"

"And Shorty and Leroy with 'em!" Jeb exclaimed. "What do we do—go help 'em?"

"Are up crazy?" Riley responded. "It looks like half the town's marchin' 'em down the street, and they've all got guns."

Their excitement caught the attention of everyone else in the saloon and soon Floyd, Wilma, and Mabel were at the door to see what the two young outlaws were looking at. "Lord have mercy," Wilma muttered.

"Micah Moran goin' to jail, I wouldn'ta believed it, if I wasn't seein' it with my own eyes."

"Cullen McCabe," Mabel stated simply.

"Which one?" Riley asked, having never actually seen the man who was Moran's nemesis.

"The big one, holdin' the rifle," Mabel answered. She looked at Wilma and asked, "You know what's happened, don't you? This town's finally got up the nerve to take it back from Micah. I swear, I never thought I'd see the day."

"What's gonna happen to us?" Wilma worried. "You s'pose they're gonna shut this place down and run us outta town?" No one could answer for sure, but she suggested somebody should go upstairs to let Tom Loughlin know what was going on, but no one wanted to leave the door at that moment. The mob in the street had reached the jail by then. "They're puttin' 'em in the jail. If they're gonna hang 'em, don't look like they're gonna do it tonight."

The two newest recruits in Moran's posse contin-ued to stare at the small mob in front of the jail, still trying to decide what they should do. "What about us?" Jeb wondered. "We ain't been here but a couple of days, but they know me and you are ridin' with Moran. You suppose they'll be comin' after us next?"

Riley was already thinking the same as Jeb. "I don't know," he answered. "But I ain't gonna be here when they do. I think it's time to light out for somewhere else. It damn sure looks to me like these folks here have decided to clean this town up."

Jeb wasn't sure. "You don't think we oughta try to help Moran get outta that jail? This was the deal we were hopin' for when we came here. To take over a whole town."

"Hell, no," Riley replied. He looked his friend in the eye. "Has Micah Moran done so much for you that you think you owe him?"

Jeb shook his head. "Well, not so far he ain't."

"That's right, and we'd best get outta here while we've still got a chance. Come on!" He grabbed Jeb by the sleeve and pulled him after him as he headed for the back door of the saloon. What few belongings they possessed were upstairs in the hotel next door. So they ran in the back door of the hotel, past a couple of prostitutes sitting on a sofa in the parlor. Taking the stairs two steps at a time, they wasted no time in picking up their saddlebags.

Bounding back down the steps, they ran past the prostitutes again. One of the women, a short, plump blonde named Effie, was prompted to ask, "What in the world has got into you two boys?" When told to go to the front door and see for herself, she and her friend did so. But when they turned to ask the two retreating possemen what was happening over at the jail, Jeb and Riley were already out the back door.

Running for the stable, they still had concern that there might be somebody guarding it, since they couldn't know how well organized this obvious uprising of the town's honest folks might be. They found, however, that there was no one. After their horses were saddled, they decided to take one of the packhorses. Then, thinking they might as well take their pick of the other horses there, they took their saddles back off and each of them picked out a better horse to ride. Riley was quick in choosing Micah Moran's black Satan. "I've been admirin' that horse ever since we've been here. Ol' Micah ain't gonna miss him where he's goin'."

"Where we headed?" Jeb asked, still not sure they were doing the right thing.

"I don't know," Riley answered, "just away from this place."

"And head in which direction?" Jeb countered. "There ain't nothin', no town of any size, within a hundred miles of here. We've been on the run ever since we left Tucson. And I've been thinkin' about the setup Micah had here and how it all came undone when Cullen McCabe showed up. That ain't but one man we need to take down—Cullen McCabe—and if he's done for, there ain't a nickel's worth of grit in the rest of the whole town. And think about those two buzzards, Shorty and Leroy. They ain't no competition for you and me, especially if we kill Cullen McCabe. He's the devil drivin' Micah loco. We get McCabe and we'll be Micah's top dogs. Then when he builds his posse back up, we'll be right there as his right and left arms."

"I don't know, Jeb," Riley said. "A lot of what you're sayin' makes sense, if it would work out in our favor."

"I'm sayin' there ain't much risk in it for me and you, if we hide in this stable and wait to see who shows up here tonight. Think about it. McCabe's gotta put his horse somewhere, if he's gonna be here all night. And I expect he will 'cause they put Micah and them in the jail. He walks in here with his horse, he's dead. Couldn't be much easier. He ain't no different from any other man, he's just got the rest of 'em spooked."

"I don't know, Jeb," Riley repeated. "It sounds pretty good. I reckon it could happen like you say, but I still got a natural feelin' in my gut that says run while you can."

CHAPTER 18

In the only way left for him to rebel, Moran suddenly sat down in the street before the jailhouse steps. He refused to get up and walk into the jail. When Beau told him to get up on his feet, Moran replied. "Go to hell. I ain't goin' in that jail."

"Couple of you men, give me a hand here," Beau said, since Cullen showed no signs of responding to the petulant outlaw. Buck Casey and Martin Pearson stepped forward right away, and with Beau's help, they carried Moran inside the jail and pitched him roughly on the cell floor. Preferring not to be thrown around like a sack of potatoes, Leroy and Shorty walked in with no show of resistance.

Once the cell door was locked, Art Becker could not pass up the opportunity to ride Moran a little. "Hey, Moran, how's it feel to be on that side of the bars? There was some water in one of those buckets, if you get thirsty tonight. And I know I left a little bit of pee in that other bucket. I doubt anybody bothered to empty 'em after I left here. Be sure you don't get 'em mixed up."

When the prisoners were locked inside, Beau told

them they could back up to the bars, one at a time, and he would free their hands. Shorty and Leroy stepped up dutifully and Beau untied their ropes, but Moran remained where he had landed on the floor, still defiant. Beau waited for him a few seconds, then said, "I think you'll be a helluva lot more comfortable if your hands aren't behind your back all night, but I ain't got time to waste on you. Too bad one of your friends in there with you can't untie your hands, since you're the only one in handcuffs."

Not unexpectedly, Buck Casey saw fit to comment, "I reckon you're gonna find out if Shorty or Leroy is your best friend when you gotta use that pee bucket."

Evidently, that problem hadn't occurred to him, for he barked, "All right, all right, I'll back up to the bars." He struggled to his knees, then was helped onto his feet by Leroy to suffer the further indignity of standing against the bars to have his hands freed.

With the prisoners secured and the volunteer guards in place, Cullen and Beau were ready to go across the street to the Cork and Bottle. There was no way of knowing what to expect from the two remaining members of Micah Moran's outlaw posse. So they decided it best to approach the saloon cautiously. With weapons drawn, they split up and moved quickly toward the building. When there were no shots fired, they continued up on the porch, past Stan Molloy's rocking chair, to stop at the door. Cullen pushed it halfway open to take a look before entering. There was no one in the saloon but Floyd and the three women, all with their eyes focused on the door.

"If you're lookin' for Riley Pitts and Jeb Dickens," Floyd said, "they lit out for parts unknown when they saw what was happenin'." He looked around him.

"The place seems right empty with all Moran's boys gone. Always nice to see you, though, McCabe. Can I pour you a drink?"

"Reckon not. Thanks just the same," Cullen answered. Hearing a footstep on the stairs, he turned immediately, his rifle aimed that way, ready to fire, until he saw Tom Loughlin on the steps. "Beau," Cullen said, "this is Tom Loughlin, he's the owner of this saloon." To Tom, he said, "You might wanna get to know Beau Arnett, here. You might be seein' more of him around town." Cullen knew it was premature, and he was betting strictly on a hunch, but he felt strongly that Beau could wind up with the marshal's job in East City.

"McCabe," Loughlin said. "Are you closing us down?"

"Me? No, I ain't closin' you down," Cullen responded. "I've got no authority to close anybody down. That's up to the town council to decide, or the marshal, when they get one." He glanced at young Beau Arnett, then added, "I expect they won't waste any time appointin' a new one. It'd be my guess they ain't thinkin' about closing you down, now that Moran's gone, as long as you're figurin' on runnin' an honest business, like O'Sullivan does." He took another quick look up toward the top of the stairs. "No, sir, what I'm interested in right now is whether or not two young outlaws are sittin' in one of those rooms upstairs waitin' to put a bullet in me."

"Floyd told you the truth," Loughlin said. "Those two young men fled the building when they saw what was happening."

"Well, they finally made one smart decision, didn't they?" Cullen responded.

"You don't want to take a look upstairs, just to be sure?" Beau asked.

"No," Cullen answered. "I've got no reason to doubt Mr. Loughlin's word, but you go on and take a look if you think we oughta be more thorough." He was convinced the two had run when they had the chance. Beau, however, was not, so he went upstairs to make sure. While Beau was upstairs, Cullen's gaze fell upon Lizzie. "I don't believe I ever thanked you for not shootin' me in the back with that shotgun the last time I was in here." Lizzie shrugged in response.

"I was the one hollered at her not to shoot," Wilma said.

"And I wanna thank you for that," Cullen said. Back to Lizzie then, he said, "One of your former employers and his two friends are in that jail across the street. I'm wonderin' about the chances you might cook 'em a little breakfast in the mornin' before we transport 'em to Ravenwood."

The skinny little woman curled up one side of her lip, much like an ill-tempered hound dog. "I didn't much like cookin' for 'em when they was here," she said. "Who's gonna pay for 'em?"

"Who paid for prisoners' meals before?" Cullen asked. When she said the town council, Cullen said, "That's who will pay for 'em again. You can ask Deputy Arnett what time he wants 'em fed. I expect he'll work with you on the time. It ain't much of a trip to Ravenwood." He paused when he saw Beau coming back downstairs.

"I reckon Mr. Loughlin is a man of his word," Beau said. "Nobody upstairs, but I figured it couldn't hurt to check." He studied Loughlin for a few long seconds, then was tempted to ask, "How did you happen to go into business with Micah Moran?"

"I've been asking myself that question for the last two years," Loughlin answered. As far as Cullen was concerned, the man need say no more. He imagined Loughlin might be one of the happiest people in East City to see Micah Moran arrested.

When Cullen and Beau returned to the jail, they told all the volunteers that they could go on home now and leave the guard duty to them. "We're gonna bunk right in here with 'em to make sure they stay put," Cullen assured them.

"Be sure you do," Joe Johnson said. "'Cause if they get out, they're liable to kill every one of us."

Overhearing his remark, Moran called out from the cell, "You can count on it, Johnson."

"You men have made a big step tonight toward buildin' a fine, peaceful town that has a lot better chance now of attracting families and businesses," Cullen reminded them. "That's worth takin' some risks for and that's what you did. Beau and I will see that they all get to the jail in Ravenwood. And the court will decide what happens to 'em from there, but they're gone from East City for good. The next thing is to put an honest man in the position of marshal, a man like Beau, here, who ain't afraid to inform troublemakers they ain't welcome in East City."

When he finished giving his little speech, his volunteers started drifting away, most of them back to O'Sullivan's to celebrate what Buck Casey called East City Independence Day. One of the ones who lingered a bit longer was Art Becker, who told Cullen that he was going back to his stable to see what kind of shape Moran's men had left it in. "You and Beau are gonna sleep here tonight. You want me to take your horses to the stable with me? I'll feed 'em some oats if I've got any left and water 'em good, so they'll be ready to go in the mornin'."

"We'd appreciate that, Art," Cullen said. Then he had another thought regarding the two young outlaws, Pitts and Dickens. He was sure they had run for it. There wouldn't be any reason for them to hide out in the stable, waiting to ambush him or Beau when they brought their horses in. On the other hand, they might be as crazy as Moran. And poor Art, Cullen had already caused him to come close to being hung. "Tell you what, I'll go with you and help you take care of 'em. Okay with you, Beau? I won't be gone long."

"Okay with me," Beau replied. "Take your time. I'll take good care of these fellows."

"You worried about those two that cut out?" Art asked him as they led the horses back toward the stable.

"No, hell no," Cullen lied. "Those boys are already a long way from East City and wearin' out a couple of horses. Jake's just been kinda nervous lately, so he might not behave himself."

"I'm pretty good with nervous horses," Art said, well aware that Cullen was concerned for his safety. He found it amusing that the big solemn man had a soft spot in his grim bearing.

"Well, Jake's different. Let's hold up here a minute. Wouldn't hurt if I took a quick look before we go waltzin' in the front door. Stay right here, I'm gonna walk around to the back of the barn." He handed Art the reins he was holding and left before he could protest.

* * *

Inside the stable, Riley Pitts and Jeb Dickens sat in the dark tack room, counting on the possibility that Cullen McCabe might bring his horse to the stable. Riley had held out for a long time, thinking the best option for him and Jeb was the one that had first occurred to them naturally. And that was to ride hell-bent for leather away from East City while they had a chance to escape. Jeb was just as convinced they were passing up a golden opportunity to make a move that would set them up as key members of a new outlaw posse. The final decision was made when Jeb was so sure of his plan that he flat refused to go. "You go ahead on," he told Riley, "and no hard feelin's. Maybe you'll be back when things are like they're supposed to be again in East City."

Riley had just stood there, looking at his friend for a long moment before giving in. "Ah, hell, Jeb," he had said. "We've been partners since we was old enough to hold a gun. You wouldn't know your right boot from your left one, if I weren't there to tell you. I'm afraid if I leave you here by yourself, you're liable to shoot yourself in the foot. Hell, maybe you're right, so we'll wait here awhile to see if anybody does show up. Then we'll cut outta here like we oughta done in the first place."

"I knew you'd come to your senses," Jeb crowed. "It just takes longer with you than it does with most folks."

Now, the better part of an hour had passed since they had fled the hotel with still no sign of anyone approaching the stable. "Damned if it ain't dark as a whore's heart in here," Riley commented. "There ain't no light a-tall comin' in that little window." There was a lantern sitting on the workbench at his elbow, so he said, "I'm gonna light this lantern and turn it down real low. I'll set it on the floor and that oughta give us enough light so we don't bump into somethin' in here." When Jeb started to question the wisdom of that, Riley said, "Can't nobody see it from the outside." He lit the lantern and turned it down until it was almost out. Then he set it down on the floor, over in a corner. "See, that helps a little, and nobody can see that from the front of the stable."

"You reckon one of us oughta go set up by the back door of the barn?" Jeb wondered. They were presently standing on either side of the small window over the tack room workbench. It was the same window that Cullen and Art had looked out to see Shep Parker and Shorty Miller bringing their horses back to the stable after the shooting of Ace Brown.

"Ain't nobody gonna be bringin' their horses in the back door of the barn," Riley replied. "This is the best spot right here. We can see anybody comin' in the front of the stable, and we've got the protection of four walls in this little room, if anybody's lucky enough to shoot back. They'll have to lead their horses right by this window, if they're gonna put 'em in a stall."

"When he comes walkin' in here with his horse, which one of us takes the shot?" Jeb asked. "I'm thinkin' the man who shoots Cullen McCabe is liable to carry that story with him wherever he goes. Might be a heavy burden to tote." As soon as he said it, Riley laughed, knowing his friend as well as he did.

"You're tellin' me you wouldn't give your left ear to be that man?" Riley japed. "And be that famous gunfighter that shot Cullen McCabe?" He chuckled again.

"I'll tell you what, we'll both shoot him at the same time. Nobody'll know which one of us killed him, so we'll both be famous."

Jeb laughed with him. Then, after he thought about it for a minute, he asked another question that occurred to him. "You know, I never heard of Cullen McCabe before we came here to East City. You ever hear of him?"

"No, I never have," Riley admitted.

"The way Micah is always talkin' about him, and Shorty and Leroy, too, I just thought we hadn't heard of him over in Arizona Territory before. He might not be anybody at all, just a thorn in Micah's ass."

Riley could see that Jeb was genuinely disappointed. And he couldn't help thinking they could have been miles away from here by now. "Ah, what the hell, we'll both shoot him, anyway. It'll sure as hell tickle Micah."

"Hush! Somebody's comin'!" Jeb whispered. They both leaned across the workbench to get as close to the side of the window as they could, squinting to see through the open shutter.

"Can you see 'em?" Riley whispered back. "I don't see a damn thing." It had gotten considerably darker since they first selected the tack room as their ambush site.

"No, I can't, either, but I heard a horse snort," Jeb insisted.

"That don't surprise me," Riley countered, "since we're settin' in a stable full of horses."

"No, damn it, I'm tellin' you I heard a horse snort out there. There's somebody comin' to the stable—or they're just sittin' out there somewhere in the dark."

"Well, we ain't got much choice now," Riley said. "We'll just sit here and wait till they show up."

As Cullen had expected, the back door to the stable had been left unlocked, so he slipped inside and knelt against the side of the last stall. He waited there for a while until his eyes adjusted to the deep darkness inside the building and he listened. No sounds reached his ears but the infrequent nickers from the horses. When he could see a little better, he moved forward between the stalls, stopping again to listen when he was about twenty feet from the tack room door. He knew that was the best way to make a quick check for an ambush. From the little window in the tack room, he could see if there was anyone waiting in the front of the stable. After another pause, he was about to move again when he heard something that didn't come from the horses. In a crouch, ready to move forward, he knelt back down to listen. There was nothing for a half a minute, and then, there it was again. This time he knew what it was. It sounded like whispering. And it came from the tack room. He knew then that someone had the same idea he had, to cover the entrance to the stable from the vantage point of the tack room.

He didn't have to guess who it might be. There were only two people it would be. He had been wrong when he thought Dickens and Pitts would run when they had the chance. Being extra cautious now, he eased forward again to see if the tack room door was closed. *Damn*, he thought when he found that it was. He was going to have to figure a way to get them out of there. If it wasn't Art's barn and stables, he'd let all the horses out again and set the place on fire. The thought of Art caused him to worry that he would not wait for a signal, and in a little while, he'd get tired of waiting and lead their horses on into the stable. Anxious to head that off, he backed away to the door again.

As soon as he was out the back door, he ran a wide circle back through the trees to where Art was waiting. "Cullen?" Art called out softly when he saw him coming through the shadows.

"Yeah, it's me," Cullen answered. "We've got us a little welcomin' committee waitin' for us in the tack room. I expect it's those two young men I thought were halfway to Kansas by now. Least, I think it's two in there, unless it's somebody talkin' to himself."

"I swear," Art said, "I'da thought they'd have better sense than that—to wait around to try to shoot somebody. It's gonna get crowded in that little cell room back at the jail."

"We've gotta figure a way to get 'em outta there first. And that ain't gonna be easy. That room's a regular little fort." He thought for a few seconds. "I'll see if I can separate 'em, get one of 'em to come out if I can. Course, I'd like to get both of 'em outta there, but one might make it easier to get the other one out. As long as there's two of 'em in there, they can watch the window and the door."

"How you gonna get one of 'em out?" Art questioned.

"I'm gonna get the horses in the stalls stirred up— see if that'll do it. Here's what I need you to do. Tie the horses here in these trees and you take your rifle and find yourself some cover where you can watch the front of the stable. If they make a run for it that way, it'll be up to you to stop 'em." He figured that would give Art a part in the action without him thinking he was just trying to keep him safe.

"You can depend on me," Art responded. "I'll be ready for 'em."

"I know I can," Cullen said. He started to leave, but stopped and went back to his horse to take the coil of rope from the saddle. "Never know when some rope might come in handy," he said, and left to return to the rear door of the stables. Once inside again, he repeated his first entrance, and when his eyes were adjusted again, he moved forward to the position where he had first heard the whispering. He wanted to confirm that both Riley and Jeb were still in the tack room. It took a few moments, but eventually he caught the sound of a whispered exchange. Satisfied, Cullen moved back into the stalls, looking for something to use as missiles. He hit the jackpot in a couple of stalls. Thankfully, since Art was not there to clean out the stalls, there were convenient piles of horse turds to pick from, most of them dried and hard. He grabbed a bucket from a nail in a pole and filled it with the drier road apples. Then he climbed up on the stall rails where he could lob pellets into several stalls.

His first few throws at the horses' hindquarters made them stir around a little, but the more he threw, the more nervous the horses became. Pretty soon the other horses began to respond to the stirring around of those being constantly pelted.

Inside the tack room, Jeb and Riley suddenly stopped to listen. "What the hell is that?" Riley wondered when he heard horses moving around. "Somethin's got after the horses."

"Maybe a fox or a skunk or somethin' has got in the stable, lookin' for somethin' to eat. They'll quiet down in a minute, or I'll go see about it," Jeb said. So they waited, but the confusion in the stalls only got worse with snorts and whinnies coming to their ears in the tack room. Before long, the two men in the tack room could no longer ignore it. "I'll go," Jeb volunteered. "Somethin' might be after our horses."

"You be careful," Riley warned him. "There might be somebody back there."

"I will, but if there was somebody back there, they woulda had to come by the window." He thought for a moment, then added, "Unless that back door ain't locked."

"Maybe you oughta take that lantern with you," Riley said.

"Druther not," Jeb replied. "If there was somebody in the stalls, they'd see me comin' if I'm holdin' a lantern." Slightly amused by Riley's concern, he said, "Move that keg of nails over against the door, just in case, and I'll knock three times when I come back. All right?" He went out the door then, smiling to himself when he heard the sound of the nail keg rolling up against the door behind him.

Out in the alleyway between the stalls, Jeb moved very slowly toward the back stalls, where most of the disturbance seemed to come from, waiting for his eyes to adjust to the darkness. The process was slowed considerably due to the faint light that the lantern had provided in the tack room. Almost to the back door, he could see nothing that would indicate anyone was in the stable but himself. Completely unaware of the ominous figure that had stepped out of a stall as he passed by and was now behind him, walking step for step. Jeb stopped when he reached the door. "Damn, it was unlocked," he muttered softly, the words barely out of his mouth when he was suddenly locked in a powerful embrace. His arms were pinned to his body by one powerful arm wrapped around him, while Cullen's other hand clamped over his mouth. Like a mountain lion surprising an unsuspecting rabbit, Cullen lifted the slighter man off his feet with his right arm and pushed him on through the open door. Outside, Cullen rode him to the ground to land on his belly. And before Jeb could realize what had attacked him, Cullen pulled his hands behind his back and tied them together. When Jeb started to yell, Cullen slammed him with an open hand to the back of his head, driving his face into the dirt, effectively muffling any sound Jeb tried to make.

Sitting on the middle of Jeb's back, Cullen used his skinning knife to quickly cut Jeb's bandanna off his neck, not wasting time to untie a knot. He stuffed the bandanna in Jeb's mouth, then quickly cut a length of rope to hold it in place. With that done, he roped Jeb's feet together and tied them to his hands. When he had him all trussed up like he wanted, he said, "You had your chance to run, but you didn't have enough sense to take it. You damn fool, I wouldn't have come after you. Now, I'll see if your partner wants to come with you."

With far less caution now, Cullen walked back to the tack room and knocked three times on the door. Almost immediately, he heard the keg of nails moving back to its original position beside the door. Riley opened the door, and when he did, he found himself facing a dark figure that looked twice the size of his partner. He realized too late that the shadow had a pistol aimed at his belly. Too stunned to react, he took a step back and Cullen matched it with a step forward to keep his .44 only a foot from Riley's gut. "Are you gonna take this the easy way, or are you gonna die here tonight?" Cullen asked, and before Riley could answer, he reached over and pulled the shocked outlaw's gun from his holster.

"I'll go quiet," Riley quickly replied.

"Turn around," Cullen ordered, and when Riley did, Cullen pulled his hands behind his back and trussed him up like he had with Jeb—with two variations. He didn't gag him and he tied his ankles, but with a short length of robe between them—hobbled like a horse—so he could walk, but he couldn't run. "All right, let's go get your partner." With his hand on the back of Riley's neck, Cullen guided him out the door and down the alleyway to the back door. "Which one are you?" Cullen asked. When Riley told him, Cullen told him the same thing he had told Jeb. "You two shoulda run when you had the chance."

"I told him that," Riley felt the need to say.

Outside the door, they found Jeb lying close beside it. Cullen guided Riley a few feet beyond that and told him to stop. Then he holstered his .44 for only a few seconds while he reached down, picked Jeb up like a sack of potatoes, and threw him over his shoulder. "All right, Riley," he ordered. "Start walkin' toward the front of the stable." Riley did as he was told. When they were approaching the front, Cullen called out to Art, "We're comin' out, Art! Hold your fire!"

Art stepped out from behind a tree. "Come ahead on, I got you covered," he sang out. Then he stood, astonished, as he watched Cullen approach, herding one of the outlaws in front of him and carrying the other one on his shoulder.

Art watched, totally amazed, as Cullen unloaded Jeb, almost gently on the ground. "Keep your eye on this one," Cullen said, nodding toward Riley, "and I'll untie his partner, so I don't have to carry him to the jail." While he was at it, he removed the bandanna from Jeb's mouth. "We might as well leave the horses tied right where you got 'em and walk these two to the jail first."

"I swear," Art said, "you boys sure shoulda run for it when you had the chance."

"I told him that," Riley said again. Jeb wanted to answer him but was still spitting dirt out of his mouth.

"Well, damn," Micah grunted when he saw Jeb and Riley marched into the jail by Cullen and Art. The two young bank robbers from Arizona were the last chance he had hoped for. After he heard they had escaped, he told Shorty and Leroy that there was still a chance they might not see the inside of the Ravenwood jail. He was especially hopeful when McCabe sent all the volunteer guards home to celebrate. With only McCabe and the deputy left to guard them all night, and the possibility they might take turns sleeping, Riley and Jeb had a good shot at springing them. If not during the night while they were in jail, they might decide to wait in ambush on the ride to Ravenwood in the morning.

"We got two more for you, Deputy," Art announced to Beau. "That oughta 'bout do it. You've got the entire East City marshal's posse right here in this little jailhouse. Don't look so dangerous now, do they?"

"These the two that ran out the back of the hotel?" Beau asked Cullen. "I didn't think there was any chance of seeing those two again. Where'd you find them?"

"Yep," Cullen answered. "They were set up down there in the stable, waitin' to ambush us when we brought the horses in." He looked over at Moran, standing near the front of the cell. "You ought not be too hard on 'em, Moran. Looks like they had it in their minds they were gonna set you free. We had to trick 'em to get 'em outta there."

It was too much for Moran to keep his mouth shut. "You'd better hope and pray I don't get set free, McCabe. 'Cause, if I do, you're a dead man."

"Good to know," Cullen responded. "If I see you out walkin' on the street somewhere, I'll cross over to the other side to avoid gettin' killed."

When they got the two new prisoners untied, Cullen and Art stood by with weapons drawn while Beau unlocked the cell and put them inside. When he was finished with that chore, he nodded to Cullen to follow him and walked outside the marshal's office. Art followed Cullen out. When he figured they were out of earshot, Beau told Cullen what was on his mind. "Two of us escortin' Moran and two others on horseback isn't much of a risk, but I'm thinkin' five prisoners are a little harder to handle. I'm not sayin' we can't do it. But as dangerous as Moran is, I think it wouldn't hurt to be a little more careful."

Not sure what he was getting at, Cullen asked, "What have you got in mind?"

"Well, I saw a jail wagon parked behind Jim Farmer's stable," Beau said. "It's been settin' there for a while now and it looked to be in good shape. I don't know who it belongs to. My guess is the Rangers, or the army, but I think it wouldn't hurt to borrow it for this little trip tomorrow—make it a lot easier on us. And I think everybody wants to make sure Micah Moran makes it to that jail in the morning."

"Sounds like a good idea to me," Cullen said right away. "You're sure right about how important it is to get Moran to court."

"I expect we can delay our trip a little while in the morning and I'll ride over to see if Jim will let us borrow it," Beau suggested.

"Hell," Art spoke up, "I'll go over and get it tonight and drive it back here in the mornin' in time for breakfast. Jim won't mind. If he does, I'll take it anyway, and a team of horses to drive it."

"You sure you don't wanna wait till mornin'?" Cullen asked. "It's way past suppertime."

"Yeah, I'm sure. I'm stayin' at the house with 'em now. Rena will fix me somthin' to eat before I go to bed." Art walked back to the horses with Cullen. He stepped up into the saddle and headed to Ravenwood, while Cullen took care of the horses.

CHAPTER 19

As Art had promised, he showed up before Lizzie had finished cooking breakfast for the five prisoners and Cullen and Beau. By the time everyone had eaten, they were more than ready to climb into the jail wagon, having been motivated by the condition of the one slop bucket. Even with no door on the front of the jail, there was very little ventilation to help with the odor left after Lizzie's red bean soup for supper the night before. The main culprit was Leroy, who had mixed his soup with too many parts corn whiskey. It resulted in a complete evacuation remedy for constipation, much to his fellow inmates' distress. Cullen and Beau were fortunate to retreat to the porch out front. When Art arrived, Cullen asked him who took care of the jail as far as cleaning up and so forth.

"Moss Turnipseed did the cleanin' when Ace Brown was deputy," Art said. "Buck Casey said that Moss quit when Ace got shot and he didn't know if he was gonna keep the job when Molloy took over. Anyway, Moss didn't show up while I was in jail. Buck said Moss ain't been back since the door got kicked in."

Cullen looked at Beau. "You might wanna remember

that name. You never can tell, you might end up in this office."

"If I do, there's gonna be a helluva lot of fixin' up to do on this place," Beau replied. Cullen was satisfied that Beau didn't flat out quash that idea.

When all was ready, the prisoners seated in the jail wagon, Tom Loughlin, Floyd, Lizzie, Wilma, and Mabel came out to watch their departure. Even though the hour was early, they were joined by a couple of prostitutes from the hotel next door, as well as some of the town's early-rising merchants. A dark, angry Micah Moran, once mighty ruler of the town, sat scowling in the front of the wagon—like his fellow passengers, his ankles locked in irons and attached to a long chain. Buck Casey, who was not about to miss Moran's last parade out of town, was there to wish them a pleasant trip. Driving the team of horses, Art Becker sat up tall, beaming with pleasure, undaunted by the knowledge that Moran would murder them all if he could get free. Cullen and Beau rode along beside the wagon, one on the right, one on the left, as Art drove the horses toward the wide creek that served as the county line. As far as he was concerned, it was a short ride that was a long time coming, and cause for celebration.

On the other side of the creek, they followed the road to the town of Ravenwood. Art drove the wagon down the main street of Ravenwood and pulled around behind the courthouse that housed the jail on the bottom floor. He pulled the horses to a stop before the door to the jail where the jailer, David Rakestraw, stood waiting. With him, Marshal Tug Taggert and guard Pete Caster were ready to help take the prisoners into custody. Sharing many of the sentiments of the townsfolk of East City, Tug Taggert hoped he was witnessing a new day in the development of the twin towns—in spite of the county line that flowed between them.

"McCabe," Tug Taggert stepped forward and greeted Cullen as he dismounted. "This is David Rakestraw and Pete Caster. They'll be takin' care of our guests, right through the trial and sentencin'." Both men stepped forward to shake hands with Cullen while Taggert continued, "McCabe is a special agent from the governor's office and largely responsible for cleanin' out that mess of outlaws in East City."

"I had a lot of help," Cullen said. "I think the folks in East City just decided it was time to take back their town. They might even be ready to be a part of Ravenwood."

Unnoticed by Cullen, Art Becker, upon hearing Taggert's remark, bolted upright in the driver's seat of the jail wagon and turned at once to stare at Cullen. "Well, I'll be go to hell," he muttered aloud, but not so loud that anyone could hear. He was afraid he couldn't wait to talk to Cullen about what he just heard.

"I'm pretty sure Judge Raven will be tickled to hear that," Marshal Taggert replied in response to Cullen's remark. "And after we get these boys tucked away in a cell, I'll be goin' to tell the judge they're locked up."

That served as Art's signal and he jumped down from his seat, hurried around to the back of the wagon, and unlocked the door. Then he stood back while the prisoners climbed out of the back of the wagon. When they were out, Cullen, Beau, and Taggert all stood with weapons drawn to watch as Art unlocked each prisoner's ankle clamp. Almost swelling with pride for having a part in the transport of the prisoners, he went quickly down the line. Last to be unlocked, Micah Moran could not maintain his stony silence. "You little rat," he growled softly. "I shoulda hung you right away." Art said nothing in return but responded with a wide smile and a nod.

The five prisoners were marched into the jail through a set of double doors, past a small reception area, then through a reinforced door that led to the cellblock where they would be held until split up and put in two separate cells. When the cell doors were all locked, Taggert said, "I'm goin' to let the judge know they're here. I'd like you and Beau to go with me," he said to Cullen. "I know he'll surely wanna talk to you." Cullen figured as much.

Taggert and Beau waited in the reception area while Cullen went back outside with Art. "Taggert wants me to go talk to the judge with him, so I won't be goin' back right away," Cullen told him. "So if you're headin' back to East City, don't think you gotta wait for me."

"That's all right, Special Agent McCabe," Art responded with a grin too big for his face to contain. "I'll go take Jim's wagon and horses back to him, then I'll wait and go back to East City with you."

"Hey," Cullen said, "don't be fooled by that special agent crap. I reckon that's just somethin' Taggert thought up to keep anybody from lookin' into the men I shot. Hell, before you know it, they might wanna keep me in jail for murder."

"Right," Art replied, still with the grin on his face,

"whatever you say. But I'll still wait to ride back with you. I'll meet you right back here by the jail."

"All right. I don't know how long I'll be, though."

He went back inside and he and the two Ravenwood lawmen went up the back stairs that led to the courtroom above the jail. Cullen followed them through the empty courtroom, then down a hall to the judge's office, where they were met by a clerk in the outer office. He asked them to wait while he informed the judge of their arrival. *Pretty fancy for a judge,* Cullen thought, *almost as ritzy as the governor's office.* Maybe, he thought then, it was because the judge was also the mayor, plus he had donated the land for the city. In a few minutes, the door to the judge's office opened and Harvey Raven came out to greet them. "Come right on in, gentlemen." He turned around then and led them back into his office. After an introduction to Cullen, Raven invited them to sit down. "Marshal Taggert has told me how busy you've been on the other side of the creek, McCabe. And I have to say, you sure have made some progress. I understand these five men you brought in today are all that's left of the Micah Moran posse. Is that a fact?" He waited for Cullen to confirm that, then continued. "Well, I'll say job well done. We'll schedule a trial for all five of them right away. I'm going to need you at the trial, of course. But I'd like to have someone from the town of East City, too, as witnesses to the unofficial hangings and killings. Can you suggest who that might be?"

"Well, sir," Cullen responded, "right off hand, I'd say probably the mayor, Abe Franks, and maybe Joe Johnson. He owns the general store. They've both seen their share of the lawless men that have been flockin' there."

"That should be all we'd need, since we've got a man in custody here who attempted to kill Marshal Taggert. Sam Polek's his name and he's willing to testify that Moran sent him and two other men to kill the marshal. That's enough for a death sentence for Moran right there."

"He was a hardcase for a while there," Taggert interrupted. "But he changed his tune in a hurry when he found out Moran was out of business and he might escape a noose if he testified against him."

"That's right," Raven said. "He refused to give his name, but the marshal was able to find out who he was." He paused then to say, "Good work, Marshal Taggert." Taggert winked at Cullen as the judge continued. "There's another important issue to discuss and it prompts me to ask you a question, Mr. McCabe. What's going to keep East City from continuing its old lawless ways as an attraction for outlaws all over the territory?"

Cullen shrugged and said, "I don't know if anybody can guarantee that won't happen. But the only way it has a chance of changin' from its old reputation is to put a good man in the marshal's office and for the town to back him up. There'll still be the lawless drifters hittin' town for a while, till the word gets out that the marshal in East City won't let 'em stay. But I think the town council over there is ready to support a good, honest marshal right now."

"Any chance you might be that marshal?" Raven asked.

"No, sir, no chance. I'll be movin' on as soon as the

trial is over." He nodded toward Beau. "You've got what I think is a pretty good man for that job, if your marshal doesn't mind losin' his deputy right after he finally got one."

Beau immediately sat up more upright upon hearing that and gave Taggert a questioning look. Taggert smiled back at him. "What do you say to that?" Raven asked the marshal.

"I'd say he'd make a good one. The short time I've had him, I figured he was strong enough to be more'n a deputy." He chuckled then and added, "I thought he might bump me outta my job, if he stayed here very long." He looked back at Beau again. "I don't know if he wants that job or not, but I think he can handle it."

With all eyes on him now, Beau did well to hide his excitement. "I reckon Marshal Taggert knows I'm ambitious," he stated calmly. "But I believe I am qualified to do the job, and I would be determined to make East City as safe a town as Marshal Taggert has made Ravenwood." His response brought smiles all around.

"That sounds like the solution to the problem, then," the judge said. "There is only one little hitch, though. It ain't our problem. We can't appoint a marshal for East City. Their town council has to do that. And with the troubles we've had in the past, they might be too much to reconcile."

"If you want my opinion," Cullen volunteered, "I think the town council is ready to take that step, and I think they're in a hurry, to boot. Of course, you and Mayor Franks and maybe the council members will have to meet and work together. But I don't think there's a likely candidate for the marshal's job in the whole town of East City—no one I think could handle it, anyway. I expect they'd be glad to hire Beau. He's already made the arrest of the five we just brought over here, so they've seen that he can get the job done."

"We need to arrange that meeting as soon as possible," Raven said. "Can you talk to Abe Franks to see about scheduling it?"

"I'll suggest something better," Cullen replied. "Art Becker drove the jail wagon over here. He's a member of the town council, owns the stable over there. How 'bout we have Art go to the mayor and talk about meetin' with you? I'll go with him, but that way, at least the suggestion would come from a member of the East City council."

"Excellent idea," Raven said. "I'll wait to hear from you."

They filed out of the judge's office and went back downstairs. When they walked out of the jail, Taggert couldn't resist japing his deputy. "So you're talkin' about quittin' on me, are you? Ain't been settin' in the deputy's chair long enough to get the seat of your pants warm, and already talkin' about leavin'. I knew I shouldn't'a let you and McCabe work together—put big ideas in your head."

"Ah, come on, Tug," Beau japed, "you know you've been tryin' to figure out how to get rid of me from the first day." Getting serious then, he thanked Taggert for his recommendation, then turned toward Cullen. "I appreciate what you said in there, McCabe. If I happen to get that job over there, I'll do my best not to disappoint you."

"I wouldn't have said it, if I wasn't sure you're the

man for the job," Cullen said as Art came around the corner of the courthouse on his horse.

He pulled up beside Cullen's bay gelding. "You ready to go?"

"I reckon," Cullen answered, and stepped up into the saddle. "Art and I will go straight to the hardware store to talk to Abe Franks and I'll let you know how that turns out, and you can tell the judge," he said to Taggert. Taggert nodded his understanding.

On the way back to East City, Cullen explained to Art why he wanted him to go with him to see Abe Franks. "Kinda makes it more a request from a member of your own town council, and not folks in Ravenwood tellin' you what you oughta do." Art understood and was more than happy to go with him. Cullen could see how pumped up Art was becoming to be involved in almost every phase of the takeover of their town. *He might get to feeling so important that he'll get up the nerve to pop the question to Hortense Billings*, Cullen thought. He had to smile when he pictured it.

Abe glanced up to see Cullen and Art walk in his store. Cullen was aware that it was the first time he was met with a friendly smile from the usually serious hardware man. He guessed it was a friendlier feeling covering the whole town since Micah Moran was carted unceremoniously out in a jail wagon. He was aware that it was a day that many of the people there thought would never dawn. "We got some things we need to talk about," Art announced, before Cullen had a chance to speak. So Cullen let him go on with it.

"What things is that?" Abe responded.

"Now that we've got rid of the outlaw trash down at the Cork and Bottle, it's time to talk about the future of East City." Not accustomed to such serious talk coming from Art Becker, Abe glanced at Cullen, questioning, but Art continued. "Me and Cullen have been talkin' to the mayor of Ravenwood and I think it's time the two towns had a little meetin' to decide how we're gonna get along together. And Judge Raven said he thought that was a fine idea. What we need, first of all, is a strong, honest marshal, and me and Cullen have found a good man for the job. Ain't that right, Cullen?" Cullen nodded, indicating that it was so. Art went on. "Might not be a bad idea to hire a deputy to help him, too."

That caused Cullen to raise his eyebrows. Art had come up with that one on his own, but he had to admit it might be a wise decision at that. Having evidently run out of words at that point, Art simply held his hand under his chin, pretending it was a knife. Then he made a slashing motion like a man slitting his throat, to signify he was done talking.

It was not until then that Cullen spoke. "Art's pretty much covered what we came to tell you. The point is, Ravenwood is ready to help East City get back on its feet, now that Moran is gone. The man Art said was a good prospect for marshal is well qualified to do the work you need. You've already met him, Beau Arnett. He was the arrestin' officer. Course, it's up to you and the council to decide if you wanna offer him the job. So if you think it's worthwhile to meet with Judge Raven, he's ready to talk whenever you say. I told him I'd let him know what you decided."

Abe didn't answer right away. He was still somewhat astonished by Art's aggressive civic interest, a quality never exhibited before in any council meetings. The downfall of Micah Moran's posse of outlaws had happened so fast that there had not been time to examine the concepts of the actual arrest and imprisonment. Abe could not now deny a feeling that Moran should have been detained in the East City jail, tried by a jury of East City citizens, and executed by hanging in East City. Instead, a law officer from an adjoining county came to this town and arrested the felon, then took him to that county for trial. It was difficult for Abe not to feel that Ravenwood was once again trying to dictate East City's business. He said as much to Cullen.

Cullen heard him out, expecting that might be Abe's reaction. "I understand why you might feel that way, Mr. Mayor," he said. "That's why Art and I came directly to you to explain. I think I oughta tell you right off that Mayor Raven made it plain to us that he only wants to cooperate with you on the arrest of Moran. And I'm sure he'll turn him back over to you folks, if that's the way you have to have it. But the fact is, right now, we don't have a jail suitable to hold five prisoners." He glanced at Art and said, "And I reckon that's my fault. But Ravenwood has a secure jail, and they have a judge. And he wants me to tell you that he expects to involve you in Moran's trial, as well as the other four's trial."

"Of course, I'll have to talk to the rest of the council," Abe said. "But the fact of the matter is we need to take some action fast. And in my opinion, it's time to call off this feud with Ravenwood, so you go ahead and tell Raven that I'll meet with him. And the sooner, the better," he added. "Just let me know when and where. I'll see if I can round up the rest of the council for an emergency meeting right now."

"I reckon I can help you with that," Art volunteered.

CHAPTER 20

After leaving the hardware store, Cullen mounted up again to take the word back to Judge Raven, while Art stayed behind to get the word to as many of the other five council members as he could. When Cullen arrived at the courthouse in Ravenwood, the judge was conducting a trial for a man accused of cattle rustling. When the judge's clerk whispered in his ear that Cullen McCabe was waiting to deliver Mayor Franks's message, Raven called for a short recess and went to his office immediately to talk to Cullen. It was an unmistakable sign to Cullen that Raven was anxious to come to an agreement. Cullen left the judge's office with a request for a meeting in O'Sullivan's Saloon the following morning at ten o'clock.

"That'll work fine for us," Abe said to Cullen when he delivered the message. "Tell him it's a deal. We look forward to meeting with him." When Cullen started to leave, Abe stopped him. "And, McCabe, I'd like for you to be here, too."

"Yes, sir," Cullen replied. "I'll be here. I'll tell him to bring Beau Arnett along, too, just in case you wanna talk to him." He left then to go back over the creek to deliver Abe's confirmation of the meeting. "It's gettin' on about time to eat something," he said to Jake as they crossed the creek once again. "I might as well visit the dinin' room at the hotel and have myself a good meal." He had considered going to Hortense Billings's boardinghouse, since he was planning to take his room back until the trial was over. But he knew Annie was not in the habit of fixing a big noon-time meal, and he felt like celebrating with a full dinner today. Things were going along better than he could have expected when he first arrived.

After dropping off his message at the courthouse, he went to the hotel dining room, expecting to find Tug Taggert there, since his office door was locked when he rode by. Beau was with him and they both waved him over to join them. Marcy Manning caught him in time to remind him of the "no-weapons policy" before he got far. "Mr. Cullen McCabe, if I remember correctly," she greeted him as she took his arm and guided him back to the weapons table. "We're glad you came back to visit us."

"Me, too," he said. "I hope you've got something good to eat. What's the special today?"

"Roast beef with mashed potatoes and gravy," she answered, "and I recommend it."

"Sold," he said, and continued on to the table.

"Heard you were already back earlier this mornin'," Taggert said when Cullen sat down.

"Yep, I've been ridin' back and forth over that creek all mornin'. Abe Franks said okay to the meetin' and it's set for ten o'clock tomorrow mornin' at O'Sulli-van's in East City. And that's the last of my final announcements, so it's up to you folks now."

"I reckon Judge Raven will be schedulin' that trial as soon as he can," Taggert said. "He'll have to give everybody time to get ready for it, I expect."

"Accordin' to what he told me just now, he's plannin' on goin' to court day after tomorrow," Cullen replied. "He said the trial is just a formality for the sake of showing every man, no matter how evil, deserves a day in court. He said, if he wasn't here, Beau and the folks would probably have hanged him in East City when he arrested him."

"I reckon we'd best get some ropes ready, Beau," Taggert said. "He gonna try 'em all at the same time?"

"He said there'd be two separate trials. Moran's gonna be tried by himself because the charges against him are worse than the four gang members." Cullen shrugged. "I expect those two young boys will most likely to just get some prison time in Huntsville. Maybe Shorty and Leroy might get a rope, though."

"What are you plannin' to do after this, McCabe?" Taggert was interested to know. "You gonna hang around awhile?"

"I'll hang around till the judge says, *Guilty, death by hangin'*, then I'll be in the saddle and gone," Cullen answered him. "I've got a place down south of Austin that always needs some work, and I've been here longer'n I figured I'd be." The meal was finished with Cullen saying, "Well, I'll see you at the meetin', Beau." He left them with that and headed back to East City.

"What's the matter, Moran?" guard Pete Caster asked. "Ain't our food good enough for you? You ain't ate half of it. Maybe you're used to fancier grub than we serve here."

Micah Moran placed his plate and fork on the pass-through in the cell door, but kept his coffee cup. "I ain't finished with my coffee yet."

"I don't reckon you're enjoyin' your little stay in our establishment, are you?" Caster continued, having nothing better to do. "I heard you had some setup over there across the creek, owned the whole damn town." He smirked and added, "Well, you ain't gonna have to put up with these poorly accommodations very long. They'll be hangin' you pretty soon."

"That's what I hear," Moran said. "You heard right about me ownin' the town. I did, all right." He shook his head sadly. "It's a damn shame, though, all that money . . ." His words trailed off and he shook his head again.

"All what money?" Caster asked, always interested to hear about money.

Moran just stared at him for a long moment before answering. "It's just a damn shame," he lamented again, "all that money. And I was fixin' to leave this part of the country. I had more than I coulda ever spent in my lifetime. And then to get arrested before I could leave. Just a damn shame."

"How much money are we talkin' about?" Caster asked.

Moran cocked his head back, as if suddenly wary of talking too much. "Well, I don't know if I should . . ." He paused for a few moments, then shrugged. "Hell, I don't reckon it'll hurt to tell you, if you'll keep it to yourself." He nodded toward the cell at the end where his posse was. "I don't want them to hear us.

They might not understand how hard I worked for that money."

Itching to find out how much he was talking about, Caster asked again, "How much was it?"

"Caster, ain't that your name? Well, Caster, if I told you, you wouldn't believe there was that much money in the world. Ain't no need to tell you, you can't get it, nobody can, now that I'm locked up in here, waitin' to die." He hung his head sadly. "It's just a damn shame."

"Don't nobody know where you kept it?" Caster asked.

"Hell, no. I wasn't about to tell anybody where that money's hid." He paused and looked right and left to make sure he wouldn't be overheard. "Caster, I'm talkin' about six hundred thousand dollars. If those boys down in the other cell had known about that money, I'd be a dead man right now. I shoulda left when I had half that much. Half was more than I'd ever need." Another shake of the head and he repeated, "Just a shame. Nobody will ever see that money."

"Seems a shame to take a secret like that to the grave," Caster remarked, "when somebody could use it." Moran was right, that was more money than Caster could imagine.

Moran cocked his head back as if wary. "That's my money. I ain't gonna tell anybody where I hid that money—give it to somebody for doin' nothin'." He paused to let Caster think some more about that much money, then he pretended to be thinking out loud. "It'd be different if I could buy my freedom with it. I'd spend half of it in a minute, if I could do that.

But I can't, so the money's goin' to the grave with me."
He could almost see the wheels turning in Caster's
head as the guard thought about what he could do
with half of that money.

"Hell, you must think I fell off a turnip wagon,"
Caster said. "There ain't that much money in Texas."

"Well, there's gonna be that much money buried
under Texas and it's gonna stay there 'cause I lied,
cheated, and stole to get that money," Moran declared.
"And I ought not even told you about it. How 'bout it,
you think I could have another cup of coffee?" he said,
as if done with the subject.

"I reckon so. Gimme your cup." Moran stuck it
through the bars.

He watched Caster as he left the cell room. *He's
thinking hard about it*, he thought. *I'll know for sure, if he
comes back with more coffee.*

It wasn't long before Caster came back, and he got
a reception from the four prisoners in the large cell at
the end of the row when he passed by with a full cup
of coffee. "Hey, Guard," Leroy Hill said, "how 'bout
bringin' us some of that coffee?"

"Ain't none left in the pot," Caster answered. "You
had your coffee with your dinner." His response left a
stream of complaints and cursing in his wake, which
he ignored.

"Why, thank you kindly, Caster," Moran said most
graciously as he took the cup through the bars.

Caster remained there for a couple of minutes
before speaking. "I was thinkin' about what you said
about all that money you got hid."

"Is that right? What about it?"

"You know, you said you'd be willin' to split it with
somebody who could get you outta here alive."

"Yeah, I reckon I would split it with somebody for my freedom," Moran declared. "You know somebody who might be able to do that?"

Caster lowered his voice to almost a whisper. "I could do it, if it was worth my while, but how do I know you ain't japin' me?"

"I guess you don't, but I'm a desperate man. I ain't got time to play games with somethin' as important as my life. If I thought you could really help me get outta here, I'd be glad to make you a rich man for the rest of your life, unless three hundred thousand ain't enough for you to make it on. It'll sure as hell do me. I can tell you that."

"Maybe you could tell me where it's at, so I could go get it and have it ready when I get you outta here. That way, I'd know for sure you were levelin' with me. I could have a horse waitin' for you and we'd split the money and both say good-bye to this town."

Moran smiled and shook his head. "I swear, Caster, you must think you're takin' a fool for a partner. You open up that strongbox and see all that money, you might forget your way back to the jail. It'd be awful temptin' and nobody would believe me if I said we had a deal." He let the simple guard sweat that for a couple of minutes while he sipped his coffee. "I reckon I can understand you wantin' some kind of guarantee that I'll pay up. I'll tell you what I'll do. I've got the key that unlocks the strongbox where that money is waitin' to be dug up. I'll let you hold on to it until we get away from this jail and go get the money." He reached in his pocket and pulled out the key to his room in the Cork and Bottle. "Here it is. I'll let you carry it now. That oughta let you know I trust you to get me a horse and a gun belt and a shovel. As soon as you get me outta here, we can go get the money. That's all I need. When we dig up the money, I can buy anything else I need." He watched Caster beginning to sweat with his indecision and he prodded him a little more. "Long as you've got this key, I can't get into the box. If you don't come through with your end of the deal, you don't know where the box is buried." He paused a minute, then acted as if to return the key to his pocket.

"Wait a minute!" Caster exclaimed. Then glancing right and left in case anyone was looking, he held out his hand and took the key. He immediately balled his fist around it so no one could see it. "It's a big key," he remarked foolishly.

"It fits a big strongbox, partner," Moran replied.

"I'll be seein' you, partner," Caster returned.

The meeting at O'Sullivan's went as Cullen had hoped it would. The representatives from both towns were ready and anxious to work with one another to increase the development on both sides of the creek, hopefully to combine it as one big city eventually. It ended with handshakes and wishes of good luck. Abe asked Beau Arnett if he would stay awhile afterward to discuss the job opening at the marshal's office. Afterward, all members of the council voted to offer Beau the job and he accepted on the spot. Acting on Art Becker's earlier proposal, Buck Casey was offered the deputy's job, depending upon Beau's approval. Buck said he would accept the position as long as he could continue his blacksmith business. Beau allowed as how he could work with that, since he mostly wanted a deputy as backup when he needed one. Cullen suggested to Beau that he might want to talk to Hortense Billings when he was ready to move over to this side of the creek. The only thing left was the trial of Micah Moran the following morning and then it would be "so long" for Cullen, who was more than satisfied with the success of this assignment for the governor.

When the meeting broke up, Cullen and Art went back to Hortense Billings's boardinghouse for the noon meal, seeing it was already close to noon. She and Annie were expecting them. Annie promised she would fix something special to celebrate the liberation of East City. So Cullen and Art left Abe Franks and Joe Johnson in a discussion with Tom Loughlin regarding the operation of the Cork and Bottle from that day forward. They decided to board up the hotel next door. It was actually owned by Micah Moran, so there was no one to object to the closing of what was actually a whorehouse, except, of course, the whores, who would be hard pressed to find gainful employment or be forced to leave town. This didn't apply to Wilma and Mabel, who were defined as *saloon girls*.

Nine o'clock the next morning the courtroom was filled with spectators who wanted to get a look at the ominous outlaw marshal who had turned East City into a haven for outlaws and a hell for honest citizens of that small town across the creek. At approximately five minutes after nine, David Rakestraw and Pete Caster escorted a sullen and smirking Micah Moran up the back stairs from the jail and into the courtroom. Caster made direct eye contact with the prisoner only once, and that was when he unlocked his cell, but it served as confirmation that he was still of a mind to arrange his escape.

At roughly ten minutes after nine, Rakestraw, who acted as the court bailiff, called out, "All rise." Judge Harvey Raven walked in from a side door. As Raven had told Abe Franks and Marshal Taggert, it would be a very short trial. There would be no lawyers involved. He would question the witnesses himself and present the case to the twelve-man jury, selected from Ravenwood citizens. He called as witness Art Becker, who testified about his false arrest, sham trial, and sentence to hang. After Art, he called Sam Polek, who testified that he was a member of Moran's posse and Moran sent him to Ravenwood to murder Marshal Tug Taggert. The only change of expression on Moran's face came when Polek testified. He openly scowled at him, but Polek merely smiled back. Raven then called upon Abe Franks and questioned him about the harassment of the merchants and the shootings in the streets.

When Raven asked the foreman of the jury if they had reached a verdict, he said that they had and they hadn't needed to leave the courtroom to reach it— guilty of murder in the first degree. The judge went right on into the sentencing of the prisoner. "He shall be hanged by the neck until dead, tomorrow morning at six o'clock. Court adjourned."

Cullen watched as Pete Caster and David Rakestraw got Moran up from his chair. As they walked him by Cullen and Art, Moran broke his silence long enough to curse Cullen. "I'll see you in hell, McCabe."

"Lookin' forward to it," Cullen answered, as Moran's guards roughly pulled him away to disappear into the stairs leading down to the jail reception area.

"Damn!" Art exclaimed. "I swear, I believe I could feel the hate comin' outta that man. If looks could kill you, that look he gave you woulda done the job."

"I reckon he's got reason to want me dead," Cullen responded. "It's kinda the same way I feel about him." He didn't express it, but the reasons came to his mind, the cruel murder of the whore Lila Blanchard, and Roy Skelton, then the senseless attempt to do the same to Art.

"Well, we'll get here bright and early in the mornin' to watch the bastard swing," Art said as everybody filed out of the courtroom.

"I reckon," Cullen replied. As far as the job was concerned, it was finished, and there was no real need to watch the hanging. He could start back to Austin right away, but he personally needed to see Moran dead before it would be finished. "I'll leave Jake in your stable tonight and we'll ride over here in the mornin'. We can tell Annie she won't have to fix breakfast, then after the hangin', we'll eat breakfast at the hotel dinin' room. I'll pay. Whaddaya say?"

"That sounds like a dandy idea," Art responded. "We'll have to tell Annie the cookin' weren't as good as hers, though."

"McCabe." Cullen turned when he heard his name called and saw Judge Raven coming toward him. The judge offered his hand and said, "It would be highly remiss of me not to thank you for your part in what took place here today. Of course, Marshal Taggert told me about your reason for being here and I intend to write Governor Hubbard to let him know we appreciate his response to our requests."

"'Preciate it, Your Honor. Hope everything works out for you folks on both sides of Walnut Creek." He

turned to leave, only to be met with the wide-eyed
grin on Art's face. "Let's just keep this between you
and me, Art. Ain't no need to say anything about it
to anybody else."

"Right," Art beamed in response, "just between me
and you."

Outside the courtroom, Cullen found Tug Taggert
and Beau Arnett waiting for him. Several men from
East City, led by Abe Franks, including Buck Casey
and Cary O'Sullivan were also eager to talk to him,
but waited until he had finished with the two Ravenwood lawmen. "Art says you're planning to leave for
Austin just as soon as the hanging's over in the morning," Abe Franks began. "We're thinking it's not right
for you to just up and leave without a chance for the
people of East City to thank you for what you've done
for our town. So . . . Cary, here, is inviting the council
to a celebration at his saloon tonight, and you are officially summoned to attend, right after supper."

It was possibly the last thing Cullen wanted, but
under the circumstances, he felt it would be downright unappreciative to decline. So, he thanked them
graciously and said he would certainly be there. That
business settled, Abe and Cary O'Sullivan climbed
aboard Cary's buggy and the others took to their saddles for the short trip back across the creek.

CHAPTER 21

Although Pete Caster had agreed to provide Moran an opportunity to escape, he was still not sure he could go through with it. The thought of three hundred thousand dollars was almost more than he could comprehend. What were the chances he would be hunted down and made to pay the penalty? He had no morals to trouble him. He had stolen before. His only concern was getting away with it. He had set the escape plan in action, two horses tied behind the work shed behind the jail. As Moran had requested, there was a gun belt with a .44 revolver hanging on the saddle horn of one of the horses and he had propped a shovel against the wall of the shed. Even so, he was still undecided whether to go through with it or not and he tried to imagine how large a stack that much money would make. He stuck his hand in his pocket and squeezed the key Moran had given him, thinking of the life he could lead with such wealth.

Supper was served early at the jail, so the cook and his helpers wouldn't be so late in cleaning up the kitchen. Ted Preston, the night guard, had already checked in and was drinking coffee in the kitchen, shooting the breeze with the cook, as was his usual habit. "Go ahead and drink your coffee," Caster said. "I'll pick up the last plates." He went back through the reception area, which was now deserted, and hurried through the door to the cell room. *It's now or never,* he was thinking, still trying to make up his mind.

When he got to Moran's cell, he found him standing at the door, waiting for him. Detecting the look of uncertainty in Caster's face, Moran was immediately concerned. "You're takin' a step to becomin' a wealthy man, partner. Nothin' but the good life after we step outta this place."

Caster hesitated one last time, then decided he deserved the good life. He took the key to the cells from a hook inside a cabinet on the wall near the door, his movements catching the curiosity of the four prisoners in the double cell. When he walked back to Moran's cell, he handed the key to him to placate his guilty feelings. That way, he could always tell himself that he didn't unlock that cell, Moran did it. And Moran did it quickly. In a couple of seconds, he unlocked his cell. "Hurry!" Caster urged, now fully committed to the escape. "The night guard's in the kitchen. He'll be checkin' in here in about five minutes!"

"Right," Moran replied, and started for the door to the reception area. "Unlock that door!" Caster ran ahead to do it.

"Hey! What the hell's goin' on?" Shorty Miller blurted when he saw Moran and Caster running toward the door. "You goin' to get hung now?"

"Not tonight, boys. Not ever. Here, come on out and join us." He tossed the cell key into their cell, then he and Caster went through the door to the reception area. "That'll be enough to keep your night guard busy for a little while. Who else is here?"

Already panting nervously, Caster fumbled with the outside door from the reception area. "David Rakestraw's in his office on the other side of the kitchen," he said.

"Good, lock this door," Moran commanded, then with a laugh, said, "We don't want no prisoners to get out." Once outside, he looked right and left while Caster locked the door. "Where are those horses?"

"Behind that shed yonder," Caster said, and led the way.

"Damn, Caster, you did a good job," Moran said when he saw the two horses behind the shed, saddled and ready to go. The first thing he did was grab the gun belt and strap it around him. "What kinda weapon you got here?" He drew the weapon, a single-action Army Colt .45 with a four-and-three-quarter-inch barrel. "This'll do," he said, and checked to make sure it was loaded. Seeing the shovel leaning against the wall, he said, "Here, I'll take that. Let's get goin'." Caster put a boot in the stirrup and prepared to step up, never knowing what hit him. The first blow with the shovel landed against the base of his skull, knocking him to the ground. Thinking he had been shot, he struggled to get on his knees, only to be knocked down again. "There ain't no money, you damn fool," Moran gloated. When Caster still tried to roll over on his back, Moran continued to swing the shovel until there was no sign of life left in the unfortunate guard. "I killed a lot of men," Moran said, standing over him to be sure. "But you're the first one I ever killed with a shovel. I woulda shot you, but I didn't want anybody to hear the shot."

With time precious now, he quickly looked the horses over to see which one he preferred. He picked the one Caster had planned to ride, a dun gelding, primarily because it had a much better saddle. Leaving the dun tied at the shed, he led the other horse a few yards away then gave it a slap on its rump, causing the horse to trot away. After it realized it was free, the horse continued on toward the street. Satisfied the horse was going to continue in that direction, Moran set out in the opposite direction, thinking that whoever chased him wouldn't know which tracks to follow. He rode the dun behind the buildings on the main street until coming out on the street at the south end of town. With no sign of anyone after him so far, he reined the dun back and rode out the south road.

It made no difference to him if he left Ravenwood from the north end or the south end. He had but one intention, and that was to circle back to East City. He had a powerful score to settle with East City, but foremost was his passionate desire to kill Cullen McCabe. When he thought about it, he decided it was lucky that the riderless horse ran north. It meant that he would circle back to come in the south end of East City. Consequently, it would be easy to check on Hortense Billings's house first, before he even got to town. If things continued to go his way, maybe he would find McCabe there. He had no thoughts beyond killing the man he held responsible for destroying the gang of ruthless outlaws he had assembled and ruled over. He knew he would never be whole again until he had this man's blood on his hands. Only then, could he storm back into East City and take back everything that had been taken from him.

* * *

"Enjoyed the party, boys," Cullen announced. "But if I'm gonna get up early in the mornin', I expect I'd best get along to the boardin'house and get to bed."

"What's your hurry, Cullen?" Buck asked. "It ain't every day we get to celebrate the hangin' of as big a crook as Micah Moran."

"I reckon that's true," Cullen answered, "but I'd like to bite off a big chunk of that ride back to Austin after it's done. And I don't wanna be totin' a head that's throbbin' like a toothache."

"I'll go with you, Cullen," Art spoke up. "You still gonna take your horse to the house tonight?"

"Yep, I'll just leave right from the house. After the hangin', I'll ride back to the stable with you and pick up my packhorse."

"I expect I'll call it a day, too," Abe Franks declared. "Six o'clock in the morning comes pretty quick."

"Looks like Judge Raven coulda called it for tomorrow afternoon just as easy," Buck complained. "Reckon he wanted to make sure Moran caught the early train to hell?" That brought a chuckle as Cullen and Art said their good-nights.

"I still ain't figured out why that man decided to take on Micah Moran and the whole damn posse," Buck wondered aloud, watching Cullen as he went out the door.

While Art did a few little things that needed doing before he locked the stable for the night, Cullen saddled Jake. Waiting for Art to finish up, Cullen took a look at Jake's shoes. "I ain't been payin' enough attention to you these last few days, have I, boy?" He stroked the big bay's neck. "I think you're gonna need some new shoes not long after we get back."

"You've been livin' with nobody but that horse for too long," Art joked when he came out the back door and heard Cullen talking to Jake. "Does he ever talk back to ya?"

"Jake can't talk, but sometimes he'll write me a note," Cullen came back at him.

"You can ride on ahead, if you want, I'll be along," Art said.

"I'll walk. I ain't in a hurry. I'll lead Jake on that narrow little path, as dark as it is."

"Might be the smart thing to do," Art said as they started out on the path, leading their horses. "It gets dark as hell in these trees at night, but I've walked it so many times you'd think I could make it with my eyes closed."

"If I'da thought about it, I mighta told you to lead the way, but it ain't so dark that I can't . . ." That was as far as he got before the muzzle flash ripped the darkness in front of him and he heard the sound of the pistol shot at the same time he heard the impact of the bullet against Jake's breast. Taken completely by surprise, he tried to react as quickly as he could, as a second and a third shot thudded into Jake's shoulder and side. Desperate, he yelled for Art to take cover while he tried to pull the startled horse to the side of the path. With one loud scream, the bay gelding stumbled and fell, never to get up again. Still the shots rang out, pausing only a few seconds when the shooter quickly reloaded. Cullen could feel the burning anger scorching his veins as his assailant continued to shoot, hitting the dead horse again and again. It was too much for Cullen to take. He jerked his rifle from the saddle sling. Something told him that somehow it was Micah Moran. He had killed Jake, and he would pay for it, come hell or high water.

"Stay down, Art!" he yelled as he rolled over into the bushes beside the path. Then standing up, he plunged through the thick juniper bushes, firing at the muzzle flashes as fast as he could pull the trigger and crank in another cartridge. With bullets flying around him now, Moran concentrated his fire at the new target provided by Cullen's muzzle blasts. No matter how many times he fired, Cullen kept coming for him, his rifle blazing shot for shot, impervious to the hot lead flying all around him. Moran was forced to back up, unable to stop the infuriated maniac charging him.

With no thought other than total vengeance, Cullen advanced a step at a time, cocking and firing with each step, ignoring the impact of a slug in his shoulder, then another in his side. Advancing and firing at the pattern created by Moran's muzzle blasts, nothing could stop him from doing what he was determined to do. Until, finally, his target of muzzle flashes went out, leaving a darkness that hovered over the form of Micah Moran, lying facedown in the weeds beside the path. Two handguns lay empty a few feet away. There was still a flicker of life in the body, for Moran struggled to pull himself away from his executioner. Cullen jammed his boot into the dying man's side and rolled him over on his back. Then he held the barrel of the Winchester 73 only inches from his forehead. "Don't shoot no more," Moran gasped painfully. "I'm done for."

"You no-good piece of shit," Cullen snarled. "You went too far when you shot my horse." He pulled the trigger to send Moran to join the rest of the evil spirits in hell. Completely spent from the fury of his rage, he took a step backward and flopped down to sit beside the body. This was how Art found him.

It was several long minutes before Art realized the shooting was over. So stunned was he by the sight he had just witnessed, that he had never thought about firing at Moran, himself. The image would be forever branded on his memory of the infuriated avenger charging straight into the hail of gunfire—shucking one empty cartridge after another from the Winchester—daring his adversary to kill him. He wondered if anyone would believe him when he told them of this night when Cullen McCabe walked straight into a hail of gunfire, impervious to the shots that struck him, until Micah Moran was dead.

"Cullen?" Art finally called softly, fearing he might be dead. "Are you all right?" Cullen didn't answer. So Art held back, watching the dark figure sitting motionless there, afraid that Cullen might still be in the grips of the terrible rage that had engulfed him and might, without thinking, turn upon him. "Cullen?" Art called softly again.

"He's done for," Cullen finally answered, seeming to be the same solemn man Art had come to know. "He's gotta have a horse around here somewhere. We'll have to find it and drag his body up on the hill, there." He pointed to a bluff where the creek cut around a stand of willows. "I expect the judge will want Tug or Beau to take a look at it, to make sure it's Moran. We'll also need to drag Jake away from the path, somewhere a little farther from the house, I reckon. And I'm gonna need to buy a horse from you, if I'm gonna start back to Austin in the mornin'."

Art stood there, looking at him, amazed, as he called off the things to be done. Finally, when Cullen paused, Art said, "Cullen, I'll take care of them things. First, we gotta take care of you. You're bleedin' from two wounds I can see. Have you got more anywhere I can't see?"

"No, I reckon it's just the two," Cullen answered.

"Can you walk?" Art asked. Cullen said he could and got up from the ground. "Come on, then," Art said. "We'll go to the house and fix you up."

"That you, Art?" Franklin George called out from the kitchen door when he saw Hortense's hound dog run to greet the two men, each leading a horse into the yard.

"Yeah," Art answered. "It's me and Cullen."

"What was all that shootin' back down that way?" Franklin asked. "We didn't know what was goin' on, so I've been watchin' the backyard with my shotgun ready."

"I need to get Cullen on into the house, he's been shot, but I ain't sure how bad yet," Art said.

"I don't need any help," Cullen insisted. "I've gotta take care of this horse first."

"Get on in the house and tell Annie to heat up some water," Art said. "I'll take care of the damn horses." When Franklin wanted to know how Cullen got shot, Art told him to just get him in the kitchen and he would tell him after he took care of the horses.

Franklin held the door open for Cullen, and when he walked by him, he uttered, "Damn, Cullen." By that time, however, Hortense and Annie were aware of the situation and promptly took charge of it.

"Oh, dear Lord," Hortense exclaimed when she saw his bloody shirt. "Sit down and let's take a look at it." She paused. "Or do you need to lie down?" He said that he didn't and sat down on a chair and submitted himself to the care of the two women. Franklin stood by and watched, eager to hear the story, after Cullen told him there was nothing else to fear. He didn't get the details of the shooting until Art came in from the barn, however.

Cullen's concern was the fate and the whereabouts of the other four prisoners. He was sure there was no one else involved in the ambush that had just happened. It was his guess that, if the others had also escaped, they would have been more interested in fleeing than seeking revenge upon him. For that reason, he was satisfied to wait until morning to find out. So he sat quietly while Annie and Hortense cleaned his wounds and bound them to stop the bleeding. He had been lucky—a miracle, according to Art—to have suffered nothing but minor wounds. The only one that had potential to cause a problem was the shoulder wound, where a bullet was still lodged. The wound in his side was superficial, no more than a deep crease of about five or six inches long. At Annie's insistence, he agreed to go to see Dr. McNair in Ravenwood in the morning to let him dig the bullet out of his shoulder. He figured he had to go to Ravenwood, anyway, to see what happened after he left the courtroom. As long as he was going, he decided to take Moran's body back with him. Art insisted upon going with him.

"There ain't no need for you to go," Cullen said, "since there ain't gonna be a hangin'. I ain't hurt that bad, and you've got work you need to do at the stable. But I need your help to put Moran's body on that horse." He paused before adding, "And you need to sell me a horse."

"You can take your pick of anythin' in the stable," Art said at once. "But I'm goin' with you, or I ain't gonna sell you a horse."

Cullen smiled. "You're a hard man to do business with."

The next morning found Cullen's shoulder stiff and sore, causing him to do almost everything one-handed. Fortunately, the bad shoulder was his left one, but it fell upon Art to extract Cullen's saddle out from under Jake, helped by Moran's horse and Cullen's one good arm. Knowing Cullen as a man of very few emotions, Art could still detect obvious evidence of deep sorrow on the part of his friend as they shifted Jake's carcass around. It was not so much what Cullen said, it was more what he didn't say. Without knowing the circumstances that caused Cullen McCabe to cross his path, he had no way of knowing that Jake was all Cullen had in his life. It was obvious, however, that the big bay gelding had meant a lot to him.

They went to the stable then, where Cullen selected Jake's replacement. Art suggested the black horse, named Satan, that had belonged to Micah Moran, but Cullen chose a lively dun gelding that had belonged to Sam Polek. Art allowed that Polek was as dumb as a pinecone, but he did ride a good horse. They led the horses back along the footpath to get Cullen's saddle on the dun, then managed to load Moran's body onto Cullen's sorrel packhorse. After a breakfast that Annie insisted they should have, they started out for Ravenwood.

In spite of the fact that Beau Arnett wanted to try to track Micah Moran as soon as it was light enough to look for tracks, Tug Taggert wanted to raise a posse to go after him. His reasoning was that he intended to hang Moran as soon as he caught him and he wanted witnesses to the hanging. Consequently, they were not yet ready to ride when Cullen and Art showed up with Moran's body. "Well, I'll be . . ." Tug started. "So the rotten dog went after you. Looks like he managed to throw a couple of shots at you."

"Nothin' serious," Cullen said. "What about the other prisoners?"

"We found 'em in the cell room, walkin' around outta their cells, but they're all back in and scheduled for trial tomorrow." He went on to tell them about finding Pete Caster's battered body behind the shed. "Hard to say whether Pete was helpin' him escape, or Moran somehow got the jump on him. Whichever it was, Moran beat his brains out with a shovel." Cullen nodded and started for his horse. "You gonna hang around for the trial of the other four?"

"I expect not," Cullen answered, and climbed up into his saddle.

Art lingered a few moments as they both watched Cullen ride off toward the doctor's office. Tug glanced over at Moran's body and commented, "He sure as hell shot him full of holes, didn't he?"

Art nodded and answered, "He sure as hell did." A vivid picture returned to his mind of the night before and the relentless stalking by the infuriated avenger wading through a sea of angry bullets. "I'll tell you one thing, it sure don't pay to shoot that man's horse."

TURN THE PAGE FOR AN EXCITING PREVIEW!

**Johnstone Country.
How the West Was Really Won.**

HE WHO LIVES BY THE GUN . . .

Shotgun Johnny Greenway thought he'd hit rock
bottom when he lost his wife and son,
hung up his badge, and hit the bottle.
But a pretty young woman gave him a second
chance. Offered him a job riding shotgun for the
Reverend's Temptation Gold Mine.
Gave him a reason to live. But even she can't save
him when the Starrett gang tries to rob the gold—
and Johnny is accused of killing their leader . . .

. . . DIES BY THE GUN

When the dust clears, Shotgun Johnny is wanted for
murder. The dead man's father has powerful
friends, including a town marshal who's Johnny's
personal enemy. The dead man's father wants
vengeance. The town marshal wants the girl.
Both men want Johnny dead. With a $2,000 bounty
on his head—and half the county trying to kill
him—Johnny's got to prove his innocence.
Not in a court of law. In a trial by shotgun . . .

**National Bestselling Authors
William W. Johnstone
and J.A. Johnstone**

SHADOW OF A DEAD MAN
A SHOTGUN JOHNNY WESTERN

On sale now, wherever Pinnacle Books are sold.

Live Free. Read Hard.
www.williamjohnstone.net

Visit us at www.kensingtonbooks.com

CHAPTER 1

A whistling bullet gave Johnny Greenway a clean shave across his left cheek before it hammered into a fir tree just behind him with a loud *thwack!*

The blue whistler was followed by the hiccupping report of a Winchester rifle followed in turn by a man shouting, "There he is!"

Johnny leaped down the steep forested slope. He dove forward as two more bullets plumed dirt and pine needles around him, these shots coming from the slope on his right.

He rolled up off his left shoulder, smoothly gaining his feet.

A large granite boulder with a V-shaped crack in it stood between him and the two men running up the slope toward him. He unsheathed both of his sawed-off, ten-gauge, double-barreled shotguns, which he wore in custom-made holsters on each hip, thonged on his thighs. Taking each savage popper in each gloved hand—he lovingly called the matched pair of handsome, walnut-stocked, Damascus-steeled death-dealers "the Twins"—he rocked the heavy rabbit-ear hammers back with his thumbs and stepped into the crack.

He grinned savagely as he extended the left-hand shotgun through the opening. The men running toward him, within fifteen feet and closing fast, breathing hard, dusters whipping around their legs, stopped suddenly. Their lower jaws dropped to their chests when they recognized their own annihilations in the ten-gauge's round, side-by-side maws, as black as death and as deadly as a lightning bolt.

Johnny squeezed the shotgun's left trigger.

Ka-boom!

The man on the left screamed and threw his rifle straight up in the air as the pumpkin-sized blast of ten-gauge buckshot picked him up and threw him down the slope as though into the jaws of hell itself.

"Nooo!"

The objection of the second man hadn't entirely left his lips before the cannonlike blast of the Twin's second barrel picked him up while blowing a big bloody hole through his middle and sent him hurling down the slope with his pard, his cream, bullet-crowned Stetson with a snakeskin band dancing along the ground beside him.

Two more bullets came whistling in from Johnny's right, one bullet nipping the brim of his black slouch hat, the other hammering the face of the boulder before him and setting up a ringing in his ears. Johnny turned to see two men running toward him across the shoulder of the slope, black suit coats buffeting in the wind.

Both men jacked fresh cartridges into their Winchesters' actions at the same time.

Johnny moved quickly to the far end of the boulder, away from the approaching ambushers. He edged along the rock, heading downslope, then turned right to move around behind the boulder, putting it between him and his pursuers. He heard the two men's running footsteps on the boulder's far side, and the anxious rasping of their breaths.

"Where'd he go?" one asked the other, keeping his voice low but not so low Johnny couldn't hear it.

Johnny moved quietly toward the V-shaped crack in the middle of the rock.

"I don't know," said the second man. "I think he headed downslope."

"No, he didn't." Johnny angled his second Twin through the V-shaped crack and grinned. "He's right here."

Both men, standing a few yards upslope from him and slightly to his right, whipped around in surprise, one cursing and raising his rifle. The curse hadn't entirely left his lips and he hadn't entirely gotten the rifle aimed at Johnny before Johnny's right-hand Twin spoke the language of death.

It spoke it again, a second time.

The thundering echoes of the double blasts were still vaulting around the canyon as both men lay in shredded, bloody piles against the incline, shivering out their last breaths, their blood-splattered rifles flung out on the ground around them.

"There he is! There's that Basque devil!"

The voice had come from up the forested slope, maybe fifty yards beyond the dead men. Johnny looked up that way to see two horseback riders moving toward him, weaving through the pines and fir trees. They had to hold their horses to lurching trots on account of the trees and deadfall debris around them, but they'd seen him and they were making their way toward him, one just then raising a carbine and firing.

The bullet smashed against the cracked boulder, to Johnny's right, kicking up a fresh ringing in his ears.

Johnny stepped behind the boulder and, keeping the large rock between him and the men moving down the slope toward him, ran down the declivity toward a creek meandering along the bottom of it. While he ran, he quickly broke open his left-hand Twin, thumbed out the spent wads, and replaced them with fresh ones from his cartridge belt. He snapped the savage popper closed, returned it to its holster on his left thigh, and gave the same treatment to the right-hand gun.

He'd no sooner clicked the second shotgun closed than hoof thuds rose sharply behind him. He turned to see the two riders swinging around opposite sides of the cracked boulder. One flung a pointing arm toward Johnny running down the slope through the pines, and shouted, "There he is! Kill that son of the devil, dammit!"

He triggered a shot that went screeching over Johnny's head to splash into the creek beyond him.

Johnny leaped two deadfalls and wove around a large spruce as the riders thundered toward him, their horses rasping and wheezing, the hooves clattering and crackling on the debris-littered slope. Neither took much care for himself or his horse, so determined were they to snuff the wick of Shotgun Johnny.

They came roaring down the slope, horses leaping

shrubs and deadfall, zigzagging crazily around the tall columnar pines. One man, the younger of the two, was sort of groaning and yowling with his fear of the treacherous ride. The older man, whom Johnny had recognized as Trench Norman, a former saloonkeeper who'd taken to the owlhoot trail when he'd been run out of business in Hallelujah Junction by a more moneyed competitor, was cursing a blue streak and whipping his horse savagely with his rein ends.

They were still roughly fifty yards behind Johnny, who broke out of the trees now and dashed across the clearing to the deeply cut creek bed. He leaped into the cut, landing on relatively dry ground beside the water, then hurled himself forward to sit back against the bank.

He drew both Twins and raked all four hammers back with his buckskin-gloved thumbs.

Beyond the clearing he heard his two pursuers thudding and crashing through the forest. There was a great crunching and cursing din as Trench Norman must have run into a snag. The man's horse whinnied shrilly, above Norman's curses. Then the thuds of another horse rose sharply as the other, younger man tore out of the forest.

Johnny swiped his hat off his head and edged a look over the lip of the bank as the younger man, wearing a battered cream hat and dirty rat-hair coat, reined his tired, wide-eyed horse to a halt between the trees and the creek bed. He was tall and lean, with a goat-ugly face complete with a fringe of colorless whiskers drooping off his pointed chin. A wad of chaw bulged one cheek.

He looked around wildly, waving his cocked six-shooter out in front of him.

"Hello, Frank," Johnny said, raising his left Twin above the lip of the bank.

Frank Tenor's eyes found Johnny and snapped even wider when they found the double-barreled Twin bearing down on him. He yelled and jerked his Colt toward Johnny but fired the piece into the air as the fist-sized spread of double-aught buck cut through his chest and belly and threw him howling off his sorrel's right hip.

Hooves crashed in the forest to the right of where Tenor was still rolling in the brush, his screaming horse lunging forward and leaping into the creek bed to Johnny's left. Johnny drew his head and shotgun down when he saw Norman explode out of the forest, firing his Winchester carbine one-handed, cursing loudly.

"Die, you greasy, damn, sheep-diddlin' Basque!"

The man appeared on Johnny's left as Johnny put his back to the bank. Horse and rider flew straight off the lip of the bank, an arcing blur of man and mount angling out over the narrow stream. Norman's carbine stabbed orange flames as he triggered the rifle straight out from his right shoulder a half second before his pinto's front hooves splashed into the creek.

Johnny snaked his right-hand Twin across his body and tripped both triggers, sending two pumpkin-sized blasts of the double-aught steel punching through Norman's upper torso and throwing him sideways off his horse. The pinto's saddle was empty when the mount lunged off its rear hooves, screaming shrilly, and leaped up and out of the stream and onto the opposite bank, its saddle hanging down its far side.

Johnny leaned forward from the bank and raised his left-hand Twin, tightening his trigger finger. He forestalled the motion.

The twin barrels of buckshot had taken decisive care of Trench Norman, whose hatless body just then bobbed back to the creek's surface, the water around the man bright red and glistening in the early-morning sunshine.

"No name-callin' now, Trench. Ain't one bit nice."

Johnny leaned back against the bank to reload the Twins.

As he did, he listened for the approach of more attackers.

If there were more, he didn't hear them. He thought he'd seen one other rider behind Norman and Tenor, but maybe that man had seen what the others had gotten for their attempt at stealing the gold bullion Johnny was hauling down from the Reverend's Temptation Gold Mine at the base of Grizzly Ridge, and had decided that even twenty-six thousand dollars' worth of freshly smelted, high-grade gold wasn't worth a fatal case of buckshot poisoning care of the former deputy U.S. marshal and now bullion guard, Johnny Greenway, aka "Shotgun Johnny."

Johnny snapped the second Twin closed and lifted his head sharply. He narrowed his dark brown, raptorial eyes to each side of his long, hawklike nose as his concentration intensified. His thick, dark brown hair curled down over his ears to touch the long, bright red kerchief he wore sashlike around his neck, the ends of which trailed down his broad chest toward his flat belly.

The rataplan of galloping hooves sounded in the far distance, from up the ridge on his right. Johnny caressed the Twin's triggers with his gloved thumb, and his heartbeat quickened with anticipation.

"One more . . ." he said half to himself.

He shuttled his gaze to the heavily forested ridge down which he knew a switchbacking trail dropped. It was off this trail he'd camped last night. It was while he still lay in his blankets early this morning, not in his camp but nearby—only a fool slept near his cook fire in outlaw country—that his camp was attacked by one party of the many countless gold thieves that haunted this northern neck of the Sierra Nevadas.

"One more coming fast . . . heading this way . . ."

Johnny peered up the creek's opposite bank and into the forest beyond.

The trail dropping down the ridge to his right angled along the slope ahead of him, roughly following the line of the creek, before climbing another steep pass on his left. A shrewd smile quirking his mouth corners, he pushed himself off the bank, rose to his feet, splashed across the creek, then ran up the bank and into the forest.

He ran hard, holding his shotguns down snug in their holsters. He'd been raised in these mountains and moved in them as easily as any native creature. Swift as a black-tailed deer, he climbed the ridge, hearing the galloping rider closing on him, on his right, following the gentle curve of the creek as it followed the crease between steep mountain passes.

Johnny's breath rasped in and out of his lungs, and his mule-eared boots crunched pinecones and needles topping the thick, aromatic forest duff. As he followed a zigzagging course around pines and aspens, he saw the trail ahead of him, straight up the steep slope, sixty yards away. Through the trees on his right, he glimpsed the galloping rider, who'd descended the northern ridge now and was racing along the flat.

Soon he'd be directly above Johnny.

Johnny grimaced as he pushed himself harder, breathing harder, wincing against the pull in his long legs . . .

The trail was ten feet away.

Five . . .

The rider was a sun-dappled figure galloping toward him on his right, twenty feet away.

Johnny leaped onto the trail, drawing both his stubby cannons from their holsters and raking all four hammers back as he aimed straight out in front of him. The rider came around a bend and, seeing Johnny before him, gave a startled cry and leaned far back in his saddle, reining his horse to a skidding halt.

He was trailing a pack mule, and the mule stopped abruptly, as well, braying up an indignant storm.

It was especially hard for the beast to stop, with all the gold it was packing. At least, the thief *thought* the mule was packing gold.

Gold that belonged to the lovely Sheila Bonner, owner of the Hallelujah Bank & Trust . . .

Johnny smiled as he aimed down both shotguns' double maws at the thief's head. "Hello, Rance. Long time, no see. Where you off to in such an all-fired hurry? With my mule, no less . . . ?"

CHAPTER 2

Rance Starrett's eyes blazed with both fear and fury as he stared over his horse's twitching ears at Shotgun Johnny Greenway bearing down on him with his savage Twins. Starrett held his reins up taut against his chest. His horse, a fine gray brindle, had turned one-quarter sideways to the trail, so Starrett's six-shooter, holstered on his right hip, faced Johnny.

When Starrett glanced from Johnny toward the bone-gripped Colt, Johnny said, "Go ahead. Give it a try, Rance. See how far you get before I muddy up the trail with your bloody hide."

Johnny wouldn't hesitate doing just that any more than he'd hesitated before perforating the other men in Starrett's raggedy-tailed pack. Starrett, a good-looking cuss in his late twenties, belonged to a moneyed patriarchal family headed up by Garth Starrett, one of the largest ranchers on the northeast side of the Sierra Nevadas. Starrett's Three-Bar-Cross sprawled across nearly an entire county, and what land he didn't own in and around Hallelujah Junction, he was likely making a play for.

Not a legal play, either . . .

Starrett had no truck with legality, only money and power. He'd passed along his own values to Rance, who hadn't amounted to much. From the time the kid was old enough to wield a gun and ride a horse, both of which he did pretty well, he'd been a fire-brand who'd gone from cattle rustling to stagecoach holdups to rape and murder and now, finally, to rob-bing the gold run from the Reverend's Temptation to the Bank & Trust in Hallelujah Junction. Garth Star-rett's wealth and power had always been able to get his worthless son out of even the deepest trouble— even two murder charges backed up by eyewitnesses, and the rape of a pretty young schoolteacher. Not to mention the rapes and killings of several parlor girls.

Such crimes had been covered up before they could be reported. But Johnny had heard about them. Most had heard about Rance Starrett's black-hearted dealings.

His father wouldn't get him out of the snag he'd just landed in here, however.

Johnny had been reading Rance's mind. He could see the wheels turning in the man's shrewd, amber eyes set deep beneath sun-bleached blond eyebrows. He was thinking that not even Shotgun Johnny would kill Rance Starrett. Not Garth Starrett's oldest son. Not even Shotgun Johnny had the oysters to pull such a stunt, even after Rance had been caught with his proverbial hand in the cookie jar—or leading Johnny's mule packing twenty-six thousand dollars in freshly milled gold.

Or so Rance thought.

At least, Johnny would hesitate to kill him. Hesitate long enough for Rance to drag that smoke wagon out of its hand-tooled black leather holster and shoot Johnny from point-blank range.

"Not worth it, kid," Johnny warned. He shook his head, a thin smile tugging at his mouth. "Them panniers aren't even packin' gold."

The churning of Starrett's cunning mind paused and incredulity ridged his brows. "Huh?"

"What? You think I'd actually leave the gold in the camp when I myself had skinned out away from the fire?" Johnny grunted a caustic laugh. "You damn tinhorn."

"You're lyin'," said Starrett, cocking his head to one side and narrowing a skeptical eye.

"Go on," Johnny said, glancing at the mule standing behind Starrett's edgy horse. "Check it out for yourself."

Starrett turned back to Johnny, and he narrowed his eyes again. "All right. I just will!"

"Go ahead. Slow. One fast move, and your pa will have one helluva time recognizing your shredded carcass."

"Stand down, you Basque devil. You so much as muss the part in my purty hair, my pa will have you run down and whipped like the sheep-dip-smellin' greaser you are!"

Johnny ground his molars at the insult. But, then, he was used to such condescension. He'd been born Juan Beristain and he and his Basque parents and brother—of Spanish and French descent—had herded sheep around the Sierra Nevadas until a venal cattle rancher had murdered his family and made Juan an orphan. Juan had been homeless until another cattleman, Joe Greenway, had adopted him, changed his name to make his life easier, and given him a good home on his Maggie Creek Ranch between Reno and Virginia City.

Still, Johnny had to use every ounce of his self-control not to jerk young Starrett out of his saddle and bash his head in with one of the Twins.

"I'm not goin' anywhere, Starrett. I'll be right here, holding my purty Twins on you while you take a look inside them packs. If you so much as sneeze in the direction of your pistol, you'll look mighty ridiculous with your head rolling around in the brush."

Starrett spat in disgust then swung down from the saddle. He cast Johnny a glare of raw disdain then walked behind his horse to the mule, who brayed its apprehension at the whole affair.

"Shut up, you broomtail vermin!" Rance yelled at the mule.

Angrily, he freed the straps of the pannier mounted on the wooden pack frame and peered into the stout canvas sack. He froze, scowling. He glanced at Johnny, his amber eyes hard and cold, then reached into the pack. He pulled out a rock a little smaller than his head and slammed it onto the ground so hard both horse and mule jumped a foot in the air.

The mule brayed its indignance.

The horse tossed its head and whickered.

"A half-dozen men are dead for nothin', Rance," Johnny said. "Not that they wouldn't have gotten their tickets punched sooner or later. I don't think there was a one of them I hadn't sent to the territorial pen when I was still packin' a moon-and-star."

Rance turned to face Johnny square. "Where is it?"

"I'll show you." Johnny smiled. "Just as soon as you throw down that hogleg . . . nice an' slow . . . and put

your wrists together so I can tie 'em. You'll be joinin'
me back to Hallelujah Junction."

"You think so, do ya?" It was Rance's turn to grin.

Johnny's spine tightened. At the same time he'd
seen the mocking grin enter Starrett's gaze, he'd heard
the faint crunch of a stealthy footstep behind him.

Rance lifted his chin to shout, "Back-shoot the son
of a buck, Chick! *Back-shoot him!*"

Johnny dropped like a wet suit off a clothesline.

As he did, a rifle barked behind him.

He rolled onto his back and, half sitting up, fired a
barrel of each Twin into the man who'd stolen up to
within fifteen feet of him.

Chick Ketchum's torso turned to bloody pulp as
both loads sawed into him. He danced away as though
taken by a sudden, catchy tune he'd heard on the
morning breeze, and waltzed straight off to the pearly
gates while his potbellied body, clad in greasy buckskin trousers and a patched hickory shirt, collapsed
on the trail.

"Ah, *hell*!" were Chick Ketchum's last words cast out
on a loud, deeply disgusted exhalation.

"Now, that was plumb stupid!" Johnny whipped
around to where he'd expected to see Rance Starrett
bearing down on him with his Colt. Only, Rance
wasn't bearing down on anything except possibly a
meeting with ole Saint Pete.

Johnny climbed to his feet. Holding his Twins
straight down by his sides, he stared down at Starrett.
The firebrand lay sprawled on his back in the middle
of the trail. He looked as though he'd been staked out
by Indians, spread-eagle. He had his pistol in his right
hand, but he hadn't even gotten it cocked before

Chick Ketchum's bullet had plowed into the dead center of his chest.

Heart shot.

One that had been meant for Johnny and likely would have hit its intended target if the witless Starrett hadn't given Ketchum away.

Now Starrett stared, wide-eyed in death, straight up at the sun angling down through the high crowns of the pines lining the trail. The sun reflected off his pretty, thick, strawberry blond hair and his amber eyes. He had a dumbfounded expression on his face, but then, that was nothing new to Rance Starrett. Johnny believed Starrett had been born with such an expression, so it was only fitting he'd go out with one, too, not having learned one damn thing on this side of the sod.

And now he wouldn't.

Kind of a shame in a way—to die little smarter than how you'd started out. But it wasn't like the kid, having been born into a wealthy family, hadn't had plenty of opportunities. He'd just chosen the wrong fork at every turn in the trail.

Bad seed.

"Well," Johnny said. "Let's get you back to Hallelujah Junction. I reckon the least I can do is turn you over to your pa for a proper burial."

He'd be damned if he'd waste time on gathering the others. The predators could dine on them. That's what the tinhorns got for running with the lowly likes of Rance Starrett.

The next day, Shotgun Johnny reined his cream horse to a halt on a promontory-like shelf of rock jutting out over the Paiute River in the Northern Paiute River Valley, and was glad to see that the little boom-town of Hallelujah Junction hadn't missed him while he'd been gone.

At least, if it had, it showed little sign. Even from here, on a high shoulder of Mount Sergeant from which the town was little larger than Johnny's open hand, he could hear the tinkle of pianos and the occasional roars of the mostly male crowd being entertained in the two opera houses that abutted each end of the bustling little settlement, like bookends.

It was late in the day, almost night, and the light had nearly faded from Hallelujah Junction's dusty streets. That which remained owned a dull yellow patina edging toward salmon. Smoke from cook fires swirled like diaphanous white snakes amidst all those purple-green shadows and yellow and salmon sunrays, sometimes obscuring shake-shingled rooftops.

The sun had fallen behind the high western ridges of the northern Sierra Nevadas, and those crags, along with the slightly lower ones in the east, caused the sun to rise and fall later in the day, and for shadows to linger. Now those shadows had swallowed the town, and that was just fine with the burly miners, hardy shopkeepers, enterprising market hunters, professional gamblers and cardsharps, wily prospectors, oily con artists and snake oil salesmen, and coquettish soiled doves who'd settled in for the year, facing the long mountain winter ahead.

Settled in but not settled down.

They were all stomping with their tails up, judging by the din that Johnny could hear from his high perch, by the clumps of men milling on the streets between the saloons and gambling dens and parlor houses, of which there was virtually one for every man who'd come out here, braving the remoteness and relative lawlessness to seek wealth and adventure or to at least have a damn good time trying for either or both.

There were a few pistol shots, as well, rising above the low roar of generalized boomtown cacophony.

Those would likely either mark the unrestrained appreciation of the acting abilities of whatever troupe was in town, entertaining the crowds in one of the opera houses, or possibly a not-so-friendly dispute in a smoky, ill-lit gambling den tucked back in one of the less-than-respectable watering holes or houses of ill repute.

A girl's terrified scream vaulted up from the smoky, darkening settlement, reaching Johnny's ears high above and on the opposite side of the wide, black river. A man's angry shout followed, followed in turn by yet another pistol shot.

Silence returned.

A piano had fallen quiet during the apparent dustup but now it started again, and the general revelry continued in Hallelujah Junction, as well—life moving on as it always did even if a dead man and/or possibly a dead woman was being hauled out of one of the saloons or parlor houses to one of the town's three undertakers. Possibly, a crazy drunk with blood on his hands was now being led away to Town Marshal Jonah Flagg's jailhouse. The poor deceased Jake or Jill would be fitted with a crudely nailed together wooden overcoat and buried quickly the next day in the town's bone orchard on a knoll to the southeast.

The culprit would soon follow after a celebratory hanging on the main street of the town, complete with barking dogs, laughing children, and a four-piece band. Six feet under he would go, another hastily erected wooden cross on Boot Hill.

Out of sight and out of mind.

Why ruin a good time with thoughts of death when it could occur so quickly, and so often did? Gentlemen, ladies—enjoy yourselves! The next round's on the house! Shuffle those cards, place your bets, roll those dice, spin that wheel!

Like clockwork, another raucous roar rose from a darkening roof, just then catching the last salmon rays of the now-defunct sun as it sank into the deep waters of the distant and unseen Pacific. A dog barked somewhere down there among those darkening streets. In the shadowy mountains on the town's far side, Johnny heard the mournful wail of a single wolf and the ratcheting cry of a late-hunting eagle.

He glanced over his shoulder at Rance Starrett's blanket-wrapped carcass resting belly-down across the saddle of Starrett's brindle gray, to the right of the mule packing twenty-six thousand dollars in gold bullion from the Reverend's Temptation. The gold was headed for the bank owned by the becoming Sheila Bonner.

Sheila.

Just the thought of the beautiful woman warmed Johnny's heart. He'd been in the mountains for six long nights—three nights up and three nights down—camping under the stars, only the night wind and the distantly howling wolves and the mule and his horse, Ghost, for company.

Well, last night he'd had Starrett's horse for company, as well. And Starrett himself, though the dead firebrand hadn't said much up there where Johnny had hung him upside down from a tree, so predators couldn't get at him. Johnny was glad he hadn't said anything. When the dead would start speaking to him, he'd know he'd been alone in the mountains too long.

"Come on, Starrett," Johnny said, nudging Ghost on down the shelf and back onto the trail that would take him down the mountain, across the wooden bridge spanning the river, and into the nocturnal town. "Let's get you settled in for the night. I gotta check in with the boss."

Visit our website at
KensingtonBooks.com
to sign up for our newsletters, read
more from your favorite authors, see
books by series, view reading group
guides, and more!

Become a Part of Our
Between the Chapters Book Club
Community and Join the Conversation

Betweenthechapters.net